The Valley Walker

T. W. Dittmer

Copyright Information

Disclaimers

This book is a work of fiction. Period.

To Sunshine

Waking the Dragon

He'd been used.

He was a soldier, fighting in a war he truly believed in, so devoted to its cause that he was willing to sacrifice everything. But doubts rose in his mind, and then he knew for sure. He'd been manipulated by men so empty they could only think of profit and power, men who exploited the toil and suffering of others to their own advantage.

The knowledge shook his faith in the cause of the war, his belief that he was doing the right thing. His honor was all he had left and, with nothing to hold him, he fell away from the world, into the cold mists of an endless valley. He wandered aimlessly there, lost and broken, until a kind old woman found him and took him to her home.

It was a place where time meant nothing, a split-bamboo hut high in the mountains of Laos. The hut was built in a clearing, surrounded by lush forest growth fed by rich, moist earth. A slight breeze pushed in through the open door, and he took in the heady aroma of the countryside. It was a musty and fertile perfume, like the under the covers smell of a waking woman.

It was cool here, but the warmth of the fire offset the chill of the packed earth floor and moist mountain air. The flames died down and a layer of smoke formed above his head, then expanded until it filled the room and nipped at his eyes. Behind him, the old woman droned a chant and beat her little drum. Her raspy voice and the primal rhythm of her singing gave him a moment of peace, but he knew it couldn't last.

It didn't. He remembered.

He was at home in the darkness. Invisible.

The Claymores were set. The ball bearings waited in their epoxy beds, ready to be hurled on their way by the C4 at their backs. When his victims moved into the kill zone, he turned his head, closed his eyes and squeezed the detonator.

The strobe of light flashed pink through his eyelids. His brain was jarred by the hollow crump of the blast. Beneath him, the ground bucked.

The force of the shockwave slammed his teeth together and rippled the vegetation around him.

The ball bearings ripped through everything. Shredded vegetation. Tore through the wood of the carts and rubber of the tires. Destroyed equipment and mutilated bodies. They penetrated the ammo boxes, causing secondary explosions. Expending munitions pinwheeled crazily through the air.

The chaos grew until it was deafening. The sounds of the projectiles hitting people, striking and tearing flesh, splitting and shattering bone — these sounds should have been lost in the madness, but somehow weren't. He heard each of these small, wet noises individually.

Branches and leaves were again shredded, as machine parts and human pieces and dirt and chunks of wood and shards of metal tore through them. The smattering, pattering began as pieces fell down through the trees, followed by thumps and light thuds as they struck the ground. Then, an unnatural silence broke through the ringing in his ears.

The panicked shouts of the survivors began. The cries and moans of the wounded rose in volume, then dwindled away to the bubbling sighs of the hopeless. His spirit walked out through the destruction — his handiwork — among the dead and the dying. He let them reach out to him, let them touch him, and he reached out to them.

They were just soldiers, all of them, sent to endure hardship and terrible wounds and death.

Just like him.

The killings were an act of war, a war he fought with as much decency as possible, but a war exploited by men who had no integrity at all. These men had no faith in the war's legitimacy, but participated because it was to their advantage. Even in this far-off place, he could see and hear those scheming men — the head shaking over his confidence the war could be won — the smirk and cruel laughter at his innocent belief that a soldier's sacrifice should be respected.

The memory tore at him like razor wire — not a clean cut, but a ragged gash that would never heal — so painful he couldn't bear it. He fell away again, back into the valley.

*****

The old woman stopped her chanting when the young man fell over on his side and went into spasms. His feet whipped on the floor like he was running. One arm stretched out and his fingers clawed at the floor as he tried uselessly to drag himself away. His clean army clothes were being soiled on one side as he thrashed on the dirt floor.

His spasms stopped and he grew still on the floor. Very still. The old woman put down her drumstick and reached out to him. He was as cold as death.

Tears flowed from her milky eyes and she wiped at them with the coarse cloth of her sleeve. She wore the traditional hemp clothing of the mountain people, the Hmong. The fabric was the same blue-white as the mist in the valley, and wisps of hair that protruded from her scarf matched her clothing.

"Oh, my son."

She wasn't his birth mother, of course. He was white, while she was Hmong. And she was far too old for him to be her son.

She was so old, in fact, that she didn't know her age. She only knew that she was one of the old ones, that no one alive could remember her being born, that her placenta was buried beyond the river, many days to the north beneath the snow. The place of her birth.

She had no children of her own, had never married, and was still a virgin in her old age. This was not the way of her people, but from the time she was a young girl, she'd been different from other females. While other girls in her village learned to be… and eventually became… wives, she found happiness in her friendship with the spirit world. She saw no reason for this as she grew up, nor was she repelled by the normalcy of the others. It just happened that she was different.

No, he wasn't her birth son. She'd adopted him as her own when she found him wandering in the mists of the valley. He'd sensed her kindness and reached out to her blindly, seeking something he didn't know the name of, some direction for his lost and drifting soul. His pain and anger engulfed her old heart, and his broken spirit brought tears to her nearly dead eyes. She enfolded him, held him to her sagging breasts and rocked him like a newborn, then took him to her home in the mountains. He was in pain now, but the men who had done this to him would pay.

She clucked to herself, frowned and shook her head. It would be a long and painful journey for him. He would carry the knowledge of the cruelty of man, and the load would be heavy. But she'd started making things ready to help him on his journey, a mission she began even before she found him.

She didn't know the exact time span of this undertaking. The time was not measured. The effort was not work. She'd simply done what was required, with absolutely no thought of the cost, for this had to be done with attention to every detail, no matter how small. Looking back, it was almost as if her entire life had been lived for this very moment, when the soul of her adopted son hung in the balance.

The old woman turned and examined her preparations.

Paints and brushes were lined up on a crude wooden shelf. Except for one very special pigment — the last pigment she would use — the paints were made from local materials — the water of a nearby stream, clay from the good earth, plant oils, and petals of native flowers. The brushes were made from branches cut from a tree, tipped with hair from the tail of a water buffalo. A big canvas was stretched tight over an entire wall of her little house, made of the finest hemp cloth she could find, purchased with opium grown in her garden.

With a grunt of approval, the woman nodded. Everything was ready. She chose a clay jar of paint and a brush, dipped the brush in the paint and began.

Stretching high on the canvas, she made the first great arc, then stepped back and closed her eyes. Even without seeing it, she knew that it was exactly right. With all doubt gone, she gave herself over to the work, not guiding her hand, but letting the purpose of the painting direct its course. Again she worked with no thought of time or effort, moved with the current of the river that was this undertaking. She chanted and sometimes closed her eyes to visualize the spirit the painting would take on.

As the form took shape, she felt its power nearing, the same way she could feel a person coming to stand over her shoulder. When she felt the spirit of the form touch her, felt its breath on her forehead and heard its heartbeat, she again stepped back to take in the life of her work.

On the wall before her was the form of the Great Za, the Great Dragon that had made its way into the mythology and religion of every continent and race on earth. Its wings were not fully spread, but drawn high and in toward the body, as the dragon fell on its prey. The five great talons on all four feet were extended, ready to sink into the flesh of its foe. Its head was drawn back to strike, the razor sharp fangs visible in its open maw, shining white and pure against the darkness of its mouth. Its nostrils were flared. Its ears were laid back and its eyes clearly focused on the object of its attack.

This was not the benevolent dragon of Chinese tales, not the protective Naga of Laotian mythology. Nor was it the evil dragon of Western religious belief that rained havoc and destruction on innocent people. It was a dragon from the depths of her son's soul, a beast born of the power of his anger.

It was a beautiful image, but it was still incomplete.

The old woman dragged a small stepstool before the painting. She picked up the last unused brush, the smallest of all the brushes she had made, with a tip as fine as she could make it. Removing the stopper from a small clay vial, she dipped the brush into the vial that held the one very special paint.

When she withdrew it, the brush was wet with a red pigment made from cinnabar, an element that held the power of life and rebirth. It was the brightest cinnabar she could find, blood red cinnabar she had ground to a powder with her own tools, then carried from the North when her people migrated here.

The hemp bag she made for her son was already dyed with the same pigment. It hung empty from a leather thong around his neck now, but would soon be filled with the force of his young heart.

With a grunt, she stepped up on the stool and focused her attention on the eye of the dragon. The pupil was a vertical slit in the iris, and in the middle of the pupil a translucent shape reflected light. The woman could feel the warm moisture of the beast's breath on her shoulder as she leaned in toward the eye with her brush. She could feel the life ready to be born as she closed her eyes and brought the brush upward.

She touched the brush to the center of the reflection in the pupil, and the spirit of the dragon was released.

✱✱✱✱✱

Something brought him out of the mists of the valley, a point of light that shined through the darkness of his misery.

He reached out to the light and wrapped his fingers around it. His hand glowed with the light he held, the bones visible through the pink glow of his flesh. He opened his hand and the light lay in his palm like some shining jewel. The gem of his honor.

Inside this glowing nugget he saw the spirit of his youth, pure and without pretense. He saw the labors of his young heart, the struggle to determine right from wrong in a world where black and white had blended to a soiled and dirty shade of gray. He closed his hand tightly on the gem, vowing to never let it go.

A spark of anger flashed inside him, anger that his honor had been used so callously. From that small spark, the anger grew to an ember, then flared up into flames, a fire that warmed him and stirred him to move. His eyes opened. He was on his side on the dirt floor. He sat up and looked around.

The old woman who called him her son was chanting and beating her drum again. On the wall behind her was a painting of a dragon. The dragon's eyes glowed, and it breathed in rhythm with the drum. Raw power came from the creature in waves, power that he felt flowing into his damaged heart.

The earth began to move, and the sound of a deep, resonant horn came from the mountains around him. The pitch was so low that it was almost inaudible, but he could feel it in the air around him and the ground he sat on. The sound grew in intensity until the entire mountain the hut was built on vibrated with its sound and echoed its harmonics.

Then came the feeling, the stirring of something deep inside him. Birth.

His head thrummed with the ancient rhythm of the struggle for purpose. He felt life at his temples, life that took on movement and advanced through his being. He looked at his forearms, saw veins rising to the surface, moving and taking shape. The veins took on form, the form of the Great Za, the Great Dragon of the ancient legends his adoptive mother sang about.

The dragon rose up inside him, drawing power from his anger, movement from his thoughts.

Facing the Dragon

Chapter 1

He reached out, found the space that lay between places, slipped through it, and he was there.

Mason, Michigan. He stood quietly for a while, soaking up the atmosphere until he was saturated with memories. The grain elevator was still there. Beyond that, the County Courthouse stood tall and proud. North of the Courthouse, the tops of the trees in Maple Grove Cemetery were visible. Home.

Many of the places looked the same, but everything was moving faster than he remembered. An endless stream of cars whizzed by. Horns honked and tires squealed in protest. Everyone seemed to be in a hurry, racing ahead with cell phones to their ears. The pace of life had definitely changed since the last time he stood on this street, but the men who'd used him hadn't.

They still exploited war and the suffering of fellow human beings for profit and power. The thought of people who could be so cold and heartless brought a weariness he didn't think he could carry. It bore down on him until his spirit sagged under the pressure, weighed on him until it threatened to drive him to his knees.

He caught himself before he faltered, reached up and pressed the shape of an object beneath his shirt. The object was a red hemp bag that hung from a leather thong looped around his neck, the bag his mother had dyed with cinnabar and given to him in the mountains of Laos. It was filled now with the essence of his heart, his need to do the right thing, the shining gem of his honor. Just by pressing the bag tighter against his skin, its power flowed into him and renewed his purpose. With a final glance at the tops of the trees above Maple Grove Cemetery, he murmured the words he'd adopted as his mantra decades ago.

"Two salt tablets, a canteen of water and push on."

He shifted the weight of his weariness higher on his shoulders, leaned into it, and pushed on.

He was on his way to the drugstore, actually a large convenience store that happened to have a pharmacy inside. He was going to the drugstore because Special Investigator Terry Altro would be there. It was where they would try to kill her.

Inside the store, he made his way through the crowd of shoppers to the back where the pharmacy was. The pharmacist wore silver hoop earrings and an array of silver rings and bracelets, a proud proclamation of her Hmong heritage. The thought of the Hmong brought a smile to him and he passed it along to her, in thanks for the kindness her people had shown him.

His smile was rewarded with a puzzled look, a furrowing of her eyebrows and a pursing of her lips, as she wondered why he would give her this recognition. She didn't recognize him, but she would have heard the stories. In just a few moments she would know the stories were true.

He continued moving slowly through the store, studying the customers, looking for Teri Altro. When he found her she was at the book rack, scanning the back cover of a paperback.

She was dressed in a light gray skirt and a starched white cotton blouse. Her sleeves were rolled up on her forearms and a large round watch with a wide leather strap was on her left wrist. She wore no jewelry. Her skirt wasn't figure hugging, just tight enough to give promise, long enough to cover her knees. The clean, no-nonsense look of her attire was completed with black platform shoes and a black leather shoulder bag that sat on her hip.

A handful of her auburn hair was pulled back and banded into a short ponytail that stuck out from the back of her head, like a Samurai's top-knot. The remainder fell naturally from a center part to just below her ears. She had dark gray eyes, the color of cold steel, but with long, thick lashes that softened them.

Her eyes pulled at him, and he moved a few steps so he could see them better. They were wide and alert, set above wide cheekbones that curved in to smooth cheeks. Her cheeks sloped

14

out again to a good chin with a slight dimple. She wasn't wearing any makeup.

The muscles in her calf danced as she tapped a foot on the floor. Then in quick, decisive movements, she shook her head and reached to replace the book in her hand with another. It took only a few seconds for her to reject that one and replace it with yet another.

He compared what he saw with intelligence he'd gathered and decided he read her profile correctly. She was a driven woman, confident of her own ability, impatient with the pace of life, unforgiving of the lack of drive she sometimes saw in others.

But in her presence, he felt something an examination of data could never reveal. In her single-mindedness she had pushed others away and isolated herself, her feelings subdued by the mission that drove her. Her once tender heart had been seared in the flames of sacrifice, on the altar of her all-consuming purpose.

He looked deeper inside her and saw the sun darkened, gangly-legged girl of her youth, walking barefoot along a sandy path on the bank of a river. Her hair was lightened by the sun and long bangs hung down over her eyes, almost hiding them. With eyes shining bright in her innocence and happiness, she looked out from beneath her bangs to something only she could see. Her arms wheeled in a swimming motion as she walked, and her full lips vibrated in a child's imitation of a motor. She hummed tunelessly to herself, lost in her own private world, indifferent to any observation, yet so perfectly beautiful in her young girl awkwardness.

The events in her life that had caused the abandonment of such peace and happiness, the loss of such purity and innocence, saddened him. He wished he could remove the calluses formed in layers around her heart and set the spirit of the young girl free again. It was still there, beneath the armor she wore so easily now, still visible behind those steely eyes.

That lost spirit cried out to him and his own spirit flew to hers. Teri Altro felt him regarding her hidden recesses. She would not look back into his heart, but she felt him reaching out to hers. She knew.

Her shoulders slumped, and she shifted from one foot to the other, uncomfortable with his probing. Then she straightened her posture, put her hands on her hips and raised her eyes to him, determined to face him down. But there was no time. They were coming to kill her.

Three men were coming — no, there were four — blindly approaching on their mission of murder. They were empty men who would go about their mission with no more thought or feeling than a pointed rifle, pawns used in a game beyond their shallow comprehension. The strings that controlled these puppets reached across thousands of miles, spanned oceans and jumped mountains. These men were soldiers of General Khun Pao.

Khun Pao, a drug lord who ruled a vast heroin empire from his sanctuary in the mountains of Laos, was sending his men to kill Teri Altro. He couldn't let that happen.

He pulled two objects from beneath his shirt, a rectangular ivory tile and the red hemp bag that held his honor. Then he grasped the bag and focused on the place where the dragon waited. The droning and drumming began to resonate deep within him. His head thrummed and his temples began to pulse with the ancient rhythms his mother had taught him.

The beast stirred in him, then came fully awake and began prowling. He released it and rode it toward the imminent conflict. The action of the moment would now begin, would accelerate into violence at a pace that could never be controlled. The violence would take on a momentum of its own, would continue unrestricted until its energy was fully spent.

He turned away from Teri Altro to face the killers, but when he did she followed at a distance — not wanting to be touched, but still wanting to see. Teri Altro stepped into his world and followed as the dragon took him.

Chapter 2

Teri Altro knew the man was staring at her, but she was used to that. She'd competed in gymnastics all through her school years, from sixth grade until law school. Altro still trained her body hard, and had kept her gymnast figure, including the tight gymnast butt men like to eyeball so much. If she gave just the right arch to her back and pulled her shoulders back, it would pull the skirt and blouse tighter to emphasize her figure. That would give him something to gawk at.

But that wasn't how Altro worked. She didn't slump to hide her figure, but she didn't strike poses to flaunt it, either. Teri Altro didn't use her body to get ahead, and she didn't let men push her around because she happened to be a female. She did all the pushing.

Altro was a Special Investigator for the Michigan Attorney General's Office, with her own office in the G. Mennen Williams Building in Lansing. She had an assistant taking care of the office while she was working for the newly formed Drug Interdiction Task Force. It was a temporary assignment, but when the AG asked Altro to join the Task Force she jumped at the chance. This position was the culmination of a career driven by near fanatical, single-minded purpose.

Special Investigator Teri Altro lived to put drug dealers behind bars.

That drive left no place in Altro's future for a family, which was the reason for her stop at the drugstore. Her birth-control prescription needed to be refilled, and she always stopped here to do it. It was supposed to be ready and waiting for her but, due to some glitch in the system, it wasn't. Too impatient to sit and wait but unwilling to come back later, she decided to check out the book rack while her prescription was filled.

The guy kept staring. Altro kept her attention on the book rack.

She absently fingered the stubby ponytail that stuck out from the back of her head as she scanned the back cover of a book. Dissatisfied with the storyline, she put it back and reached for another, still playing with her hair. She knew her hair was too short for a true ponytail, that it looked a bit ridiculous sticking out the way it did, but that was the point.

Bunching up that handful of hair and removing her business suit jacket was what she did every night in the parking lot. It was her private declaration that she was off the clock, a small rebellion against the pains she went through to maintain her professional appearance. Her work uniform.

The one part of her work uniform she never left behind was her shoulder bag. It held some of her personal items, of course, but it also held her Attorney General Office credentials, her BlackBerry and her gun. Altro never went anywhere without the gun.

She'd purchased the weapon after her parents were killed when a hopped-up drug addict robbed their jewelry store. An arrest was made and the accused was taken to trial, but the comedy of errors in court left even Altro doubting the man's guilt. The murder of her parents and the apparent ineptitude of the District Attorney's Office altered her life.

The first act of her new life was to apply to law school. The second was to arm herself. The Lady Smith 3913 automatic fit nicely in the outer compartment of her shoulder bag. The gun was always right there on her hip, always loaded with 100 grain Hydra-Shoks. Man stoppers.

The guy kept staring. He was one aisle over, and he even took the few steps to the same aisle she was in to see her better. Altro kept trying to ignore it, but his staring started to bother her. It wasn't just that he was looking. It was something else.

She felt like he could see inside her, could see her secrets. It began to disturb her, and then to embarrass her. She felt naked in front him and, though she was proud of her body, her cheeks burned at the thought. Her eyes moved restlessly, aimlessly along the book rack. She shifted uncomfortably from one foot to another, like a school-girl caught in a naughty act by her parents.

Then she got angry. That any man would stare so openly, would pry like that into her secret places. The walls she'd methodically built around her were a barrier beyond which no one was allowed, especially some stranger in a drugstore.

She put her hands on her hips and raised her head to give him her best scowl, but he wasn't looking at her anymore. He was gazing at some point in the distance. Her eyes followed the line of his stare, but she couldn't see anything that would hold his attention.

She measured him, taking in his faded blue jeans and scuffed leather boots. His long-sleeved chambray shirt was baggy, and so faded it was almost colorless. He was older, definitely over fifty. Average height but thin, maybe five-ten but less than one-fifty. His hair was gray and cut short. Crow's feet dug deep around his eyes, matching the lines at the corners of his mouth.

The only notable thing about him was the battered leather briefcase he carried. Other than that, he was nothing special, just some guy in the drug store.

But as she studied the man who had so boldly examined her, he reached up to his neck with his free hand and pulled on a couple of cords looped around his neck. Two items attached to the cords slid up and out from inside his shirt. One of the items was a white rectangular pendant that almost looked like a game tile, the other a fist-sized bag made of some kind of coarse red cloth. He let the objects fall on his chest, then reached for the red cloth bag and grasped it. The world shifted, and Teri Altro lost her place in it.

A subtle feeling, a sound or deep droning, began around her. It was like a giant foghorn sounding in the distance, the pitch too low to be heard, but the vibrations so intense her feet tingled. She felt the ground shift beneath her feet, like a light earthquake was occurring, and spread her feet to shoulder width to keep her balance. But this wasn't an earthquake. It was eerie, as if the entire area was changing focus, disturbed from its natural place. Other people in the store felt it too.

The middle-aged woman at the register pressed both hands on the counter as her eyes darted around the store. Customers grabbed at shelves. Someone dropped a bottle that broke on the floor. An elderly man at the pharmacy turned around and teetered from side to side, then raised his arms to keep his balance. Behind the elderly man, Altro saw a pharmacist, a young Asian woman.

The pharmacist didn't seem to be bothered. She was gaping, wide-eyed, at the man who'd been staring at Altro. One hand was to her mouth, which was opened in an exaggerated O, while her other hand was at her throat. And as Altro watched her, the pharmacist raised her hand from her mouth to her forehead and smiled.

Altro looked at the man again. He was still staring into the distance and, as she watched him, a vein started throbbing on his left temple, swelling in and out with his pulse. A rhythmic vibration began in the air, coming in waves that fell into time with the throbbing vein. Then the entire store began to pulsate, ebbing and flowing in her vision to a primal drumbeat in the air.

The man moved over a few aisles to the outer aisle of the drugstore, then turned toward the entrance. Altro saw a vein on his right temple that throbbed and pulsed like the one on his left. He walked down the aisle toward the store entrance, still gazing into the distance, still clutching the red cloth bag. Near the end of the aisle he stopped, and it dawned on Altro that he wasn't any farther away than when he'd turned and walked down the aisle. She'd dropped the book in her hand and followed him, walking down the aisle she was in on a parallel course.

He was very close to the entry door, but partly hidden behind a revolving display of sunglasses. She was three aisles over, maybe fifteen feet away from the doorway, the check-out counter just across the main entry aisle from her.

The man raised the red cloth bag up higher and gripped it tighter. Veins bulged on his hand and his knuckles went white.

The throbbing vibration grew more intense, the droning foghorn louder. More veins emerged on his face, snake-like shapes that pulsed and squirmed in rhythm with the vibration beating the air. His face was alive with them.

Then he let go of the red cloth bag and cocked his head, like a dog listening to a distant sound. The foghorn and vibration died suddenly, and an unnatural silence enveloped the building. It was so quiet that Altro could hear herself swallow. Her breath came in a hoarse rasp. Her pulse pounded in her ears, so loud that she threw a panicked look around her.

It looked like time had stopped in the drugstore. The middle-aged woman at the check-out had stepped back from the counter. She was motionless, her hands held to her ears, her eyes squeezed shut. Customers were frozen in place, hands held out to block some unseen force, mouths locked in grimaces. The Asian pharmacist, however, was completely unaffected. She'd come around to the customer side of the pharmacy counter, smiling as she made a deep bow to the man with the pulsing veins.

When Altro looked at him again, the veins on his face stopped their movement, then stretched and straightened, extending in dark blue lines on his skin. The lines shifted to create forms, shapes that darkened to the indigo color of the veins, so dark they were almost black. The shapes and coloring became an image on his face, a mask of tattoos.

It was an abstract depiction that only came into focus as Altro stared at it. Then teardrop shaped eyes and crudely portrayed fangs became clear, and gave it an identity. The portrayal was still more symbolic than concrete, but Altro had no doubt what it was. She could feel it as much as she could see it. It was a dragon's head.

The dragon mask turned its face to the store entrance. The automatic door hissed open and three Asian men walked in, carrying short-barreled pump shotguns with pistol grips. One man turned back to face the entryway. The other two took a few steps toward the interior of the store before one of them spotted Altro, put a hand on the other's shoulder and pointed at her.

The two men gripped the shotguns with both hands and began raising the barrels toward Altro. She was already reaching for her gun.

Chapter 3

Altro's gun was secured in her shoulder bag with a single snap, just like a holster. It was a quick draw, but not quick enough. She just got her hand on it when the masked man shot all three of the gunmen in the back of the head.

Her vision was distorted, but frames of utter clarity flickered through, where she could watch the action unfold in slow motion. A video replayed, frame by frame. The motions he made appeared effortless, a well-rehearsed ballet that Altro caught in glimpses through the wavering distortion.

His briefcase was gone, and he had a pistol in each hand. He stepped behind the two men facing her and shot them both at the same time. The impact of the slugs shoved their heads forward and the pressure buildup in their skulls made their eyeballs bulge out of the sockets.

He turned, pivoting smoothly on the balls of his feet as he swung around to his next victim. He took a step and the gunman facing the store entrance was right in front of him, not three feet away. He shot this man before he had any chance to react, or even flinch. The hair on the back of the victim's head was blown flat, then fluffed out and caught fire. A fine red mist, mixed with bits of bone and brain matter, blew back over the barrel of the pistol in the tattooed man's hand.

It all happened so fast neither of the men facing Altro had time to get their barrel level and aimed at her, and she was still trying to draw her own gun. The automatic door hadn't even closed behind the gunmen yet.

The masked man stepped around his third victim and started toward the exit. The ejected shell casings were still in the air, and he flicked one casually out of his way with the pistol in his right hand. By the time Altro had her gun out, he was gone.

Shell casings rattled on the floor. The dead men leaned forward, their ankles twisted and they fell like trees cut for lumber. The automatic door closed on the body of the gunman that was lying in the store entrance with a light thump, then hissed open again.

*****

Just outside the drugstore, a white panel van waited with the engine running. The driver flinched and started to turn his head at the sound of the gunfire, but froze when the masked man reached in through the open window and pressed the bloody barrel of a pistol to his temple.

"Look at me," the masked man said.

The driver turned his head slowly until he saw his face, then gasped and closed his eyes tight, like a frightened child. The driver was Hmong, one of Khun Pao's men. He had heard the stories.

"Tell your masters I'm here. Tell them the men they sent to kill the woman were nothing to me. I hold their sniveling souls now, in a black bag that admits no light. I will take them to the other side and feed them to Ndsee Nyong, the Soul Devourer. He will enjoy their foul flavor."

The driver gasped. The tattooed man continued.

"Khun Pao thinks he is safe in his sanctuary, but there is no safe place for him. I'm coming for him. I'm coming for all of you. The Soul Devourer will tear at your entrails and suck them down like noodles. He will pick his teeth with your bones for centuries. You will be in blackness forever."

The driver couldn't speak, just sat and shivered. The tattooed man nudged his head with the pistol.

"Go now. Tell them."

The driver's hands trembled uncontrollably until the tattooed man nudged him with the pistol again. Then he managed to put the van in gear and drive off.

The tattooed man had pushed himself deliberately out of balance. He had thrown himself into the violence with relish and, in the aftermath, he savored the fire the dragon's power gave him. The sticky warmth of the would-be killers' blood on his hands was pleasant to him. He would kill them all.

Then he thought of the woman in the drugstore, Teri Altro. Even with the fire burning, he felt drawn to her, felt the closeness of their spirits, the interweaving of their lives. His mind raced back through time to find the beginnings of their connection, but couldn't. He didn't understand the affinity he felt with this woman. It just was.

Knowing he couldn't deny their destiny, that the woman's draw was too strong, he decided that he would try to show her.

*****

Altro was trying to catch her breath when the tattooed man walked back into the store, the pistols still in his blood-spattered hands. Her surroundings shifted. The foghorn began sounding again. The air vibrated and throbbed. He seemed to be moving toward her through heat waves that rose from the floor, and she saw him step over a body in flickering glimpses, like watching him under the flashes of a strobe light.

The dragon mask stared at her. She thumbed off the safety and raised her gun with two hands, targeting a point on his chest above the red cloth bag.

As she pointed her gun at him, a wisp of smoke came from the bag, rose up into the man's chin. The dragon-mask tattoo blurred and faded, then materialized as a three-dimensional dragon's head. It wasn't an abstract image on his skin now, but a living organism — a separate being, but still part of him.

Then the dragon head separated completely from his, floated up and hovered above him. The wisp of smoke from the bag followed it, then became a steady stream that poured out and swirled around the man. Through the haze of smoke, Altro watched as the body of the dragon became visible inside him, then grew larger until it emerged from his body.

This wasn't a cute purple dragon from a children's fairy tale, with a lump of a body and smiling mouth. This dragon was angry and powerful, with laid-back ears, flared nostrils and fangs bared in a snarl. The creature's front paws rested on his shoulders, and its wings spread in an arc above him. The long, serpentine body coiled once around the man, and the scales of its sides expanded and contracted in rhythm with the primal throbbing that beat the air.

Altro was terrified. She held her gun on him and backed away, but he followed. She retreated into the store, but the man kept coming, bringing the dragon with him. Finally, she backed into something and could go no farther. The creature leaned forward and stretched its neck to bring its head closer to her, so close that she could feel its breath, hot and moist on her face.

"No!" she yelled.

The man stopped, locked eyes with her, and Altro immediately felt like she was falling, as if she'd stepped off the edge of a cliff. She couldn't move her limbs. Her arms and legs felt three times their actual size, useless sacks packed with wet sponge. Once again Altro felt her soul being exposed to his merciless examination, but this time she could feel him opening himself to her. She could see inside him.

She saw violence — intentional, driven violence. She felt anger — white hot, blinding anger. Winding around everything she saw and felt were the coils of the great dragon that seemed to be part of the man. The power of the dragon grew stronger, bore down on her until, with a quick intake of breath, she flinched away. Her finger jerked at the trigger in reflex and the gun jumped in her hands. The man dropped his pistols, stumbled backward and fell. Her world imploded.

A roar came from the maw of the dragon, then turned into an ear-piercing scream of pain that shredded her mind. A tearing sound split the air, a great canvas being ripped, the universe torn. All the glass in the store — the windows, the check-out counter, the refrigeration units — it all disintegrated into fragments not much bigger than grains of sand, blew out into the air, then compressed back into itself.

She felt a vacuum as the shattered glass blew outward, like being in an airtight room when the door was yanked open. Intense pressure, like the door was slammed closed, followed as the glass compacted inward. Her hair and clothing fluffed out, then flattened against her in response to the changing pressure.

The glass was back in its original form for a second, looking like nothing had happened. Then it dissolved in place and gravity took over. The tiny pieces slid down into the cases and onto the floor — sparkling diamond chips that rattled their way downward.

*****

He watched Teri Altro as she held her weapon on him, and knew she would shoot him. She wasn't breathing. Her heart had stopped. He tried to reach out to her again, but she could not see him. Rather than disarm her, child's play for him, he decided to take the bullet. It would become part of him.

Her finger convulsed on the trigger and the weapon discharged in slow motion. He took the bullet, but it was the look on her face that caused him pain. Her fear of him was so agonizing that he started sliding away immediately. He stumbled backward, lost his balance and fell, landing hard on his bottom. A stack of bagged charcoal was at his back, and he leaned against it.

27

Teri Altro kept her weapon trained on him, the fear still in her eyes. The Hmong pharmacist rushed in, knelt and blocked him from Altro's view until she slowly lowered her weapon. He turned to the pharmacist and saw the spark of recognition in her eyes.

"You are him? You are the Valley Walker?" she asked.

He was almost gone, but managed to hold up the rectangular ivory tile he wore. A dragon was engraved on it.

"This tile is my sign," he said. "Show it to your elders. They will know what to do."

She slipped the leather thong the tile was attached to up over his head, wound the thong around the tile and hid it in the pocket of her smock. Her hand went to his forehead and he felt her strength, realized she was trying to keep him there. He could not stay, but croaked out his question.

"You are shaman?"

She smiled and bobbed her head, but he could not return her smile. The mist was closing around him. He reached for the red hemp bag and held it with all his might. And then he fell away. Away from the pharmacist, away from Teri Altro, away from the world.

*****

Altro lowered her gun and stepped to the side so she could see around the pharmacist. He was leaning back against a stack of bagged charcoal and one of the pharmacist's hands was on his forehead. The thrumming vibration in the air had stopped. The dragon had vanished, like the monsters of childhood nightmares disappeared with daylight. With her pistol still in her hands, she took a step and leaned in for a better look.

She jumped back when one of his hands darted up and grasped the red cloth bag again. The muscles in his forearm corded up. He flopped over on his side. His arms went rigid. The

28

cord that held the red cloth bag snapped, but he still clutched the bag in his hand. The other arm reached out and his fingers clawed at the flooring. His feet began scrabbling on the tile floor, like he was running in his sleep.

The pharmacist began what sounded like a chant, but her voice was so soft that Altro could barely hear. Gradually, the man quieted. His feet stopped scrabbling, and his arm quit reaching and pulling. Reality crashed back into Altro's world.

She could smell the gunpowder and burning hair, could taste it in her mouth. Car alarms were sounding in the parking lot. The entrance door grated across the broken glass to close on the body, then reopened. The woman at the register opened her eyes, looked down at the bodies and screamed. Customers started yelling. Another woman screamed and cringed away from a man who put a hand on her shoulder. People pulled their cell phones and punched at them with clumsy fingers.

Altro just stood there, her mind beaten numb and senseless by what happened. Two Mason Police officers rushed in before she thought to safety her weapon and put it back in her bag.

In minutes, the store was crowded with uniforms from the Mason Police and Ingham County Sheriff departments. They were trying to get everybody out of the store, but allowed Altro to stay when she pulled her Attorney General credentials. Two paramedics brought in a stretcher and their gear. Altro tried to make her way over, but a county deputy held his arms out, blocking her. She held up her credentials again, but the deputy just shook his head. All she could do was snatch glimpses as the paramedics worked on him.

Chapter 4

Bill Mallory took Altro's call in his hotel room. She didn't tell him much, just that there'd been an attempt on her life at a drugstore in Mason. When he asked if she was okay, she went quiet for a while and he could hear a lot of racket in the background. People yelling. Car alarms. Eventually, she said she was okay, that a man had stepped in to stop it. Halfway through his second question, Mallory realized Altro had hung up on him. He took a breath and stared at his BlackBerry. Altro didn't like him, and probably resented having to call in to him, but she had good reason.

Mallory was the titular leader of the Drug Interdiction Task Force, directly appointed by the Governor of Michigan, supposedly because of his long career in Army Intelligence. Mallory *had* served over 30 years in the 519th Military Intelligence Battalion, and liked to think that his service counted for something. But he wasn't the Governor's first choice. If outside forces hadn't pushed the Governor, Altro would be in charge.

The Task Force, which had only been in existence for a few days, was created to stop the flow of heroin into Michigan's two largest college campuses. The first overdose occurred a month ago, in a Michigan State University dorm room. By the time the cause of death was determined, five more Michigan State students had died. At that point, Mallory began paying very close attention to news updates on the drama.

It was like a disease, and the contagion spread through East Lansing quickly. More deaths came. In dorm rooms and frat houses, in apartments around the school and, once, in a student's bedroom at his parents' home. Then the University of Michigan became infected. Students started dying in and around the city of Ann Arbor.

The heroin was everywhere at once. Campus security and local law enforcement were overwhelmed by the influx. The speed with which the drug flooded the two campuses reminded Mallory of the way heroin had poured into U.S. military bases in Vietnam. And this version was evidently just as pure as the "skag" that had caused the ruin of so many American GIs. Potent enough to be smoked, even better when snorted. Potentially lethal if used while drinking alcohol.

Mallory had booted up his computer to do his own research, but kept his television on and tuned to the news. The media cashed in on the tragedy, interviewing stricken parents and running a touching biography of each victim after the story of their overdose. Politicians, eager to display their concern to potential voters, wrangled for spots on special broadcasts.

One half-hour special, in particular, caught Mallory's attention. It featured an interview at a posh estate in Virginia. Before the broadcast, Martin Woodley's name wasn't well known in Michigan, but Mallory knew it would be spoken at dinner tables across the state afterward.

Martin Woodley looked good on television. He was tall, perfectly groomed, and splendidly dressed. With his strong features and aristocratic bearing, he was the kind of man that could take command of a room with just his presence. The interview was staged in his study, enabling Woodley to impart his wisdom while seated in his favorite leather club chair.

In the cultured baritone of the manor born, Woodley expounded at length on the problem. The reporter mentioned Woodley's knowledge and understanding of the situation, which led to Woodley's humble explanation. He'd been fortunate enough to serve as the "Drug Czar" for two previous presidents, and was now the chairman of "Free America," a non-profit organization dedicated to the eradication of illegal drug use.

Free America happened to be a major sponsor of the special broadcasts, and at least one commercial for the organization ran during every station break. A toll-free number and Free America's web address were displayed in lettering large enough for the elderly to read. All donations were tax-deductible.

At the end of the interview, an emotional Woodley called on Karen Listrom, the Governor of Michigan, to do everything within her power to stop the flow of deadly drugs. His voice had just the right tremor as he offered his services, and the services of Free America.

"Governor Listrom, young people are dying. They are the future of America, and we must protect them. I stand ready to serve, and place the resources of Free America at your disposal."

An hour after the interview, Mallory received a phone call from the Pentagon. His quiet retirement in a small town outside Grand Rapids, Michigan was disrupted. He packed his bags and set his home phone up to forward calls to his cell. When Governor Listrom called, he was already settled into the Holiday Inn Express, just south of Lansing. It would be a quick drive to her office in the Capitol Building.

He met with Listrom that evening. It turned out to be an awkward experience for him, though Listrom did her best to put him at ease. He found her quick, competent and likable, but to his discomfort, physically attractive.

Her striking good looks and classic dress made him ashamed of his off-the-rack suit, number three buzz-cut and scarecrow build. His glasses kept slipping down his nose. Listrom's aide served coffee, and Mallory was afraid he would slurp or drop the delicate china cup.

"Thank you for meeting so quickly with me, Bill," Listrom said.

Mallory nodded and pushed his glasses up on his nose.

"My pleasure, ma'am."

"This is about the heroin problem we have," she said.

"Of course, ma'am."

Governor Listrom eyed him for a few seconds, then related the formation of the Drug Interdiction Task Force. A public announcement would be made the next morning, and the team chosen as quickly as possible. The Task Force would have a representative from the FBI, the DEA, the Michigan State Police, and the Michigan Attorney General's Office.

Mallory nodded, and Listrom continued.

"You probably think this is all political posturing, an attempt to make it look like we're doing something," she said.

When Mallory didn't reply, the Governor's mouth twitched at one corner.

"It's not," she said. "Their primary duty will be coordinating the efforts of the various law enforcement agencies involved, but I want them to do more than that. I want them to push the investigation."

Mallory still didn't say anything. She went on.

"The members' names will not be made public, nor will the location of the office they'll work out of — what we're calling the Task Force Team Center. They will not be my mouthpiece for the press."

Mallory raised one eyebrow and Listrom returned his gesture. Then she gave him the high-inside pitch.

"Martin Woodley strongly recommended you to lead this task force, Bill. He called me personally, praising your background in Army Intelligence. He sent me a copy of your service records, in fact, to persuade me."

It didn't surprise Mallory that Woodley had been given access to his records, but it did when Listrom recited from memory.

"Thirty-five years in the Army's 519th Military Intelligence Battalion. Vietnam, Grenada, Panama, Kuwait, Afghanistan and Iraq. Early promotions recommended throughout your career. Retired as a full-bird colonel. Too many decorations to recount."

Mallory sat rigid. The Governor smiled.

"Very impressive, Bill. So impressive that I agreed with Woodley. We should, at least, consider you."

It was embarrassing, but Mallory managed to keep his expression neutral. Listrom studied him for a full minute before she went on.

"Do you know Martin Woodley, Bill? Are you affiliated with him?" she asked.

"No, ma'am. I don't know him, and I'm not connected to him. I've certainly heard of him."

"Then you understand the position I'm in."

Mallory nodded. He knew that Martin Woodley's contacts in the defense industry had helped Governor Listrom bring hundreds of good-paying jobs to Michigan. So many defense companies had opened up shop in Michigan, in fact, that the Governor's PR people were calling the cities north of Detroit the "New Defense Corridor." It was a major campaign talking point for Listrom. The Governor owed Martin Woodley.

"I know he's a powerful man," was all Mallory said.

Listrom's mouth twitched again. Then she started grilling Mallory, a rapid-fire interrogation on his knowledge of the heroin overdoses that went on for thirty minutes. At the end of this curt examination, she asked him what he thought of the situation.

"My biggest concern is this," he said. "Why would the sellers target college students? They had to know there would be an extreme public reaction."

Listrom leaned back in her chair and smiled again.

"I see why Woodley recommended you, Bill. You do your homework." Her smile grew broader. "And you can think."

Mallory tried not to blush, but wasn't successful. The praise she gave him and her smile — especially her smile — were getting to him. But Listrom got serious again, staring at him for a full minute before she asked her question.

"Can you do this, Bill?" she asked. Then she waved a hand in the air. "No, it's evident you can. *Will* you do this?"

"What do you want me to do, ma'am?"

"I want this heroin stopped."

The corner of her mouth twitched again, more pronounced this time. Then she slapped a hand on her desk. Hard.

"But that's not all I want," she said. "Somebody's behind this, Bill. I want their damn head on a platter."

"And your position, ma'am?"

The Governor took a deep breath. "Do what you can, Bill, but put a stop to this."

For the first time, Bill Mallory smiled at Governor Listrom. "Yes, ma'am. I'll do it."

When Mallory met with the Governor two days later, he was just as uncomfortable as before. His suit still felt cheap and ill-fitting. His glasses still kept slipping down his nose. He still felt clumsy, and the china coffee cup still looked like it would shatter if he breathed on it too hard.

Listrom looked even better than she had the time before. The string of pearls she wore was offset perfectly against her bright blue knit dress. Her gray eyes probed him from behind her designer glasses as she told him where the Task Force Team Center was set up. When she slid a form across her desk, he was glad to have something else to look at.

"That's a standard non-disclosure agreement, Bill, the same one the FBI uses."

Mallory didn't bother reading it, just scooted his chair up to her desk and signed. Listrom then pulled four files from a drawer and plopped them on the desk.

"This is your team, " she said. "They'll be reporting to you at the Team Center this afternoon. These people aren't field agents, but they certainly aren't toadies. They're the best technical people I could get."

He was looking at the files, so she cleared her throat to get his attention.

"Don't be offended, Bill, but you're bright enough to realize you weren't my first choice to lead this task force."

He didn't take offense, just nodded in agreement. Martin Woodley. Her position.

"I can see you're not a pushy person, and I want this investigation pushed hard. To guarantee that, I made sure one of the team members is a hard driver. She was my first choice to lead the task force, in fact."

Listrom smiled. "You'll know who I'm talking about as soon as you meet her."

With that said, Listrom pushed across a legal-size envelope with his name printed on it. He opened it up and looked inside.

"The keys are for the outside door of the building and your desk," Listrom said. "There's an ID card, which you'll need to get in and out of the building. Your logon ID and password for the computer system are written down on that piece of paper, those and the code to disable the building alarm."

Mallory nodded. He'd figured that out on his own.

"The BlackBerry is already set up for you," Listrom said. "It and the landlines in the offices will be used for all official verbal communications. If you have problems, don't hesitate to call me. My private number's programmed into the BlackBerry."

Mallory blushed at the words "private number" and stuffed the BlackBerry in his pocket. He started putting the files in his briefcase to avoid making eye contact, and was glad when she looked at her watch and stood to indicate the meeting was over. Then she walked around her desk and held out her hand. He took it, and she held his hand with both of hers, looking into his eyes as she spoke.

"As far as my political position goes, Bill, just do your job. My career isn't nearly as important as stopping these deaths."

He pulled his hand away from hers and made a hasty retreat.

When he started his car, his hand still felt warm from when she'd held on to it. He liked Karen Listrom, and it made him feel good when she praised him and called him Bill. She seemed impressed with his service in the Army, but he wondered what she'd think if she knew the truth. His Army records didn't tell everything. With the Army, they never did.

Chapter 5

It wasn't far to the Task Force Team Center, just nine miles from the Capitol Building, but it still took Mallory almost thirty minutes to make the drive. His mind wasn't on the road, which got him turned around a couple of times. He was thinking about Martin Woodley, mulling over Woodley's place in the formation of the task force and his recommendation that Mallory lead it.

The Team Center was a small brick building in an industrial park, seven miles outside of Lansing, just off I-69. The asphalt parking lot would hold maybe twenty vehicles. There were security cameras mounted on light poles, and two more above the entrance door. No signs identified the building, just a number above the door.

Mallory opened the outer door with the key and stepped into a small vestibule. The inner door had an electronic lock with a card reader. He used the laminated ID to card himself in, spotted the alarm panel and punched in the number to disable it.

A unisex bathroom was next to the vestibule, so he decided to get rid of some coffee. With that out of the way, he took a look around. The whole place looked and smelled like money had been thrown at it. The smell of fresh paint and new carpeting saturated the air. Everything was new.

The vestibule led to an open office area, where four brand-new desks were set up with lamps and landline phones sitting on them. A big flat-screen monitor took up a portion of one wall, and a laminated table was set up underneath it. To the side of the open office space, a large room was set up as a break room, with a refrigerator, ample counter space and a sink for washing dishes. A laminated table with plastic chairs was set up in the middle of the break room.

Two more rooms were at the end of the office area, and Mallory walked over to check them out.

One room was a computer room, with a rack-mount server against one wall and a wireless router installed above the door. The room was stocked with top of the line electronics. One whole wall was covered in shelving, which held state-of-the-art wireless cameras and routers. Spare power supplies, extra cables, splitters, amplifiers and hot-swappable hard drives. All new.

The other room was a private office. A computer monitor, phone and lamp were on another new desk. A flat-screen TV was mounted on one wall. As leader of the Task Force, Mallory figured the office was his. He sat down, fired up the computer and logged on. After he'd found his way around the system and changed his password, he shut it down, pulled the files of his team members from his briefcase and scanned them. With that finished, he wandered over to the break room to see if there was a coffeepot. There was. He was rummaging through the cupboards, looking for cups and coffee, when he heard the vestibule door open.

"Hello?" a voice called. "Hello?"

Mallory walked out of the break room. A tall, dark man with a scimitar mustache held out his hand.

"I am Abdul Korszctani, of the FBI," the man said. His Middle Eastern accent was pronounced. "Everyone calls me Doolee."

Abdul Korszctani was a Pakistani immigrant, originally recruited by the FBI as a linguist. But, with a degree in physics and extensive knowledge of weaponry and heroin production, he'd been transferred to Scientific Analysis. Mallory shook his hand.

"Doolee?"

The man grinned and nodded. Mallory found himself smiling back.

"I'm Bill Mallory, Doolee. I was about to make some coffee."

Doolee shook his head adamantly, and waved his arms like he was trying to hail a cab.

"Oh no. I will do it. You are the boss, sir."

Doolee put his laptop case on a desk, took off his sport coat, then went to the break room. He was puttering around in there when a blonde-haired Asian man walked in.

His hair wasn't just blonde, but an almost iridescent canary yellow, and cut so it stuck out from his head like a scrub brush. With his wrap-around sunglasses, he looked to Mallory like some Asian punk from a cheap martial arts movie. He reminded himself he wasn't in the Army anymore and walked over to extend his hand.

"Bill Mallory. You must be Sam Lu of the DEA."

Sam took off his sunglasses and took Mallory's hand.

"That's me, sir."

The file said Sam was fluent in Mandarin and Vietnamese, but Mallory caught no trace of an accent.

"Doolee's making coffee, Sam. Pick out a desk and make yourself at home."

Sam looked over to the break room, where Doolee smiled out at them. Sam nodded back, then decided on the desk next to the one Doolee had taken. He put his laptop case on the desk and, gazing at the flat-screen on the wall, let out a low whistle.

"Seventy-two inches," Sam said. He walked to the screen and examined the back, then turned back to Mallory with a grin. "Cable's already hooked up. I can connect the computer network to it, no problem."

Sam went back to his desk, sat down and opened his laptop. He fiddled with it a minute, then went over to the room with all the computer equipment.

"Server room," Sam said. "Nice setup."

Sam had a Bachelor's in Computer Science and a Master's in Database Administration. He worked as a computer scientist and linguist at the Detroit DEA Division.

"The wireless isn't connected yet, sir. You want me to get us up and running?"

Without waiting for an answer, Sam headed into the server room. A couple of minutes later, another member of his team walked in.

She was young, blonde and television commercial pretty. Her clothes looked like they came from stores with names Mallory couldn't pronounce. Mallory untied his tongue and introduced himself. He didn't know whether to offer to shake hands or not, but the young woman held out a hand with perfect nails, painted a light purple to match her dress. He took it, worried that he would crush it, but her grip was firm.

"I'm Jessica Harmon, sir, from the Michigan State Police."

According to the file, Jessica Harmon earned her Bachelor's in Criminology at 20 and her Master's in the same subject the following year. Her five year career with the State Police began in the intelligence unit, giving weekly briefings on crime trends. Within a year she was compiling the reports instead of just reading them.

Her smile was radiant and her voice sounded like a teenager's. Mallory had no choice. He had to smile back. Doolee came out of the break room, grinning and holding out his hand.

"Abdul Korszctani. Please call me Doolee."

Jessica giggled and Doolee grinned even wider. Then she tipped her head from side to side, and her shoulder length hair flowed perfectly with the movement. Doolee was captivated.

"Doolee? I like that," she said.

Doolee looked like he was ready to float away. Then Sam charged out of the server room, pushed himself between Jessica and Doolee and extended his hand to her.

"I'm Sam, Jessica. DEA."

The testosterone was getting out of control.

"Why don't you pick out a desk, Jessica?" Mallory said.

She put her laptop case on the desk farthest from the door, then hung her purse on the chair. The purse, like everything else about her, was color coordinated. Jessica was looking around the place and smiling at everyone when the other female team member came in.

This woman wore a dark gray business suit with a starched white cotton blouse. A hefty shoulder bag rested on her right hip.

Her left hand held her laptop case. Mallory walked over and extended his hand.

"I'm Bill Mallory. You must be Special Investigator Teri Altro."

Teri Altro didn't take his hand, but recoiled and took a step back from him. "Just Altro," she said.

She looked everybody up and down and tapped a heel as she waited. Sam and Doolee gave their names, and she nodded. When Jessica gave her name with a beaming smile, Altro scowled. Then she walked to Mallory's office, looked in and turned to him.

"You take the office, Mallory?"

Mallory nodded. Everyone else was calling him sir, but Altro evidently wasn't going to. She looked the place over, then stomped back to the desk where Jessica had her laptop and purse.

"Well, if you get the office, then I want this desk." She glared over at Jessica. "This your stuff, Princess?"

Jessica trotted to the desk, scooped up her laptop and purse, and smiled at Altro.

"Sorry, Ms. Altro. I'll take the other one."

The way Altro commandeered that desk was the first glimpse Mallory had of her stubborn willpower, but it fit what her file said about her.

Because of her drive and GPA, Altro was hired straight out of law school by the Michigan Attorney General Office. In just two years she worked her way into the Criminal Division, then earned her own office and the Special Investigator title.

Altro had a law degree, but didn't sit at the counselor's table. Instead, she coordinated investigations for the prosecutors. Right then she was investigating her desk, opening drawers, then slamming them closed, frowning about something.

"Why don't we all get some coffee?" Mallory said.

Doolee had found some cardboard cups, cream and sugar. Everything was laid out on the counter. They all fixed their coffee and started filing out. Altro stood outside the break room with a black ceramic coffee mug in her hand, waiting for them to leave before she would go in.

They ended up at their desks with coffee in the cardboard cups, Altro with hers in her black ceramic mug. Mallory sat on a corner of the table under the big flat-screen television and took a whiff of the coffee. It smelled strong enough to strip paint. Everybody took a tentative sip.

"Whoa!" Sam gasped. Jessica coughed and screwed up her face. Mallory shuddered and looked over at Doolee, who was grinning again.

"Good, no?" He turned to Sam. "It will grow a moustache on your lip, Sammy Lu."

Jessica giggled and pushed her cup away.

"No thank you, Doolee. I don't want a moustache."

They all turned to Altro, who took a drink and nodded to Doolee.

"Good coffee, Doolee. Damn good."

Doolee raised his eyebrows and smiled at Altro. For a second, Mallory thought she may smile back. But she didn't, just nodded her head again. Doolee leaned back in his chair and stroked his moustache. Mallory decided to get things going.

"We'll get to know each other as we go along, but you should know who I am."

Altro's upper lip curled into a snarl. "We don't need touchy-feely introductions, Mallory. We were all briefed on who you are and everybody got a look at the file on you." She raised her eyebrows and tilted her head toward Jessica. "I think we can all read?"

Jessica bobbed her head and beamed like she'd just received a compliment.

"We need to get this show on the road," Altro said.

It was Wednesday afternoon, the fifteenth day of April. Two days later, they tried to kill Altro.

Chapter 6

Mallory was staring at his BlackBerry. Altro had just reported that someone tried to kill her, then hung up on him. He shook his head, called the other Task Force members and told them to report back in.

When he arrived at the Team Center, Doolee was already in the break room, making the nerve-fraying coffee Mallory had quickly become addicted to. Mallory was pouring himself a cup when Sam Lu came in, pushing his wrap-around sunglasses up on his forehead. Mallory took a deep breath when he saw Sam's ridiculous yellow hair, but Doolee walked out of the break room to welcome him with a high-five and the poetic greeting he'd started using.

"Sammy Lu... How are you?"

The team was still getting to know each other, but Doolee and Sam had quickly bonded. The two even went out for drinks last night — Doolee had renounced Islam and developed a taste for liquor — and their friendship was cemented in the uninhibited honesty brought on by alcohol. The tall, dark Doolee, with his proud scimitar mustache, and the diminutive, sallow Sam formed an unlikely pair, but neither of them seemed to mind.

Mallory walked out of the break room with his coffee, thinking about giving Jessica another call when she walked in, looking fresh and feminine as always. He smiled like an idiot at Jessica, then got everyone's attention by holding up one hand.

"Listen up, people. Someone made an attempt on Altro's life — at a drugstore in Mason."

He shook his head at the worried looks.

"She's okay. A man stepped in and stopped it. The locals are on the scene, but I want you people to go to work on this."

They looked at him, waiting.

"We need information. Get it. I'll give the Attorney General the news."

He went into his office, closed the door and called the AG. Mallory reported solely to the AG, who was scheduled to meet weekly with the FBI and the DEA. A report would then be given to the Governor. When he finished talking to the AG, he checked his email and scanned the news channels. There was nothing on television yet, so he turned it off and thought about what had happened.

The attempt had occurred in a public place, a drugstore that would probably have security cameras. The press would be all over this, but there was one sure way to control the information made public. Mallory picked up the landline, called the FBI's Satellite Office in East Lansing and eventually was connected to the Senior Resident Agent there, Thomas Furlow. Mallory explained the situation to Furlow and said he wanted the Bureau on this case right away.

Furlow said he would call the Detroit Field Office, that their Evidence Response Team would have to come from Detroit. He'd send two agents to the scene immediately, and would interface with the Mason and Ingham County departments personally. They'd worked well with both departments in the past, and he didn't think there would be a problem.

"Keep a lid on this, Furlow," Mallory said. "The location of the Team Center isn't public and the Task Force members' names aren't either. We want to keep it that way."

It was almost an hour before Mallory left his office and walked into the Team Room. Ex-military and an avid cop show addict, Mallory had started off calling the open office area the Squad Room. Altro had ridiculed that, said that it sounded idiotic. Jessica lined up behind Altro, while managing to be polite and deferential to Mallory. Doolee and Sam agreed with Jessica, of course.

So it was the Team Room. He sat at what had become his customary place, on the corner of the table under the flat-screen, pushed his glasses up and waited to be acknowledged.

"All right. What do we have so far?"

Sam spoke up, consulting his laptop with his feet up on his desk, as usual.

"For starters, we have three corpses, the guys who were going to kill Altro. They're all Asian. No big surprise there."

Because of the heroin's purity and moisture content, Sam had already concluded the drug was coming from the Far East, probably Southeast Asia. Doolee, who was knowledgeable about the heroin industry in Pakistan and Afghanistan, agreed.

"No IDs on the bodies," Sam said. "All dressed in casual clothing like clean-cut Americans. Ingham County deputies printed them and got DNA samples. They're on the scene now, and the locals are stepping aside."

Mallory nodded. Mason was a town of about 8,000, located just southeast of Lansing. It was the Ingham County Seat, so the sheriff's department, the jail and the courthouse were all nearby.

"One of the deputies said all three bodies had pretty distinctive tattoos on their forearms," Sam continued. "They'll post photographs as soon as they can."

Mallory cocked his head to one side. "Who's the guy who stepped in to stop it?"

"We don't know, sir. Like the men he killed, he had no ID. No wallet, no driver's license, not even any cash. White male in his fifties or sixties. Five-ten. Light build. County took prints and got blood samples. All the evidence is still at the scene."

"Won't he talk to them?"

"I guess Altro shot him. He's at Sparrow Hospital in Lansing now. Jessica called Sparrow, but they couldn't give us any information yet."

Mallory frowned at that, but Sam continued like it didn't mean anything.

"I called Altro. She was still talking to the county deputies at the scene. Said she needed to rent a car, because all the glass was blown out of hers somehow. She's coming in, but may go home to clean up first. I guess she owns a condo right there in town."

Altro and Jessica were the only members of the task force who weren't staying in hotel rooms. Altro was already working at the Attorney General office in Lansing, and owned a condo in Mason. Jessica worked at the State Police office in Lansing and commuted from her parents' home in the town of Leslie, south of Mason.

"Oh yeah, she also said she was going to stop by the hospital," Sam said. "She wanted to check on the guy she shot."

Doolee was shaking his head as he spoke up.

"That is not good, sir. For her."

Jessica raised her hand and chimed in.

"Doolee's right, sir. She must be pretty shaken up. Maybe you should give her some time off, a day or so."

Sam shook his head. "Altro's one tough cookie, Jessica," he said. "And we need her in here. There were a number of witnesses, but none of them remember anything about the shooting. Some of them were even ranting about an earthquake. They ended up being sedated and taken to the hospital for observation."

Jessica's shoulders slumped, but she nodded in agreement.

"Speaking of witnesses," Sam continued. "One of them is missing. The drugstore pharmacist."

"Does the store have security cameras?" Mallory asked.

Sam nodded. "Lucky for us, it's an updated system, 120 frames a second and four cameras. The action should be really clear. I guess the store had some trouble with shoplifting and management had it updated. I talked to the locals at the scene and helped them download everything."

"Let's run it then. I want to see this."

Sam worked at his laptop and the display was fed to the large flat-screen on the wall behind Mallory. The first video was from the camera covering the store entry door from inside. Sam fast forwarded until he came to the shooting, backed it up and started again. They watched the action unfold until the shooting, which raised murmurs from the others.

"Whoa, whoa! Stop it right there," Mallory said. "Back it up and rerun that. Can you slow it down some?"

Sam played it again, at half speed. The murmurs rose again, louder and more agitated.

"Can we check this out, Sam?" Mallory asked. "This can't be right. Nobody moves that fast."

"No kidding," Sam said. "You want me to do it now, sir, or just keep going?"

Mallory motioned for Sam to continue. Running the video at one quarter speed revealed even more. Doolee jumped to his feet, approached the screen and pointed to the images. Unlike the others, he was actually smiling.

"You see this? These men come in carrying shotguns, like big cowboys. But this man steps right into them. See? His stance and position are perfect."

Jessica's brow was furrowed and her blue eyes were open wide. The young woman raised her hand and, after Mallory acknowledged her, she asked the question that was on everyone's mind.

"What kind of guy can do something like that, sir? Special Forces maybe?"

Sam broke in. "He's gotta be hired muscle. This looks like the start of a drug war to me."

Jessica raised her hand again, and Mallory again acknowledged her. She pointed to the screen where the man was reentering the drugstore.

"Why would he come back in then, Sammy? Why would he save Ms. Altro's life in the first place? I mean, it's pretty clear that he did. Anyone capable of that could do the killing after she was out of the way."

Sam frowned, but nodded. Mallory motioned with one hand.

"Roll it again, Sam, from when he first walks in. At normal speed. Maybe we can pick up something."

The feed started again and ran through to the timeframe when Altro shot the man. Doolee jumped to his feet again and Sam stopped the video.

"That is a good stance for Altro," Doolee said. "Considering the way he backed her up. But her shot is all herky-jerky. She is lucky she hit the man, sir."

"Lucky?" Mallory asked.

Doolee's face went all hang-dog and he shook his head. "You are right, sir. It may be a problem. They may reprimand her."

"Right, Doolee, but what's going on after her shot?" Mallory asked. "That looks like some kind of explosion. That's probably what blew out the glass in Altro's car."

Doolee was getting back into his seat as he spoke. "We can check that, sir, no problem. Explosions always leave residuals. But I see no flash. No smoke. This does not make sense."

Mallory squinted at the screen. "What about the shootings, Doolee?"

"Very little blood, sir. See this, when the shooter comes back in? This dead man in the door does not bleed. Look in the doorway. There is no scatter, no blowing out from an exit wound, just from the entrance wound." He turned to Sam. "Run the video again, Sammy, the part where he shoots them."

Doolee stroked one end of his mustache while Sam fiddled with his laptop, then pointed to the screen and continued. "These men are dead when they hit the floor. See these two men? The way they fall down? See the knees buckle, the arms drop? Their nerves are all cut. Without the bullet to the back of their heads, these men would just collapse. But the impact pushed their heads, hard enough that they fell forward."

Doolee paused for breath. "And see, sir? Look closely at the shooting. Almost no recoil. He must be using light loads to have so little recoil."

Mallory nodded. Doolee was right. The weapon didn't jump much in the shooter's hand. The cartridges would have to contain less gunpowder than a normal factory load for that to happen.

"What kind of weapons do you think he has there?" Mallory asked. "They look like the old Army forty-five to me."

"Yes, Colt M1911A, I think. See how thin they are? Single-slide action and single-feed magazine," Doolee said.

Mallory nodded, then turned to Sam. "Okay, Sam, let's roll that part again."

The shooter came back into the store and Altro shot him. After the shot, she was just standing there, holding her weapon on the man, and didn't lower it until the pharmacist came between her and the shooter. The man was leaning against a stack of charcoal, the pharmacist bent over him with a hand on his forehead. Then it looked like he had some kind of seizure and, when it stopped, the pharmacist bent over him again. In the pandemonium at the end of the incident, with police and EMTs arriving, the pharmacist simply walked out of the store.

"That's our missing witness. Find out who she is, Sam."

"Already done, sir. The locals got her name and address from the store manager. Her name is Thang Neng Mai. She's a Hmong refugee out of Laos. Lives there in Mason. Local uniforms are on their way to pick her up."

Mallory took some time to think, pushing his glasses up on his nose.

"All right, people, keep working it. I don't like the way this is shaping up. There's too much we don't know. We have to find out who the shooter is to even begin to make sense of all this."

Doolee's BlackBerry buzzed and he spoke to the caller for a few minutes before he ended the call.

"Altro, sir. She wants me to go to the scene. It is a good idea. I can make a visual check for explosion residue."

Mallory patted his jacket pocket. His BlackBerry was there. Altro was deliberately bypassing him.

Jessica raised her hand. "I'll go with you, Doolee. Maybe Ms. Altro could use some company."

Doolee broke into a brief smile, but then shook his head. "She wants you to stay and call the hospital, Jessica, for permission to tap into their security system. She also wants a video feed of the man's room."

He then turned to Mallory. "Sir? Altro wants a uniform on the hospital room. And for you to call the FBI. She wants them to do the scene. I think this is a good idea too, sir."

Altro was putting Mallory in his place, telling him what to do. Well, Governor Listrom had warned him about how pushy she was. He didn't bother telling the rest of them he'd already called the Bureau. It wasn't important at this point.

"Right," Mallory said. It *was* a good idea for Doolee to check things out. The FBI was the best at assessing a crime scene and gathering evidence, but their thorough methodology took time. He wanted information in a hurry. "When you go to the scene, take Sam with you. I want him to check the video equipment."

He held one hand up for them to wait, and pushed his glasses up on his nose while he thought. "Take both of your vehicles, and give one to Altro. I don't want her held up waiting for a rental."

Sam took his feet off the desk and shook his head. "No need, sir. She's got a rental already on the way."

"Okay. But before you go, put the videos on the server so we can all get to it. Every camera."

"Already done, sir."

Mallory nodded and turned to Jessica. "Jessica, call the Lansing Police about a uniformed guard on the shooter's room for me."

Mallory went back into his office, found the surveillance video on the server and opened it. The phone on his desk rang and he paused the video. It was the Governor. She'd heard about the incident and was concerned. Mallory was again impressed with how genuine and personable the woman could be, even while she worked quickly and got straight to the point. And he really liked the way she called him Bill.

Mallory updated her, then got back to the surveillance videos. As he watched the feed from the camera behind the pharmacy, he came to the timeframe where Altro shot the killer.

He stopped the feed when he saw the shooter staring at Altro just before she shot him. A vague feeling of recognition ran through him.

He unconsciously began rubbing at a thick scar that ran across his chin, a scar he'd picked up long ago, when he was a young Second Lieutenant in Vietnam.

Chapter 7

Twelve time zones away, in the mountains of northwest Laos, the morning was chilly. Khun Pao's bones ached from the cold, and he yelled for the girl to put more wood on the fire. She complied, then stood in front of him with her eyes downcast, waiting to see if there was more he wanted from her. He shoved her away so violently that she fell to the floor. He was busy.

Khun was talking on his satellite phone to an underling in the United States. It was too early for business, and he was angry at the disturbance to his patterns. But when he heard the news, fear replaced his anger. He spoke loudly and abruptly to hide it.

"He said this? He said my name? How did he happen to be there?"

He listened, then yelled into the phone.

"He had the signs of the dragon? You're sure of this?"

The underling was positive. Damn the eyes of the devil! The man who wore the dragon signs had cost him a fortune over the years.

"And you let him escape? You fool!"

Of course it was not the underling's fault his men had failed. They were no match for this man. He was the Valley Walker. The stories about him among the Hmong were legendary. They said he walked with the dead, that he left no footprints. Khun didn't want his subordinate to sense the fear that was creeping into his belly, however, so he continued his tirade.

"What about the woman? Did you at least complete your mission?"

Khun Pao listened, but his mind was on other things. He would have to call the dung eater, the cursed white man in the United States who thought the whole world belonged to him. Khun detested Martin Woodley, but the call had to be made. Business was business.

The dung eater had offered Khun the chance to expand his exports of heroin to the United States, even helped with a transportation scheme that would facilitate the quantities planned. Khun was taking a loss on his product right now, the cursed white man's doing again, but had plans to turn that around. The underling was asking him something, but he cut him off.

"Forget the woman. She is the dung eater's problem. The killing was his idea."

Khun disconnected and made the call to the dung eater.

*****

Martin Woodley wasn't eating dung. He was nestled in a leather club chair with his feet resting on a matching ottoman. A glass of single malt whiskey sat on the side table.

The network news was running on the television, but he was only half listening to the feel-good piece, some nonsense about saving an endangered bird. When the programming was interrupted for a special broadcast, he put his hand on the remote.

"Violence erupted in the quiet town of Mason, Michigan today."

Woodley picked up the remote and turned up the volume. This was what he was waiting for.

"A shootout occurred when three men walked into a local drugstore with sawed-off shotguns. The FBI has taken over the scene, and they're being tight-lipped about what exactly occurred, or what the three armed men were after. But, thanks to our network of viewer reporters, we learned that an unknown man stepped in and foiled their plans, whatever they were. He killed them, folks. All three of them."

A picture of a man came up on the screen. His eyes were closed and he was lying on his side on a gray tiled floor.

"We were also able to obtain this exclusive photo of him. Authorities still have not identified the man..."

Woodley hit the pause button on the remote and leaned forward in his chair to study the photo.

It's him.

The whiskey on the side table was meant to be sipped, but he drank it down in one gulp. His valet was gone for the night, so he stood, crossed the room to the bar and poured more. He took a deep drink, plodded back to his chair and sat heavily. After watching the rest of the report, he went to his computer to gather information. The material he scanned confirmed what he'd already seen and heard.

Woodley considered the situation. Mallory, the man in charge of the Task Force, was reliable. Bill Mallory had always done what he was told, and would continue to do so. That insured Woodley's untouchable position. But the assassination attempt had failed, and the reason it had failed was extremely troubling. Something had to be done.

He had two men he kept on retainer for situations like this one. Brain and Sledge, his technical consultants. He picked up the phone and made a call.

Brain answered on the first ring. "Good evening, sir."

Woodley kept his voice conversational. He was good at maintaining outward appearances, the façade for public consumption.

"Good evening, Brain. I'm afraid we have a problem. Our old nemesis from Southeast Asia has surfaced."

The line was silent for a beat while Brain took that in. "You're sure of this, sir?"

"Khun Pao called to tell me. I didn't believe him, but I just saw his picture on television. He killed three of Khun's men sent to eliminate Teri Altro."

"How did Khun hear of it?"

"He let the driver live."

There was a pause as Brain digested this.

"A message to Khun?"

"Exactly. There is a bright side, however. She shot him for some reason. He's in a hospital in Lansing, Michigan now."

"Shot him?"

"Doesn't seem possible, does it? Nevertheless, it happened. I'd like you and Sledge to get over there and look into it."

"Of course, sir."

He could hear the clacking of computer keys.

"There's a flight out of Dulles in less than two hours. We'll be on it, sir."

"Good. I'll send you the information as it comes in, including who to contact when you get to Lansing. Keep your distance from the action, but make sure the outcome is in our favor."

A pause for effect.

"Make sure they finish him."

Chapter 8

Altro slumped in the rental car, trying to bring some semblance of reality to the violence in the drugstore. What she thought she saw couldn't have actually happened. It was a trick of the mind, an aberration of her thought processes.

No doubt, she'd shot a man. She'd tried to push her way in closer as the paramedics worked on him, but lost that battle. The Sheriff's deputy who took her gun was brisk with her, and told her it would be sent to the State Police Forensics Lab for ballistics tests. She had to submit to a gunshot residue test, even though she openly admitted to discharging her weapon.

The shockwave she'd felt was real, too. The evidence of glass exploding — disintegrating, really — was scattered through the store and parking lot. Her own car, a Cadillac XLR convertible, couldn't be driven because of the broken glass. When she retrieved her suit jacket from the car, it was covered with tiny fragments and she had to shake them off.

And the man she shot had definitely killed three armed men. She'd watch them bag the bodies while she gave her statement to a deputy, relieved she didn't have to walk around them on her way out of the store.

All of that was real enough, but everything else about the man she'd shot escaped reality. The way she'd felt him reaching into her — the throbbing veins — the tattoo mask — the dragon that came out of him — the ease and speed of the killings... It couldn't have happened that way.

Altro shook her head and started the car. She thought about going home to clean up, then shook it off. She had to get back in to the Team Center. First, though, she needed to go to the hospital. A mental replay of the episode convinced her she wouldn't have had her weapon out in time to protect herself. The man had saved her life, and she'd shot him in a moment of schoolgirl fright. She had to check on him.

All she knew was that the ambulance took him to Sparrow Hospital. She pulled out of the parking lot, jumped onto US 127 and headed north to Lansing, pushing the rental for all it was worth. Altro was used to the acceleration and quick handling of her XLR. She loved to drive fast, and the V-8 in the two-seater never failed to give her a nice rush. The XLR was her pride and joy. Her baby.

The sedan provided by the rental company, however, drove like an obese cow. When she pulled into the parking lot, the car's spongy brakes couldn't keep up with her aggressive driving, and she nearly drove through the barrier gate. She swore, backed up to take the ticket that marked her time in the lot and glanced at it. It was 7:42.

An elderly woman at the information desk consulted a computer, then said all she could tell Altro was that he was brought into the ER earlier. He hadn't been admitted to the hospital. Altro walked over to the ER waiting room to see if he was still there. It was busy.

People were waiting in line to be logged in, or sitting in plastic chairs. Children cried while parents tried to keep them quiet. Other children ran around unattended. She looked through the doors to the ER proper, saw an orderly bringing in a patient on a gurney. Doctors and nurses were rushing about and shouting to each other.

Altro stood in line for fifteen minutes, but the nurse at the counter would only tell her that he was in the ER. When Altro produced her credentials and tried to bully her for more information, the nurse just shrugged and threatened to call security.

Altro chided herself for not calling ahead. She still wasn't thinking straight. Her stomach growled, and she realized that she hadn't eaten since noon. In the hospital cafeteria, she wolfed down a stale sub with a cup of rancid coffee. She went to the bathroom, looked at herself in the mirror and saw her hair was still in the stubby ponytail. That had to go. When she finished brushing out her hair, she took a closer look. Her eyes were hollow and dead.

She leaned against the counter. Her head drooped. She'd shot a man.

It was one thing to shoot at targets, another thing to actually pull the trigger on a human being and watch him go down. One thing to think about the need to defend yourself, but something altogether different to actually see people killed. To see human matter spraying, smell the powder and hair burning.

Women came in the bathroom and left. Altro leaned against the counter with her head down, hoping she hadn't killed him. Her BlackBerry buzzed. It was Mallory.

"I'm on my way."

Altro splashed water on her face and dried it off with a paper towel, then straightened her shoulders and hiked up her shoulder bag. She flogged the rental sedan to the Team Center, wishing she could shove a cattle prod up its tailpipe to make it move faster.

*****

He was surrounded by urgent voices. Hands removed his shirt and tried to take the hemp bag that held his heart. He couldn't let it go. More hands probed him and attached things to his chest.

"Clear!"

Cold, wet pressure on his chest, then a jolting that arched his back and made him grind his teeth. The voices grew louder and more strident.

"Clear!"

The jolt again. And again.

Gradually, the voices grew quiet.

"We have to call it. He's gone."

58

The voices left him. He drifted away, deep into the valley. There was only cold and darkness until he felt rolling movement. The movement stopped. He heard a soft *ding* and the sound of doors sliding open. An elevator.

Then he felt the presence of Teri Altro. She was near, and just that was enough to warm him, to give him hope. His eyes opened, which shocked a man standing there.

"Shit!"

The man's hand squeezed his, touched his face, his chest. His eyes closed again. More rolling movement, faster now.

"Doctor, this guy's still alive! His eyes opened. He's warm."

The voices returned. Hands probed and prodded him again. Things were attached to him. A needle pricked the back of his hand. Something was forced down his throat. He endured it all.

He felt Teri Altro leave, but she had come. She cared. It was enough.

Chapter 9

Sam and Doolee jumped up when Altro walked into the Team Center, but she ignored them and stumped stoically to her desk. The two men followed at a distance, but Jessica intervened and, for once, Altro was grateful for the way the Princess could bend men into pretzels.

The room fell into an uneasy silence until Mallory walked out of his office. He started toward Altro's desk, but she chased him off with a scowl and shake of her head. He took his place on the edge of the table.

His cheap suit jacket was off, with the tie tucked into his shirt to keep it out of the way. His gray hair looked like he'd gotten it buzzed at one of those chain barber shops recently. His clunky glasses slipped down on his nose, making him look like an absent-minded school teacher. They were waiting on him, but he still cleared his throat and held up a hand to get their attention.

"Okay, people. Did you find anything at the scene, Doolee?"

Doolee shrugged his shoulders. "I saw no evidence of an explosion, sir, but the FBI is there now. They will check for residuals. There are no flash marks, though, no shockwave pattern. An interesting problem."

The silence hung as Mallory tried to digest this. "Okay," he said. "Let the FBI do their job. They're about the best there is for evidence collection and analysis. What about the weapons the shooter used?"

"It is like we thought," Doolee answered. "Old M1911A. And the rounds, too. The cartridges left in the magazine had a very light charge. Israeli air marshals use light loads like this, so there is no collateral damage to the passengers or plane if they shoot. The bullets were hollow points. Very thin jacket with cuts in them. He made the rounds himself, no doubt."

"So what do you think, Doolee?"

Doolee was smiling as he gave his assessment. "There was a briefcase he carried the weapons in, and I looked inside, sir. No more rounds or magazines, only enough to do this job." His smile grew to a grin. "Sir, this man knew what he was doing."

Altro was well aware of Doolee's knowledge of weapons. Actually, it was more than just knowledge. The man would be considered by many to be a genuine gun nut, in fact. He'd noticed the weight of Altro's gun in her shoulder bag, asked to see it and complimented her choice, even offered to go to a range with her. How anyone with a degree in physics acquired such a love of tools designed to kill people was beyond her.

Mallory nodded, stared at his feet for a few seconds, then shifted on the corner of the table. "Sam, what about the security equipment at the store?"

"It's quality equipment, sir," Sam answered. "Less than three months old. The installation looked okay, as professional as anything is these days. I couldn't find anything that would cause a glitch in recording speed."

Altro knew they had to be talking about the impossible speed with which the man killed the would-be assassins. Sam was a genuine bit-head, the kind of guy you asked to speak English when he talked about computers. Hell, if Sammy said there was nothing wrong with the equipment, then there was nothing wrong with it.

Sam consulted his laptop and went on. "I went over the recordings again, but couldn't find any problems there either. I just don't have an answer for the video."

Throughout this exchange, Altro was staring at her desk, but could sense Mallory peering at her.

"Altro, what do you think? You were at the scene. You saw this guy in action."

Every head in the room turned to see her reaction. When she raised her head, it was clear that they half expected her to break down and start crying. Far from it, she'd actually been deep in thought, rolling the events and her impressions around in her mind. She wanted to be able to talk about this as logically and honestly as possible, but there was just no logic to it.

"He just looked like some guy in the drugstore at first," she said. "I knew he was watching me, but he wasn't checking me out, if you know what I mean."

They knew what she meant, all right. She'd caught each of the three men there trying to figure out what she would look like in something more revealing than her business suit. She'd thought about scolding them, talking about some necessary sensitivity training, just to make them squirm. But it really didn't bother her when men looked at her. She usually just ignored it, like she'd tried to ignore the man in the drugstore.

"Then things got really weird."

Their expressions began closing down, doubt appearing in their eyes, and she couldn't blame them. She herself didn't know what to think about what happened.

"No, let me finish here," she said. "You saw the security video."

Everyone nodded.

"Well, then you know how bizarre the whole incident was."

There where nods around the room again. Skirting the mystical atmosphere that overtook the event, she plunged ahead.

"When he moved up to the front of the store, it was like he changed. At first he was just some guy, but then he turned into this killing machine. I mean, it looked to me like he intentionally moved up there to intercept those guys, like he knew they were coming."

Mallory interrupted her.

"So you think the shooter was there on purpose, Altro?"

She didn't like the term "shooter." The man saved her life. But Mallory's face was open and waiting, so she just nodded.

"It looked that way to me."

"Why would he do that? Do you know him?"

"No, I've no idea who he is. Why he would be there in the first place."

"We're thinking he must have had some special training," Mallory said.

"Training?" she barked. "I've never seen anything like what happened. Those guys he killed didn't have a snowball's chance in hell. He was out the door before the bodies hit the floor."

"I know," Mallory said. "I studied the video for half an hour."

Altro shivered. In spite of herself, she could picture veins writhing and throbbing on the man's face, veins that morphed into a mask of tattoos.

"Was there a good shot of his face?" she asked.

Altro saw a ghost of something flicker across Mallory's face. Fingering an old scar on his chin, he nodded, but changed the subject.

"Why would he come back inside, Altro? He was as good as gone."

"I don't know. He just walked back in and straight over to me."

Then came the question she had no answer for.

"You felt you had to shoot then?"

A dumb, mechanical nod was all she could manage.

"I talked to the AG, Altro," Mallory said. "He said he'd personally stand behind you in any investigation into the shooting. The man just killed three people. He was still armed and presented a threat, backing you into the building like that."

Then Mallory pointed a finger at her.

"You should have some police protection."

Altro shook her head. "No way. I'm not having somebody follow me around."

"Be reasonable, Altro. Those guys were going to kill you." She shook her head again, but Mallory pushed it. "I've already talked to County and they agreed to do it. They want the overtime."

But she was adamant. "Look, Mallory, I've got a law degree. I know my rights as a citizen. You can't force police protection on me. Call them off."

Mallory stared at her for almost a minute before he nodded his surrender. He stood up from his perch on the table, looked at his watch, and started fingering that scar on his chin again.

"Okay, people," Mallory said. "The only reason I wanted to talk to Altro was to get her take on the shooter and what happened. I don't want us staying too late. We'll have to be in tomorrow." He turned to Altro. "Altro, you can refuse police protection, but I want you to take the morning off."

Doolee leaned over and motioned to Altro as Mallory walked back to his office. His voice was a whisper.

"Altro, what is this? Why did you shoot that man?"

She shook her head. There was no rational explanation. Her gun had just gone off. She stood up, rolled her chair over next to Doolee's desk and plopped down in it. She liked Doolee — hell, everybody liked Doolee — but she definitely wanted to keep this conversation quiet.

"I don't know. The whole thing was so... It was eerie."

Doolee just looked at her and waited for a clearer explanation. Sammy and the Princess were both looking their way, but Altro couldn't help herself. The memory of the dragon, the man killing the would-be killers so damn easily. It all played again and again on her mind's big-screen, in vivid color and surround sound.

"And this guy... This guy..."

A grin flashed across Doolee's face, but he wiped it off and rapped softly on his desk.

"Altro? Are you okay?"

She hadn't known Doolee long, but she'd never seen a face more animated. His expression could be twisted in anger, bright and full of life, dreamy and far away, or like it was right now. His face seemed to have elongated and his eyes drooped, making him look like a Bassett Hound.

This was not going to happen. She stood up and put her hands on her hips. "I'm good, Doolee. Just what the hell do you expect after that?"

She glared around the room. "Come on, people. Let's run this guy down. Find out who the hell he is."

Nobody moved, so she continued. "What'd we get on his prints?"

Jessica gave her the bad news. "The FBI is taking charge of the scene, Ms. Altro, so we probably won't get anything on the prints for a couple of days. My guess is we won't hear anything on the DNA samples for a week."

"The hell we won't, Princess."

She swiveled her glare back to Doolee. "Light a fire under them, Doolee. Have them run a tox screen on the corpses, too. I want to know if they had any of this heroin in their system."

Doolee nodded and picked up the phone. Altro didn't let up, but kept the charge going. She turned back to Sam Lu.

"Sam? Did we get anything on the men he killed?"

Sam had his feet up on his desk again. He took them down and turned to Altro. "No ID yet, but this is interesting. The corpses all have the same tattoos."

Sam diddled with his laptop and a picture of the forearm of one of the dead men came up on the flat-screen. It showed a tattoo that covered the entire forearm. Two lions facing each other and holding the globe of the earth in their paws.

"And they were dressed conservatively, but they all had on these shiny new Nikes."

The screen changed and a picture of one of the corpses came up. The man was wearing tan slacks, a plaid cotton sport shirt and iridescent basketball shoes. Altro didn't know what Sam was saying, so she turned to him. He was staring at his laptop screen, his face screwed up in concentration. Then he shook his head and continued.

"Also, the parking lot camera of the drugstore shows a van bringing in the guys he killed. Our shooter actually went out to the van, and it looked like he was talking to the driver."

So that's where he went. Why would he do that? And, like Mallory said, why would he come back in?

Trying to avoid being sidetracked, Altro stared at the floor, tapping her foot while she thought. Out of the corner of her eye she saw Sam staring at her butt and turned her head, just enough to make him worry about getting caught. He raised his eyes back up to her head just as she turned to face him again.

"That's not enough, damnit! See if you can make out the plate number. Do some kind of computer magic on it."

Sam ducked back to his laptop, and Altro turned to Jessica again.

"What about traffic cameras? They're everywhere now. Did any of them pick up that van after it left the drugstore?"

"I'll find out, Ms. Altro."

Altro snapped her fingers. "Well, get on it, Princess."

She glared around the room some more, but everyone had their nose to a laptop or a phone to their ear. There was no use in browbeating them further. As she walked stiffly away from Doolee's desk, she saw him smiling to himself. She looked over at Jessica and Sammy, who were smiling to themselves too.

Altro knew that all of the commands she'd just given were already being taken care of by the FBI. The Bureau would leave nothing to chance, but there would be no way to hurry their investigation. They did things in their own time.

At her desk, she dug out her laptop, took a deep breath and brought up the drugstore video. She ran through the shooting scene, biting the inside of her cheek as she watched it play out. The dragon didn't appear on the video, but that didn't surprise her. She shook her head, disappointed at her imagining demons.

"I just can't believe how fast he killed those guys," she mumbled.

Sam broke away from his laptop and turned to her.

"116.6 milliseconds, roughly. About a tenth of a second."

Jessica sucked in a breath, loud enough that everyone turned to look at her.

"Is that possible, Sammy?" Jessica asked. She sounded like a schoolgirl, as usual. "Where'd you get that number?"

Sam shrugged his shoulders.

"Well, the shootings took up fourteen frames in the video. At 120 frames per second, it works out to 116.6 milliseconds."

Altro turned to Doolee and got his attention. He ended his call, hung up and arched his eyebrows.

"Sam says he killed those guys in a tenth of a second," she said. "Will the damn gun even fire that fast?"

Doolee nodded his head and broke into a grin. "Oh, yes. It is no problem for the weapon." He paused, pursed his lips and stroked his mustache, then shook his head. "But for the shooter? No. I don't see how it is possible."

Chapter 10

The men called Brain and Sledge sat apart from the others in the airport. Their clothes were meant to blend in with the other travelers. Sport jackets and slacks, button-down shirts with no tie. Their loafers were easy to slip on and off as they went through airport security. Their only luggage was a carry-on that would easily fit in the overhead. They were seasoned travelers, on their way to another stop in an endless series of stops.

Brain was just over six feet, and had the easy grace of a practiced athlete. His gray hair was cut short, but still managed to look stylish. His face was hard and chiseled, the face of an aging actor. Cold gray eyes assessed the other people waiting at the departure gate at Dulles International as he worked on his electronic tablet.

In contrast to Brain's height and fit build, Sledge was short, bald and more than a bit overweight. His chubby face sported a neatly trimmed gray mustache and goatee. His soft brown eyes gazed out from behind rimless round glasses. As they waited for their flight to be called, he removed his glasses and wiped them with a cleaning tissue taken from a foil envelope.

"So why the hell are we going to Lansing?" Sledge asked.

Brain leaned over to his partner and spoke in low tones. "I just heard from Woodley. Khun's men tried to kill Special Investigator Teri Altro today."

Sledge put his glasses back on and raised an eyebrow. "Tried?" he asked. "She should have been delayed at the drugstore so the shooters could have an easy job of it. We paid good money to have that happen."

Brain nodded. "Well, they failed."

"What a bunch of morons," Sledge said. "How could they screw that up?"

"Somebody stepped in to stop it," Brain said.

Sledge sat up straight in his chair. "Who?"

Brain had a picture of the man on his tablet. He was on a gurney, with his eyes closed. When Sledge saw the picture, he snatched the tablet and stared at it.

"Shit. I was hoping he was dead."

Brain took the tablet back and shook his head. "Evidently not. There were four men sent, three shooters and a driver. He killed the three shooters with a shot to the back of the head."

Sledge nodded his head slowly. "His signature from the old days."

Brain nodded and let his partner digest this. The chubby man chewed it over.

"Where is he now?" Sledge asked. "Do we know?"

"The Altro woman shot him. He's in a Lansing hospital."

"Shot him? How the hell could that happen?"

Sledge was getting too loud. A woman seated a few rows over looked their way. Brain made a motion with one hand to quiet him, then shook his head. "It's not clear, but we're going there to check things out."

"We're going to finish him off, right?"

Brain grimaced. "That's easier said than done. We've never been able to accomplish it in the past. We couldn't even catch sight of him."

"But we know where he is now," Sledge said. "And he's wounded."

The nine p.m. flight from Dulles to Detroit Metro arrived at 10:32, and the two men were in the rental car by 11:15. With little traffic, they made the drive from DTW to Lansing in less than 90 minutes. It took another fifteen minutes to find the place they were looking for, and they walked into Tommy Mo's Winged Lion with time to spare. Closing time for the bar was still more than thirty minutes away.

After the customary stares when they walked in, the two men were ignored. They ordered a beer and sat down at a table to observe their surroundings. It was a small place with dim lighting and tiny Asian waitresses wearing skimpy, low-cut outfits. They were the only white men there.

Just as they finished their beers, a waitress placed two more on their table. She smiled broadly, placed a hand on Brain's shoulder and turned to point at a man sitting in a booth at the rear of the bar. He was a tall, middle-aged Asian wearing a gray sports jacket over a black silk shirt.

Brain picked up his beer and raised it in a toast, then motioned for the man to join them. He shook his head and motioned for the two of them to join him in the booth instead. Brain placed a bill on the table for their first beers, and the two rose and made their way to the booth. They slid in across from the man, who nodded his head and waited for them to settle in.

"Good evening, gentlemen. I wanted to welcome you to my establishment."

The man's accent was barely noticeable. His tone was friendly and he smiled, but his hooded eyes were cold and calculating. He didn't offer his hand.

"You're Tommy Mo?" Brain asked.

Tommy nodded, then lit a cigarette, oblivious to any objections his customers may have.

"Nice place you have here, Mr. Mo. We actually came here to meet you," Brain said.

Tommy Mo's eyes revealed nothing, so Brain leaned in.

"I'm Brain. My partner here is Sledge. Martin Woodley sent us."

Tommy Mo smiled, but his eyes remained cold. He held his hands out like the Pope at a blessing.

"I've been expecting you gentlemen. What is it that you need?"

Chapter 11

Sleep just wouldn't come for Altro. The bizarre events at the drugstore snapped her back awake every time she started to nod off. At 5:30, she gave it up and called the hospital. They wouldn't tell her much, only that the man she shot had been transferred to intensive care. She had to go to the hospital. She had to see him.

At 6:55, she stormed into ICU. An exhausted looking clerk sitting at the desk barely acknowledged her. Altro slapped her credentials on the counter and demanded to know which room the mystery man was in. The clerk yawned and gave her the number.

There was a Lansing uniform outside the door, reading a magazine and drinking coffee. The cop looked bored and barely awake, but at least he was there. Now that the moment to see the man who had frightened her so badly was here, Altro was thankful for the cop's presence.

The man had saved her life, but the whole event was so confused that she was still trying to determine what had really happened. Instead of clarifying things, the discussion at the Team Center had only served to highlight the unknowns. The only thing she knew for certain about the patient was that he took the lives of three men in a heartbeat. Less than a heartbeat.

She identified herself to the Lansing uniform, straightened her shoulders, and strode into the room. He was propped up in the bed, with tubes and wires running everywhere.

A tube protruding from his mouth went to a device on a stand that popped and hissed rhythmically, a machine breathing for him. Wires snaked from under the blanket to a monitor. A tiny speaker beeped in rhythm with his pulse. A screen recorded the jagged lines of his heartbeat and respiration. One arm was at his side with an IV attached to the back of the hand, and a wire ran from a device clamped like a clothespin on that index finger. His other arm was lying on his chest, and in that hand was the red cloth bag he had clutched in the drugstore.

The open door let in some light, but the only illumination in the room was the glow from the monitors, and she couldn't see the man's face well. She moved to the side of the bed and bent closer for a better look. His eyes snapped open. Altro jumped back and bumped into the monitor stand. The machine wobbled on its stand and started beeping. An alarm sounded at the nurse's station outside, and a nurse hurried in as Altro was turning around to the door.

"Ma'am, you'll have to leave. This patient cannot be disturbed under any circumstances."

Altro didn't argue, but followed the nurse outside in stiff obedience. The nurse was petite and probably in her thirties. Her nametag read Gupta.

"I need to talk to you about the patient. What's his condition? " Altro said.

"Are you a relative?"

Altro knew that patient information would normally be given only to family members, but she also knew where hospital administration would stand on this. She dug into her shoulder bag and pulled her credentials again.

"I'm from the Michigan Attorney General's Office. Do we need to call administration?"

The nurse frowned and shook her head. "I just came in, but let me get his records. I'll join you in the waiting room."

Altro went to the waiting room, where a news anchor was rehashing yesterday's drugstore shooting on television. When the program broke to a commercial for Free America, Altro found the remote and turned it off. Nurse Gupta came bustling in with a large electronic tablet. Altro glared and tapped a foot on the floor while the nurse scrolled through the records.

"He's on full life support protocol," Gupta said.

Altro frowned. "Will he live?"

The nurse didn't reply, but continued her examination of the records. Altro held her impatience in check.

"Evidently there was no pulse or respiration detected when they brought him in last night. Body temp at 32 C and falling. They called it at 6:30 p.m."

"Called it?"

"He was gone, ma'am. They tried everything."

Altro stared at the nurse.

"They were taking him down to the morgue when his eyes opened," the nurse said. She consulted the tablet. "This was at 7:45. They were backed up in the ER and couldn't get to him until then. The aide taking him down said his eyes opened, then noticed his body temp had gone up. He ended up back in ER at 8:00."

Altro frowned. She'd been at the hospital then and they wouldn't tell her anything. No wonder.

"He was stable when they brought him here," Gupta said. "But he's regressed since then. Comatose, and body temp is falling again. If there's no improvement, someone will have to make a decision soon."

"What? You mean, let him die? I just saw his eyes open."

"His eyes opened? You're sure, ma'am?"

"Positive. That's why I bumped into the monitor."

The nurse looked at her watch, then thumbed data into the tablet. When she was finished, Altro asked the question most prominent in her mind.

"What about the gunshot wound?"

The nurse went back to the tablet for a minute. "There's nothing here about a gunshot wound."

"What are you talking about? There has to be a gunshot wound."

Gupta cocked her head. "No, ma'am. No gunshot wound."

Altro shook her head. He'd been less than ten feet away when her gun went off, but she must have missed him completely. She'd seen him go down, watched him go into shock and pass out. Then she remembered his arm reaching and his feet scrabbling on the tile floor. He didn't pass out. He must have had some kind of seizure.

"There were notes about some old gunshot wounds," Gupta said. "Is that what you're asking about?"

"What?"

The nurse scrolled to an x-ray and tipped the tablet so Altro could see it.

"See? There are three old bullet wounds in his chest, and the exit wounds in his back. Looking at the locations, I don't see any way he could have lived through them."

Altro could see the broken ribs, but couldn't discern the entrance and exit wounds. She didn't say anything. The nurse cocked her head again.

"That's not what you meant, is it?"

Altro changed the subject to avoid any more scrutiny from Nurse Gupta.

"I have to see the patient again."

She strode back to the hospital room with Gupta tight on her heels. In the room, the nurse looked at the monitor display.

"His body temp is back up again. That's good." She looked at her watch. "I have to attend the shift-change meeting, but I'll be back in about twenty minutes. In the meantime, don't touch anything."

Gupta left the room, leaving Altro alone with the man who'd terrified her so badly that she shot him… or shot at him. He didn't look menacing at all now. In fact, with the tube in his mouth and the IV running from his arm, he looked helpless, a man close to death.

Altro sat down in the chair next to the bed, torn between relief that she hadn't shot him and worry he may die anyway. She was seriously questioning her own emotional and mental stability when the patient sat up in bed and started pawing at the tube that protruded from his mouth.

She jumped up and knocked into the monitor, just as she had earlier. The machine started beeping and the alarms went off at the nurse's station again, but were quickly silenced. She heard scuffling noises at the door and turned, expecting to see Gupta coming back. Instead, two Asians hurried in, a man and a woman.

They were wearing hospital scrubs, surgical masks, and white smocks. The woman was pushing a wheelchair, and Altro automatically stood off to the side.

An old woman hobbled in behind them. Hell, she wasn't old. She was ancient. Her walk was a tottering gait that spoke volumes of the pain she must feel. She was dressed in some kind of off-white, ceremonial clothing with a matching scarf. A babble of sobbing sounds in a strange language came from the old woman and tears rolled down her cheeks. She shuffled to the head of the bed, raised her arms in the air and started a heart-piercing keening.

The woman in hospital garb pushed the wheelchair to the other side of the bed and locked the wheels.

"I'll get him disconnected, doctor," she said.

"Hurry, nurse," the doctor said.

The nurse nodded and bent over the man, then peeled back the Velcro that held the tube coming out of his mouth in place. When she pulled the tube out the man went into a fit of coughing, then waved an arm at the doctor. The nurse ignored this and started pulling off the various wires that were connected to the patient. When she had removed everything, she transferred the IV bottle from the stand on the bed to a stand on the wheelchair. The man again waved a hand at the doctor, and Altro turned to watch.

The doctor was just standing there, watching Altro. He put his right index finger to his mouth, then bent over the patient, placing his ear to the man's mouth.

The old woman teetered over and put her arms around the patient, and the doctor struggled to keep his ear to the man's mouth. The doctor broke away, put his hands on Altro's shoulders and peered into her eyes. When she flinched and backed away from him, he spoke to the nurse in an Asian language. The nurse rushed to the door, shouted something in the same language, then scurried back.

When the nurse began helping the patient into the wheelchair, Altro turned back to the doctor with a question on her lips. He pulled her and spun her around in one quick movement, then pinned both her arms behind her with just one of his. With his free hand, he clamped a cloth over her mouth and Altro could taste the sweetness of chloroform. She raised a leg to stomp down on his foot, but he shifted his weight and pressed a knee against the back of her weight-bearing leg. Her knee buckled, and she ended up in a half-sitting position on his knee.

The sobs of the old woman turned to echoes. The world went gauzy white, then gray, then black.

Altro awoke sitting upright in a vehicle, a van or big SUV. She was sitting crossways, buckled into a one-person seat. The "doctor," with his surgical mask now gone, was sitting on a plastic box next to her. She had a splitting headache, and pressed her thumbs to her temples.

"You have a headache?" he asked. "It is from the chloroform. Here, take this."

He handed her a bottle of water, then held out two tablets.

"Don't worry, they are ibuprofen." He motioned to the back of the vehicle with his head. "He would not let me hurt you."

Altro turned and saw the patient on a gurney. *She was in an ambulance.*

The "nurse" sat facing the gurney on a bench seat that was installed on one side of the vehicle. With her surgical mask removed, Altro recognized her as the pharmacist in the drugstore yesterday. The old woman sat back there with them, mumbling to herself in a raspy voice. She held a small drum on her lap that she rapped lightly with a stick, in rhythm with her mumbling.

The man sitting beside Altro spoke. "I am Colonel Nguy."

The pharmacist turned to Altro. "Why did you try to shoot him? He saved your life."

Altro didn't have an answer, so she turned away and looked out the window. She could tell where they were, not far from the hospital, heading north out of town on US 127. The man next to her, the Colonel, pushed the ibuprofen in front of her face. She shook her head, but took a drink of the bottled water. As she was drinking, there was a flash of movement and a sting in her thigh.

The man pulled a syringe from her leg and, smiling, took the water bottle from her hand.

"You will fall asleep now."

She felt the drug almost immediately. In a gauzy haze, she watched the man place a pillow between her head and the vehicle window, and she leaned into it. With the effects of the drug in full swing, the pillow felt heavenly, and Altro thought that it was very nice of him to do that.

"Thank you," she mumbled.

Chapter 12

The plan was to have Tommy Mo's men kill him while he was helpless in the hospital. It was baffling that the Altro woman managed to shoot him, but Brain and Sledge intended to take advantage of the situation. They knew they should stay as far away from the hospital attack as possible, but their reasoning was slanted because of their history with the man. They just had to be there when Tommy Mo's men took him down.

At 7:30 a.m. Brain and Sledge walked in the front door of Sparrow Hospital like they belonged there. In the lobby they looked at the directory, milled around for a few minutes, then took a seat in the waiting area to watch the show. When Tommy's men entered, they stood up without thinking about it.

There were six of them. Two were dressed in hospital scrubs covered by white doctor's smocks. The other four were dressed in casual clothing that looked like it came from J. C. Penney's — chinos, button-down shirts and sport coats to hide their guns. They were all neatly groomed and the lion tattoos on their forearms were hidden, but there was no way to hide those iridescent basketball shoes.

The two "doctors" were supposed to bluff their way into the patient's room and push a syringe full of insulin into his IV. The other four were backup, armed with handguns in case things went wrong. It was a weak plan, but there hadn't been enough time to draw up anything better. Brain and Sledge would not be part of any action, and the men that took part in it were all Khun Pao's. They were expendable.

One of the "doctors" looked at the directory, then all six men headed for the elevator. When the elevator took them away, Brain and Sledge sat back down.

Brain turned to Sledge. "It won't be long, now."

It wasn't. In less than a minute the elevator returned, all six men piled out and rushed for the exit. One of them already had a cell phone to his ear and was jabbering away in Hmong as they trotted past the lobby. Brain and Sledge stood up again, and Sledge yelled at the men.

"Where you stupid fucks goin'? You can't be done yet!"

Several people in the lobby looked their way and the woman at the information desk stood up. Tommy Mo's men ignored the outburst and hustled out the door. Sledge kicked at a plastic chair and sent it tumbling across the waiting area. Brain put a hand on Sledge's arm.

"Calm down. Something must have gone wrong. Let's go see if we can find out what it was."

The two of them followed Tommy Mo's men out of the lobby and saw the reason for the panicked departure. Two police cruisers were parked at the entrance to the ER with their lights strobing. As Brain and Sledge headed to the parking lot, four more squad cars gunned into the area and slid to a stop.

Chapter 13

Mallory got the call from Agent Furlow at 0745, just as he was walking into the Team Center. Altro had been abducted.

"I thought your people were protecting her," Mallory said. He'd called Furlow from his office last night after Altro refused police protection from Ingham County. "They were supposed to be discrete, not lose her altogether."

"Bowman, our Special Agent in Charge from Detroit took it over. I didn't have any choice in the matter," Furlow answered.

"Give me his number."

First, Mallory called the other Task Force members to tell them. They were already on their way in. Next, he called the AG to give him more bad news. As he was explaining Altro's refusal of police protection and his call to Agent Furlow as a step to counteract it, the rest of the team came in. Jessica was talking on her BlackBerry as she walked. Sam got on his laptop right away, and Doolee picked up his landline. As soon as Mallory finished with the AG, he stepped out to the Team Room.

"We're on it, sir," Sam said. "Jessica's talking to the hospital right now. We'll get everything from their security cameras. Doolee's calling the Lansing Police to get as much information as he can."

Mallory went back into his office and called SAC Bowman. Bowman was staying just north of Mason with the Evidence Response Team and four other field agents from Detroit while they worked the drugstore shooting. Though Mallory had the greatest respect for the FBI and their investigative skills, he thought Special Agent Felix Bowman was slippery and oily. He tried hard to be personable, using Mallory's first name and insisting on being called Felix. When Mallory reprimanded him for losing Altro, the man talked non-stop for almost twenty minutes before he got to the point.

"I had my people keep a very loose tail on her, Bill," Bowman said. "That way they wouldn't be seen by someone making a move, but still be right there when something happened. They were waiting in the parking lot."

"You mean you used her as bait."

Bowman hemmed and hawed for another ten minutes, but Mallory was done with that conversation. After he hung up on Bowman, he got a cup of coffee, then headed for his spot on the corner of the table. Sam and Jessica had put together a video sequence of the security cameras at the hospital by then, and Sam started running it without being asked.

Five men and two women, all Asian, walked into view of the cameras in ICU. All but one, an elderly woman who was in some sort of ceremonial garb, wore white doctor's coats over green medical scrubs and surgical masks. Two of the men took out the Lansing Police officer with what appeared to be chloroform, while two more took out the clerk at the desk. Then one man and the two women went into the shooter's room with a wheelchair. The remaining four men loitered around the nurse's station, with one hand in their doctor's coats.

"Hold it," Mallory said. "Why is the clerk at the station the only medical personnel there?"

Sam stopped the video and Jessica spoke up.

"I already asked about that, sir. It was right at shift change. They always have a meeting where the outgoing shift relays patient information to the incoming shift. These people timed it just right."

Doolee stood up and walked up to the screen. He pointed to the woman in scrubs who was now at the hospital room door, waving an arm at the men who waited outside.

"This woman is the pharmacist from the drugstore," Doolee said. "Do you see her earrings and bracelets?"

Mallory wasn't sure if what Doolee was saying was correct, but they could get to that later. He nodded and told Sam to roll the video again.

One of the men hurried off and then returned to the room with another wheelchair. After a few minutes, the shooter and Altro were rolled out of the room in wheelchairs, covered in blankets. The group exited uncontested through the ER. The outdoor cameras showed the shooter and Altro being loaded into an ambulance parked just outside the ER.

"Can we track down the ambulance?" Mallory asked.

Doolee was back in his chair. "We already tried tracking the markings, sir. It's a genuine ambulance company, but they say that ambulance was reported stolen last night."

Mallory frowned, and Doolee continued. "But this thing, it makes no sense. Why would they take Altro?"

Sammy shrugged his shoulders. "They were there to take the drugstore shooter, and Altro just happened to be there. They didn't want any witnesses."

Mallory couldn't see the logic in that and shook his head. His glasses slipped down his nose, and he had to push them back up before he replied. "They could have just put her out, then. That's what they did with the Lansing cop."

Heads nodded around the room, and Mallory continued. "So why were they there? They could have killed him on the spot, if that's what they were after." He twisted around and pointed to the flat-screen. "You're sure about the pharmacist, Doolee?"

Doolee had no doubt. "Yes, sir. I studied the videos. She had those earrings and bracelets."

Mallory thought for a few seconds, fingering the scar on his chin. Jessica sat up straighter in her chair, raised her hand, and waited to be acknowledged. Mallory nodded at her.

"The pharmacist stepped between Altro and the shooter at the drugstore, sir. She took a big chance doing that. Then she shows up at the hospital to take him away. I think she's protecting him. I think all of these people are protecting him."

Sammy agreed. "They were thinking more guys with the lion tattoos would show up to kill him while he's helpless in the hospital."

Jessica nodded, then looked to Mallory. He waved a hand at her to continue.

"That's what I'm thinking, that their primary motive seems to be protecting the man. But like Doolee says, why take Ms. Altro? It's clear from the drugstore videos, and from Ms. Altro's account, that he deliberately stepped in to save her life. Did they grab her at the hospital to protect her again?"

Just then Mallory's BlackBerry buzzed. It was Agent Furman, and he went to his office to take the call. Forty minutes later he was back with a fresh cup of coffee. He got their attention and gave them the news.

"Okay people, the FBI has taken Altro's abduction as an active case," he said. "Along with the attempt on her life. We're already feeding all of our information to them, but make sure everything gets posted to the case files, no matter how small it may seem."

He waited for them to nod in agreement, then continued. "Also, we have another lead. It seems that someone got a picture of the shooter in the drugstore, probably a cell phone. They sold it to one of the networks, and the guy's picture is all over the country now."

Sam and Doolee groaned. Mallory raised a hand for silence. He pulled the yellow sticky note he'd written the information down on from his pocket and consulted it as he talked.

"A woman who saw his picture on television this morning called the Mason police and identified him as John Michaels. Said she married him back in the sixties. Her name is Andrea Shellers, her maiden name I guess. They must have divorced."

He took a sip of coffee and went on. "Ms. Shellers lives in Mason. I called the Mason police and talked to them. The Chief of Police knows her personally, and agreed to let us interview her at the police station there. That works out well for us, since the location of the Team Center isn't public."

"What time, sir?' Sam asked.

"Eleven hundred hours," Mallory answered. "That's eleven o'clock in the morning."

Doolee snorted and punched Sam on the shoulder. Sam just shrugged and looked at his watch. Mallory continued.

"Sam and Jessica, you'll ride down with me. Doolee can stay here and hold down the fort. Jessica, I want you to join me in the interview. I need a female in there. Sam, I want you to check their recording equipment. Make sure everything is copacetic."

"Copa-what?" Sam asked.

"Sorry," Mallory said. "Old Army slang. I need you to make sure everything works. It's a small town, and I want to make sure this is done professionally."

"Has the FBI interviewed her, sir?" Jessica asked. "If they have, we should have access to their recording."

Mallory shook his head.

"Agent Furman from East Lansing talked to the Mason Police Chief and her on the phone, but the Detroit SAC listened to the recording and didn't think it worth following up. Said the woman sounded hysterical to him." He frowned. "I think we should talk to her, but we'll have to go easy. The Mason police chief said it sounded like she was already close to breaking down."

Chapter 14

It took about 20 minutes to drive to Mason. Mallory drove, with Jessica in the front passenger seat. Sam sat in the back, thumbing his BlackBerry.

The police station was an unimposing brick building, just off the town square. The interview room was small, with a video camera on a tripod at one end of a laminated table. Sam looked the camera over and, after checking out the controls in the radio room, declared that things were ready to roll. Mallory sent him back to the radio room to monitor the recording.

The Chief of Police brought Andrea Shellers in himself. As he escorted the woman to her seat, Mallory couldn't stop himself from looking her over. She wore a navy blue pant suit, a gray silk blouse, and what looked like genuine alligator skin boots and purse. Her hair and nails looked recently done, her complexion and physique well cared for. When she was seated, the Chief patted her on the shoulder. She looked pale and disoriented.

"Thanks for coming in, Andrea," the Chief said. "Can I get you something to drink before you start?"

She shook her head. The Chief gave Andrea's shoulder a squeeze, raised an eyebrow at Mallory and left. Mallory opened the interview, hoping she could get through it.

"I want to record this meeting, Ms. Shellers. Is that all right with you?"

She nodded her head like an automaton, then finally found her voice. "Who exactly are you people?"

Mallory thought she may respond better to Jessica. He nodded at her, a prearranged signal for her to take over. Jessica gave Andrea Shellers a warm smile before she answered.

"We're part of the new drug task force, Ms. Shellers. You may have heard about it."

Shellers' eyebrows arched. "It's been on television. You think this is all about drugs?"

"We don't know that, but we're still trying to find out, ma'am."

The woman took a deep breath and nodded slowly. She looked like she was doing better, so Mallory nodded at Jessica. She produced a crime scene photograph and held it up. It was just the man's head, but his eyes were closed and it was clear that he was on a stretcher.

"Ms. Shellers, are you sure this is your ex-husband?"

Andrea Shellers shook her head strongly, almost violently. Her eyes darted around the room, and her voice rose in pitch and volume. "There must be some mistake. It can't be him."

Jessica gave Mallory a look. It was clear the woman was confused, losing control, and they tacitly agreed to give her some time. After a long pause, Ms. Shellers seemed to regain herself and nodded resolutely. Her voice was firm when she spoke.

"His name is John Michaels."

"When was the last time you saw him?" Jessica asked.

"It was March of 1969."

Jessica sighed and reached out to touch the woman's forearm. "You haven't seen him since then? This must be so difficult for you."

Shellers didn't say anything, so Jessica gave her a minute.

"Is there anyone else he could have contacted? Does he have family in the area?"

"He was an only child. His parents are both dead. His mother died of cancer, and his father followed her two years later."

"Do you have any idea why else he would be here?"

"No, but he did grow up here," Ms. Shellers said. "We both did. We were high school sweethearts, and were married in June of 1968, while he was home on leave. That was just before he went to Vietnam."

Mallory jumped back into the conversation.

"He was in the service? Which branch?"

"He was in the Army. He enlisted, and then volunteered for Vietnam."

"We need his full name, Ms. Shellers," Mallory said. "We'll want to see his 201 file, his Army records. I'm sure there were many soldiers named John Michaels."

"His middle name is Walker. John Walker Michaels."

Walker.

Mallory's thoughts wandered. He shifted in his chair, then stared at Ms. Shellers as he fingered the scar on his chin for a minute. Jessica coughed to bring him back to the present. He smiled weakly at Jessica, then turned back to Andrea Shellers.

"Do you remember where he was stationed in Vietnam?" he asked.

"I don't even remember if he ever told me."

"Do you have any letters from him while he was stationed there? The return address would tell us."

Her right hand rose and rubbed at her temple in a circular motion. "I'm not sure. I got rid of a lot of things."

Mallory thought about it for a while. "We may have Jessica come by later to look with you, if you don't mind."

She sat mute, still rubbing her temple.

"Do you know anything about his time in the military, ma'am?" Mallory asked "His tour in Vietnam?"

Her hand went back to her lap and grasped at her purse. "Not really."

"Was he Special Forces, Ms. Shellers?"

"No."

Mallory persisted. "Are you sure he wasn't a Green Beret — or a Ranger?"

"I don't think so. Why?"

Mallory tried to be as tactful as possible.

"Ms. Shellers, he killed three men in the drugstore yesterday. He killed them very quickly, very efficiently. We think that would require special training."

Andrea Shellers' shoulders sagged.

"I knew the military had changed him. Radically. He just wasn't the same."

She turned to Jessica. "When he came home from Vietnam, nothing was right about him. His tour wasn't over yet, and he was still in his fatigues — filthy, like he'd just stepped out of the jungle. He hadn't shaved."

Mallory raised a hand off the table top, his index finger pointing in the air, but the woman ignored him and kept her attention on Jessica as she continued.

"He'd changed completely. I thought he must be doing drugs. I kept thinking that the Army had done this to him, that Vietnam had done this. We all knew what was going on over there... the drugs... the atrocities."

Mallory scowled and bit the inside of his cheek. People thought they knew what went on in Vietnam, but they didn't. They only knew what the press and Hollywood told them.

"We argued," Ms. Shellers said. "I did all the talking, really. He just sat there, but not really there at all. I tried to convince him that he should leave the Army. I didn't want him participating in that ugly war."

She stared at her hands in her lap for a few seconds before she continued. "He didn't even answer me. I asked him to go away — demanded it, really — and he did. He hadn't been there more than an hour, but I just couldn't stand to have him near me anymore."

This caused more shaking of her head and another wild look around the room.

Jessica spoke softly. "Have you had any contact at all with him since then? Alimony payments? Anything?"

The woman shook her head some more, then started sobbing. Her shoulders shook and she hid her face in her hands. After a few minutes, she pulled a hanky from her purse and dabbed at her eyes. She was clearly breaking down. Her nose was red, with a bubble of mucus bulging from one nostril. Her eyes were puffy and her mouth drooped on one side.

"This can't be him. I mean, it's him — but it can't be him!"

She sobbed some more. Her voice was constricted and becoming shrill.

"No! No! No! I can't talk about this anymore! I shouldn't have come here!"

Mallory and Jessica looked at each other. Jessica shook her head at Mallory, and he made the decision.

"Thank you very much for coming in, Ms. Shellers," he said. "Would you mind if we contacted you later with questions? We'd like to look at those letters, if you have them."

Andrea Shellers took a full three minutes, dabbing at her eyes and nose with her hanky. Finally, she stood and pulled a business card from her purse. She handed it to Jessica.

"My office and home phones are both there. My email addresses, too."

She started to leave, but stopped at the doorway. "I need to see him. About an hour ago, I called the hospital, but they said I couldn't. They wouldn't tell me anything."

Mallory shook his head. "I'm afraid that's not possible, Ms. Shellers. He was taken from the hospital this morning."

Her entire body sagged and her voice cracked when she responded. "Taken? Where?"

"We're still trying to find out."

Andrea Shellers' shoulders shook again for a long minute. Then she dabbed at her nose with the hanky again. While she was crying, Jessica retrieved a business card from her purse, then rose and moved to the woman, placed a hand on her forearm. "Do you want us to drive you home, ma'am? We'd be more than happy to."

Shellers shook her head. "No, I'll be all right. I walked over."

Jessica gave the woman's forearm a squeeze, then held out the business card. "Well, if you think of anything that you feel may be important, please contact us." Shellers took the card. Jessica spoke softly to her. "My email address and phone number are there. I'm available any time, day or night, even if you just want to talk."

When the woman was gone, Jessica tilted her head to one side and sighed.

Sam came into the room. "Well, that was short."

Jessica turned to Mallory. "I think she's holding something back, sir."

"You think she's hiding something?" Sam asked.

"I wouldn't call it hiding," Jessica said. "But there's something she's not telling us about her ex."

Sam rolled his eyes. "Tomato, tomahto."

Mallory was lost in thought, rubbing the scar on his chin.

"Sir?"

It was Jessica. She and Sam were standing there, waiting for him to respond.

"Okay," he said. "But I think she needs some time to recover from the shock of all this. We can try to talk to her later at her home. Maybe she'll be settled down and more comfortable there."

Sam spoke up. "I'll call Doolee. Have him contact Agent Furlow in East Lansing to get warrants for her financial and phone records."

Mallory nodded absently. *John Walker Michaels.*

Chapter 15

It was night in Laos. Khun Pao was still sitting on his stool next to the fire, eating rice from a clay bowl with his fingers.

Khun had spent the entire day inside, stoking the fire and drinking lao-lao. The rice whiskey normally lit a fire in his belly, but today he continued to shiver. Fear had come alive in him, crawling in his belly like worms through a corpse. The Valley Walker had made it very clear. He was coming for Khun.

At the end of the day, when he was close to toppling off his stool from drinking so much lao-lao, Khun had grown furious with himself. He swallowed the venom of fear and forced the bile of hate into his heart. It was a feeling he enjoyed, and he called to the young girl to make the rice for him. The fear showed clearly on her face when she served it to him, and Khun fed on her fear.

He put the bowl on the floor, stood and knocked the girl down. She lay there whimpering, and he kicked her in the ribs, then in the face. His boot split her lip and loosened a tooth. The sight of her blood inflamed him to kick her in the face again. That kick broke her nose, and Khun kicked her again. Her face was torn and disfigured now, a sight that made him smile. The girl was getting old anyway, almost fourteen. It was time for her to be shipped off to the brothels in Cambodia and a fresh girl brought in. When she crawled her way out of the room, Khun ignored the trail of blood and went back to his rice.

The grain was formed into the rough shape of a human being, a ritual of the Dark Hmong. The actual practice of cannibalism had died out among the Dark Hmong long ago, replaced by the ritual of human-shaped rice. Khun was one of the few Dark Hmong left in Laos, an ancient cult that shunned goodness and wallowed like pigs in the slime of darkness. As his belly filled, he felt his power returning. He was still a powerful man.

Khun Pao had grown very powerful in the opium trade during France's colonization of Laos, even more powerful during America's Vietnam War. His opium had been floated down the Mekong all the way to the delta, then trucked up to Saigon. In laboratories operated by the Cowboy gangs of Saigon, the opium was processed into the Number 4 China White heroin the Americans hungered for.

Later, when the Cowboys got too greedy, he cut them out of the deal. The processing laboratories were relocated to Laos, making his profit higher. The finished product was floated down the Mekong to Cambodia, then carried by human mules into South Vietnam. The cargo was delivered to men wearing aviator sunglasses and South Vietnamese Army uniforms in Bin Longh province.

The heroin business was still profitable. He commanded his own army of men who followed him without question. Khun finished his rice, tossed the clay bowl on the floor and picked up his bottle of lao-lao. After a deep drink of the fiery liquid, he turned to the door and bellowed.

"Bring me the witch!"

One of his soldiers stepped inside, his eyes wide with fear.

"Bring me Neng Jou, the Dark Shaman!" Khun yelled. "Bring her to me!"

The soldier hurried out to do Khun's bidding, and Khun smiled. The Dark Shaman would know what to do. She would help him bring an end to the Valley Walker's meddling.

Chapter 16

Everything was fuzzy. Altro couldn't seem to grab hold of whatever she was reaching for. Someone was knocking. She started coming around. She looked at her wrist, but her watch was gone. The knocking came again.

She was lying on a single bed in a small room. She swung her feet over the side of the bed and looked around while the knocking continued. A wave of nausea hit her, and she resisted the urge to lie back down. Someone had taken her shoes off and placed them neatly under the bed. She put her shoes on and looked around for a window, but the room had none. It was coming back to her. The hospital.

"Ms. Altro?"

The knocking. She cleared her throat.

"Where am I?"

The door opened to an Asian man in dress slacks and a sport coat over a knit shirt. His battleship gray hair was short, his facial features squared off like he was cut from a block of stone. As Altro focused on him, she thought he looked familiar.

"Are you feeling well?" he asked.

She wasn't. The nausea hit again, and her question was squeezed out between gritted teeth. "Who are you?"

"I am Colonel Nguy. You are safe here. Feel free to use the bathroom, through the door there. I will make some coffee. Then we must talk."

The door closed before she could protest, and Altro could hear it being locked. She looked around the room, searching for her shoulder bag, but it wasn't there. With nothing she could do short of banging on the door and screaming for help, she went to the bathroom.

The Colonel returned in a few minutes, holding a tray with a flaky roll, a decanter of coffee and two cups. His posture was erect, but his movements smooth. Instead of bending over, he bent at the knees to put the tray on the bed stand. He poured her a cup of coffee and handed it to her as she sat on the bed.

"Do you remember me from this morning, Ms. Altro? I escorted you from the hospital."

It came back to her. The "doctor." She remembered him introducing himself to her in the ambulance. The nausea must be from the drug he'd injected into her leg.

"Escorted? You kidnapped me."

"I am sorry, ma'am. I will not hurt you, rest assured. I only brought you because he told me to."

The man in the hospital. The man she shot, or thought she shot.

"Who is he?"

His reply didn't answer her question.

"I have brought something for you to eat, Ms. Altro. I know you must feel a bit nauseated right now, but take a few bites. It will help you shake off the effects of the drug."

He waited for a few minutes while she picked at the roll and drank some of the coffee. The coffee didn't have the kick of Doolee's brew, but it was good. Very good. The Colonel watched her closely, and when she was getting her feet back on the ground, he started talking to her again.

"I apologize again, ma'am. I know this must be very difficult, but he insisted we take you with us. I could see that you wouldn't come easily, so I put you to sleep. Is there anything I can do to make you feel more comfortable, more secure?"

"You can begin by telling me what the hell is going on here. I don't know where I am. I don't know who you are, or who the man who had you bring me here is."

"I'm afraid I can't tell you where we are, Ms. Altro, but you are safe here."

Colonel Nguy poured himself a cup of the coffee, then shrugged his shoulders.

"Me? I am Colonel Nguy Bo. You can call me Bo... or, if you prefer, Colonel Nguy. He is my friend... my brother."

94

"Colonel, your brother killed three men yesterday. Those men he killed were hired killers, professionals, and they didn't have a chance. Not a damn chance. Now it looks like he had me kidnapped."

The Colonel nodded his head after he sipped at his coffee. "Yes, ma'am."

"Who is he, Colonel? Who is he working for? Is this the beginning of a drug war?"

"Ms. Altro, this is certainly not a 'drug war', as you are thinking. Walker works for no one, except his family and people."

"Walker? That's his name?"

The Colonel shook his head. "His middle name. The nom de guerre started in Vietnam and has stuck with me all these years."

"You met him in Vietnam? You're Vietnamese?"

He nodded. "I was once a Colonel in the People's Army of Vietnam, what the Americans called the North Vietnamese Army. I was a dedicated communist and fought in the war against the American Forces. Later, I surrendered to the U.S. Army for... Let us say tactical reasons. I became a scout for their army, what was called a Kit Carson Scout. I met Walker while serving in this capacity. He was a young soldier who asked me to teach him the language and customs of Vietnam, but it was not long before he was teaching me. He taught me much, but the most important thing he taught me is that no matter which side wins a war, the soldiers and their families always lose."

The Colonel drank more coffee before continuing. "The hill people, the Hmong, have adopted him as one of their own. The Hmong are different from a practical man like me. They call him Ha Mu Dsee Nung, which roughly means Man Walking in Valley — or Man Walking Beyond — Valley Walker — or Beyond Walker."

He raised a hand, palm toward Altro, and waggled it. "It is hard to translate because the thoughts of the Hmong are so different from mine, so spiritual. They see the world in ways that I cannot."

The Colonel shook his head and went on. "Many people in Southeast Asia were in awe of him, and still are. Many people feared him, and still do."

"Do you fear him, Colonel? Do you think he is dangerous?"

"Ma'am, you know he is dangerous. You saw what he did in the pharmacy." Then the man shook his head emphatically. "But no, I do not fear him. As I said, he is my friend, my brother. He is, without doubt, the most honorable man I have ever met. I would do anything for him."

The Colonel finished his coffee, excused himself and left Altro pondering what she had just been told. Though they had once been enemies, the colonel seemed to worship the man he called Walker. She was sure that he would do anything for him, no matter how farfetched or difficult. And it was clear that Walker had become the Colonel's mentor, a teacher and sponsor that the Colonel idolized. Altro chewed those thoughts, and was just finishing her second coffee when Nguy returned, looking apologetic and smelling of cigarette smoke.

Altro suddenly wanted a cigarette. She had started smoking in law school but, for what must be the twentieth time, had quit smoking a month ago. The overwhelming desire for the rush of nicotine still came to her at predictable times. When she had coffee in the morning. When she had a glass of wine in the evening. Or when she smelled the smoke on someone else.

The Colonel tapped her shoulder to break her reverie, produced a black cloth bag, and indicated she should put it over her head.

"I must take you to see him now. He wants to speak with you."

Chapter 17

With the black cloth hood on her head, Altro had no choice but to let Colonel Nguy take her arm. He held it lightly, gently guiding her as they moved through the building. She heard him open a door, which he moved her through, then the soft click of it closing. The Colonel removed the hood and smiled at her, then stood aside.

They were in the entryway of a candlelit room, more than fifteen feet on each side. Opposite the entry was an opening that appeared to be a darkened hallway. On what must have been the outside wall were two windows, covered with heavy drapes. The hardwood floor looked like it had been waxed and polished, and reflected the soft glow of the candles. In the middle of the floor was a thin, two-foot square pad. Sitting cross legged on the pad was the man Colonel Nguy called Walker, the man who effortlessly killed the three thugs sent to murder her.

A number of candles burned in a circle around the man. A wisp of smoke curled up from a brazier behind him, a squat, cast-iron heater that must be stoked with wood. The air in the room was warm, and the pleasant tang of wood smoke saturated the air.

Sitting on a stool to one side of the room was the old woman who was at the hospital. In the candlelight, her clothing was more blue than white, the color of mountain clouds. She was beating the small drum and droning on like she had in the ambulance earlier. The pharmacist was there, kneeling beside the old woman and nodding her head with the drum beat. The timbre and volume of the old woman's voice rose and fell as she tapped at the drum, in a primitive tempo that reminded Altro of the rhythms she felt and heard in the drugstore yesterday.

On the wall behind them hung an intricate painting of a dragon, a frightening resemblance to the dragon that had emerged from him in the drugstore. The beast seemed to breathe in time with the old woman's drum and quavering voice. At the center of the dragon's eyes, red dots glowed. Altro drew in a long breath in an effort to stay in control.

The old woman stopped beating her drum and chanting. The pharmacist stood, walked over to them and bowed slightly to the Colonel. She stepped into her shoes, which were placed at the side of the door, and left.

Colonel Nguy removed his shoes, placed them to the side of the door and wordlessly indicated that Altro should do the same. Without her platform shoes, she was about the same height as the Vietnamese. He started to put his hands on her shoulders, stopped himself and smiled kindly.

"He will not hurt you."

The man on the mat spoke. "My old friend, Bo. It is good to see you."

"I have brought Ms. Altro, Walker."

"Thank you. Come. Sit with me."

The Colonel picked up two stools from beside the door, similar to the one the old woman was seated on, and gestured at Altro as he started toward Walker. She followed hesitantly, reluctant to face the man. Nguy placed the stools directly in front of the mat Walker sat on, took a seat and clasped Walker's extended hand with both of his as he leaned in toward him. He was smiling when he turned to Altro and indicated that she should sit too. She sat on the low canvas seat, pressed her knees together and looked directly at the man who had frightened her so badly she'd shot at him.

The old woman burst out in a tirade in a keening language, angrily shaking her drumstick at Altro. Sparks seemed to fly from her clothing, lightning jumping from the clouds. The old crone put down her drum and the drumstick, rose with a grunt from her stool and toddled to Walker. She bent over him, put one hand on his shoulder, and glared at Altro through cloudy eyes. Walker patted the old woman's hand while she shook a gnarled finger at Altro.

Walker spoke to her in an Asian language for a short time, and she turned and stared at Altro, her translucent eyes wide. She turned back to Walker, who nodded at her and smiled. The old woman leaned over and peered into Altro's eyes for a few moments. Altro endured the stare of those milky eyes, wondering if the woman could even see her. Then the old hag patted Altro on the wrist, straightened with a grunt and limped away, muttering to herself and clucking her tongue.

Walker smiled after the old crone, then turned back to Altro.

"The old woman, Neng Cheng, is my adoptive mother. She is a Hmong Shaman, from Laos. Her name translates to True Shaman, in fact. I suppose she would be called a witch here. She was angry with you because you shot me."

That simple statement cut deep. She felt the quick rush of anger, knew it was the result of her fear and guilt, but used it to defend herself anyway.

"Well, I didn't even hit you!"

He smiled at that, and it made her angrier.

"And what did you expect?" she said. "You killed three men. You were still armed. I had no idea what you would do."

Her anger didn't seem to faze him, so she continued, growing angrier and more afraid by the second.

"Don't you know the trouble you've brought down on yourself? You've kidnapped a member of the Attorney General's Office. You can't imagine the power that is being brought together to find me right now."

Colonel Nguy shrugged, and Walker turned his face to him.

"Maybe she is right, my friend," Walker said. "This is not the old days. Our old ways aren't welcome here."

The pause in his speech seemed eternal. Colonel Nguy waited patiently, while she fussed inwardly at the silence. When he spoke to Nguy again, it was in a lilting language she assumed was Vietnamese. Being left out of the conversation grated on her, and her patience was just about gone when Nguy stood to leave.

He turned to her, politely excused himself, then made a slight bow to Walker. When he was gone, Altro knew she needed to calm herself. She didn't want her fear and anger to taint her logic, so she examined Walker to stall for time. He sat there patiently while she looked him over.

He was not a ruggedly handsome man. His face was boyish, and the lines at his eyes and mouth looked like laugh lines in the soft flickering light. The expression on his face was pleasant and open, and she couldn't justify the man in front of her with the one who had terrified her in the drugstore. His hair was cut in the same ten-dollar style as Mallory's. Not as short, but just as cheaply and efficiently. His appearance was ordinary in every way, and her thought from the drugstore returned.

He's just some guy.

Her eyes moved from his face to his body. Loose cotton pajama bottoms covered his lower half, but his torso was bare. A wispy patch of hair grew between his chest muscles, barely visible in the dim light. He was lean and, from the way he sat cross-legged on the pad, quite limber.

Hanging from a leather thong around his neck was the red cloth bag he held so tightly in the hospital. On a separate thong hung the ivory colored pendant, a rectangular tile of about two inches by four inches. The old bullet wounds the nurse had seen on the x-ray were nickel-sized pucker marks. She leaned forward and looked closer at where her own bullet should have hit, but there was no mark. Nothing.

"You are confused, Ms. Altro?"

That startled her, and she immediately went on the offensive.

"Just what is going on? Why am I here?"

His expression turned thoughtful. She felt his presence invading her, as it had at the drugstore, and she flinched at his touch.

"May I call you Teri?"

She pushed his presence away.

"No. You may call me Ms. Altro."

He nodded stoically, and she went after him again.

"Just who the hell are you?"

"My name is John Michaels. John Walker Michaels."

John Walker Michaels. Colonel Nguy called him by his middle name, Walker. The Hmong called him the Valley Walker. He waited for her to sort it out, then shrugged and held his hands out to his sides.

"I'm sorry to introduce myself in such awkward circumstances."

"Awkward?" She raised her voice. "Awkward? What the hell are you doing here? Why were you at the drugstore?"

He drew in a breath.

"I was at the drugstore to save your life. And to kill those men, of course. The events at the drugstore were what you could call an opening skirmish."

"Skirmish? As in a war? Colonel Nguy said this wasn't a drug war."

Altro waited a few seconds, but it seemed he wouldn't answer. She grew impatient and spoke up in an effort to keep the conversation under her control.

"Mr. Michaels, I'm a member of a special drug task force. It's probable the men you killed are involved in the heroin trade."

He smiled at that.

"They are definitely involved in the heroin trade, Ms. Altro."

"And how do you know that, Mr. Michaels?"

"The lion tattoos you must have discovered mark them as being part of the organization of a man in Laos. This man reaps a harvest of poppies using the forced labor of his own people, and takes young girls from their families. The poppies are converted into heroin and the young girls are sold into slavery or prostitution, on the black market in Thailand and Cambodia. He rules over the poor mountain Hmong through fear and violence."

He paused again, but this time the pause was short.

"His name is Khun Pao." He spelled the name for her. "Remember his name, Ms. Altro. You will have to deal with his underlings."

He sounded like a college professor talking to a not-so-bright student, and Altro kept a bite in her tone to let him know she didn't like it.

"You know this man?"

He nodded.

"I know him from my life in Southeast Asia. I believe Colonel Nguy told you a few things about my time there."

"So you're starting a war against drug dealers? That's *my* job, Mr. Michaels."

"Yes, the United States has already declared a 'War on Drugs' — and, as you say, that is *your* job. But truly evil men are at work in the mountains of Laos, and here in your own country. Our own country. My country."

His head drooped until he was staring at the floor, then he raised his head and looked directly in her eyes.

"These men are completely without shame, completely without honor. They care for nothing but profit. These men will take your honor, and use it for their own ends."

His shoulders sagged, and he appeared limp and lifeless for a short time. Then one of his hands went to the red cloth bag that hung from his neck and clutched it.

"Two salt tablets, a canteen of water and push on."

"What?"

His shoulders straightened and he looked her in the eye again. There was iron in his voice now.

"Honor is all that is left in the end, Ms. Altro."

Altro saw the anger flare in him. The heat of it fell on her in waves, and her fear grew from a thin whisper of smoke into a black oily cloud that choked her. A vein in his left temple protruded, started to pulse. The vein became veins. More veins rose from his arms, writhing and pulsing.

The tattoo mask. The dragon.

"Mr. Michaels?"

The veins kept squirming, began to take on shapes. She shouted, her voice echoing off the walls and floor.

"Walker?"

He heard her voice. It penetrated to whatever world he'd gone to, and she waited on the edge as he calmed himself. He breathed slowly, his belly extending and receding with each breath. The veins receded, and he seemed to be back in control. His head rose and fell with one final deep breath and he spoke, his voice calm and measured again.

"The drug dealers are only puppets, Ms. Altro. They do as they're told. It's the power behind them that must be dealt with."

Not yet in control of her fright, her voice was softer and less strident than before.

"That's our intention," she said. "We plan to stop the heroin trade at the source."

Altro watched as he thought about what she said. Again, it looked like he wouldn't answer, but his answer was only slow in coming. Eventually, the professor continued his lecture.

"The profits from the sale of drugs on a massive scale bring power, Ms. Altro. Yet the sale of drugs on a massive scale can only come through power. Think of where that power lies."

She had to get this back under control.

"You leave the war against drug dealers to me and the Task Force, Mr. Michaels. I'm grateful for your intervention, but you can't just kill people like that."

He sighed audibly before answering her.

"It was necessary. I had to kill them, and in that manner, to let their masters know I am here. I even let one live, so he could take a message to them. There could be no doubt."

She'd seen the fluid ease with which he killed the men. He could have immobilized them and captured them. Hell, he could have clipped their fingernails and given them a shoe shine if he wanted to.

"You *had* to kill them? I don't believe that. I saw how easy it was for you."

"I have no regrets about what I did, Ms. Altro. The world is better off without them."

"If we had those men in custody instead of bodies in the morgue, we could have questioned them," she said.

He just shook his head. "You should be relieved, Ms. Altro. Those men won't come for you again. They will be looking for me now."

She didn't want to give him too much credit, so she didn't answer. Neither of them spoke for a while and the silence in the room grew until it pulled at her physically, like the silence before the violence in the drugstore. She began to lose control of her fear again. Beads of sweat trickled down her sides. A shaking was creeping into her hands, and she clasped them together on her lap, pressed them against her drawn together knees.

"Mr. Michaels, the whole shooting incident seemed… Well, it didn't seem real. It was like some kind of black magic."

He said nothing. The intensity of his gaze made her press her knees together harder. Though she was afraid of the direction the conversation was taking, she couldn't control the hunger that was gnawing at her. She needed to know more.

"In the drugstore…" she said. "There was a sound, almost a feeling rather than a sound. There were tattoos on your face."

He still said nothing. She fidgeted on the low seat until she couldn't stop herself and blundered on.

"Everything happened so fast," she said. "But it seemed to go on for a long time."

Finally, he spoke… a question.

"And why do you think it seemed that way to you?"

She had no real explanation. The video showed the impossible speed, yet during the action she had watched and heard it all unfold in slow motion.

"You stepped into my world, Ms. Altro. You felt me looking into you, and when I turned away, you stepped into my world and followed me."

Logic denied it, but she remembered how she'd dropped the book and followed him down the aisle, the way time had lost its place in the world. Everyone else in the store had come to a standstill, while only she and the pharmacist remained in time with the man called Walker.

He was reaching for her again, invading her. She pushed him away, but couldn't regain a solid grip on reality. Her mind whirled and lurched, grasping desperately for something solid. She couldn't catch her breath.

"Are you all right?"

She looked at him and resolutely nodded her head, not wanting him to see her fear and confusion, knowing he already did. Her thoughts defied her will and betrayed her, even as she nodded.

No, Goddammit! I'm not all right. I think I'm losing it here. I can feel you looking into me. Touching me. I'm scared to death of you.

"Breathe, Ms. Altro."

She took a deep breath and it helped. Her shaking gradually subsided.

Teri Altro looked at John Walker Michaels, afraid of what she saw happening inside her. From the time of her parents' death, she had anchored her life in the driving purpose of her mission, avoiding the morass of emotional entanglement. Now she sat before this man who had drawn her out of the cold safety of her own world and into his. She was lost and adrift. She was exposed.

"I was trying to help," he said. "I'm sorry it frightened you. I was trying to calm you, to let you see."

"Let me see? See what?"

The man's eyes suddenly filled with tears. When he spoke, he was sobbing and barely got the words out.

"To see *me*. I would never hurt you."

He looked down, then held a hand up and began taking deep breaths. While she waited, Altro tried to imagine his need to convince her of his good intentions, a need so overwhelming that he had her kidnapped. When he'd regained his composure, he looked up at her again.

"You are part of it now, Ms. Altro," he said. "You always have been."

What?

But he was reaching out again. She tried to deny him, but his presence grew stronger inside her. She drew in another breath but it did no good, and when she spoke her voice quavered like a child's after crying.

"What are you doing? What's happening?"

She clawed frantically away from him, but her attempt was useless. She felt his emotions — *his emotions, damnit!* — overcoming her. They crashed over her barriers and rushed into her. She fought it, but the invasion continued relentlessly... until it was complete.

She could feel the raw exposed emotions that swirled in him, and now in her. The anger, pain and violence. The love and tenderness. The pride and the shame. She could feel his heart beating with hers, could feel his breathing ebbing and flowing with hers. Their most basic life functions moved in sync, together.

"Can you see now, Ms. Altro?"

Though her eyes had closed, she *could* see. She could see him. She could feel him. The anger and violence were still there, but behind that she saw his simple quest to do the right thing. The very basic goodness of the man brought an almost physical warmth that reminded her of the heat of her parents' fireplace on a cold winter morning.

She felt like she had known this man all of her life, but no... even before that. Like time had no meaning in their relationship, as if they'd been together before time even was. Before *they* even were.

Teri Altro had left her life of cold logic behind. She was in Walker's world now. Her eyes opened and she saw that he was smiling at her.

"That is why I had you brought here. I wanted you to see me. I tried to show you in the drugstore, but all you could see was the anger that burned in me."

Understanding came to her, and she was no longer afraid of him, could plainly see just how happy this made him. They smiled at each other, then lapsed into the easy silence of people who no longer need to hear their own voices, each comfortable in the other's presence.

That comfortable silence was broken when an Asian woman entered the room from the darkened hallway, smiled politely at Altro and stood at Walker's side. She held out a plain gray cotton long-sleeved pullover for him, and he raised his arms while she dropped it over his lean frame. The woman had a scar on one side of her face, a line that ran down through one eyebrow and ended on her cheek.

The woman gave Altro an appraising look, went down on one knee and placed a hand protectively on his shoulder. Walker placed his hand on hers, looked up at her and smiled. When the woman spoke to him in a lilting language that Altro couldn't understand, Walker shook his head and patted her hand.

"Please speak English for our guest, Ka."

The woman bobbed her head and smiled at Altro.

"Forgive me. I was telling him that he must go to the Mountain of Hawks and Swallows."

She saw Altro's confusion and explained. "I was telling him he must rest."

Walker squeezed her hand and replied. "You are right, as always."

He turned to Altro.

"This is Ka. She was in a terrible situation in Laos. I was able to have her brought here, to the United States."

He turned his face upward to the young woman.

"This is Teri Altro, Ka."

The woman again appraised Altro, colder this time, and she moved so she was between Walker and Altro. He raised her hand from his shoulder gently, then rose to his feet with an effortless, fluid movement.

"I must rest now. Colonel Nguy will take you back when he returns. For now, Ka will take you where you can be more comfortable."

He held out a hand and she rose to take it, grasped his hand in both of hers and pressed it in a desperate squeeze. Warmth flowed from his hand into hers, moved up her arms and settled deep in her chest.

Teri Altro didn't want to leave. She held tightly to his hand, and he reciprocated, reluctant to release her. She knew this, but together they knew he had to. He smiled again, and then he pulled his hand away.

She felt the loss immediately. His warmth was gone and she wanted it back. He put his hand on her shoulder, started walking her away from the center of the room toward her shoes.

"Go back to your world for now, Teri. Your friends on the Task Force will need you."

His use of her first name made her want to stay with him even more. She wanted to hold his hand and talk to him some more.

"You saved my life and I tried to shoot you. I'm sorry."

"I have been a soldier, Teri. I know how these things happen. It had to be this way. I am just glad I had the chance to meet you, to talk to you."

Then his face turned deathly serious.

"Be careful, Teri. Dangerous men will be involved in this, men much more dangerous than Khun Pao's thugs."

His shoulders sagged visibly, and he took his hand off her shoulder to take hold of the red cloth bag. His head slowly drooped, and the hand that held the bag fell to his side. Ka came from behind them, and her hand took the place of his on her shoulder. She spoke in a low voice as she continued guiding Altro toward her shoes.

"We must go."

Altro retrieved her shoes and followed Ka away, still reluctant to leave his company. They walked across the room and past him toward the hallway. She stopped at the end of the room and turned around to see him once more before she left. He still stood there with his head hanging.

Then he fell to the floor like a rag doll. Teri Altro dropped her shoes, ran and knelt at his side. Ka remained at the doorway.

"I will get Grandmother," Ka said.

When Altro knelt by him, she saw that one of his hands had grabbed the red cloth bag, the way he clutched it in the drugstore. The muscles in his forearm were bunched and chorded, his knuckles white. She grasped his hand that held the bag and looked at his face, saw his eyes wide open. Time stopped, then became a river running in no set direction. She was carried along helplessly, like a leaf in its flow.

The terrible noise of the explosion rocked her. Then the shock wave struck her, blew dust and grit and leaves past her.

She watched the destruction in fascination, unable to turn her face from the horror. Contrails sailed crazily away from the column as the projectiles caused secondary explosions in the ammunition carts. Equipment and branches and leaves and body parts were blown through the surrounding brush and trees... up to ridiculous heights... away, away.

The screams and moans of the wounded began, then withered away to the pitifully weak cries of the dying. Her spirit walked out to the destruction. The dead called to her, reached out to her.

Teri Altro gasped and looked around her. Though her ears were still ringing from the chaos, she was back in the candlelit room with John Walker Michaels. She held tightly to his hand, which was still clutching the bag. Then the seizure came, like it had in the drugstore.

He rolled to his side and his other arm reached out. His fingers clawed at the hardwood floor but could find no grip. His bare feet scrabbled like he was running, but he went nowhere. After some time, his hand stopped reaching and his feet quit running in place.

He became cool to her touch. She held on to his hand with both of hers but it did no good. He grew colder and colder, as cold as death. His coldness seeped into her, and she began shivering uncontrollably.

When the old woman finally arrived, Ka was kneeling beside Altro. The old crone saw Altro quaking, stooped and looked into her eyes. Clucking her tongue, she put a hand on Altro's shoulder and gave a squeeze. In the awkward shuffle that is peculiar to the ancient, she retrieved her little drum and the drumstick. Then she began a soft chant and started to beat the drum. Teri Altro slowly stopped shivering, and John Michaels grew warm again.

Ka's hand touched Altro's shoulder. She turned her head, stood with Ka and gazed down at him. She still did not want to leave him, but the woman placed a hand on her shoulder and firmly led her away.

"He has fallen away. Grandmother will bring him back."

Chapter 18

"I was going through Andrea Shellers' bank records, sir, looking for alimony payments from her ex. Nothing like that, but I thought you might want to see this."

Mallory looked at his computer screen as Sam Lu's voice came over the speaker. It showed the transactions for Shellers' private bank account for May of 1970. There was a check written to Anders Funeral Home highlighted, and another to Maple Grove Cemetery.

"She took out a loan to cover these. Three months later, she made a 5K deposit and paid off the loan."

He looked out the window of his office to the Team Room, where Sam had his feet up on his desk with his laptop balanced on his thighs.

"I wonder who she buried?" Mallory wondered.

"There's no one in the cemetery's office today, sir, but I can get that information on Monday if you want me to."

Mallory thought about having the Mason Police bring in the cemetery manager, but rejected the thought. Sammy continued.

"She runs an upscale clothing store in Mason now. *Andrea's.* The business account is held in the same bank."

Mallory's screen changed. More checks were highlighted and Sam continued.

"There are regular checks made out from her personal account to a Methodist church there in Mason. She must be a churchgoer."

"Any trouble getting the information, Sam?"

"They had to bring in the bank manager since it's Saturday. He cooperated up to a point, but stressed the fact that Shellers is an upstanding member of the community. A good customer."

Mallory nodded. "Okay. Anything from her phone records?"

"All pretty boring, sir. We're still trying to get through to someone at the National Personnel Records Center in St. Louis about John Michaels' 201 file. There's nobody in the office today. I guess the NPRC keeps civilian hours, with weekends off."

"No progress?"

"Doolee's calling the FBI in St. Louis. Maybe they can do something."

Mallory looked at his watch.

"Tell Doolee and Jessica to make an appointment to see Ms. Shellers. I want to find out about any friends he had back in school. We can have the locals interview them, in case he contacted them."

"Right, sir. They can ask about those letters you wanted to see, too. To see what unit he was in. Jessica can call her. She'll have the best luck."

Mallory nodded absently. The woman did respond well to Jessica, considering the circumstances, but just about everybody responded to Jessica. Everybody but Altro, that is.

Chapter 19

Andrea Shellers sat on her wraparound porch, holding a picture of her and John in her lap. It was an old eight by ten black and white in a cheap frame, taken just before their wedding. Beyond the Courthouse, she gazed at the tops of the trees in Maple Grove Cemetery, wondering how any of this could be real.

Her phones had been ringing constantly, both her house phone and her cell. It was a number she didn't recognize, but she thought it was the Task Force people, wanting to talk to her again. She just couldn't, so she turned the ringer off on the house phone, turned off her cell and put it in a drawer.

It was almost dark, but still warm enough to sit outside. People were taking advantage of this run of splendid spring weather. Children played on the sidewalk with an amazing variety of colorful, plastic toys. Their parents sat vigilant on lawn chairs, or worked at trimming shrubs or weeding flower beds. She heard a lawn mower running, and the strident racket of a gas powered trimmer.

A gray sedan pulled up at the curb in front of the house and an Asian man wearing a sport coat, dress slacks and very shiny shoes got out. He looked up and down the street, nodded to two more Asian men in the back seat and approached her house with his hands in his coat pockets. She stood to greet him as he stepped up on her porch. When he saw the picture she held, he nodded at it and smiled kindly at her.

"Hello, ma'am. My name is Colonel Nguy. I am a friend of John's."

"John? Have you seen him?"

He gave her a slight bow and smiled again.

"Yes, I have seen him. He sent me. May I come in and talk to you?"

She hesitated a few seconds before she agreed.

"Of course. Come in."

She led him inside, shut the door behind them, then led him into the living room and pointed to a chair as she sat on the sofa.

"Please, sit down."

He remained standing and shook his head, his hands still in the pockets of his sport coat.

"No thank you, ma'am. John sent me to take you to him."

"I beg your pardon?"

The Colonel's face lost its kind smile, and she could see the granite of his character. "The men who tried to kill the woman from the drug task force… He says they will come for you. He wants you to be safe. I'm here to take you to him."

"Take me to him? Where?"

"He is in a safe place, ma'am. He sent me to take you there, so you will be safe also."

Andrea looked down at the carpet and shook her head.

"Is it really him?"

She heard him take a deep breath.

"Ma'am, these are very dangerous men. You will not be safe here. These men will come after you."

It was so far-fetched that she didn't know what to say. She looked up to the man as he spoke to her again.

"Please, ma'am. Come with me."

"I can't just go."

The Colonel sighed, then his face turned to stone again.

"I cannot leave without you, ma'am. He sent me for you."

Andrea looked closely at the Colonel and could see he was telling the simple truth, that he would not leave without her. He appeared ready to physically drag her along, if necessary. His hands were still in his coat pockets, and she wondered if he had a gun in there. Then his face took on a softer look.

"Andrea? John cares for you very much. That is why he sent me."

Those words broke her reluctance, and she stood.

"How long should I be prepared to stay?"

"Just come now, ma'am. There may not be any time."

She opened the closet in the foyer and retrieved her purse and a jacket. The Colonel held the picture in one hand and helped her slip her jacket on with the other. He handed the photo back to her, then held the front door as she walked out on the porch. After she locked the door, the Colonel led her to his car and held the door politely for her. The two Asian men in the backseat smiled pleasantly as she got in.

When they pulled away, she held the picture tightly to her chest and looked back at her home, wondering if she would ever see it again.

Chapter 20

Ka led Altro down the hallway to a small eat-in kitchen. "I will make us some tea," she said.

Altro sat and tried to recover from the shock of Walker's attack as Ka puttered at the stove. The scar on Ka's face looked like a drop of acid had dribbled down through her eyebrow and landed on her cheek, somehow missing her eye. The teardrop shaped scar on the woman's cheek was like a beauty mark, making her seem more exotic.

When the tea was ready Ka gave Altro a cup. "Colonel Nguy is concerned about you," she said. "He said you look tired, that you should eat something. I'm afraid I don't know what we have."

Altro was tired, but she didn't want tea or something to eat. Some of Doolee's coffee and a cigarette is what she wanted.

Ka reached up into a cabinet and retrieved a plate, then went to an old refrigerator and looked inside. There were more of the rolls the Colonel had served to Altro earlier, and Ka put one on the plate. Altro took a bite, then realized how hungry she was. She dug into the roll while Ka took her seat. After devouring the roll, Altro turned to Ka. She had so many questions.

"Will he be all right?"

Ka smiled. "Grandmother will take care of him."

"Are you sure?" Altro said. She shuddered. "He was so cold."

Ka patted her hand like she was reassuring a child who didn't understand why the goldfish was gone. Her face was so open and her touch so warm that Altro didn't pull her hand away.

"You don't understand," Ka said. "He is between the places now, deep in the valley. I would tell you not to worry, but I worry too. Our people think of him as invincible, the Valley Walker, but you can see he isn't. He is so tired. Sometimes the pain is too much for him and he falls away."

The pain is too much and he falls away? Altro felt her stomach turn. The same thing happened to him in the drugstore when she shot at him. She could almost hear the scream of pain that came from the dragon. Had she caused him that much pain?

She was staring at her teacup when Colonel Nguy walked in, leading a very frightened looking woman. The Colonel released the woman's arm and smiled.

"Andrea, this is Ka. She will see to your comfort, as much as possible." He gestured to Altro. "And this is Ms. Altro. She is from the drug task force."

He turned back to the woman he'd brought in and nodded his head, almost a bow.

"Ladies, this is Andrea Shellers."

Ka jumped up and almost ran to the Shellers woman. She gave her a fierce hug and stood back with her hands still on her shoulders.

"Andrea, I am so happy to meet you at last. Father has talked so much about you, but you are more beautiful than I could have imagined."

Looking the woman over, Altro had to agree that the woman was attractive, in spite of her bewildered and confused expression. She was well dressed, and evidently took good care of herself. But who was she?

Shellers pushed Ka firmly away, then looked around the poorly furnished room, taking in the cheap cabinets and chipped Formica table top. She looked at Altro, who nodded at her. She took in Ka with a frown on her face.

"You have me at a disadvantage, Ms. ... just who are you?"

Ka frowned. "Please sit down, Andrea. I will make you some tea. There is so much we need to talk about."

Shellers pulled out a chair and sat at the table. Her face went from suspicion to confusion, and her voice became quietly frantic. "Colonel Nguy said John was here. Is it really him?"

Ka looked away as she spoke. "It is him. He has slipped away, but he will be back."

As she started making tea, Ka turned to Altro. "Are you tired, Teri? I know it has been a trying day for you. If you like, I can take you somewhere you can rest while Andrea and I talk."

Ka was trying to give Shellers privacy, but Altro wanted to learn more about John Michaels and the Shellers woman.

"I'd like to stay," she said, and watched the Shellers woman to gauge her reaction. Shellers ignored Altro and kept her glare locked on Ka. Ka smiled at Altro, clearly happy to have some support.

"Yes. Please stay, Teri." Ka's smile broadened and then she laughed. A musical laugh. "It will be nice, we three women talking."

Shellers continued to stare at Ka as she placed a cup of tea in front of her. Ka sat down across from her, next to Altro.

Ka smiled at Shellers. "It is herbal tea, Andrea, with no caffeine. I imagine you are tired. It must be frightening for you, everything that has happened. Is there anything I can do to help?"

"You were going to tell me who you are," Shellers said.

Ka took a sip of her tea and began.

"I am Ka. I am Hmong, from Laos. I met John in the mountains of Laos in 1976 when I was 12 years old. My village was fleeing the Laotian Army. The lowland Laotians hunted us all, because our people made war on the North Vietnamese. Father was trying to help us, but the Army of Vietnam and the Russians were helping the Laotian Army. We could only run, and try to escape to the refugee camps in Thailand."

Ka's voice was starting to shake, and her hands became nervously busy. She took a deep breath and a sip of tea to calm herself before she continued.

"We managed to escape the army on the ground, but Russian planes came. They sprayed our camp with a chemical. It was yellow and stuck to everything. My people called it the 'yellow rain'. It burned the skin."

Altro watched Ka touch the teardrop burned into her cheek.

"When the planes dumped the chemicals, Father... John gave his poncho to me, but some of the chemical leaked through his poncho, on my face."

Altro wondered where John Michaels had hidden from the "yellow rain," but Shellers spoke bluntly and coldly.

"I see the burn mark on your face. Now tell me why you keep calling him Father. His name is John."

Ka lowered her head and slowly nodded. Her voice was no longer light and lilting, but quiet and somber when she spoke. Her head remained lowered.

"John managed to get the survivors from our village to a refugee camp in Thailand. Many died on the way, my entire family among them. But in the refugee camp, he arranged to have me brought to the United States."

Altro broke in. "So when did he get you here to the States? How?"

Ka raised her head, and her pride was evident in her smile.

"A Frenchman in Bangkok handled all of the logistics and paperwork. John adopted me in 1977. I was brought here as his daughter in 1978."

Altro watched the anger, grief, pain and confusion chase each other across Shellers' face. In a few moments, anger won the contest and the woman glared at Ka as she leaned forward in her chair.

"You're his daughter?"

Again Ka lowered her face, then nodded. Tears fell to the table and she dabbed at them with a paper napkin.

"I'm so sorry, Andrea. Father told me you had no children before you sent him away."

No children? Sent him away? Were Shellers and Michaels married?

She had her mouth open to ask about that when Colonel Nguy walked in again.

This time he was accompanying a young woman, a girl really, carrying a baby. Ka jumped up from her seat, ran to the girl and threw her arms around her neck. She gave the newcomer a

119

hug and kissed her on both cheeks before she stepped back. The two began to chatter away in a tonal language, the pitch of their voices rising and falling musically.

The young woman handed the baby to Ka, who held it tightly to her chest before pulling the blanket back just enough to see its face. The baby was evidently sleeping. There was more excited conversation between Ka and the mother, this time quieter, so the baby wouldn't be roused. Altro could almost understand the words being spoken in admiration of the baby… how it had grown, how lovely it was. She stopped herself from sneaking a peak.

The Colonel was already gone, evidently eager to leave this women's business to the women. Ka turned to Altro, and in turn to Shellers.

"I'm so sorry. I have forgotten my manners. This is Bao. She is Hmong, from Laos, also. Bao does not speak English yet. Father had her brought to the United States too."

Altro looked over this young mother. She was taller than Ka, at maybe 5 feet 8 inches. Her hair wasn't the deep jet black of most Asians, but was almost blond. Her eyes were the most shocking trait, a deep blue that looked absolutely incongruous next to her dusky complexion.

Ka saw Altro's puzzled look. "She is descended from the original Hmong, the Old Ones. Grandmother, Father's adoptive mother, is also. She had the light hair and blue eyes when she was young. You met her earlier, Teri."

Altro had been called by her last name for so long — in law school, at the Attorney General's Office, and now by members of the Task Force. She'd been Altro since her undergrad days, and now this woman she'd just met was calling her by her first name. Teri. It was a bit strange, but Ka was so open about everything it felt natural.

"Yes, she was so angry. But now… " Altro said.

"She was just worried about Father, because you tried to shoot him. But she could not stay angry at you. She is very old and wise, and powerful in her way."

Andrea Shellers' anger boiled over.

"I've been dragged to this rather tawdry place by the 'Colonel,' who seems to be John's faithful servant. Now I'm sitting at the table drinking tea with people I've never met, like some ludicrous church social!"

She turned her pale face toward Altro.

"And you! You tried to shoot John? What are you doing here?"

Altro's anger flared, but she didn't have time to answer. Shellers pointed a finger at the new arrival and continued.

"And why did the Colonel bring this girl here? Did John adopt her too?"

Ka turned slightly away, and handed the baby back to Bao. She stood and made tea for Bao, taking her time. Shellers twisted in her seat and cleared her throat, but Ka still didn't answer. She placed the tea before Bao and placed a hand on the girl's shoulder. She didn't sit, but turned to Shellers with a look of resolve on her face.

"I will tell you the story of Bao, Andrea. Please understand that much of what I tell you is only what I have heard, stories that have reached us from Hmong in Laos and Thailand. But parts of the story were told to me by Father. Other parts by Bao herself. So I know these parts are factual."

Ka started running her hand along Bao's hair, smoothing it. She stopped herself, placed her hand on Bao's shoulder again, and began.

Chapter 21

Lo Bao was the beautiful daughter of a family from the once powerful Lo clan of the Hmong. The name Bao means butterfly, and the girl lived up to her name. She flitted from one beautiful flower of life to another, drinking freely of the nectar of her carefree existence.

Her father was well to do in the Hmong world, respected in the small town of Ban Konoy. The town was on a main highway, not far up in the hills, and clean enough for a family of their high standing. They didn't live in a split-bamboo hut like the rural Hmong, but in an actual masonry house, with a pleasant courtyard where the family could entertain. Bao's mother loved her daughter more than her sons and doted on her, giving her all that she wished for. It was a pleasant life for the young girl until Chiong, a mountain Hmong of power, came down to their village seeking some excitement.

This mountain Hmong, a petty drug lord with violent men at his disposal, spotted young Bao and was immediately struck by her beauty. The young woman had the light skin and hair of the Hmong of legend, and her bright blue eyes overwhelmed the older man. He sent for the girl's family to announce his plans to marry this exquisite creature, but the girl's mother would have none of it. The mother was beautiful in her own right, for she had the same features as her daughter, and was plainly spoiled by her husband. The woman bluntly said that no daughter of hers would ever wed a crude old man from the hills.

Humiliated and angry, the drug lord killed the parents, took the young girl by force and returned to his place in the mountains. Once there, the man tried to impress the girl with his power and wealth, for he was hopelessly overcome by her innocence and beauty. He showered her with expensive gifts and brought in two old women to care for the house. For two full weeks, the man tried to win Bao's heart, only to be rejected again and again. Finally, after a fellow drug lord laughed at his helplessness, his love for the young woman turned to hate.

After that, Bao was raped and beaten regularly by Chiong. Every time the man passed, he would strike her. The girl was covered with bruises and her clothing soon turned to filthy rags. The man had taken back all her gifts and refused her more clothing. She cowered in the back of the split bamboo hut in an effort to avoid the man, but he came to her and raped her whenever the idea came to mind.

Being Hmong, Bao's tender heart was made up of more than one soul. Now, because of Chiong's cruelty, her heart was shattered. All of her souls but her primary soul, her Winjan, had deserted her and gone to the other side. The once lively girl was without hope, hanging by a thin thread to life, with no spirit left.

To the northeast of the town of Ban Konoy, in a clan village with no name, Walker heard of the abduction of young Bao and was moved by the story. He had just come down with his mother from her private camp and was listening to the hearts of the Hmong, the people who had adopted him into their race. He sat next to his adoptive mother, Neng Cheng, in a split bamboo hut on simple stools placed close to the fire pit in the middle of the dirt floor.

With him and his mother were some elders of the village, who were discussing the plight of the Hmong with their adopted son. They told Walker how the drug lord Chiong took Bao to his compound in the mountains close to the Vietnamese border, near Dien Bien Phu. His mother launched an angry outburst about these self appointed overlords and their lack of honor and manners, ending the harangue by hawking into the fire. The fire reacted as if a teaspoon of gasoline had been thrown on it, the flames momentarily flaring to the ceiling. The village elders drew back in fear and cast worried looks at the old woman, but Walker was filled with pride that a woman of such power and spirit had chosen to adopt him.

A week later, Walker sat hidden in the shadows of an overhanging ledge, on the slope that looked down on Chiong's compound. The man was giving orders about the business of his opium business when a small ragged figure came out of his hut. Chiong strode to her, knocked her down with his fist and began kicking her viciously. When he tired of this, he left the young woman lying in the dirt, walked back to his men and took up his conversation with them as if nothing had happened. The girl rose to her feet after a few minutes, and went into the woods in back of the house to tend to her business. She returned around the other side of the building, in an effort to avoid Chiong, then ducked into the building without the man noticing her. The door closed softly behind her.

Later that day, when the sun was near the end of its downward slope, Walker walked into the clearing of Chiong's settlement with four Hmong in his company. The four Hmong were armed with AK47s and crossbows. Chiong's underlings quickly surrounded them and interrogated them. Walker did not tell them his name, but said he was there to speak to their master. His business was with Chiong.

Walker joined Chiong in his hut and sat with him next to his fire pit drinking lao-lao. After exchanging banal pleasantries and conversation, Chiong came to the point.

"Why are you here? What do you want of me?"

Walker tilted his head toward the darkness at the back of the room where Bao was hiding.

"I would like to purchase the worthless woman who weighs you down with her presence," Walker said.

Chiong roared with laughter and drank more lao-lao. At the sound of his laughter, a fat young dog came from the darkness at the back of the room, wagging its tail. Chiong kicked at the dog and laughed loudly again.

"This woman is not for sale. Like the dog, I keep her to beat her. Her pain gives me pleasure."

Walker contemplated this simple answer.

"I can give you a good price."

With a snort, Chiong shook his head. "Her pain gives me more pleasure than any money you could pay."

Walker tried to appeal to the man's spiritual side.

"My friend, do not do this. The spirits will become angry that you carry so much hate in your heart."

Chiong spat on the floor. "I care not for any spirits. I live by my strength. I will keep her."

When Chiong said this, Walker became angry. The dragon stirred, then snarled. A vibration coursed through the ground and a deep low humming sound, like the ever-present sound in a Buddhist temple, began, then rose in volume until the drug lord's hut shook. Chiong tried to speak but couldn't. Drool dripped from the corners of his mouth.

"You would not sell me the woman, Chiong," Walker said. "You said you live by your own strength. Now I will just take her, for I am stronger than you. Then I will take your soul to the other side and give it to Ndsee Nyong, the Soul Devourer. I will laugh as he rips your heart into shreds. You will be no more, Chiong, and no offspring will ever come from you."

Chiong continued trying to speak, but the vibration in the earth grew so strong that he toppled from his stool. The drug lord managed to get himself on all fours and looked up at Walker, who was still sitting on his stool.

"Now you look like the dung eating dog you are," Walker said. "Bark for me."

A yip of a bark come from Chiong's mouth and his back end wiggled as he wagged his tail. His tongue rolled out and he began to pant. The proud drug lord raised his face to Walker and he whined. Walker took pity on the poor creature.

"Sell me the woman, dog," Walker said. "I will give you two bars of silver. And your life."

Chiong yipped in agreement and wagged his tail. He panted and looked up at Walker in adoration. Walker sensed Chiong's complete submission and stroked his head to show his approval.

"Good dog."

The sale of the woman was completed, but Chiong was no more.

Back at his mother's home, Walker watched as his mother performed the ceremony to return the girl's lost souls. The old woman straddled a bench, the trusty winged steed she rode to the other side for the rescue. Four elders from the village were assisting the ceremony, nodding to the shaman's chanting.

Bao lay in bed, her sweaty head tilting from side to side in rhythm with the drum. Small cries sounded in her throat, and her eyes shifted behind closed eyelids. There was nothing more Walker could do. He rose and left the house, confident his mother would bring the young woman back to this world.

When Walker returned the following day, young Bao was sitting on a stool, eating. White strings were wrapped around her wrists, to keep her souls together in her body until she gained strength. The old woman sat next to her speaking softly. Walker sat next to his mother and placed a hand on her shoulder.

"You have done well, Mother."

The old shaman shook her head and spoke softly. "Her soul is complete now, Son, but it will be hard to keep it so. The poor girl is pregnant. She carries the seed of the animal that did this to her."

Walker was struck hard by this. He needed to think, to decide if any honorable thing could be done. He said goodbye to his mother and left for his own house.

As the sun was setting, Walker came back to his mother's house and saw the old woman sitting on a stool next to young Bao. The two women were watching the sunset and talking quietly. Bao had tears rolling down her cheeks as she looked up to acknowledge him.

"You women, good evening. It is a beautiful end to the day."

Neng Cheng spoke softly. "It is beautiful, Son. Sit with us."

Walker approached the purpose of his visit slowly. "Mother, a man needs something in his life. Without it he searches endlessly."

"Yes, that is the way."

"I have been thinking of taking a wife. What do you think of this?"

"My heart would be happy, Son. I have waited for this day."

"I was thinking that young Bao here would make a good wife. She is of a good family, and she is so beautiful that I am helpless in her presence."

At this, young Bao drew in a quick deep breath and jumped to her feet. She started to sob and tears ran down her cheeks. Walker stood beside her and placed a hand on her shoulder.

"Will you think of this, Bao? I will return in a week for your answer."

With that, Walker left. Bao looked questioningly at the old woman, and Neng Cheng smiled broadly at her.

The couple was married in a traditional ceremony a month later. An ancient man played the Geng, a Hmong instrument made of hollow tubes. The song the old man played told the story of how Walker found this beautiful woman and saved her from Chiong. It made many of the guests weep openly, but young Bao smiled as she danced.

Chiong's compound was deserted when Walker returned. After helping themselves to anything of value, including the two bars of silver paid for Chiong's woman, Chiong's men had moved on to form their own little empire. The compound seemed haunted now, the only inhabitant left was the crazed dog that ran endlessly around the area, barking and wagging its tail. Chiong

Walker shot the dog through the heart with a crossbow, then burned the body. On the other side, he captured the souls of the dog and stuffed them into a black bag that admitted no light. He took the souls to Ndsee Nyong, the Soul Devourer, and watched as the monster greedily ate them. Ndsee Nyong gnawed lustily on the souls, snuffling like a pig in the yard.

Above the sound of flesh ripping and bones cracking, a hoarse screaming could be heard as threads of the primary soul of Chiong, his Winjan, were torn away from his son that lived in the body of young Bao.

Walker nodded. He would let his own Winjan be tied to the boy, in place of Chiong's. The boy would grow up strong and healthy, untouched by the darkness of his natural father's heart.

Chapter 22

At the end of Ka's story, Altro was stunned. There was no way to determine how much of it was true, but what these people thought of the man they called the Valley Walker was apparent.

Andrea Shellers reacted quite differently. She stood up, then teetered from side to side until she leaned over and put her hands on the table. There were tears in the woman's eyes and her voice was soft.

"He married this... this girl?"

Her mouth opened and closed but no words came out, only a soft mewling. Her wide open eyes flitted back and forth between the three other women in the room. When she finally found her voice, it pierced the air.

"But it can't be! It's just not possible!" She held her hands out from her body and shook her head, her voice lower now. "None of this is possible."

The woman tried to continue, but just stood with her mouth open. Ka took her hand.

"I'm sorry for the shock all of this must have been to you, Andrea. You must be exhausted. Let me take you to your room."

✱✱✱✱✱

Andrea didn't resist as Ka led her from the room. When they left the kitchen, from a room down a darkened hallway, she heard a droning sound and the beating of a drum. Andrea unconsciously pulled her hand from Ka's and turned to the sound, then walked toward it, unable to stop herself. The room was dim, but as she moved slowly into it, her eyes began adjusting to the lack of light. The sight that materialized made her stop in her tracks.

On a square mat, in the center of a room with a polished hardwood floor, sat a figure that appeared to be John, her very own John Michaels. Candles encircled the mat and a closed cast-iron brazier smoked in back of him. Sitting to the side, her face illuminated by the candles, was an ancient and withered woman. The old woman was chanting and beating a small drum, her eyes closed, her head nodding in rhythm with the drum.

The room began to vibrate and a deep tone, deeper than the lowest note from an orchestra's bassoon, rose from the bowels of the earth. Andrea's body began swaying in rhythm with the drum. In a trance-like state, Andrea approached the figure and saw that it was indeed John. As her eyes adjusted to the dim lighting, she began to see him clearly, and panic overcame her. She tried to turn and run but was rooted to the spot, unable to budge. Gravity overcame her and she sank to her knees immediately in front of him, the edge of the mat beneath her knees.

His torso was covered with tattoos, but the tattoos weren't just pictures on his skin. They writhed and coiled and slid to the rhythm of the old woman's drum and the vibration that permeated the air. The images stopped their movement, then merged into a physical entity, a living, breathing dragon that seemed to grow from him. The beast turned its head toward her. Its yellow eyes focused on her and the tongue of the creature flicked out, testing the air for her scent.

A strangled cry came from her throat, and John opened his eyes. She looked into his eyes and felt herself falling into emptiness, an abyss that seemed to have no bottom. As she fell, the roar of the dragon followed her, the volume of its roar increasing until it overcame her hearing, and there was only a ringing in her mind.

Deeper and deeper she fell, and her screams echoed from the darkness around her.

Then, appearing from the darkness, she saw John's face. His arms came from the blackness to hold her, and her fall was slowed, eventually arrested. His embrace tightened around her until she could feel his warmth flowing into her body. She let herself be held and rocked, and felt herself growing sleepy. The last thing she remembered as she slipped into slumber was his voice.

"You're safe here, Andrea. It's enough for now."

Chapter 23

After Ka and Shellers left, Altro watched young Bao as she rocked the baby that had begun to stir. Through the kitchen window, Altro could plainly see it was dark outside and started to stand, thinking she would look out and try to determine where she was. But a deep vibration began in the building. The great foghorn started sounding in the earth.

On the edge of her seat, Altro turned to Bao, and the girl was smiling at her. The young mother started cooing to the baby, and when the vibration grew so strong that the cupboards rattled, Bao pulled the covers from the child's head. She held it out and up, away from her, as if to give the baby a better view of the world.

Ka walked back in, and Bao and Ka chattered to one another, both of them smiling broadly as the foghorn sounded and the building vibrated and shuddered. Then the vibration stopped, and the two women chattered more as Ka sat down. Ka noticed that Altro was left out of the conversation.

"I apologize, Teri. Bao and I were so excited that I forgot my manners again. But you felt it, didn't you? Grandmother has brought him back."

She'd felt it, all right. She could almost see the dragon. Then Ka leaned in and spoke quietly.

"Please don't be angry, but I have to tell you this before you go. When I saw you with Father, I was envious. I was jealous. I could feel the bond he has with you."

There was nothing Altro could say to that. There was no way to explain it. Ka sighed and continued.

"Before he adopted me, I wanted so much to be his wife, you know. In our culture, in the old country, it was commonplace for a young girl to marry. A man would often have more than one wife, and families could be very large. But he always continued to treat me as his daughter."

Ka smiled ruefully, then shook her head slightly.

"Of course I couldn't accept being the second wife any longer. I have grown up and changed over the years. This is America, after all."

Second wife? Altro frowned. She wasn't keeping up. But Ka reached out and touched her hand.

"And now I worry about Bao. She is so young. She cannot understand." Ka sighed and smiled at the same time. "But you can see she is happy. And she has us, the clan, the extended family. We will take care of her. She and her son will always be loved."

Altro turned and watched as Bao began nursing the baby. It had started fussing and the girl opened her blouse and took him to her breast. The openness of these people shocked Altro, but at the same time she found it warming.

She couldn't stand being touched, except when her body demanded it. Yet the way these people were always touching each other appealed to her. In fact, when the old woman and Ka had touched her shoulder, when Ka had patted her hand, she'd felt something she hadn't felt in a long time. The desire to be close to someone.

For years there'd been no room in her life for more than passing physical relationships, let alone thoughts of a family. Now, here she was, watching the baby sucking on his mother's breast, contemplating what it would be like to raise children, wondering what it would be like to have a baby suck on her breast.

Colonel Nguy walked back into the room, smelling of cigarette smoke again. *God, that cigarette smells good.* He gave Altro his kind smile, the granite gone from his face.

"I can take you back now, Ms. Altro."

As she turned from the table to stand, the Colonel, still smiling kindly, stuck Altro in the shoulder with a needle and emptied the contents of a syringe into her. She hadn't seen the syringe in Nguy's hand until the needle was plunged into her shoulder.

"Goddammit, Colonel! Again?"

The Colonel just kept smiling, and the drug started working. He was suddenly such a nice man that Altro actually smiled back.

"We can't let you know where we are, Ms. Altro."

He raised her to her feet and handed her the black cloth bag.

"Here, put this over your head, and we will take you to the car. It will be better if you are seated and belted in before you fall asleep."

The black bag was probably unnecessary. Even with one arm draped over the Colonel's shoulder and the over Ka's, Altro had no idea how she made it to the car. Whatever the Colonel gave her, it was good.

Chasing the Dragon

Chapter 24

Brain and Sledge were sitting in a booth at the Winged Lion, sipping beer while they relayed the latest information to Tommy Mo.

"Did you know that Walker has a woman in the area, Mr. Mo?" Brain asked. "He was married to her in the old days. She lives in Mason now."

"How did you learn this?" Tommy asked. "Does the dung eater have someone planted on the Task Force?"

Brain frowned. If Woodley ever learned about the Hmong calling him the dung eater, there would be hell to pay. "You don't need to know that," was all he said.

Tommy lit a cigarette and thought about it. "She could be leverage."

Brain nodded. "Definitely. Your men should pay her a visit."

*****

At the Task Force Team Center, Mallory had spent a lot of time staring at the wall, thinking things through. He also made a thorough examination of the Task Force server's filing system, checking who had access and what level. When he was sure what had to be done, he made some changes to the system.

Finished with that, he looked out through the door. The others were still at their desks. It was 2100 hours, 9:00 p.m. to these civilians. Jessica was just hanging up her landline when he walked out of the office.

"I still can't get in touch with Andrea Shellers, sir," she said. "I left messages, but she hasn't returned my calls."

"Altro would get a warrant," Sam grumbled.

Mallory shook his head. "I don't want to cause her any more trouble."

Sam frowned and shook his head.

Doolee was hunched over his laptop, unresponsive. Mallory stepped behind him and looked over his shoulder. He was running the video of the drug store shooting. Mallory cleared his throat. Doolee finally looked up and acknowledged Mallory.

"Sorry, sir," Doolee said. "I was wrapped up in the video."

"He's wasted hours on the thing," Sam said.

Jessica shook a finger at Sam. "Sammy!" she said.

Sam scowled for a second, then cleared his face and nodded his head. "Sorry, Doolee."

Doolee just grinned. "Sammy and I have talked about it. He does not want to listen."

"We know something's wrong with it," Mallory said. "Have you spotted something new?"

"It is interesting," Doolee said. He pointed to the flat-screen and turned to Sam. "Can you put it on the screen?"

Sam groaned, but in less than a minute the video was up, on pause. "What section do you want to see?"

"The shooting, of course," Doolee said. He stood up and moved closer to the screen. The video started running. The three gunmen came in the entrance.

"Stop it," Doolee said. "Back it up, perhaps ten seconds. Then run it at a slower speed."

Sam groaned again, but did as Doolee asked. The shooter, who they knew as John Michaels now, walked to the end of the aisle at the outside of the store. Altro walked down her aisle, looking at him. Michaels had one hand wrapped around something hanging from his neck, something that looked like a bag made of cloth. Then he let go of it and turned to the door. The gunmen walked in. One turned back to cover the entry door. Altro was reaching into her shoulder bag for her gun.

Doolee was pointing at the screen. "See how the gunmen, Altro and Michaels are moving, but everyone else is stopped?"

The woman at the checkout counter was frozen. All the customers they could see were locked in place. They watched the shooting scene through, continued to the part where Michaels came back in, backed Altro into the store and she shot him. The pharmacist came into view and moved between Altro and the man she shot. Everyone else in the store was still motionless, and stayed that way until after Michaels had some kind of seizure.

"See?" Doolee said. "Only a few people are moving. The rest are immobile through the entire event."

Sam groaned. Jessica gasped. "What do you think this is, Doolee?" she asked. "How is that possible?"

"I don't know," Doolee said. He made an arcing motion with one hand. "But something is bent." Then he started grinning. "It is a beautiful problem. It would explain why none of the witnesses except Altro remember the shooting."

Doolee was grinning so big that Mallory thought his face would split. The video was stopped with Altro standing there, still holding her gun. Michaels was on his side on the floor. Mallory stepped up to the screen and stared at it. Then he made a point of looking at his watch. "It's past nine o'clock, people," he said. "Go home."

Doolee arched his eyebrows. Jessica looked shocked. Sam mumbled something Mallory couldn't make out. They didn't want to go, but Mallory stood firm until they locked up their desks and filed out. As soon as they were gone, he went back in his office and called up the video of the drugstore incident on his computer.

Running the feed from the camera behind the pharmacy, he came to the sequence where John Walker Michaels stared at Altro before she shot him. Rubbing at the scar on his chin, he zoomed in and studied the red cloth bag hanging from a cord strung around the man's neck.

Mallory opened his briefcase and pulled out a phone. It was a cold phone, a burner. There were three more just like it in his briefcase. He made the call, and Buzzard answered like he always did.

"Yeah."

"Possum here."

"Possum? What woke you up?"

There was no time for pleasantries. Mallory got to it. "You know the new drug task force in Michigan?"

"I've heard of it," Buzzard answered.

"Well, I'm leading it."

Mallory heard Buzzard's coarse laugh for a few seconds before the man broke into a fit of coughing. Mallory waited until the coughing stopped before he went on.

"Listen up, Buzzard. Walker's here."

"What the hell? You sure about that?"

"I'm sure. He had one of my people snatched this morning."

"Huh." Mallory heard the distinctive click of a Zippo, followed by a short pause as Buzzard took a drag on his Marlboro. "What the fuck for?"

"It's not clear, but I think you should get some people over here."

"Damn straight," Buzzard said. Then he chuckled. "Walker, huh? That motherfucker."

Chapter 25

At 2:00 am, a car pulled to the curb in front of Andrea Shellers' home. Two men dressed in dark gray clothing and ski masks got out, closed the doors softly and moved silently to the rear entrance. The plan was to pick the lock, sedate Shellers and deliver her to Tommy Mo.

As they rounded the corner of the house, there was a metallic click followed by a low thrumming sound. One of the men grasped at a short arrow that protruded from both sides of his neck. The arrow, actually a crossbow bolt, had severed his carotid arteries and a red halo of mist pulsed around his head, highlighted by the glow of a streetlight. A strangled, gurgling sound came from his throat as he went to his knees.

His associate turned to flee, but was struck in the thigh with another bolt. He went down immediately, tried to scream, but a gloved hand clamped down on his mouth. Two men pulled him to his feet and dragged him back to the car, a hand still covering his mouth. They opened the driver's door and shoved him into the seat.

"Keys," one of the men said.

He shook his head as much as he could with the hand over his mouth. One of the men went back to the body on the lawn and retrieved the keys from a pocket of the corpse. When the keys where handed to the man in the car, he dropped them on the floorboard and made muffled moans. One attacker retrieved the keys and shoved them into the ignition. The other whispered in his ear.

"Tell your masters that you are dead. All of you."

The hand at the man's mouth finally moved away. As he opened his mouth to scream, a wooden dowel was shoved between his teeth. A hand was shoved under his jaw, forcing it closed. Another hand went to the back of his head, grasped his hair at the back of his head and tightened to a fist.

"Bite on this and be quiet."

Even more terrified, the man complied.

"Go home to your masters, like the whipped dog that you are," the voice said. "The Valley Walker will be coming for you."

Biting on the dowel to keep from screaming, the man started the car and put it in gear. He drove away using his left foot, the crossbow bolt still protruding from his right thigh. The pain was so intense that he didn't notice he was being followed.

Chapter 26

At the Ascott Sathorn in Bangkok, a French expatriate answered the call on his satellite phone. He was dressed in a silk robe over silk pajamas, soft-soled slippers on his feet. He was smoking one of the fine cigars that gave him such pleasure these days.

Jean Barouquette was the son of an officer in the French Expeditionary Forces that had occupied Vietnam and Laos. His father had stayed behind in Thailand after the fall of Dien Bien Phu, and made a small fortune trafficking in arms. It was during that time that Jean was born to a beautiful woman of French-Vietnamese lineage, but the woman left Jean and his father for a man of greater wealth and promise. Jean had been raised by his father, but with the help of willing women who came and went.

Though he was a French citizen, Bangkok had always been home to Jean. He'd carried on his father's business, expanding into legal holdings in restaurants and real estate around the city. The family business had come a long way from its beginnings at a banquette in the smoky Madrid Bar. He had a plush office and a secretary now, but for an old friend, he would always conduct business from home.

"Walker, it's good to hear your voice. I saw the report on the news. You are well?"

A pause as he listened, followed by a brief smile. Then he pursed his lips.

"Then the intelligence was correct. They delayed the woman at the drugstore so they could assassinate her there."

He nodded his head at the answer, then shook it at the thanks given.

"No thanks are needed, my friend. I am happy to assist you, and my computer people are always eager for a challenge."

The two men spoke in a combination of French, Thai, Vietnamese and English. This pidgin was the language of almost all illegal business conducted in Thailand. The Frenchman took a puff on his cigar, sat down at a side table and listened intently. He then pulled an electronic tablet from a robe pocket, placed it on the table and scrolled with one hand.

"Yes. The weapons are already available, warehoused here and there, as you specified. What else can I do?"

He put down his cigar and entered the information on his tablet as Walker unfolded his plan.

Chapter 27

When Mallory carded himself into the Team Center at 0730, everyone else was already there. It looked like they'd been there a while.

Doolee was on the phone. Jessica was hunched over her laptop and Sam had his feet on the desk, his laptop on his thighs.

Mallory got himself a coffee, went to his spot on the corner of the table, leaned back and cleared his throat to get everyone's attention.

"I talked to the FBI on the way in. Still nothing new on Altro's kidnapping."

Sam actually took his feet down off his desk. "Jesus Christ! It's been 24 hours!"

Mallory waved an arm at him to settle down. "You people are in early. What are you working on?"

"John Michaels," Sam said. "Trying to figure him out."

Mallory nodded. *No kidding.* "Did you come up with anything?"

"I got nothing from the serial numbers on the pistols he used in the drugstore, sir," Doolee said. "I will check with the military next."

Jessica raised her hand. Mallory nodded at her.

"His fingerprints and DNA drew a blank, sir. There's no record of him having a passport, entering or leaving the country, or even having a driver's license. That's all going through the computer records. Since it's the weekend, the search through paper records will have to wait until tomorrow."

"We still haven't heard from the Army records people," Sam said. "Same reason. It's the weekend. And if he was in the Army back in the 60s, those records will still be on paper too."

Mallory started rubbing the scar on his chin. "Anything new on the men he killed in the drugstore?"

Jessica shook her head. "Still nothing on their IDs. Sammy got the plate number on the van used in the drugstore shooting. The plates were reported stolen three days ago. The owner checks out okay."

"Any hits on traffic cameras?"

"No, sir. They must have used country roads and side streets."

Mallory mulled it over. These people knew what they were doing.

"Okay. What about the heroin distribution?" Mallory asked. "Any patterns there?"

Jessica worked at her laptop and a map of the area came up on the display behind Mallory. He stepped aside and pushed his glasses up on his nose. There were blue and red dots scattered on the map. Jessica flipped a hand at her hair and sat up straighter in her chair.

"The blue dots are security checkpoints set up by local police departments and campus security. The red dots are the locations of student deaths, sir. Twenty-seven. There haven't been any overdoses for almost a week. The local police and campus security say the checkpoints are having an effect, but I think it more likely the dealers are waiting for another shipment."

Mallory raised an eyebrow. Jessica was proving as bright as her record indicated.

"What about the DEA or FBI?" Mallory asked. "Have they come up with anything solid yet?"

"No, sir. The DEA has four agents working undercover, but they won't disclose their location. The FBI says their investigation is still solidifying."

"Okay. Jessica, keep working the intel as it comes in," Mallory said. "But Altro's abduction is the FBI's case. Let them handle it. I'll keep you updated."

Sam groaned. "I guess you're right, sir. The FBI *is* the best, but they're too damn slow. We need to do something."

Jessica turned to Sam. "You're worried about her, aren't you Sammy?"

"I know she's a hard ass, Jessica, but I like her."

Jessica smiled at "hard ass," then turned serious again. "I'll think she'll be okay, Sam. I just don't think the people who took her and Michaels would hurt her. I mean, he saved her life for some reason."

She looked up at Mallory. "Right, sir?"

Mallory grimaced, but nodded. *Walker.*

Chapter 28

In the mountains of Laos, night was just beginning to fall. Khun Pao was again sitting on his stool by the fire drinking lao-lao. He was waiting for the arrival of the witch, Neng Jou. The Dark Shaman.

While he waited, he fumed about Walker. First he had stepped in to stop the murder of Altro. Then the attempt at the hospital went wrong, and now the plan to kidnap Walker's woman had failed. He drank enough lao-lao to drop an elephant, then smoked a bowl of his finest opium, but it didn't help. A new girl had been brought to him, a tender one, but even her fear couldn't suppress his rage. He'd just sent the girl away when Neng Jou hobbled in the door.

Like Neng Cheng, the mother of the Valley Walker, she wore the traditional Hmong clothing and scarf made of hemp. Unlike the True Shaman's clothing, however, the Dark Shaman's clothing was completely devoid of color. Everything she wore was a dingy, sooty black, a reflection of the darkness she walked in.

The Dark Shaman sat down on the stool Khun offered with a rattling grunt. He offered the old woman a jar of lao-lao and a pipe filled with smoking opium, then waited for her to be comfortable. The old woman put the pipe on her lap and took a healthy drink of lao-lao. Then she turned to Khun.

"The Valley Walker troubles you again," she said.

Khun growled low in his throat. "The man's heart defies thought. He is always a step ahead of me. It is why I sent for you. His magic is too strong."

"You must send Nab," the hag said.

Khun thought it over, then nodded his agreement. Nab was his best man in the States. His name meant "Snake", and Nab lived up to his name. He killed as coldly and ruthlessly as any viper. Nab was in Minneapolis, Minnesota, but could be in

Lansing quickly. Khun put down his lao-lao, picked up his satellite phone and made the call. Nab was on his way.

The witch had picked up the pipe of opium and was waiting for Khun to light it for her. He used his butane lighter, holding the flame to the black ball while she inhaled. The Dark Shaman exhaled a cloud of smoke into the air. The cloud whirled and shifted, changed itself to form the image of a snake that coiled around the hag.

"I will give Nab power," she croaked. The snake breathed and hissed.

Khun smiled for the first time that day.

"Open the gates of hell, woman. I will meet the Valley Walker there."

Chapter 29

When Altro woke up she was still in her clothes, but in her own bed at home. She sat up and took stock of herself. The drug Colonel Nguy gave her had pushed her into a deep sleep, and must have worn off hours ago. Other than being hungry, she felt surprisingly refreshed.

Her BlackBerry was disassembled on the nightstand, with the battery and SIM card lying on top of the case. Next to her BlackBerry were her watch and the key for the rental sedan. Her shoulder bag was leaned up against the nightstand. She installed the SIM card and battery in the phone and turned it on, then called the Team Center. Mallory's phone was busy, so she tried Doolee. He answered on the first ring.

"Altro?"

"Yeah, Doolee, it's me. I'm at home."

"Are you okay? Are you hurt?"

"I'm good. Tell everyone I'll be in as soon as I can. I was drugged."

Again. Colonel Nguy and his needles.

"I will call an ambulance, Altro. I will come myself."

"No, Doolee. Listen to me. I'm fine now. Call your buddies at the FBI. They'll want to go over everything here."

She hung up on Doolee while he was still talking, then walked to the door that opened to the garage. The ugly rental sedan had been left in the lot at the hospital when she was kidnapped, but was parked in her garage now. Someone must have driven the car over from the hospital and put it in the garage for her.

A conscientious kidnapper?

Altro took a quick shower and dressed. She had just finished eating a cup of yogurt when the doorbell rang. When she went to answer the door, she saw an envelope sitting on the small table next to the door in the foyer. The envelope had her name on it, printed in stylized lettering. Sitting next to the envelope was an ivory colored pendant, attached to a leather thong. It looked like the one Walker had been wearing.

She picked up the envelope and opened it. The few lines were printed in the same style lettering as her name on the envelope.

Teri,

I would be very pleased if you would accept my tile.

It is my sign. The sign of the Valley Walker.

Show it to any Hmong person, and they will help you in any way they can.

You're family now, Teri. You are part of the whole.

John Michaels

The doorbell rang again. Still holding the note in one hand, she picked up the pendant with the other. The Valley Walker's tile. His sign.

A dragon was engraved on what looked like genuine ivory. It was the same dragon she'd seen come from inside him in the drugstore, the same dragon as the painting on the wall that frightened her so badly.

After meeting John Michaels and seeing who he really was, the dragon on the tile wasn't frightening to her. The tile was warm in her hand, comforting, in fact. She squeezed it and her mind drifted. She smelled wood smoke and heard his voice. The doorbell rang again.

"Just a minute," she called.

Teri Altro read the note again, slid it back in the envelope and put it in the inside pocket of her suit jacket. His tile went in one of the outside pockets so she could touch it easily. This was private, between her and John Michaels. None of the FBI's business. Somebody banged on the door.

"All right!"

The FBI had arrived in force, in two SUVs and a sedan. While the Evidence Response Team put on their coveralls and booties, Altro stood on the front porch with one hand in her jacket pocket, fingering the tile. Across the street, the retired couple came out on their porch to gawk.

SAC Felix Bowman walked up to her and introduced himself, holding his hand out for a full ten seconds while he waited for her to take it. She disliked Bowman immediately. He was unctuous and condescending, clearly a man who was doing penance working with the peons while he waited to assume his rightful place in the FBI hierarchy. Altro had worked with the Bureau several times over the years, but had never met the Detroit SAC. He must have seen a golden opportunity for self-promotion to leave his office in Detroit.

She went back inside to let the Evidence Response Team know where she'd been, and pointed out her clothes piled on the floor next to the bed. They gave her some flak for not keeping their crime scene intact, but she just barked at them to get to work. A photographer started taking pictures, and a technician dusted her shoulder bag and the items in it while she waited. The technician quickly announced her bag and its contents clean of any prints, even her own. Altro wasn't surprised.

A medical tech took her vitals and a sample of her blood, which was bagged and tagged. After being declared fit for duty, she went back out to the porch where Bowman waited for her. The garage door was open. Two men in white Tyvek coveralls were going over the rental, dusting for prints and vacuuming up any fibers that may have been left by the people who put it in the garage.

Bowman wanted to go to the FBI satellite office in East Lansing to debrief her, but Altro didn't want that, and argued for going to the Team Center. Bowman wouldn't back down, even when she gave him her best glare and threatened to call the Attorney General. She called Mallory to let him know, and Mallory asked to speak to Bowman. After a short conversation, Bowman handed the BlackBerry back to her.

"I guess we'll be going to the Team Center after all," Bowman said.

She wondered, briefly, what Mallory had said to Bowman to convince him, but the ivory tile was warm. Her hand slipped inside her jacket pocket.

Since the rental was being examined, she had to ride with Bowman. On the way to the Team Center, the man ran his mouth constantly, using her first name when he addressed her. Altro said nothing to him. She tuned him out and kept one hand in her jacket pocket, fingering the ivory tile.

Chapter 30

Andrea Shellers didn't wake up refreshed. She was in a strange bed, in a strange room. As she realized where she was, the vision of John in the darkened room, the vision of the dragon, came back to her. She drew up her knees, pulled the covers to her chin and shivered.

But her mind couldn't dwell on that for long. It pushed away the things beyond her ability to grasp, things beyond anything she wished to know. Instead, she reached for and clutched desperately at one thin thread. *It was him.* She rose from her bed, driven by a need to see him.

While she showered, the thought of how she was brought here, how alien people had become the focal point of John's life, returned. She stood in the stream of hot water and wept. When she could cry no more, she completed her shower, toweled dry and wrapped herself in the robe hanging on the bathroom door. It was her own robe. It occurred to her that she had just used her own soap and shampoo, in her own special containers from her home, in fact.

When she left the bathroom, she smelled freshly brewed coffee. On the nightstand next to the bed sat a tray with an insulated decanter and a coffee cup. She poured herself a cup from the decanter and sipped, recognizing the flavor as her favorite blend. While drinking the coffee, she looked around the room, missing her own home. But there on the other nightstand, next to the picture of her and John, was her Bible. She went to the closet, found a good part of her wardrobe inside. Her shoes and purses were lined up neatly. These people had somehow brought some of her personal things to make her more comfortable.

She dressed and made her way to the kitchen. There she found Ka and Bao, sitting at the table drinking tea. Unable to face them, she retreated to her room and remained there for the rest of the morning, reading her Bible. Someone, she assumed it was Ka, brought a tray of food and left it at the door. Not really hungry, she picked at the food and tried to be angry again. She just couldn't.

Andrea began to regret the way she'd treated people who'd been nothing but kind and polite to her. The tragic stories of Ka and Bao had touched her deeply, but she'd been hurt by being excluded from John's life. Even though she had pushed John out of her life, the innocence of Ka and the beauty of Bao made the pain sharper. She'd raised her voice and let them know, without a doubt, that she didn't accept them.

Now she felt ashamed, and was embarrassed by her behavior toward the two women. She didn't know how she could face them, but knew she had to do something. Andrea straightened her appearance and strode from the room, intent on trying to set things right.

She almost walked over an ancient woman who stood in the hallway. She was dressed in snow-blue ceremonial clothing, and Andrea realized it was the same old woman who'd been in the candlelit room last night, beating the drum and chanting. The memory of the darkened room where John had come alive with dragons, demons to her, returned. Her breath came in quick gasps. The old woman took her hand and smiled.

To Andrea's surprise, a calm came over her. She looked closer at the woman, and saw the kindness hidden behind her translucent eyes. The old crone led her to the kitchen, where Ka was sitting alone with a cup of tea in her hands, and Andrea wondered if Ka ever drank coffee. The two exchanged unintelligible words. Ka rose from her seat and gave Andrea a light hug.

"Sit down, Andrea. Would you like some tea?" Ka said. Her voice was quiet.

The old woman jabbered to Ka for a minute and the two of them smiled at each other. Then the old crone patted Andrea on the shoulder and shuttled from the room. Andrea watched her leave, wincing at her arthritic gait.

"What did she say?"

Ka laughed, the music coming back to her voice. "She said you were wondering why I don't drink coffee."

Andrea was shocked, but not really surprised. "She knew what I was thinking?"

Ka laughed again, more music, and Andrea began her attempt to make amends. She smiled as warmly as she could and put a hand on Ka's arm.

"I think I'd like some more coffee, Ka. Can you show me where the pot is?"

Chapter 31

The Team Center was buzzing with questions when Altro walked in with SAC Bowman. They were all asking the same questions, more or less, resulting in an escalating level of happy confusion. She'd almost made it to her desk when Mallory stepped out of his office. He saw Altro and walked over to welcome her back, smiling and pushing his stupid glasses up on his nose. Forgetting her aversion to physical contact, he held out his hand to her, then actually apologized when she didn't take it.

Altro was in a hurry to get Bowman out of there, so she was pleased when Mallory stepped back from the group, put his pinkie fingers in the corners of his mouth and whistled shrilly. He pointed with one arm to the break room.

"All right people, we need to get a debriefing from Altro, so let's make our way to the break room. We'll get it recorded, and you can ask questions afterward."

Mallory turned to Altro. "Sam and Jessica set up cameras while you were driving over."

"I still think we should have gone to the Bureau's East Lansing office, Bill," Bowman said.

Mallory shook his head. "I wanted to do it here."

Sam made a short trip to the computer room, then they all filed into the break room. Altro saw cameras installed in two corners as she took her seat.

Her recitation was as brief as she could make it. The mention of Andrea Shellers created some discussion, and after they explained to Altro that she was John Michaels' ex-wife, Altro finally thought she understood the tension in the air during Shellers' conversation with Ka. She ended the narration with her waking up at home. Everyone waited for a few minutes to see if she would say anything more.

Doolee poured himself a cup of coffee, then one for her and Mallory. Sammy got himself a soda from the refrigerator. The Princess stared openly while Altro sat there with one hand in her jacket pocket, fingering the tile. When it became apparent she was finished, Bowman smiled his politician's smile.

"Teri..."

Altro released the tile and held her palm out to cut him off right there. She'd had just about all she could take of this clown.

"My name is not Teri to you, Felix." She made his name sound like Feeeeeelix, and pushed the sarcasm through her voice. "Call me Altro, or Ms. Altro. I don't care which. Just get it through your thick skull that I am not Teri to you."

Sammy and Doolee put a hand to their mouths to hide their grins. Mallory smiled openly. Princess Jessica ducked her head and stared at Altro. The slam just rolled off Bowman like water rolls off an oily hamburger.

"Ms. Altro then. I want to have a facial composite expert come over so we can get a make-up drawing of the man that abducted you. The Colonel. What was his name?"

She didn't want to do that, so she shot a look over to Sam before she spoke. He had his feet up on the table, and his laptop was balanced on his thighs. She needed to bring more people into this and sidetrack Bowman.

"He said his name was Nguy, but Michaels called him Bo. You're of Vietnamese descent, Sammy. Can you explain that?"

Sam said that in Vietnam, the family name always came first. Nguy was probably his family name, and Bo would be his given name.

"So we should be calling you Lu, instead of Sam, or Sammy?" Altro asked.

Sammy blushed. "No, I had it changed so my given name comes first when I became a citizen. I'm an American, Altro. Call me Sam."

That did the trick. Feeeeeelix looked completely sidetracked, and Altro wasn't surprised it had been so easy. But Sammy wasn't done yet. He took his feet down from the table, and leaned forward over his laptop toward Altro.

"Altro, I need to get this straight. They snatched you from the hospital, right? You said the guy was in ICU, on full life support, right? And you talked to him, what, a few hours later?"

She knew where Sammy was going with this, but nodded anyway and looked around to gauge reactions. Jessica was concentrating on every move she made. Doolee was grinning like he had some hidden secret. Mallory was rubbing at the scar on his chin and studying the table. Feeeeeelix just looked stupid.

"They took my watch, so I'm not sure of the time. We talked for... I don't know... maybe thirty minutes. He stood up and shook my hand. He seemed fine. Pretty thin, but healthy enough. He does have three old bullet wounds in his chest."

She pointed out the location of the wounds on her own chest. "Here, here, and here."

"But what about where you shot him?" Sammy asked.

She ignored Sammy's staring at her chest and shrugged her shoulders to minimize what she had to say. "I must have missed him. There was no bullet wound there. The nurse at the hospital told me there was nothing in the medical charts about a new bullet wound."

Sammy turned to look at Doolee. Doolee grinned. Sammy ran his hand over his outlandish yellow hair. Jessica pouted and Mallory looked out the window. Feeeeeelix still looked stupid.

"What the hell? How could you miss him, Altro?" Sammy asked.

Altro didn't know herself how she'd missed him. She shook her head and waved her hands in the air. Sammy started in again.

"Okay. Let's bypass the weirdness for now. But you said you were just taken back home again?" He snapped his fingers. "Just like that?"

"I know. I know. But he said he never intended to keep me there."

Jessica raised her hand. Altro pointed at her and nodded.

"Then why did he take you there, Ms. Altro? Did he tell you that?"

She didn't know if she wanted to tell them, but it was out. They were all looking at her and waiting for her answer. As she thought that over, she reached into her pocket and fingered the tile.

"He told me he had me taken there just so he could talk to me, so he could tell me he would never hurt me." The tile was warm. "I believe him."

She stared down at the table, but could feel their eyes on her. It was quiet. She released the tile and raised her head. Princess Jessica's face held a look of intense concentration.

"Did he give you any indication as to why he killed those men, Ms. Altro?" Jessica asked. "I mean, what was he doing there in the drugstore in the first place?"

Altro's hand slipped inside her jacket pocket and clutched the tile again.

"I asked him that. He told me that he went to the drugstore to save my life, and to kill those men. Those are almost his exact words. He said he had to kill the men to make sure their bosses — no, his exact word was 'masters' — so their masters would know it was him."

Jessica was almost talking to herself.

"So he's starting something and wants to make sure somebody knows it. He's drawing attention to himself, announcing the fact that he's here."

Altro looked closely at the Princess, a bit surprised by her grasp of the situation. Jessica wore a pale pastel blouse, with lacy trim around the neck and sleeves. Her slacks were more than tight enough to reveal her perfect figure, and the matching pumps added length to her legs. The makeup she wore accented her high cheekbones perfectly, and her jewelry was... Well, it was pretty, damnit! The woman was the picture of femininity.

She then considered her own conservative clothing, the starched white blouse with the business woman's suit. Charcoal gray today. Everything she wore and didn't wear was meant to downplay her own sexuality, to avoid the female stereotype. She realized that she'd misjudged the young woman's intellect because of the very prejudice she worked so hard to avoid.

"You're right, Princess. He said they'd no longer be concerned with me. They'd be looking for him now."

Doolee was grinning that devilish grin of his and stroking his mustache. "I would like to meet this man."

Altro's mind wandered, and she started thinking out loud. "The same man that gave me the chloroform took me home. Colonel Nguy. A very nice man if you take away his needles. He said he'd been in the North Vietnamese Army but later served with Walker in the American Army as some kind of scout... a Kit Carson scout, he called it."

Mallory squirmed in his chair, and it caught her attention. He was staring at the table again, rubbing that scar on his chin.

"I want everyone to realize how much these people respect this man," Altro said. "I think they would do anything for him."

Altro paused, remembering her conversation with John Walker Michaels, the intertwining of their hearts and minds. She fingered the ivory tile, remembering. Jessica was still staring openly at her, that same look of concentration on her face. It was making her uncomfortable, but she went on.

"These people have all experienced violence and deprivation beyond what any of us could imagine."

She raised a finger for emphasis as she continued.

"That could make them very dangerous, but I don't think they're a danger to us, or to any civilians. These people, Walker himself, they were kind and courteous to me. They're all very protective about him, and he's the same way with them. It's a very close-knit group, a family really, including the Colonel that kidnapped me. He told me himself that he considers Walker his brother."

Mallory was staring at the wall. "Walker," he mumbled. "Colonel Nguy and Walker."

"It's his middle name, Mallory," Altro said. "Colonel Nguy called him Walker, said that's what he was called in Vietnam."

Altro waited for some response from Mallory, but he just sat there, staring off into space and rubbing that scar on his chin. Bowman oozed his way back into the conversation.

"Ms. Altro, your view of the kidnapping seems to place the perpetrators in a very positive light."

She took her hand out of her pocket, shook her head and glanced at her watch. "Your point?"

"I think you may have been unduly influenced by the abductors. I'd like to have one of our psych people interview you. I'm sure you've heard of the Stockholm Syndrome."

Every member of the task force was watching her, waiting for the explosion. She didn't disappoint them.

"Stockholm Syndrome? Do you think you're talking to some pimple-faced teenager or hysterical housewife? I was only there a few hours, not long enough for Stockholm Syndrome to set in. Get your head out of your ass, Feeeeeelix."

Bowman finally looked angry. He cleared his throat and said he needed to get back to his people. His agents needed this new information so they could adjust their search parameters. The slug from Altro's gun would need to be recovered at the drugstore scene, for starters. They would also start a search for information on the daughter of Michaels, his wife and adoptive mother. Altro curtly suggested getting somebody over to Andrea Shellers' home, and made damn sure it sounded more like an order than a suggestion.

She watched Mallory, still rubbing at the scar on his chin, throughout the exchange between her and Bowman. After Feeeeeelix slid out the door, Mallory excused himself and hustled back to his office. It looked to her like he was running off to hide.

The rest of them filed out to their desks and took their seats. Altro ignored Jessica's stares and tried to remember what the hell it was she'd forgotten. She had to work hard at it. Her hand slipped inside her jacket pocket and clutched the ivory tile as she ran through the entire conversation with John Michaels, the man called Walker, the man called the Valley Walker. Then it came to her.

She released the tile, pulled her hand out of her pocket and snapped her fingers. "That's right. He said a man in Laos is behind the drugs, a man he called Khun Pao. He told me the killers from the drugstore worked for him."

Sam cocked his head to the side. "Khun Pao? I think I've heard a few of the old guys at DEA mention him."

Altro jabbed a finger at him. "Well, let's find out."

"Yes, ma'am." He smiled at her. "Good to have to you back, Altro."

Chapter 32

Everyone had their nose stuck in their laptop. Mallory was hiding in his office. Altro watched the video of Andrea Shellers' interview, but couldn't concentrate much on it. She sat there, fingering the ivory tile in her pocket. The Team Center was dead quiet when the report from the FBI came in.

SAC Bowman had been calling Mallory, but it kept ringing straight through to voicemail, so he phoned Jessica. The bureau had obtained a warrant and sent two agents to Andrea Shellers' home.

Ms. Shellers was gone. The agents gained access and found that most of her clothing was gone, too. Closets and dressers had been emptied of personal things. There was nothing in the medicine chest in the bathroom. They found little to indicate that Andrea Shellers even lived there, and nothing at all about her ex-husband. What they did find was a body on the lawn.

They'd just posted a report with pictures of the scene, the body, and the apparent murder weapon. When Sam put the picture of the body up on the screen, he got sidetracked on the shoes the man was wearing.

"Look at his shoes, Altro. They're iridescent Nikes, the same kind of shoes that were worn by the guys in the drugstore who tried to kill you."

Altro nodded and made a "let's move along" motion with one hand. He scowled, but when she just scowled back, he did what she wanted. The next image came up, showing a short, blood-stained arrow. Doolee came out of his seat. He was practically jumping up and down, grinning like a madman and waving his arms.

"That's a crossbow bolt!"

At the sound of Doolee's excited voice, Mallory dragged himself out of the office. He stared at the screen, but didn't say anything. Jessica and Sammy were jabbering while Doolee was pointing at the screen and grinning. Mallory stood mute and staring, so Altro spoke up.

"A crossbow? Of all the ways to kill someone, why use a crossbow?"

Princess Jessica raised her hand. Altro pointed at her, almost expecting the young woman to jump to her feet like a grade school student reciting an answer in a classroom. "I've done some research on the Hmong, Ms. Altro, since you said Michaels' family..." She paused and frowned. "Walker? Michaels? I don't know what to call him."

Altro rolled her eyes and put her hands on her hips.

Jessica ducked her head, took a breath and continued. "Well, you said his adoptive family was Hmong. The crossbow is a traditional weapon of the Southeast Asian hill people, including the Hmong. It's been used by them in warfare for centuries."

Altro nodded her thanks, then turned to Mallory. He just stood there. Jessica sat up straighter in her chair and continued. "The report also cited a blood trail leading away from the scene to the curb. It looks like one got away."

Mallory didn't even seem to be listening. Altro picked it up again. "Right, Princess, but my guess is that one was allowed to live, to send a message to whoever sent them. Walker told me he did the same thing at the drugstore, probably the guy he talked to in the van parked outside."

Mallory still stood mute. Jessica raised her hand and spoke up, mirroring Altro's thoughts. "They found a bottle of chloroform in the jacket pocket of the body. It sure looks like they went after Michaels' ex-wife, Ms. Altro. Maybe he had her and the others taken to wherever he's hiding for safety. You said they were all protective of one another?"

Mallory still didn't speak, but just stood there. Altro was worried. She let the room fall into disjointed babble about the incident, then stepped in front of him to get his attention. She pointed to his office and started walking. He followed meekly, looking like a condemned man going to the gallows. Altro closed the door behind them.

"What's going on with you, Mallory?"

Mallory walked to his chair and plopped down, but said nothing. He stared blankly ahead, his index finger tracing the scar on his chin. Altro hadn't gotten as far as she had without being able to read people. She also knew when to push, and right now it was time to push hard. Putting her hands on Mallory's desk, she leaned forward. In his face.

"What the hell is it with you and Walker? You know him don't you?"

Mallory looked her in the eye and nodded his head. He stood and walked to the closed door, opened it and motioned for Altro to follow him. In the Team Room, he cleared his throat.

"I want everyone back in the break room. There's something you need to hear."

Chapter 33

Sam got the computer ready to record again. Mallory sat down in the chair facing the cameras and started fingering the scar on his chin. When everyone was seated comfortably, he cleared his throat, pushed his glasses up on his nose and began.

"I met Walker, John Michaels, in Vietnam, near the Cambodian border. I was an infantry platoon leader, and he was one of my men. I never learned his real name. We just called him Walker."

He shook his head and mumbled to himself.

"Fucking spooks."

*****

The water was just over their ankles and the grass rose almost to their shoulders. The squad was milling about in a large field of elephant grass they'd been crossing when they found four trails crossing their path. The grass had been beaten down by someone or something traveling in a direction perpendicular to theirs.

Their Kit Carson Scout, Nguy Bo, was huddled with Walker in an animated discussion regarding the trails. The two men where crouching on either side of the trails, smoking cigarettes. Nguy was gesturing along one of the trails and speaking quickly in Vietnamese. When Walker responded and pointed in a direction to the side of the trails, Nguy nodded his head and started waving his arm from side to side.

Nguy had been a colonel in the North Vietnamese Army, serving as a technical advisor and liaison to the Viet Cong. Waving a Chu Hoi (Open Arms) leaflet, he'd surrendered to the

Americans near their present Area of Operations. Nguy had been debriefed by intelligence and paid handsomely for the weapons caches he pointed out to the American forces. He'd been given new American uniforms and an M16 under the Chu Hoi program. Now, because this unit was operating in the area of his surrender, he was assigned to them.

Second Lieutenant Bill Mallory was the platoon's new "Butterbar." He was fresh out of Officer Candidate School, thrown into the helter-skelter world of this platoon when their former lieutenant rotated back to the states. He'd only been in the field two days, but was already aware of the special relationship between Nguy and Walker.

Before coming out to the field, Lieutenant Mallory had looked at the 201 files of all of his men, trying to learn who they were and how to treat them. All of them but Walker. He had no file on him, and didn't even know the man's full name. Walker wore no name tag on his uniform, no unit insignia or rank either. Mallory had asked his Platoon Sergeant about Walker, but the sergeant just smiled and told him to ask the Battalion Commander.

Mallory walked up to Nguy and Walker, then waited for their conversation to finish.

"What's going on, Walker? What's he saying?"

"This looks like the real deal, LT. It's gotta be a good-sized force from the number of trails here. Looks like they're movin' something."

Walker pointed back in the direction he had been pointing when Mallory walked up to them. "They're moving fast but Bo thinks we can intercept them over there if we really hump."

"What makes you think they're even headed that way and moving fast?"

Walker shook his head and said something in Vietnamese to Nguy. Nguy muttered and flipped his cigarette butt out into the grass.

"The mud is still swirling in the trails, LT. They were just here," Walker said. "The grass is bent over in that direction. That shows which way they're moving. The number of trails says they're really bookin'. They don't like to travel all bunched up that way. Look back at our trail and compare these trails to our trail comin' in. They're wide as hell compared to ours."

"I'll radio it in," Mallory said. He pointed to a small copse of trees that rose up out of the elephant grass. "Let's move over to that rise, get our feet dried out."

Walker and Nguy talked it over, both men shaking their heads. Mallory started the men moving, then turned and looked back along their own trail. He could clearly see that their trail was narrower and the grass was bent in the direction they'd been moving.

On dry ground, Mallory radioed in to Battalion — what they'd seen and the opinions of Nguy and Walker. He was told to stand by.

As he waited for Battalion to call back, he took a look at his men. All of them had their boots off and pant legs rolled up. Some were using cigarettes to burn leeches off their legs. The ones who were done with that task just lounged around finishing their cigarettes. Some of the men started a game of cards on a poncho liner. Crazy Eights, no less. No one set up any kind of perimeter. No one had their weapons in hand. Walker and Nguy were squatting, Vietnamese style, apart from the squad. Both of them had their weapons cradled on their thighs and were looking out in the direction they said the enemy force had gone.

He wiped the sweat from his forehead with his sleeve. It had finally stopped raining, but his fatigues still hung heavy from the moisture that refused to evaporate. From the time he woke up to the time he fell into an uneasy slumber, his clothing was never completely dry. It was August, the height of the rainy season, and when it wasn't raining, the air was still heavy with moisture. Every effort, no matter how small, was multiplied by the thickness of the air. It was like moving in mud.

His Platoon Sergeant, Richards, approached, clearly unhappy about something. Richards was a tall black man from Oklahoma, thin as an oak rail and just as hard. He already had two tours under his belt and Mallory felt damned lucky to have him.

"What'd those stupid fucks at Battalion say, LT?"

"I'm waiting to hear from them."

"Well, they're fuckin' freaky, but they know what the fuck they're talkin' about."

"Who's that?"

"Walker and his buddy."

"You mean Colonel Nguy, Sergeant?"

Sergeant Richards nodded.

"Look at 'em. Squattin' and yammerin' like a couple of fuckin' dinks. It's fuckin' spooky."

"They're speaking Vietnamese. I don't know how they can be comfortable squatting like that, but they're the only ones halfway aware of their surroundings. Just what is the problem, Sergeant? You should have a perimeter set up and be keeping these men alert."

"Ain't nobody gonna sneak up on us with them two fuckers around, LT."

Richards paused and fished out a smoke from a waterproof case.

"They gettin' ready to deedee."

"What do you mean 'deedee,' Sergeant?"

"Split. Them muthafuckas is on point, like a bird dog on a covey o' fuckin' quail. Look at 'em sniffin' the wind."

"What?"

"You just wait, LT. Pretty soon you'll turn round and those two'll be gone. I don't know where the fuck they go or what the fuck they do, but they'll be gone for a week or more. Then you'll wake up one morning and they'll be back in camp, makin' fuckin' coffee like nothin' happened."

Richards turned and slouched away toward the card game, lighting his cigarette as he walked. Mallory always marveled at the unlimited capacity of his men to say "fuck". They seemed capable of carrying on complete conversations using the word almost exclusively. "Fuckin' great." "Fuckin' A." "Un-fuckin'

170

real." His personal favorite was "un-fuckin'-believable." It was an amazing linguistic feat.

The radio crackled to life. Battalion. "Charley one-three, Eagle one. Charley one-three, Eagle one. Over."

"Eagle one, Charley one-three. Over," Mallory answered.

"Charley one-three, we have evaluated your report on the trails. We don't think it deserves further consideration. Over."

"Eagle one, our Chu Hoi seems to think it's important. I agree. It all makes sense. Over."

Sergeant Richards trotted up to Mallory, grinning and shaking his head. "I told you those two fucks would take off, LT. They're gone already, sure as shit."

The radio crackled again. "Charlie one-three, your input is acknowledged, but you are not to follow up those trails. I say again, under no circumstances are you and your men to follow up those trails. Over."

"Eagle, wait one. Over."

"Who's gone, Sergeant? Gone where?"

"Walker and that fuckin' Nguy. They took off, just like I said."

Mallory left the radio and walked over to the center of the rise to look around. Once there he scanned the area, looking vainly for any sign of Walker and Nguy. When he didn't spot them, he walked to the edge of the rise and looked out over the expanse of grass. He couldn't see them anywhere. How could they be out of sight so fast? He walked back to the radio, wondering what he could possibly say to Battalion about this. He didn't see any way out of reporting it. They would show up missing sooner or later.

"Eagle one, Charlie one-three. Over."

"Charlie one-three, Eagle one. Over."

"Sir, it seems my Chu Hoi and one of my men have disappeared."

"Charlie one-three, Eagle one. Maintain radio discipline. Over."

"Eagle one, roger radio discipline. My Kit Carson scout and one of my men have left the squad's Alpha Oscar. Over."

"Charlie one-three, Eagle one. Code name Walker? Over."

Mallory looked at Sergeant Richards. Richards nodded his head and smirked.

"Eagle one, roger. Code name Walker. Over."

"Charlie one-three, Eagle one. Stand by. Over."

Mallory leaned back against his ruck. He couldn't fathom how this could happen. He looked over at Sergeant Richards, who was grinning like the Cheshire Cat. His radio operator was looking at his fingernails, obviously trying to avoid the whole issue. Several men were pretending to clean their weapons. No one met his eyes.

"Charlie one-three, Eagle one. Over."

"Eagle one, Charlie one-three. Over."

"Charlie one-three, proceed to X-ray Papa one niner Alpha. Over."

"Eagle one, say again last transmission. Over."

"Charlie one-three, Eagle one. Proceed to X-ray Papa one niner Alpha. Stand by at that location. Out."

They headed out to the Extraction Point. Three hours later the squad was choppered into Battalion Field Headquarters, which was fine with the men. It got them out of the bush, and there was hot chow. Mallory was not so pleased. He was thoroughly confused, and about to become more so.

As soon as the Huey touched down, he was summoned to Colonel Howard Steadley's command tent. It was sandbagged on all four sides, making it more a bunker than a tent. Outside was a generator, providing power for the lights and two large fans that circulated the air.

The colonel pointed to a chair when Mallory entered.

"Have a seat, Mallory. Beer?"

There was a wooden floor inside with a large area rug in the center. A table sat on the rug, with folding chairs around it. Steadley was seated at the head of the table, with two men seated to one side of him. One man was rather chubby, with evidence of premature baldness, while the other was slim and fit looking. Mallory sat down, feeling very dirty among the officers in clean and pressed uniforms. Hell, their boots were even shined.

"A beer, sir?"

"Do you want a beer, Mallory? You and your men certainly deserve it."

Mallory sat opposite the two other men. "No thank you, sir. I'd like to know what this is about, sir."

"I wanted to talk to you about Walker. You won't like what you're going to hear and, quite frankly, I'd hoped that a beer or two would soften the blow."

"Sir?"

"Walker and Nguy. I need you to keep a close eye on them."

"I'm sorry, sir. I'm afraid I still don't understand."

The Colonel looked at the two other men at the table. Both men nodded. "Listen very carefully, Lieutenant Mallory. I want you to report on Walker and Nguy to me, and only to me. You will be choppered in for the reports on a monthly basis, starting today. There will be no records kept of these reports and this conversation did not take place. Are you clear on that?"

Mallory stared at the Colonel, thinking as quickly as he could. He looked at the two men at the Colonel's side then. Clean uniforms, no name tags, no insignia, aviator sunglasses. He opened his mouth twice to ask a question, but thought better of it and closed it without saying a word. Finally, he looked back to the Colonel and nodded his head.

"Perfectly clear, sir. If Walker won't be officially assigned to us, I'd like to get a replacement for him. I'd like the platoon to be at full strength, sir."

"Good thinking, Mallory. I'll see what I can do before you're choppered back out."

"Yes, sir."

Colonel Steadley brought the meeting to a close.

"That's all, Mallory. I'll have you brought in for your next report."

It was getting dark when Mallory found Sergeant Richards sitting on some sand bags, smoking a cigarette. He started chuckling and shaking his head when he saw Mallory coming.

"You knew this would happen, didn't you, Sergeant?"

"Fuckin'-A, LT."

"Richards, you and I are going to be together for a while. I've got a lot to learn, and I need your help learning it. The quicker I learn, the more of these guys make it out of here, and the quicker your job gets easier. Let's work together and make this as safe and sane as possible. Deal?"

Richards stared at him for a while, then reached behind the sandbags and pulled two beers from an O.D. metal cooler. He handed one to Mallory and opened his own with a P-38 can opener. Mallory watched as the sergeant opened the can, ratcheting the blade to form a slit on both sides of the can, prying the slits open with the end of the device to make them wider. Mallory held his hand out for the P-38, and copied the process.

"The first fuckin' thing you gotta learn, LT, is to always carry your own P-38, your own spoon, and your own stash of TP, toilet paper."

"Noted, Sergeant. So tell me. What's the deal with Walker and Colonel Nguy?"

Richards put out his cigarette and slurped at his beer before he answered.

"Walker? He's been with us about five months. Just showed up one day. He's a damn good man to have around, but there's somethin' not right. Ya know, I don't even know his fuckin' name. I don't think the Colonel even knows who he is. He's just Walker. That muthafucka is spooky is what he is."

Richards lit another cigarette, thought about it and offered one to Mallory. When Mallory declined, Richards shrugged and went on.

"The fucker is better with weapons than I am, and he knows tactics better'n Colonel Steadley, I bet. Shit, he knows we're closin' on a base camp when we're still a ways away from the place. I don't know how the fuck he knows, but he knows."

After another drag of his smoke and a pull at his beer, Richards waved a hand in the air.

"He just drifts in and out of camp whenever he wants. Some of the guys have started callin' him *Casper*. You know. The fuckin' cartoon ghost? You'll see. He ghosts into our site in the middle of the night sometimes. Right past the guard, right through our trip flares and claymores. Like he can see in the fuckin' dark. You wake up in the mornin' and the fucker is squattin' there makin' coffee. Like I told ya."

Richards gave a soft chuckle and shook his head, his teeth shining as he smiled. "He's got this saying for when the shit gets heavy. 'Two salt tablets, a canteen of water and push on.' That muthafucka."

There was a pause as Richards finished his beer, tossed away the empty and opened another with his P-38. He belched and continued.

"Colonel Nguy? We picked him up about eight months ago. He may be a good scout, but there ain't no fuckin' way to tell 'cause he don't speak no English. When Walker showed up, he just started hangin' out with Bo all the time. Bo didn't take to him right off, but soon enough those muthafuckas was tight. Walker picked up Vietnamese so fuckin' fast, it was like he was a dink in a white man's skin. They hang out at the edge of our setup a lot, smokin' and jabberin' in their goddamn hammocks."

Mallory processed it all in silence.

"What the Colonel tell ya?" Richards asked.

Mallory could see no use in lying to Richards. "Just keep tabs on him, is what they said."

"They?"

"The Colonel and two spooks with him. I decided not to ask any questions."

"You did right, LT. I don't think you wanna step in that shit. Fuckin' spooks."

Mallory mulled this over, which gave Richards a chance to finish his beer and grab another. The man went through his ritual of opening it with his P-38 before he looked up at Mallory and continued.

"I'll tell you somethin' else, LT. Today wasn't the first time we got told not to do our fuckin' job."

"You mean when we were called off those trails, Sergeant?"

"Fuckin'-A right, LT."

"You think those trails were hot, Sergeant?"

"Fuck yeah. I don't know just what's goin' on, but they were hot, for sure." Richards took another drink. "Walker'll find out. You can bet your ass on that."

"Why would Colonel Steadley call us off then? This is a war."

"Steadley don't give a fuck about the war. He don't even care who wins, as long as he does. He don't care about nothin' but gettin' his next promotion."

"He's a soldier, Sergeant!"

Richards shook his head.

"Guys like Steadley ain't soldiers, LT. They just usin' the war to get some glory. " Richards belched again. "And they usin' us to do their dirty work. Don't you fuckin' get it?"

Mallory stared at Richards for a while, then they drank in silence, Mallory thinking and Richards letting him. Mallory finished his beer and belched. It felt good.

"Thanks for the beer, Richards. And thanks for the lesson."

He tossed the can behind the sandbags and stood.

"Where you headed, LT?"

"To get my own P-38, my own spoon and my own stash of TP, Sergeant."

Richards chuckled and nodded his head.

"Fuckin'-A right, LT. Fuckin'-A right."

Chapter 34

Mallory stood up and got a cup of coffee, sat back down, pushed his glasses up on his nose and resumed his recorded confession.

"That was my introduction to Walker." He took a sip of coffee. "I didn't see him again for months. I don't have a clue where he went. He was just gone."

*****

Walker and Nguy followed the trails out of the elephant grass to the area between An Loc and the Saigon River. There they caught up with what turned out to be twenty men carrying overstuffed packs, escorted by an additional ten armed men. They were gathered in a small copse of trees to the side of a large clearing. Walker and Nguy observed from the tree line, 800 meters away, as the men all dropped their packs and the armed escort set up a perimeter. Nguy rolled over on his back and lit a cigarette. He spoke quietly.

"These men are not Viet Minh and they are not of the People's Army."

"These men are mules," Walker said.

Nguy raised an eyebrow. "Yes, their packs are heavy."

After they watched the group for about thirty minutes, a South Vietnamese Army truck and two jeeps came across the clearing and stopped at the copse of trees. Men wearing South Vietnamese Army uniforms and aviator sunglasses got out of the jeeps and were met by two of the men in the armed escort. They squatted in the shade of the truck, lit cigarettes and conversed for a few minutes. One of the men from the escort walked to the trees and gestured toward the truck, and the mules began carrying the packs to the truck and loading them. When the truck was loaded, it left the way it came in, followed by the two jeeps. Walker looked at Nguy and gave a summary.

"Now they return to the road with the cargo. The cargo will be taken into Saigon. These men will rest for a short time and then head back to Cambodia."

Nguy looked sharply at Walker. "So? What do you think this is Walker?"

"I think this must be business, my friend. I think we should move ahead of them to the border on a parallel path. I would like to see where these businessmen travel to."

"Do you see their clothing? It is made from hemp. These men are Hmong, Walker, from Laos. I think they will return there."

"Tell me about these Hmong, Bo. Do they grow poppies in Laos?"

Chapter 35

Mallory took his glasses off and rubbed at his temples.

"I don't know where they took off to, but the scuttlebutt surrounding Walker was wild. Rumors ran through Battalion like a California brush fire. The man was rumored to be everywhere. I mean, this guy was becoming a legend. I even heard rumors of him hijacking a chopper out of Long Binh, a major base outside Saigon."

*****

The pilots and their door-gunners sauntered out to their chopper. They had come in from Lai Khe to drop off a routine F.U.O. (Fever of Unknown Origin) transfer. The docs told them the unknown fever was probably a symptom of malaria, but tests had to be run to make sure.

While they were there, they decided to check on a comrade who had picked up some shrapnel and eat a hot meal. They'd even watched *Hee Haw* on Armed Forces Television in the hospital dayroom. Now it was late, time for them to head back to reality, back to the job. If they lifted off now, they would be back in Lai Khe just after dark.

As they walked out to the landing pad, they looked over to the bunkers along the wire. They were about 100 meters away. Maybe another 25 meters beyond that, the traffic streamed endlessly on the highway. The men in the bunkers were smoking and watching the highway, listlessly guarding it because they were told to. The crew boarded the Huey, and the pilot was just starting to spool up the engine when a voice came from the back of the chopper.

"You guys headed back to Lai Khe?"

The men all turned, and saw two men at the back of the bird. A Vietnamese and an American, both in tiger stripes and wearing camouflage paint.

"Can you drop us off about twenty-five klicks northwest of Loc Ninh?"

"What the fuck? In the first place, that's outta our way. In the second place that's Cambodia, and in the third place... Who the fuck are you?"

The American shuffled to the center of the chopper. "My name's Walker. My Montagnard partner here is Trang. It'll be quick and dirty. Just drop us and split."

"Who the fuck are you trying to kid? And what's a 'Yard' doing down here in Long Binh? They're from up in the Central Highlands."

"There are six cases of Bud and a case of decent scotch back there."

The pilot waivered, looked around at his crewmates who grinned and nodded. Walker gave the final push.

"Easy cheesy, bud. In and out. And the drinks are on me."

The pilot spooled up the engines, shaking his head, wondering why he was doing this. The two door gunners gave the thumbs up to their riders.

After 30 minutes of flight, the pilot turned and shouted, "We're coming up to your LZ."

Walker leaned out the doorway, one foot on the skid. He pointed to the chopper's two o'clock and turned his thumb up. He wanted more altitude. The chopper banked easily and climbed to an altitude of twelve hundred feet. The pilot looked at his altimeter and shouted again.

"Where do you want to put down?"

One of the door-gunners tapped him on the arm and shook his head, grinning like a maniac.

"The motherfuckers jumped, sir. I shit you not. They fuckin' *jumped*."

Both the pilot and copilot craned around to look, bumping helmets. They disentangled, got coordinated and saw what the gunner said was true. The static lines of parachutes where trailing out into the night from the entry handle in the doorway, flapping against the skid. They hadn't even noticed the guys had chutes.

The pilot began a slow bank and headed back toward Lai Khe. He could use a drink of that scotch and a couple of beers to boot.

"Fuckin' spooks."

*****

The two men drifted down in relative silence with their drop zone in sight. A sliver of moon was reflected off a swampy area and they wanted to come down just west of it. The land here was flat and had large stands of forest growth with clearings here and there. They were coming down to the north of Route 74, ten kilometers (klicks) inside Cambodia.

After they landed, they checked their gear. They each had five claymores and half a dozen clackers, the devices used to create the charge to set off an electrical blasting cap. In addition, they carried their weapons and twenty extra magazines of ammunition. Trang also carried a Prick 25 radio, so Walker carried the spool of detonator chord and a starlight scope with fresh batteries. They each had two canteens of water and some iodine tablets, but they didn't carry any food. Food was more weight, and they needed to move fast. They wouldn't be out long.

They headed for the intercept point. They wanted to be settled in, waiting at their ambush at least an hour before dawn. About ten klicks to the north, they set up their claymores, spaced 25 meters apart and daisy-chained together with the det chord. A line of five ran down one side of a little-used trail, and five more ran down the other side. The second line of mines was positioned so that their spacing was interleaved with the line on the opposite side. With the claymores placed 25 meters back from the trail on either side, it gave them an effective kill zone of over 125 meters.

Trang then led the way to their waiting point, about two kilometers to the south. When they finally settled in, they were about one kilometer north of highway 74, a state road that went from Snuol, Cambodia into Vietnam. It was still hours away from dawn. They had made good time. Walker pointed to himself and then to his eyes, meaning he would take first watch. Trang settled down to catch some sleep.

Trang, a Montagnard he'd met in a village in the Central Highlands, was with Walker on this mission in place of Colonel Nguy for a reason. Walker prized the friendship of Nguy, and he was going to kill many of his countrymen today.

Two hours before dawn, Walker woke Trang. They headed out to be closer to highway 74, within sight of the column they were here to intercept.

At the same time, an AC-47 "Spooky" gunship took off from Bien Hoa Airbase, banked to the west and headed toward the position of Trang and Walker. There was no flight plan filed for this sortie. The gunship carried three 7.62 mm mini-guns. It was flown by a young Vietnamese pilot who was in training for when the planes would be turned over to the Army of the Republic of Vietnam. In minutes, it was on station for its mission and awaiting instructions from Walker.

Walker and Trang settled in, and Trang observed the trail through the starlight scope. It wasn't long before Trang saw the People's Army column, traveling slowly and carefully, in the phosphorescent images of the scope. The column would reach its final destination, Snuol, that day, beyond the reach of American forces. Walker and Trang planned to attack before it got there. As the advance party went through, Walker radioed the AC-47. Though English was the universal language of aviation, Walker spoke in Vietnamese.

"Night one, Ghost one. Over."

"Ghost one, Night one. On station. Over."

"Night one, Ghost one. Lead element just passed. Expect main column shortly. Over."

"Ghost one, Night one. Relay timing and instructions. Over."

It didn't take long.

"Night one, Ghost one. Main column in view. Proceed with firing mission on front of main column. After initial contact, fall back to station. Over."

Both men could already hear the plane approaching. The elements in the main body of the retreating column heard it too, and began to show agitation as the plane approached. Some men were raising their faces to the sky, while others started milling about in confusion. The plane banked slightly so all three of its mini-guns would be put on target.

A waterfall of tracers spouted from the plane, followed immediately by a deep buzzing sound. Three very loud warning buzzers. Between each tracer in the waterfall were four more rounds of 7.62 mm ball ammunition. Each gun was firing at its maximum rate of 4,000 rounds per minute, making the total firing rate 200 rounds per second. The Spooky gave the column three five-second bursts, each burst a bit farther up the column, then banked away before the column could muster organized return fire.

Walker and Trang watched as the column tried to regroup. With the Spooky still close enough to be heard, the leaders in the column started their prearranged maneuver of breaking away from the highway to the trail with more cover. As the column started toward a trail that ran perpendicular to the highway, Trang and Walker nodded at each other. The column would be headed for the place they had mined with the claymores.

The two men fell back to their ambush positions and Walker radioed the Spooky.

"Night one, Ghost one. Over."

"Ghost one, Night one. Awaiting further firing orders. Over."

"Night one, Ghost one. Resume contact on rear of column. Hit them hard and return to base. Out."

The Spooky moved to their northeast and gave four more five-second bursts. Green tracers reached toward the plane and they heard the hammering of a fifty-one caliber, but the return fire was futile. The Spooky responded with another long burst to push the column hard into the ambush. Walker and Trang split up, went to their individual positions on either side of the trail and wired up their clackers.

Within minutes, a lead element of four men moved quickly through the ambush area with their heads tilted back, their eyes on the sky. Soon after that, the main body of the column started to come through the claymores. The column was moving fast now, and starting to bunch up. Caution and discipline had become secondary to survival. They allowed fifteen men to pass through the claymores and then hit the clackers.

The vegetation around them pulsed in response to the shock wave. Grass, bushes and small trees were blown toward each other and the column as 7,000 1/8-inch steel ball-bearings ripped through the vegetation on either side of the trail. They were propelled from their epoxy carrier by 15 pounds of C-4, deformed into the shape of a .22 rimfire by the explosion. At the center of the crossfire of projectiles, men were mangled and hand-drawn carts carrying ammunition were shredded and exploded.

The amount of dust and debris raised with the smoke of the explosion was blinding. The screams of the wounded and the moans of the dying pierced the curtain of smoke and debris. Walker's mind drifted out among the dead and dying. Trang touched his shoulder lightly to bring him back.

They rose and began their circuitous route toward the border of South Vietnam.

Chapter 36

"The next time I saw Walker was when he showed up in a Vietnamese village named An Loc," Mallory said. "Maybe you know it Sammy. It's north of Saigon, Ho Chi Minh City now."

Sammy nodded his head at Mallory. "I've got some relatives that live near there. It's a lot bigger than a village now."

"Well, the whole area was controlled by the VC back then. Cambodia was close and the NVA were massing there in preparation for the US withdrawal. The Air Force was bombing the base camps in Cambodia with B-52's. What was called Operation Menu."

Mallory got himself some more coffee, even though he had to pour out what was in his mug to refill it. He was stalling, preparing himself.

"Anyway, when Walker came back in, it was pretty surreal. But, I guess everything about the guy is."

*****

The M113 armored personnel carriers rumbled into An Loc at 0600, then went into herringbone formation along the edge of town.

The day's pho was being prepared in every home, and the overpowering odor of nuoc mam (fish sauce) hung in the air. The big Detroit Diesel engines rattled in their rhythmic idle and, with the lack of movement, the diesel fumes soon overpowered the smell of the nuoc mam. The APC crews fidgeted on top of the tracks, peering into the dark. The fifty gunners jiggled the cartridge that was jammed under the butterfly trigger mechanism as a safety, waiting for the kak-kak-kak of an AK47 or the pulsing whoosh of an RPG. The APC crew members knew they were sitting ducks parked in the darkness.

Conversely, Mallory's men didn't usually have the firepower of the APCs with them, and were feeling invincible that morning. One of them started shining a flashlight toward the edge of the town. Sergeant Richards was quickly but quietly telling the men to get down from the tracks and set up positions on the ground along the herringboned APCs.

Richards knew that this was when an APC was most vulnerable, parked in the open, in the clear field of fire of RPGs that could be launched from unseen vantage points. The tracks were a rolling ammunition depot, carrying cases of ammo for the 50s, for the M60s, for the M16s and M79s. They also carried cases of grenades, trip flares and C4. Richards didn't want his men sitting on top of a track if it happened to go up in a spectacular explosion.

"Get down and spread out. Keep those safeties on. We don't want to toast a bunch of fuckin' civilians. And douse that light, asshole."

Mallory and Richards watched as the men reluctantly spread out and took positions in the predawn darkness. Richards pointed deeper into the town where lights were winking on.

"Fuck a duck, LT," Richard said. "We're gonna have company.

A vehicle turned on its lights, then flashed its brights on and off. Other lights switched on inside the vehicle, showing the interior of the cab and the back cargo hold. The vehicle started moving toward them, and as it approached, Mallory saw that it was a large van or small truck with a windowed rear cargo area.

Someone had given the order to shut down. Up and down the column the APCs were switching off their engines, bringing relative quiet to the area. Above the now audible conversation among the men and the noises of equipment being moved, light tinkling music floated from the approaching vehicle. Bright orange lights started flashing on top of the vehicle, like the warning flashers of a school bus. As it approached, the words "Ice

Cream" could be clearly seen, hand-painted in large letters on the side. The conversation around them turned loud and excited as the vehicle made a wide turn and pulled alongside the column, creeping along where Richards had just deployed the platoon.

Men were whooping and pointing, crowding around the vehicle and bringing it to a stop just a few yards from where Mallory stood with his mouth open. The immediate area was now lit up by all the lights on the truck, and he could clearly see his men gathering around the vehicle. He could hear Richards' raspy voice as he went into orbit, swearing at the driver.

"Get that mothafuckin' thing the hell out of here! Third Platoon, you get your sorry asses back to the fuckin' tracks!"

The ice cream truck *(ice cream truck?)* couldn't move, of course, because of the men pressing in around it, and the men had no intention of going back to the tracks. Not only was there ice cream, but inside the vehicle were a number of very attractive young Vietnamese women. They were dressed in colorful Ao Dai, their long black hair was neatly combed, and all of them were smiling widely and waving as they climbed out of the back of the vehicle. Added to the din of conversation of the men and the comical music of the ice cream truck were the musical voices of the young women. They started moving among the men, pressing their slender bodies against them and rubbing crotches to see who would be the ripest for picking.

All of the men were extremely ready and willing customers for the enterprising young women. The entire battalion had been out for ten long weeks now, going on one patrol after another, transported from place to place on the APCs.

Sergeant Richards approached Mallory shaking his head and laughing, his white teeth shining in the darkness.

"We're in trouble, LT, but I don't think the fuckin' VC'll hit us with all these civilians around. The civilians always stay away if they know we're gonna be hit. And they *always* know, LT. Lookee here, I'm gonna get up on the track and get on the radio. You might wanna do the same. Keep an eye on these fuckheads. Lord knows they all ready to rape a fuckin' snake."

Mallory took Richards' advice and clambered to the top of the track with him. He stood there, observing the men in line for ice cream and cold sodas while others slid off into the darkness with the young ladies. Still trying to digest the scene, he looked at his Platoon Sergeant with a raised eyebrow. Richards smiled again, showing those white teeth, and gave him a shoulder shrug and a thumbs up. Richards had donned the APC's radio headphones and was alternately scanning the men and looking out the opposite side of the track into the darkness.

Mallory was reminded just how little he knew about this war that wasn't a war. He knew nothing of the people here, nothing of their customs. This was his first contact at all with the civilian population. He continued to be amazed, outraged even, by what was considered Standard Operating Procedure. He was glad to have a seasoned hand like Richards to help him find his way through the maze of decisions that had to be made in these situations.

One of the women, older than the others, was approaching the APC with two ice cream cones in her hands. Somehow she moved through the milling, jostling troops without being troubled by the excited young men. She smiled a beautiful smile at each man who spoke to her and touched her, but continued undeterred toward the track he and Richards were on. When she arrived, she held up the ice cream cones and favored him with a smile that lit up the area.

"We are honored that you chose our humble town to stop for rest, Lieutenant."

Richards sat down on the edge of the track, reached down for the cones and gave one to Mallory. Mallory licked the ice cream — soft ice cream, in fact — and a chill went through him. Richards made a slight bow to the woman.

"Cam on ban, Amois."

"You are most welcome, Sergeant."

Richards beamed from ear to ear as he stood with his ice cream. The woman smiled at him and made a slight gesture with her head, beckoning Richards to go with her. Richards indicated the headphones and shook his head.

"Sin loi, Amois. I must stay."

The young woman turned to Mallory and raised an eyebrow questioningly. Mallory was speechless. This woman was truly beautiful, and her smile made him feel warm and tight inside. He shook his head reluctantly, and smiled back at her like a love struck teenager.

"Ah, the burden of command," she said. "Still, I am happy to have you and your men here, Lieutenant."

Just then a young man, no more than nineteen, put his hand on the woman's shoulder. She turned to him and smiled, and he dropped his hand. He stood there with his mouth open momentarily, then regained his ability to speak.

"We go An Loc," the young man said.

The woman cocked her head a bit, smiled and said nothing. The column was already in An Loc. They were at the edge of town, with the lead elements heading east on highway 303, toward Quan Loi.

Almost none of the men knew where they were, or that they would soon cross the border into Cambodia in what the senior officers called a Reconnaissance in Force. Mallory was about to tell the young troop to find his squad leader when the ground began to shake and a deep rumbling started to the north.

The woman's head snapped up as she turned to Mallory. "B-52s! B-52s!"

Mallory realized this civilian woman had recognized the sound immediately, while he hadn't known what it was. He'd been briefed that they would be going in behind a B-52 strike, and still hadn't known what the rumbling noise was.

More civilians gathered around in the growing light. Young boys were selling knick-knacks and various other goods to the soldiers, and children were staring wide-eyed at the young troops, begging with their eyes like puppies for candy and other treats. A buzz of the musical Vietnamese language rose as they all turned to face the continuing rumbling in the darkness.

Then a pronounced hush fell over the civilians and they started moving away from each other, parting like Moses had just raised his staff over them. The rumbling in the distance continued as the civilians split apart to make a path through the crowd. The buzz of Vietnamese began again, but it was subdued now, not the excited tones of the conversation before. The young woman looked up at Mallory again, not smiling at all now, but her eyes wide with fear. She saw the utter lack of understanding on Mallory's face and turned to Richards.

"It is Di San. Walker."

Richards nodded and jumped down from the APC, landing beside the woman. He put a hand on her shoulder and turned toward the approaching disturbance.

Walker came out of the darkness, dressed in tiger camouflage, his face darkened with grease paint. A Vietnamese Mallory had never seen followed him. Richards took a couple of strides to meet Walker, and the two of them engaged in a conversation Mallory couldn't hear. The crowd fell quiet. In the silence, Mallory realized the bombing had ended. Walker walked to the APC and looked up at him.

Mallory had seen the lifeless faces of men just out of combat, but Walker's face was twisted in grief. His eyes were alive with something, and Mallory was drawn into those eyes, felt himself seeing through them. Flashes blinded him. He heard the claymores, the screams and moans of their aftermath. Tracers sailed. The smell of burning plastic assaulted him.

He was losing his balance, falling from the APC, when he felt a hand on his shoulder, pulling him back from the edge. Richards had climbed back onto the APC. As Mallory regained his balance, Richards gave his shoulder a squeeze. Walker's face turned to stone. He gave Mallory a crisp salute and climbed up on the APC behind the one Mallory was on. The Vietnamese followed him.

Mallory was shaken badly. It was bad enough having the insanity of the stop here, his men being serviced by beautiful young women and buying soft ice cream. But the arrival of

Walker and the way the civilians gave way for him was too much. It was spooky, otherworldly.

"I told you, LT. The mothafucka's spooky."

Mallory's head snapped toward Richards.

"What the fuck else can ya say, LT?"

With that, Richards put the headphones back on. He listened for a few seconds, then shook his head.

"We gotta roll, LT. They been tryin' to raise us."

His voice turned to a bellow as he yelled into the hushed crowd.

"All right you fuckin' grunts. Mount up. Move it, move it, move it!"

The men responded quicker than Mallory would have anticipated, as if their idyllic stop had ended as soon as Walker showed up anyway. The big diesels roared to life, and the noise of a column getting ready to move out rose. Richards was spewing obscenities at the men, the APCs, the Army, and the world in general. He turned to Mallory, a maniacal grin on his face.

"Here we go on another useless fuckin' mission, LT. The NVA we're supposed to hit? They deeded out already."

After giving Mallory a second to digest this, he continued, the grin frozen on his face, his teeth still shining, even in the growing light.

"They knew we were fuckin' comin', LT. They always know. You think we can traipse around in these monsters, raisin' hell from one end of the fuckin' country to the other and them not know? With the number of radio messages sent to put this shindig together, they *gotta* know. They ain't fuckin' stupid, LT."

"But what makes you so sure, Sergeant Richards? How can you be so absolutely sure?"

Richards was almost laughing now, his sardonic grin went from ear to ear.

"Walker just told me, LT. The fucker says he just came in from Cambodia, that he caught a column boogyin' away from their base camp northeast of here. He hit 'em with a Spooky and some Claymores. Can ya dig it, LT? That muthafucka!"

Chapter 37

"That was January of 1970. My Platoon Sergeant, Sergeant Richards, was right. The NVA knew we were coming and had pulled out of their base camps. We blew all the bunkers, but the NVA were all gone. The only positive thing that got accomplished was another company recovered the body of a man that was lost during a helicopter insertion in March of 1969. They said the NVA didn't bury the body, but had it on display with a sign hanging on a string around the neck. An object lesson, I suppose."

Mallory fingered the scar on his chin again.

"It's where I picked up this scar. We rode in on the tracks, rolling over brush and small trees. A sapling that was pushed down sprang back up and hit me here. Knocked me right off the top of the APC. Out cold. I didn't want to leave the field, so our medic closed it up with butterfly sutures. He said it would leave a nice scar."

He took a drink of coffee and stumbled on.

"Walker and I were ordered back to Lai Khe at the end of the operation. We met at Steadley's Command Headquarters."

*****

"Just what the hell do you think you're doing out there, Walker?"

Mallory watched Walker as the young man considered Colonel Steadley's question. Instead of meeting Steadley's glare, he turned and looked at the two men sitting next to him. Two men in army uniforms, one fit and trim, the other chubby. The same two men who'd been with Steadley when he'd talked to him about keeping an eye on Walker. No insignia or rank, wearing aviator sunglasses indoors. Steadley called them Brain and Sledge.

Walker had put a clean uniform on for the meeting and had his sleeves rolled up above his elbows, the way Steadley liked it. Again, it occurred to Mallory that, just like Brain and Sledge, Walker never wore insignia or rank on his uniform. All of the other men in the battalion had their name tags sewn on their jungle fatigues. All of them wore their rank and unit badges. Steadley insisted on it.

"Colonel?" Walker said.

One of the men in aviators, the lean one called Brain, leaned in and whispered something in the Colonel's ear.

"We've heard reports that you've been operating up in the Central Highlands," Steadley said.

Walker kept his eyes on Brain and Sledge. "I was doing some research, sir."

Brain whispered in Steadley's ear again.

"We've also heard reports of you working with the Hmong," Steadley said.

Walker shook his head. "No, sir. You must have a faulty source, sir."

"Walker, we have a need to know," Brain said. It was the first time Mallory had heard the man speak. His accent was Northeastern, his voice calm and measured. "Are you clear on that? We need to know who the hell you are, and what your mission parameters are."

"No you don't," Walker said.

Sledge, the chubby man with thinning hair, jumped to his feet. His chair toppled over behind him.

"Listen, you stupid fuck. You'll do what you're told!"

Walker ignored him and turned to the Colonel.

"We can still win this war, sir."

Steadley shook his head, then turned to Brain and Sledge. Brain nodded at him.

"Okay, Walker. Let's talk about the war. Tell me about the NVA column that got hit inside Cambodia."

"They knew you were coming, sir. I cut a column off during their retreat."

Steadley was smoking a cigar. He put the stub down in a glass ashtray, reached into his pocket to pull out a pen and pad of paper. "What was the body count?"

Pain flashed across the young man's face, the same look Mallory had seen when Walker showed up in An Loc. Mallory watched him struggle to bring himself under control. It took a while before he answered.

"Those men were soldiers, brave men who died for a cause they believed in. And you want to count their corpses?"

Steadley arched an eyebrow, turned to Brain and Sledge and held his hands up. "I give up."

Brain smirked. "I think we're talking to Mary Poppins here."

Sledge busted out laughing. "They're just gooks, you stupid fuck."

Tears formed in Walker's eyes as he stared at the three men. "Soldiers give up everything in war, and you don't even care," he said. "You're just using us."

"Enough about soldiers. Enough about the war," Sledge said. "Get with the fucking program."

Walker actually started crying then, which made Sledge start laughing again, louder now. Walker lowered his head, and his shoulders shook with sobs. After a few moments the young man went completely still, so still that Mallory reached out and put a hand on his shoulder. Mallory jerked his hand back. Walker was as cold as a dead body.

A deep vibration started in the ground, grew until the building started shaking. Colonel Steadley's ashtray danced and slid on the table. A foghorn was sounding somewhere. The world slipped away.

The pleasant aroma of wood smoke brought Mallory to his senses. He sniffed the air and turned to find the source. Walker was standing in the doorway, about five feet away. Mallory tested the air again. Yes, the young man definitely smelled like he'd been sitting at a campfire.

Walker wasn't crying now. The look of pain on his face was gone, replaced with the glare of anger. His eyebrows arched and the corners of his mouth turned down.

"Don't let these men use you, LT," Walker said. "Don't let them steal your honor."

Colonel Steadley, Brain and Sledge were still there. The pudgy one, Sledge, was still standing with his mouth open in a silent laugh. The chair was still on the floor behind him. Steadley was staring at the spot where Walker had been sitting, his eyebrow still arched. Brain's face was frozen in a smirk. Mallory looked back to the doorway, but Walker was gone.

The others stirred, then woke up the same way Mallory had. The three of them looked around, then at each other. They shook their heads in unison, dogs waking from a nap.

"Where'd the fucking crybaby go?" Sledge asked.

Mallory didn't know, so he just shook his head.

Brain and Sledge pulled their sidearms and rushed out the door. Steadley watched them go, then straightened his shoulders, trying his best to look stern and military.

"Fucking spooks."

Chapter 38

Mallory's shoulders slumped and his head dipped so low his clunky glasses slid off and clattered on the table.

"Walker just disappeared," he said. "A few days later, I was pulled out of the field, and ended up being transferred to Army Intelligence at MACV in Long Binh. Fucking spooks."

The room got loud. Fast. Everyone but Altro had questions about Mallory's last meeting with Walker, but Mallory didn't even look up.

Altro's mind wandered while the questions got louder. She could smell the wood smoke Mallory talked about. The ivory tile in her pocket called to her, but she resisted the urge to reach in and hold it. She needed to get the subject changed. Fast. She raised her voice.

"You kept saying *fucking spooks*, Mallory. You mentioned that Walker wore no markings on his uniform. Are you saying he's CIA?" she asked.

Mallory shook his head, but didn't say anything. Sam and Jessica gaped at her like she'd lost her mind. Doolee leaned back in his chair, stroked his mustache and stared at her.

"This man is not a spy," Doolee said. "This man is something else."

"Don't even start, Doolee," Sam said.

Altro agreed. They didn't want to go there. She sure as hell didn't. She turned to Sam. "We ever get his records?"

Sam's eyebrows shot up for a second, then he squinted. His mouth went all tight and one corner turned down. Altro wondered what the hell that look was about. Then he shook his head.

"The St. Louis Police finally got in touch with a manager at the NPRC, and he went in and located them. Then he ran copies and put them in the mail. Can you believe that? He mailed them. It's the twenty-first century, for Christ's sake."

They eventually broke up and went to their desks. Mallory retreated to his office and shut the door. It was quiet when Jessica spoke up.

"Ms. Altro?"

She looked over at the young woman and nodded, then waited impatiently while Jessica worked on her laptop. "Well, what is it, Princess?"

The flat-screen on the wall came to life and Jessica pointed at it.

"I was looking at the security videos from the hospital yesterday and I found something I think is important."

Altro looked at the screen. The scene looked like it was the main lobby of Sparrow Hospital. Six men were rushing out the door, almost running. Two of the men wore white doctors' smocks. The other four wore casual clothing. Their backs were to the camera, but their dark hair and slight stature gave them away as Asian.

Off to the side, two white men stood in front of a row of chairs. They were turned toward the men rushing out the door, and one of the men was pointing and had his mouth open. The young woman kept working at her laptop and the scene changed. She'd zoomed in on the two white men.

Doolee spoke up. "Who are these men, Jessica?"

Jessica flounced her hair and pouted. "Well, I don't know."

Altro rolled her eyes and sighed. "Come on, Princess. What's this about?"

"Sorry, Ms. Altro. I got to thinking that if the people who took Michaels and you from the hospital were trying to protect him... Well, somebody else may have gone to the hospital to do him harm."

Altro nodded. It made sense. She rolled a hand at the Princess to continue.

"Okay. So I called the hospital to see if anyone had gone into ICU after the kidnapping. Nobody did, but they told me about a disturbance in the main lobby that happened at about the same time the Lansing police arrived. These two were part of it."

Altro stood up and walked over to the flat-screen for a better look. One looked to be about six feet tall, with short-cropped gray hair. The other was short and chubby, had almost no hair on his head, but a neatly trimmed gray goatee. The short, chubby one was effeminate looking, and wore wire-rimmed glasses. The taller one was trim and fit looking, a good looking guy. She turned to Sam, who was diligently checking out her butt.

"Sammy, maybe you can stop staring at my ass long enough to start tracking these guys down."

Sammy ducked his head down to his laptop. The Princess twittered. Doolee snorted.

"Get the Princess to give you the best picture she has, and send it to TSA. Have them start scanning their security shots to see if these guys came into the airport. Maybe we can ID them."

Sammy, who still hadn't looked up from his laptop, started banging away. Altro put her hands on her hips for a second, then snapped her fingers.

"Extend that search to the Detroit airport. The local bus station, too. I'll call the AG and get the paperwork started."

She sat down and picked up the phone, then turned to Jessica. "Good work, Princess."

Jessica beamed at her, and Teri Altro suddenly felt pretty damned good. She turned her face away before she smiled back.

*****

In his office, Mallory stared at the wall and thought about his last meeting with Walker, the way he'd zoned out and Walker had just appeared in the doorway when he came to. He hadn't told the Task Force members everything in his confession.

He didn't tell them about the sound of the woman's voice that echoed in his mind before the smell of wood smoke brought him around. Her voice was quavering and harsh, the voice of an old woman, and she was singing in a language similar to Vietnamese. Chanting, he thought, with the sound of a small drum beating in the background.

Nor did he mention the way Walker's clean uniform had become soiled on one side, like the young soldier had been rolling on his side in the dirt. And he certainly didn't say anything about the red cloth bag hanging from Walker's neck as he stood there in the doorway, that he was certain the bag hadn't been there before the vibration and foghorn started. It was the same bag Walker was wearing in the drugstore when he saved Altro's life.

The rest was the best he could give them, including the look of anger on the young soldier's face, the way his lip curled up in a sneer when he looked at Brain, Sledge and Colonel Steadley.

"Don't let these men use you, LT."

Mallory stared off into space for a few minutes, remembering. Then he pulled his cold phone from his briefcase and called Buzzard again.

"Yeah?" Buzzard said.

"It's Possum. Have you talked to people?"

"I made some calls. I'm in Lansing now. More are on the way."

"Good," Mallory said. "We'll probably need them. The woman Walker snatched? Well, he let her go."

"It was a woman? You didn't tell me that."

"Yeah. Special Investigator Teri Altro. She works for the Michigan Attorney General's office. Joined the Task Force."

"But Walker let her go?"

"It turns out that it was Colonel Nguy who snatched her" Mallory said. "But yeah, Nguy just let her go after she talked to Walker."

Buzzard laughed, then broke into a coughing fit. When he'd cleared out his lungs he answered. "Those two working together? This oughta be good."

"Guaranteed," Mallory said. "Listen, who's the best available? The very best. This is Walker and Colonel Nguy we're talking about here."

Buzzard was quiet for a few seconds.

"Brice Keenan's crew is in Chicago right now."

Mallory knew Keenan, had met him while doing some work in Afghanistan. He'd heard good things about his organization, Kerr-Newman Acquisition and Delivery. He smiled, as he always did, at the company name. Keenan and his crew "acquired" people, almost always a known or suspected Islamic terrorist, and "delivered" them to a U.S. agency, usually the CIA.

The irony of the company's name didn't end there. Kerr-Newman was a type of black hole, a region in space with gravity so strong that nothing can escape its grip. Not even light. The few people who knew of the company's existence sometimes joked among themselves. "People go in, and they never come out."

Buzzard and Mallory discussed Kerr-Newman at length. When they were finished, Mallory stashed his cold phone. He picked up the landline and made a call that was answered by a clipped voice.

"Pentagon switchboard. Please state the nature of your call."

"This is Colonel Bill Mallory of the 519th Military Intelligence Brigade. Retired. Put me through to General Steadley."

Mallory knew the General would take his call. He knew the General would approve of Mallory's suggestion to call in Kerr-Newman.

Brain and Sledge had recommended Mallory's transfer to Army Intelligence, pushed hard to make it happen. They wanted to keep an eye on him. Steadley had approved the transfer, then followed his career path closely, watching Mallory as he toed the line and spouted the opinions his superiors wanted to hear.

It was General Steadley, in fact, who had recommended Bill Mallory to Martin Woodley.

Chapter 39

Brain was in their room at the Radisson, sipping scotch while he examined a map of the city spread out on the desk. He'd marked the location of the Winged Lion, and an apartment building Tommy Mo told them was managed by a Hmong man.

His phone buzzed and he looked at the caller ID. It was Sledge, who was staked out at the apartment building. He sounded rattled to Brain, was yelling into the phone.

"It's me, Sledge. I'm at the apartment building that Tommy Mo told us about."

Brain rolled his eyes and shook his head. Because of his glasses and physique, Sledge was often thought to be more intelligent than he really was. There was, however, a sound reason for his alias. He was dumb as a hammer. Sledge continued yelling into the phone.

"I spotted some Hmong guys. They split up and I'm following two in a car."

"You're sure they're Hmong?"

"Hell yeah. They're wearing those traditional Hmong vests."

Brain thought that was too overt a sign, almost like the men were advertising their culture, but there could be a traditional Hmong festival going on. He leaned over the map. "Where are you now?"

He could hear Sledge grunting and cursing before he answered. "The corner of Maple and Grand River. Just turned the corner."

Brain found the intersection on the map and marked it. More cursing from Sledge.

"Shit. I can't see them anymore. I lost them while I was reading the fucking street sign!"

Brain frowned. "Do you know where the others went?"

"They went into the apartment building."

At least the apartment building had panned out.

"Okay, Sledge. Good work. Try to pick up the car again for a few minutes. If you can't, just come back to the hotel."

Brain disconnected and started making a list. He wanted to be well-prepared when they went up against Walker.

Chapter 40

Mallory had been hiding in his office for almost an hour when he walked out, holding a yellow sticky-note in one hand. They were all looking at him, but he still made a point of getting their attention, like always.

"People, listen up. A Captain Lafferty, from the Pentagon, is on his way here to review our files on Michaels. He'll be here tomorrow at ten hundred hours."

Everybody just stared at him for a few seconds. Jessica raised her hand. "What's the military want with him, sir?"

"Remember the way he disappeared in Vietnam, Jessica. Technically, Michaels is a deserter. They want to take him in."

Altro couldn't believe this. She came out of her chair and put her hands on her hips. "That was over forty years ago, Mallory. Jesus Christ! Don't they have enough to do?"

He motioned for her to sit back down.

"Altro? Everyone?" He waited for their attention, even though he already had it. "With Walker being a deserter, the Army has a legitimate right to him."

Mallory fled to his office, ending the discussion, but Altro was furious. The man had saved her life. He was an integral part of the case they were working on. Now the Army wanted him because of something that happened decades ago? She went to get a cup of coffee, and when she walked back out, the rest of them had their chairs scooted together. Sammy was pointing to his laptop as she joined them.

"This Lafferty? He *is* listed with the Pentagon. Captain *Brandon* Lafferty. He's on the staff of a General Steadley."

The Princess spoke up. "Steadley? Wasn't Steadley the name of Mr. Mallory's Commander in Vietnam?"

Sammy was still working on his laptop. "Oh yeah. Steadley works in procurement now. Reviews weapons systems for future purchase."

Just then Mallory walked out of his office again. "Altro? The governor wants to talk to you."

He waved an arm toward his office door, then pushed those stupid glasses back up on his nose. Altro could see that he'd straightened his tie and tucked his shirt in neater. She walked over. Mallory stood aside, then closed the door behind her. His landline phone was off the hook, so she picked up the receiver.

Her phone conversation with Governor Listrom lasted more than twenty minutes. Altro knew that was a lot of time for the Governor of Michigan to spend on the phone, and was impressed by it. Listrom made small talk at first, asking questions about the office, the computers and other Task Force members. When she got around to asking Altro if she was coping all right, she sounded genuinely concerned. Then she told Altro that Mallory had her private number, that Altro could get it from him and call her at any time.

Mallory has the Governor's private number?

"Thanks for taking the time to talk, Altro. It makes me feel a little better. Can you put Bill back on the line."

Bill, huh?

Altro opened the door, waved Mallory over and pointed to the phone.

"She wants to talk to you — Bill."

Mallory blushed, sat down and picked up the phone.

"Yes, ma'am."

Altro watched as he straightened his tie again and ran a hand over his cheap haircut. When he saw she was still standing there, he blushed again and waved a hand at her to leave.

An hour later, Altro was done for the day. Sam and Jessica were working away at their laptops. Doolee was talking on the phone to the senior FBI agent at the East Lansing office. Mallory was hiding in his office again. Altro couldn't concentrate on anything.

The ivory tile was warm in her pocket. It was almost speaking to her, calling her name and begging her to look at it. She started her preparations to leave.

"Ms. Altro? You rode in with SAC Bowman, didn't you?"

She looked up at Jessica and nodded her head as she locked her laptop in the desk.

"I had to. The FBI was going over my rental. Colonel Nguy was considerate enough to make sure I had transportation after he took me home, but evidently consideration isn't very high on the Bureau's priorities."

"I can give you a ride home if you want. I'd be more than happy to."

Out of the corner of her eye, Altro caught Sammy and Doolee looking their way.

"I already called a cab, Princess."

A horn sounded outside and Altro picked up her shoulder bag. She gave Jessica her "thanks, but no thanks" smile as she walked away, but the young woman's disappointment was clear. Altro felt a twinge of guilt, but pushed it back in the corner.

When she carded out, she saw two Ingham County cruisers parked in the lot. The deputies waved to her as she walked across the lot to the cab. Somebody had thought to add more security to the building.

The cab ride to her condo took over twenty minutes and she kept a hand in her jacket pocket the entire time, fingering the ivory tile. At home, she looked around, assessing the damage done by the Evidence Response Team. All things considered, the place didn't look too bad. She would have to do some dusting, clean up the smudges and fingerprint powder, but they'd done a real nice job vacuuming. Regardless, the dusting would have to wait for a while.

She trudged into her bedroom and dropped her shoulder bag next to the bed stand. She sat on the bed and pulled the note and ivory tile from her jacket. She opened the envelope and withdrew the note to read it again.

Teri,

I would be very pleased if you would accept my tile.

It is my sign. The sign of the Valley Walker.

Show it to any Hmong person, and they will help you in any way they can.

You're family now, Teri. You are part of the whole.

John Michaels

Altro stared at the note for several minutes, remembering her time with John Michaels, the man the Hmong called the Valley Walker. *Part of the whole.* She sighed and put the note and tile on the bed. The nightstand was covered in fingerprint powder.

Her cleaning service didn't come until Tuesday, and there was no way she could put up with the fingerprint powder until then. It was time to dust. The rental in the garage would have to be cleaned up too, she supposed.

When she'd finished her dusting and eaten a hurried dinner of leftovers, Altro undressed and pulled on the old tee-shirt she wore for pajamas. After reading the note again, she carefully folded it back into the envelope and placed it in a drawer of the nightstand. She didn't put the tile away. It sat there on the bed, calling her name again. She couldn't resist the urge to pick it up.

It was heavier than she would expect. The dragon etched on its surface looked like it had taken years to complete, a work of artistry and craftsmanship. A hole had been drilled in one end of the tile, and the simple leather thong going through the opening allowed the piece to be worn around the neck. After a thorough examination of the tile, she draped the leather thong around her neck and let the tile fall between her breasts.

Warmth began where the ivory touched her, then moved through her body. The aroma of wood smoke rose to her nostrils. She saw John Michaels sitting on the floor, smiling easily at her. He was on the mat, bathed in candlelight, then rose with that effortless fluid movement she would never forget. He took her hand in his, and she felt the warmth spreading through her.

She drifted off to sleep slowly, smiling at the sound of his voice.

Chapter 41

Kerr-Newman Acquisition and Delivery was a private company with only four employees, a company very few people knew existed. The company president, Brice Keenan, worked hard to keep it that way.

For the past three years, Kerr-Newman had acquired and delivered subjects on almost every continent around the world. Their last assignment had been in Chicago, where they acquired Abidin Shukor, a Malaysian fundamentalist Muslim they'd tracked for more than three months. They cleaned up a drugged and compliant Shukor, cut and dyed his hair, gave him a clean shave and clothed him in Macy's finest. After this makeover, they took him to Midway Airport and pushed him in a wheelchair to a private jet that whisked him off to a site where he would be extensively and enthusiastically questioned.

After Shukor was delivered, Kerr-Newman's employees stayed on in Chicago, living in separate apartments in Bridgeport, a neighborhood on the South Side that included the White Sox's U.S. Cellular Field.

Brice Keenan knew their time as a unit was limited. The service they provided was being raked over by the politicians in Washington, who were willing to say anything to gain favorable airtime. Hollywood had jumped on the bandwagon, making a big budget political statement movie that achieved some semblance of success at the box office. Americans were beginning to wonder if the end did indeed justify the means. Progress.

While all of this went on, Keenan's people were idling away, trying to stay sharp and getting bored. Although Chicago is a great city with almost endless entertainment and educational choices, the employees of Kerr-Newman ran on different juice than what Chicago had to offer.

Keenan was mulling the situation over, hoping he wouldn't have to disband the company altogether, when he was contacted. He picked up his cell phone and started calling his people in.

Chapter 42

Walker sat on the edge of Andrea's bed and stroked her hip. She stirred a bit and mumbled his name, unaware he was watching her sleep, listening to her breathe and taking in her scent. He tried to reach out to her, to touch her heart, but couldn't. The memory of their attempt to make a life together made him realize he never had. They were so in love then, their goals in life so far apart.

For as long as he could remember, he'd wanted to be a soldier. As a young boy, he saw them as heroes and, in the confusion of puberty, he longed for the quiet self-confidence those men exhibited. The camaraderie of men who served together in combat and their willingness to die for a cause was something not even the church could offer.

Soon after he graduated from high school, he took the chance to do something meaningful, something that mattered. He enlisted in the Army, chose the infantry, then volunteered for Vietnam. When he arrived in country, he was assigned to a unit that operated out of a base called Lai Khe. He adapted very well.

The utter simplicity of life in the bush suited him. He liked mixing the C rations with the Heinz 57 and Tabasco sauces, concocting dishes in an empty coffee can and heating them with a pinch of C4 he lit with his cigarette. To him, there was nothing so relaxing and satisfying as a cup of that acrid instant coffee and a cigarette after a day of humping the bush.

The adrenaline rush of blowing an ambush threw his senses into a mad chaos, and the post combat crash brought him back to earth empty and ready for sleep. He learned to sleep light, but still slept soundly, safe in the knowledge he was doing the right thing.

All of that changed in a hailstorm of small-arms fire that still haunted him. That firefight sent him back to the States, seeking some acknowledgement of his sacrifice. He didn't find it.

The country had changed, and Andrea had changed with it. She'd lost her belief in the cause of the war and insisted that he leave the Army. Her attitude confused him, made him wonder what had happened to the woman he married. The first time she had seen him in uniform, she had melted, fussing over him and breaking out in tears. Later, their bodies had come together in a near frenzy of tender lust.

But when he went back to her, she pushed him away. He didn't know what she needed from their relationship, but all he wanted was to be her hero. He wasn't. She hated the things he believed in. Her fear of him, the disgust for what he'd become, was clear on her face. That look of revulsion drove him away, back to Vietnam. Back to the war he still believed in. Back to the war he'd left unfinished.

It was the right thing to do. His honor was all he had left.

As he watched her sleep, a need to explain things to her filled him. So much had happened. It had been a long hump, and the way men fed on the agony of others weighed heavy on his heart. His anger had prodded him and given him power over the years, but now the anger was as heavy as the knowledge that men profited from the suffering they caused.

He was tired. He wanted to go home. The power of the red hemp bag drew him and he reached up to it.

"Two salt tablets, a canteen of water and push on."

Chapter 43

Teri Altro was trying desperately to regain the rhythm of her life, which had been disrupted when she met Walker. She rose at her usual time, 5:00 a.m., determined to go through her morning workout.

Her condo had a fairly good workout center on the lower floor, complete with a big-screen television and stereo to keep the mind occupied. There was an elliptical machine, a heavy bag, a speed bag, and a good assortment of free weights. She chose the elliptical machine, but after fifteen minutes of listlessly going through the motions, abandoned the attempt and headed for the shower.

With this completed, she turned to the closet of nearly identical business suits that were her trademark. She opted for the dark blue, dressed with her usual speed and efficiency, then ate a yogurt and wheat germ breakfast. While eating, she watched a rerun of last night's special broadcast on the kitchen television. Martin Woodley and SAC Bowman were in a three-way teleconference with a network anchor in Atlanta. Bowman was in the FBI's East Lansing Satellite Office. Woodley sat smug in the den of his palatial house in Virginia.

The questions to Woodley were all a set up for him to showcase his knowledge and speaking style. Bowman agreed with every word Woodley said, and gushed over Woodley's commitment to the drug problem that threatened to take over the country.

Woodley complimented Bowman's courage, standing up to the dangers of facing down vicious drug pushers. The drugstore shooting was discussed, with Bowman revealing that drug dealers attempted to assassinate a member of the Task Force. Woodley nodded sagely, then declared that the incident underscored the need to stop the influx of drugs into the country. No mention was made of Walker or Altro.

Woodley's rich baritone grated on Altro's nerves, and the sleazy fawning of Bowman made her want to hurl. She turned the TV off, walked into the bedroom and stared at the ivory tile on the nightstand. She'd taken it off before her attempt at a workout, but it was calling to her again.

She picked up the tile, draped the leather thong around her neck, tucked it into her starched white cotton blouse and let it fall. It slipped down below her blouse and came to rest between her breasts. The tile warmed her, the way his touch had. Her hand went to its shape and she reveled in the warmth it gave her. Her mind wandered. She smelled wood smoke.

Altro shook her head and pulled it off. The tile went back in the nightstand drawer with the note Walker had written. There wouldn't be any time for daydreaming today. She couldn't be sitting there at her desk, seeing his smiling face and feeling his warmth. There was too much work to do. She had to crawl back into her shell. Special Investigator Teri Altro straightened her shoulders, picked up her shoulder bag and charged into the day.

First she had to drive to the State Police Forensics Lab in Lansing to pick up her gun. They were finished with the ballistics tests on her pistol, and were holding it at the evidence cage. Altro missed carrying it, and hoped its weight in her shoulder bag would get her back on track.

The trooper in charge of the evidence cage hit on her, complimenting her and making a big deal out of the fact that he'd cleaned the gun for her. She looked him up and down, then turned on the frost machine. After she signed the forms, the disappointed man handed her the pistol and turned back to his paperwork on the counter.

Altro loaded it then and there, and the trooper looked up with an arched eyebrow when she worked the slide to put a round in the chamber. A nod was all he got. She safed the weapon, put it in her shoulder bag and headed out the door.

The rest of the team was already seated, noses in their laptops, when she walked in at 9:15, but she gave no explanation and made no apologies for being late. Mallory was hiding in his office, so she poured herself a cup of Doolee's buzz-producing coffee and took her seat. She dug her laptop out of the desk and checked up on how things were going on the case.

No one was reporting any progress on tracking down the source of the heroin, but there hadn't been any overdose deaths in a week. Nothing had come back from TSA about the two men seen at the hospital. Somebody would have to kick some tail on that one, and it looked like it would be her. Jessica had come across this lead, and Altro scanned the growing database for any other entries from her. She looked at Jessica's map where everything was plotted out and was struck by the professionalism. The Princess did good work.

Altro drummed her fingers on her desk as she thought about the case and everything that had happened. She didn't like where her thoughts were taking her.

The location of the Team Center and the names of the Task Force members were never revealed to the public. No one should have known Altro was even on the Task Force, let alone where she would be. But they had, and if it wasn't for Walker's intervention, she would be dead.

John Walker Michaels, the man the Task Force hadn't known anything about until he revealed himself to Altro. No, that wasn't right. His ex-wife told them his name and who he was before Altro did.

Not long after Shellers had talked to Mallory and Jessica, men were sent to her home to kidnap her. Altro was sure about that, and the evidence certainly supported the theory. But how could the kidnappers know about Shellers?

They had a leak.

Chapter 44

Martin Woodley took the call from General Steadley in his study. The cursed white man wasn't eating dung, though some would infer he was drinking it. He was sipping his morning Kopi Luwak.

It didn't bother him a bit that some considered Kopi Luwak the epitome of indulgence by those with more money than they needed. When the squeamish turned up their nose at drinking coffee made from beans pulled from the feces of caged civets, the dung eater gave them his haughtiest sneer. The whining of animal rights agitators who decried the inhumane conditions of the intensive farming methods only made the brew taste better.

General Steadley, however, was in no mood for small talk about the finer things in life. He was calling about Walker. The General wasn't happy about the progress made toward putting an end to the man who threatened to bring down their carefully constructed castle, and wanted to bring in a team of specialists.

Woodley had heard of Kerr-Newman, of course. Their exploits were widely discussed by the few who knew about such things, and their delivery rate was extraordinary. After a lively discussion, he had to agree with General Steadley.

Brain and Sledge had botched the attempt on Walker at the hospital, and the move to snatch the Sheller woman had failed outright. It was time to bring in the best.

*****

Brain couldn't believe it. Woodley was pulling him and Sledge off the hunt.

"Sir, we're close."

"Brain, I appreciate your work on this but I think we should leave it up to Steadley's people now. They're professionals at this, the best there is."

Woodley knew Brain and Sledge had no respect for Steadley, and moved quickly to smooth things over. "Look, it's actually better for us if someone else handles it. We should stay as far away from this as possible. It's to our advantage that Steadley's stepping in here."

Woodley said "us" and "we" and "our", but Brain knew he was only thinking of himself. This would benefit the man personally, would distance him even further from the violence that would certainly erupt when Walker was taken down. Brain didn't want to give up the chase, however. He tried again.

"Sir, we've come this far. Don't make us stop now."

There was a slight pause while Woodley came up with his final play, flattery and money. The man thought it worked for everything.

"I know you're disappointed, but I'll take good care of you and Sledge. You men have both been invaluable to me. You'll receive a sizable bonus when you get back."

Brain snapped his cell phone closed when the connection was broken. He tossed it on the bed, and turned to Sledge.

"We're being recalled from our pursuit of Walker. Someone from the Pentagon is taking over, General Steadley."

Sledge exploded, the way Brain knew he would.

"That stupid motherfucker?"

Brain let Sledge stew until he erupted again.

"God fucking damnit, Brain! We owe Walker big time! We're not going to back out are we?"

They did owe Walker. The years spent trying to run him down was only a small part of it. The discomfort of tracking a ghost through Southeast Asia was bad, but the loss of face when they repeatedly failed was worse. Brain poured himself some coffee before he answered.

"No way. We'll have to move out of here and dump our phones. Tommy Mo can set us up with a place, and we can get pre-paid phones just about anywhere. We'll keep an eye on the apartment building, and if the chance comes up, we'll take Walker down. Hard."

Chapter 45

Altro was eyeing the others in the Team Room, thinking about who the leak could be, when they all closed their laptops. She looked at her watch and remembered that the guy from the Pentagon was coming in this morning.

What the hell was his name? Oh yeah. Lafferty.

Captain Brandon Lafferty, the man who represented the Army's long memory. The memory of an organization that branded Walker, the man who had saved her life, as a deserter. The organization that wanted to take him in and punish him for something that happened decades ago.

Sammy took his feet down off the desk. Doolee went into the break room and started making fresh coffee. Princess Jessica went into the bathroom to tinkle and primp. Altro just knew the Princess tinkled in there. She certainly didn't pee like other people, and she sure as hell didn't piss.

The Princess timed it just right, and managed to come out of the bathroom just as someone knocked on the glass of the vestibule door. The young woman's hair was perfect. Her makeup was perfect. Her shoes and clothes were perfect. Hell, everything about her was perfect.

Jessica swiped her card to open the door and greeted Captain Lafferty with her teenager's voice. Altro struggled not to glare as Jessica took Captain Lafferty over to Mallory's office. She wasn't surprised to see the Princess turning on the charm, even less surprised to see the young captain enjoying every second of her attention.

Lafferty was grinning like a cartoon. He was so enthralled that he kept tripping over his own shoes. Patent leather, Altro noted. He was towing his laptop and a briefcase on one of those lightweight aluminum carts, and it bumped into the back of his feet whenever he swiveled his head to eyeball Jessica.

Jessica knocked on Mallory's door, and Altro saw him straightening his tie before he nodded for her to enter. Altro stood up and stalked over so she could watch what was going on.

"Sir, this is Captain Lafferty from the Pentagon," the Princess announced.

She turned and smiled at Lafferty, then placed a perfectly formed and manicured hand on his forearm.

"Brandon, this is Bill Mallory, the Task Force leader. Why don't you have a seat? Can I get you anything? Coffee or a Coke maybe?"

Altro almost gagged at the way Jessica used the captain's first name, but Lafferty just about drooled over it. He was trying desperately to keep the Princess in his sights as he sat down, and almost missed the chair.

"I'm okay. Thanks, Jessica."

After beaming and flouncing her perfect hair, Jessica turned and waltzed out the door. As soon as the Princess was out of her way, Altro stormed into the room, put her hands on her hips and started her attack.

"I'm Special Investigator Altro."

Lafferty stood up and extended his hand, but Altro didn't take it. She jabbed a finger at him instead, very close to poking him in the chest.

"I don't like the way you're grabbing our witness, Lafferty."

Lafferty squirmed a bit and put on a puzzled look. Altro continued to stare him down as she waited for his answer.

"Michaels is a deserter, after all," Lafferty said. "And as far as the military is concerned, he's damaged goods."

She barked back at Lafferty, almost before he finished his sentence, leaning forward enough to make him take a step back.

"Bullshit! That was over 40 years ago."

Lafferty took another step back and held his hands up in surrender. Mallory pushed those ridiculous glasses up on his nose and cleared his throat.

"Altro, the only use Michaels is to us is the information he can give us. I'm sure the Army will share any information pertinent to our case with us."

He turned to Lafferty, who nodded his agreement. "Of course we will, sir."

She nodded grimly. "All right, Mallory, but this is on your head. In the meantime, you're going to keep the team informed about what's going on here, right? The way you're holding this meeting sequestered in your office makes me think you're hiding something from the rest of us."

Mallory stood up, straightened his shoulders, and his face morphed into a look she'd never seen on him before. It was completely blank, with no expression at all she could read.

"That'll be all, Altro."

He ushered her to the door and closed it behind her, then closed the blinds that hung on the door window. Altro was almost shocked, and a flicker of respect for Mallory hit her. Not many people could back her down.

Not knowing what else to do, she took her seat and waited it out. Princess Jessica was watching her every movement, but Altro couldn't help herself. She drummed her fingers on the desk, tapped a foot on the floor incessantly, then finally stood up and paced the floor with her hands on her hips. The Team Room remained silent during the entire meeting.

When the door to Mallory's office finally opened, Jessica jumped up and trotted over to show the captain out. She put a hand on his forearm and brushed against him a few times as they walked, making it look like the captain was escorting her. Altro got the distinct impression that the captain wanted to kiss the Princess goodbye at the door.

It was sickening.

Chapter 46

As soon as Lafferty was gone, they all got fresh coffee and Mallory slumped out of his office. He stood there to the side of the Team Room, avoiding eye contact with anyone. Sam spoke up.

"Now that the Army's happy, I've got something that relates to our case."

The flat-screen lit up.

"I've been digging into the name that Michaels gave Altro, Khun Pao," Sammy said. "Well, I hit the mother lode. Like Michaels said, he's a drug lord in the Golden Triangle, the border area of Laos, Thailand and China. He's been in business for decades, from back when Laos and Vietnam were still French colonies."

A smiling Asian man in uniform was on the screen.

"He's a soldier?" Altro asked.

"He heads his own private army," Sam said. "Gave himself the rank of General." He waggled a hand back and forth. "Opinions vary on the size of his force, from several hundred to more than 10,000. But every analysis I looked at said he packs some real punch. Here, check this out."

The screen changed to a table filled with numbers. There was a lot of data on the screen — estimates of Khun's income, tonnage of raw opium harvested and tonnage of heroin refined.

"Jesus Christ," Altro mumbled. "Tonnage."

"Yeah, he was so big that he had his own brand marking for his heroin," Sam said.

The screen changed again to show a package of white powder wrapped in clear plastic. The wrapping was marked with a professional looking red logo. The symbol, two lions facing each other and grasping the globe in their paws, was identical to the tattoos of the three dead gunmen from the drugstore.

Sammy turned to Mallory. "Pretty coincidental, don't you think, sir?"

Mallory just stared at the screen. In the absence of any response, Jessica raised her hand.

"It looks like Michaels told Ms. Altro the truth about this guy. That he's the one behind the heroin we're trying to stop."

Sammy, always eager to impress the Princess, spoke in his best television announcer's voice. "But wait, Jessica. There's more. Much more!"

Jessica beamed at him and Sam worked his keyboard. "I came across this picture of the guy. It was part of an old *Washington Post* article, written back in the 70s."

He brought up a picture of Khun Pao with his troops, the drug lord looking proud as he walked through the ranks with a smiling white man at his arm. Jessica rewarded Sam with one of her dazzling smiles.

"Good work, Sammy. I really don't know what we'd do without you."

Altro almost groaned at the way the Princess worked the men in the team, but stopped herself. A groan actually did come from Doolee, who was evidently jealous of the attention Sammy was getting. Not one to leave anyone out, Jessica beamed over at Doolee and flounced her hair, which made him grin briefly before he asked his question.

"But who is the white man, Sammy? He looks American. Why is he there with this big drug dealer?"

Sammy zoomed in. The man's smile was even bigger. "I don't know who he is, but he sure looks happy."

Altro jumped to her feet.

"Is that Martin Woodley? Sammy, get a picture of Woodley and put it up next to this one. That sure looks like him. Younger, but him."

They all knew who Martin Woodley was. Hell, everybody knew who Martin Woodley was now. It didn't take Sammy long to dig up a recent photo. In just a few moments, the current picture of Woodley came up on the screen, confirming Altro's theory. Sammy gave a low whistle.

"That's him, all right. Very interesting."

Doolee stood up, turned to Mallory and waved an arm at the screen.

"But why is Woodley here, sir? What is he doing with this Khun Pao?"

Mallory just stared at the screen and started rubbing that scar on his chin. Special Investigator Teri Altro wasn't going to let this slide. She put her hands on her hips and barked out a clipped order.

"Sammy, I want everything we can get on Woodley. Phone records, credit cards, bank records. I want it all. Princess Jessica can help you out."

Sammy grinned over at Doolee, who rolled his eyes and sighed. Altro sat down and picked up her BlackBerry.

"I'll get the warrants started."

Mallory shook his head, pushed his glasses up on his nose and retreated to his office.

Chapter 47

Andrea Shellers and Ka talked for over an hour. Actually, Andrea listened for most of the time. The closeness of John's adopted family touched her deeply. They had all gathered here, left their own lives at the news of his being in the hospital. She thought it would be nice to have family like that, and said as much. Ka's answer was not what she expected.

"Andrea, we would have gladly come as you are thinking, but we didn't know what was happening when we came. Father had us brought here for our safety. He was protecting his family."

At this point, the old woman, John's mother, shuffled back in. Before she left with a cup of tea, she spoke to Ka in the lilting tones of her native tongue.

"Mother says to tell you that you are family, too," Ka said. "She's right, you know. He brought you here to protect you too. He still loves you."

Andrea reached her hand out to touch Ka's. The two sat in silence then, and time passed. Despite the silence, Andrea's mind continued to turn and finally she couldn't keep it in any longer.

"I just couldn't marry again. I couldn't let go of what we had." She sighed before she went on. "I had suitors, of course. I even changed my name and dated men. Some of them wanted to get serious, but no matter how hard I tried, I couldn't start over with someone else. I never really felt like there was a conclusion with John."

Ka nodded.

"It must have been hard for you, the way things have happened."

Again they fell into silence, again Andrea's mind kept spinning, and again she couldn't keep quiet.

"Now everything's changed. He's back, but I don't feel like I'm part of his life anymore. He has you and his mother. He has his son, and Bao." She fiddled with her coffee cup before she looked at Ka again. "She's so beautiful, and so young."

Ka squeezed Andrea's hand.

"Yes, Bao is beautiful, and young. But she is so young she cannot understand. He loves her, but more in the way he loves me. As a daughter."

"He married her," Andrea said.

"I think he only married her to help heal her broken spirit, and to solve her problem of having a fatherless child," Ka replied.

Andrea stared at Ka, who nodded her head and continued. "Father has told all of us about you, Andrea. He's never said a word against you, over what happened between you. In fact, Bao is in awe of you. You will always be the first wife to her."

There was silence again. First wife. Andrea knew so little about these people and their customs. In fact, she knew so little of what had become of John. She had to know more.

"You know, I don't even know where he's been, what he's done. Does he do something?"

Ka took her hand away and raised it to her mouth. "You don't know. Of course not, how could you? Do you know the Thai restaurant across the street from your clothing store?"

Andrea knew it well. She'd eaten there many times.

"The people who own it are Hmong refugees," Ka said. "Father's company owns 50 percent of that restaurant. He supplied the start-up money in return for part ownership. In Lansing, he has invested in two restaurants, three apartment buildings, and a nail salon. He is part owner of Asian businesses in San Diego and Minneapolis. And in Bangkok, Thailand, it is the same. Of course, the money could not be in his name. A friend of his in Bangkok, a Frenchman, handles it all. The same Frenchman who arranged for Bao and me to come to the States."

Andrea looked around at the poor furnishings of the kitchen. Ka saw the look.

"This is only temporary, Andrea. But with Father, everything is temporary. You must know that."

Ka's face was serious and her gaze was focused on some faraway place. Then a radiant smile lit her face and her musical laugh made Andrea smile, in spite of herself.

"Let me tell you one of my favorite stories. In fact, it is told throughout Laos, and the Hmong refugees still in Thailand. Father has legitimate business investments that support his work today, but the startup money came from the opium business."

Pleased at the shocked look on Andrea's face, Ka clapped her hands and smiled.

"Oh, I've heard this story so many times that I know it word for word."

Chapter 48

Walker and Colonel Nguy watched another exchange between the Hmong of Laos and the men in ARVN uniforms. The bearers loaded the truck and one of their armed escorts took a heavy pack from a uniformed man. The truck and jeep left, then the Hmong group started hiking toward Cambodia.

Walker and Nguy moved ahead of them. Nguy carried an XM21 sniper rifle, with a Leatherwood Adjustable Ranging Telescope and a bipod. Walker carried two army-issue .45 caliber pistols.

When the group was five kilometers from the Cambodian border, they stopped at a campsite for rest and food. The escorts set up a lazy perimeter. Evidently they'd stopped at this site before and thought they could relax here.

Roughly 500 meters out from the campsite, Nguy was already adjusting the scope for elevation and windage. He hunkered down in a spot with brush overhanging it, placing his body in shadow. His rifle had the bipod extended for stability. On the opposite side of the campsite, Walker waited with his pistols.

Nguy took the first shot, hitting a man who was seated and leaning against a tree. The shot was good enough that the man didn't even fall over. Walker moved to the edge of the camp as only he could, sliding through the grass without disturbing a single blade. He moved behind a guard and shot him in the back of the head before the guard knew he was there.

Meanwhile, Nguy had killed another guard on his side of the perimeter and was zeroing in on the next in line. This man he hit off center, and the wounded man let out a series of cries before he fell silent. Nguy backed into the brush until he was behind it, rose and quickly moved west.

The guards were staying hidden when Nguy settled into his next position. He was scanning for targets with binoculars and saw Walker appear behind another guard and shoot him in the back of the head. Not far from the victim, another man came into view as he tried to scurry back from his position. Nguy dropped the binoculars and took a quick shot which hit the man in the upper torso. The man screamed in pain and panic took over in the campsite. The guards still alive decided to make a run for the border of Cambodia.

Nguy could see the grass and brush moving as the men crawled through it. He started firing rapidly in the direction of the moving men, but lower and just ahead of their positions. Then he walked his fire closer to the movement until he heard howls of pain. Nguy emptied his clip rapidly in the area, then loaded another. Two men stood upright with their arms raised in surrender, one of the men holding a canvas pack that sagged with the weight of its contents.

Making a wide circle, Colonel Nguy moved closer to the men who still stood with their arms raised. He fired on either side of the men again, and they jumped involuntarily, then stood rooted as a further sign of surrender. When Nguy was within 75 meters of them, Walker rose up from nowhere and kept them under cover. Nguy was soon close enough to see the bodies of three more guards lying in the grass. He took the backpack from the guard and motioned with his rifle barrel for the two captives to return to the campsite.

Walker was already there.

The men who served as mules were huddled in the center of the site, pointing at Walker and babbling loudly in Hmong. Walker motioned for the bearers to sit down and relax. He pulled the waterproof container holding his cigarettes from his fatigue shirt pocket, pulled out a cigarette, lit it with his ever-present Zippo and put the smokes back in his pocket. Then he took an unopened pack of cigarettes from his other shirt pocket, tossed it to the mules and proceeded to make coffee for them.

Reaching into a thigh pocket of his fatigue trousers, he pulled out a half stick of C4 and broke off a pinch. He placed the pinch of explosive on the ground and the remainder back in the pocket. He poured water from a canteen into his coffee cup, lit the pinch of C4 with his cigarette and held the water over the flame to heat it. The burning C4 had the water bubbling in minutes.

Kneeling beside the shoulder bag, Nguy opened it, examined its contents and turned to Walker with a grin on his face. He reached inside the bag and withdrew a 12-ounce gold ingot, held it up and showed it to the huddled mules with a smile. Meanwhile, Walker went over to the bearers and squatted, holding out the cup of coffee. The men passed it around and sipped while they smoked.

Walker shrugged out of his web gear, pulled out more powdered coffee and heated more water. He began listening to the men, and began picking up their language, interrupting occasionally to look questioningly at them and motion with his hands. He threw in a few words of French with the words of Hmong he picked up, and a conversation was born.

These men were simple farmers who grew opium poppies mixed in with their corn crop. The opium was used to purchase things they could not grow or make themselves. Metal pots, fancy cloth and beads, any metal tools, crossbows and flintlocks — these all had to be purchased. The Hmong were not opium users to any great extent, but had bartered with it for centuries.

But a powerful drug lord named Khun Pao had forced them to convert the greatest part of their fields to growing opium. The farmers barely had enough to eat, and the entire opium crop was confiscated by the drug lord. Then their crop was processed into heroin and the poor men were forced to transport the product down the Mekong River and overland into Vietnam. As a final insult, Khun took their most desirable daughters for his own amusement. To ensure cooperation, the farmers' families were held hostage by the armed thugs Khun called his army.

The Hmong were at a loss. They were used to being mistreated by the lowland Lao, who considered themselves superior to the people who lived in the mountains, but these were men of their own race.

Walker listened carefully, then told them what to do. He told the Hmong to return with the guards who were still alive. Let the guards explain to their masters how they were ambushed and the profit stolen. The farmers should cooperate and describe the men who took the gold willingly, so no blame would be placed on them.

The Hmong approached Nguy, and began babbling at him and pointing at Walker, wanting to know who this man was. Nguy told them his friend's name in English, "Walker." The men repeated this word among themselves, but did not seem satisfied with the answer.

After they harangued him for a few more minutes, Nguy tried again. He tried making a walking man with one hand, two fingers waggling in an imitation of moving legs while he gave his name in English. He repeated the puppet show while saying his name in Vietnamese. Not satisfied, the bearers talked among themselves. Nguy shrugged.

After more babbling and pointing, the Hmong started calling Walker by their own descriptive nickname, "Valley Walker." The man had appeared among them like a ghost and killed their oppressors with a single shot to the back of the head, what would become his trademark execution.

This man was clearly a spirit creature that rose from the valley, the faraway place beyond this life. To them, there was no other explanation.

He was the Valley Walker.

*****

At the tale's conclusion, Ka's face practically glowed. "Father and Colonel Nguy continued their raids on the drug shipments until the Americans left Vietnam," she said. "The gold they took was eventually used for seed money."

Andrea Shellers was shocked. According to these people, he was not the innocent young man of her memories. He was something else altogether.

She reflected on how naïve she'd been about him when they'd married, how the world had seemed so simple. She'd wanted a good life, at least a normal life, from her marriage with John Michaels, but the war took that away.

The war. It took everything. It took him. The impossibility of the whole situation struck her again. She looked into the eyes of the still beaming Ka.

"But... but... how can this all be true, Ka?" She waved a hand in the air. "How can any of this be real?"

Ka's smile stayed on her lips, but the woman's eyes held the truth. When Andrea broke into sobs, Ka put a hand on her shoulder, but offered no explanation.

Chapter 49

Brain and Sledge were in the Winged Lion again, discussing business with Tommy Mo.

"Can you get us a place to stay?" Brain asked. "We need to go to ground."

Tommy Mo's eyebrows shot up. "You're being pursued?"

Brain shook his head. "Just a precaution," he said. "We'll also need to be armed. Well-armed."

Tommy's eyes grew bright and narrow. "You have found him then? He is at the apartment building I told you about?"

"Not yet, but we're sure he'll go there."

Tommy frowned. "Lodging is no problem, but you said well-armed. What do you need?"

Brain handed Tommy a piece of paper, a list of what they wanted. As Tommy looked it over, Brain thought he should soften the blow. "It's a lot, but we don't want to take chances. You, of all people, know how dangerous Walker is. We'll take good care of you financially."

Tommy looked at the list, put his arm up on the back of the booth, lit a cigarette and blew smoke at the ceiling.

"I have no doubt about that, but I am only too happy to help. Anyone who is not a friend of Walker is a friend of mine."

Tommy smiled at his own joke and motioned to a man sitting at the bar who stepped off his stool and approached the booth. He was big, huge for a Hmong, in fact. He had the easy, fluid movement and hooded eyes of a snake. The big Hmong pulled a chair over from a table and straddled it at the end of their booth, his arms hanging over the back of the chair. Brain eyed the tattoos proudly displayed on the man's forearms. Two lions crouched on opposite sides of the globe, grasping it in their paws.

"This is Nab," Tommy said. "He will work with you."

There was something about the man that Brain didn't like.

Sledge didn't like him either. "Who the fuck is this guy?" he asked.

Tommy just stared back at Sledge.

"Well, I'm not working with him," Sledge continued.

Nab smiled at Tommy. Brain half expected a forked tongue to slip from the big Hmong's mouth.

"There is no choice," Tommy said.

Nab gave Brain and Sledge a cold stare, then slid out of the chair and slithered away. Tommy nodded at another man who was seated at a table. The man came over, Tommy handed him the piece of paper with Brain's list and smiled.

"These gentlemen will need to be properly equipped. See to it."

He turned back to Brain and Sledge.

"We can discuss the financial details after this is ended. This will be an agreement between men who are seeking an end to a difficult problem."

"And the snake?" Brain asked.

Tommy took a drag from his cigarette. "You're very perceptive," he said. "His name means Snake in Hmong."

Then Tommy shook his head. "As I said, there is no choice. Nab was sent by General Khun himself."

Chapter 50

The entire staff of Kerr-Newman Acquisition and Delivery was gathered around the kitchen table in Brice Keenan's Chicago apartment. All four of them. They were watching the pharmacy security video of Walker killing the three would-be assassins on their laptops.

The icy blue eyes of John Prentiss remained at half-mast as he watched the video. This was not, however, an accurate indication of what was going through his mind. He leaned forward in his chair, and his upper lip twitched, making his walrus mustache see-saw back and forth. There was no hiding his Tennessee background as he made his assessment.

"Holy shit the bed, Irene!"

Geena Fabrizzio answered in her thick Bronx accent.

"You said it, Cornpone. Look at that Goddamn speed!"

Geena was the only female employee of Kerr-Newman and, at twenty-six, was also the youngest. Geena lived for the juice. She thrived on the adrenalin rush of action and gave little or no respect to those who cowered from it. Her skills and instincts were critical to the company's success, but sometimes Geena's instincts needed firm direction. This was one of those times.

Geena took in a deep breath that stretched the fabric of her black ribbed sweater, revealing just how erect her nipples were. She ran her tongue slowly over her lower lip as she stared at the screen. When one of her hands slipped down below the table to her lap, Keenan figured he'd better bring her back to earth. He reached over and punched her shoulder.

"Ground Control to Geena."

Geena's head snapped around and her black eyes narrowed in anger. Keenan kept his expression neutral and waited for her to settle down. Her eyes widened gradually, until she abruptly stood and stalked out of the room. She returned quickly, shrugging on a loose black denim jacket over her sweater. Geena's entire wardrobe was black.

"Sorry, Chief, but watchin' this guy makes my nips hard as a rock."

The gravelly chuckle of Asa Thomas Lincoln was like distant thunder. His rumbling voice made Howlin' Wolf sound like a choirboy.

"Just keep your claws sheathed until we need 'em, Geena."

Geena turned to Asa. "So whatta ya think, Link?"

Geena had a nickname for all of them.

"The man's a death dancer, no doubt," Asa growled. "Just look at those moves."

"Oooh, don't I fuckin' know it. It's makin' me wet just thinkin' about it."

The black giant chuckled again, then grew serious and scratched the side of his face. "Yeah, but something's not right. Why does he just stand there and let that woman shoot him? What's going on with all that broken glass? It looks like some kind of shockwave there."

He shook his head and continued. "And that speed just isn't possible. I don't know if we can take this guy alive."

Keenan let everyone digest this, then turned to Prentiss. "What's your take, Prentiss?"

Prentiss stroked his mustache as he spoke. Though he always looked relaxed, Keenan could read the tension in his posture. The southerner took a deep breath.

"He saved that lady's life, no doubt about it. It just don't seem right to me for us to haul him in."

"He's a deserter," Asa said.

"If he's a deserter, why us?" Geena asked. "The Army can send their own guys after him."

Everybody nodded and looked to Keenan for an answer.

"Okay. We don't have to take the assignment, but I think we should," Keenan said, then held up a finger. "Number one, we're the closest thing to sympathetic pursuit he'll get. Which brings us to number two." He held up another finger. "I think we have the best chance of pulling this off without anybody getting killed."

He looked around the table and got looks of approval from everyone. Even Geena looked serious.

"And you know what else? I've heard of this guy," Keenan said.

Keenan was fifteen years older than the next oldest in their group, Asa, who was 32. When he was in Special Forces, he'd heard about Walker.

"You children are all too young, but when I went through the grinder, some of the old timers — even older than me — whispered about him when the brass wasn't around. They didn't talk about him like he was a deserter or damaged goods. They talked like he was some kind of ghost warrior."

They chuckled at his old timers remark, then raised their eyebrows over the ghost warrior description. Good. There was more to this job than he'd told them, much more, but he wanted to make sure they were totally on board before he laid it all out.

"Remember people, we are not machines. We can opt out if it looks ugly." He turned to Prentiss. "If it's at all possible, we'll talk to the subject before we turn him over. We will keep our honor intact on this, I promise you."

This brought such a loud "Hooah" from Prentiss that Keenan looked around at the walls, thinking of the neighbors. He started things rolling.

"Okay, people, pack it up. Let's see if we can bring this guy in without causing World War III."

Chapter 51

She didn't hear the door open. She didn't hear his step. She didn't hear anything, yet there he was. John Michaels. Andrea Shellers blinked, jolted from her thoughts. Her right hand went to her chest and she scooted back on the bed.

"You scared the life out of me, John! No wonder these people talk about you like you're some kind of ghost."

His laugh was quiet but resonant, not how she remembered his voice at all. She was shocked at how much he had changed, or perhaps how inaccurate her memories were. He had aged, yes, but it wasn't just his appearance that was so different from her memories. It was his voice, his demeanor, the way he looked at her. He backed up and sat on a chair against the wall, ceding her space to her.

"You look good, Andrea."

She stared at him.

"Is it really you, John? I feel like I'm losing my mind."

"It's me, Andy."

She knew absolutely then. It was impossible, but she knew. No one but John had ever called her Andy.

"They say you killed three men," she said.

He didn't say anything, so she continued. "Why, John? Why would you kill those men? Why are you even involved in this?"

Andrea watched him thinking about what he would say. The pain was evident on his face when he finally spoke.

"They used me, Andy. In the war. They used us all."

"They?"

"Men without honor. Men motivated only by profit and power. They will stop at nothing."

His shoulders sagged and he shrank into himself before her eyes. When it seemed like he would just topple to the floor and disappear, he reached up and grabbed a coarse red cloth bag that hung from his neck by a leather thong. After a few deep breaths he looked back at her, anger in his eyes.

"Now they're here, and they think they can get away with anything. They sent men to your home, Andy."

She tried to control her voice, but it still came out as a strained squeak. "My home? To my home?"

The look on his face softened.

"It's why I had Bo bring you here, to protect you."

"Colonel Nguy? He and Ka told me that. They said you still care for me."

He pulled his chair closer, leaned in to her and kissed her on the top of her head. She bowed her head and closed her eyes. She felt his hand at the nape of her neck. His voice was soft and warm.

"Of course I care for you. You'll always be in my heart."

He didn't say it, but Andrea still thought it. He didn't leave her voluntarily. He had come to her, and she had sent him away. There was no way she could ever say enough. She could never explain. She tried anyway.

"I'm sorry about what happened between us, John. I'm sorry about all those things I said about you and the war. I'm sorry I sent you away."

His hand caressed the back of her neck.

"I was already gone, Andy."

She shuddered. "John? Who is buried in Maple Grove Cemetery?"

He didn't answer. It was silent for a while, and she felt his tears falling on her head. His hand melted into the nape of her neck. She looked up, and he was gone. Knowing he would somehow hear her, she spoke to the wall.

"I'm praying for you, John. I don't understand any of this, but I'm trying."

Chapter 52

Altro couldn't get the warrants for Woodley's records. She argued with the Attorney General himself for twenty minutes, walking the floor with her BlackBerry to her ear. Sam was assiduously checking out her butt while she paced, but she didn't bother to call him on it, just continued her pacing and arguing.

She raised her voice enough that Mallory came out of his office. Mallory had a Bluetooth headset in his ear now and, as he watched the show, a phone chirped in his pocket. He touched a finger to the headset and went back to his office.

She shook her head and went back to the Attorney General, who finally tired of arguing with her and hung up. Altro plopped down at her desk and fumed. She was pissed, but the AG was right. There just wasn't enough evidence for a warrant. She'd jumped the gun.

Sam put his feet up on his desk and started working at his laptop. Doolee stared at the flat-screen, where Woodley's picture was smiling at them. Jessica gave Altro a sympathetic look, but when Altro just glared at her, turned back to her laptop. They were still sitting there, moping, when Mallory came out of his office again.

"The Governor's coming over," he said.

Mallory went back in his office. Altro saw him take the Bluetooth out of his ear and put it in a desk drawer. Then he put a phone in the drawer and closed it. The phone wasn't his state-issued BlackBerry, the device all state employees used for official business. On a state-issued BlackBerry, every call was logged. Every keystroke was recorded.

She stared at Mallory, thinking again about Task Force information being leaked. He stood up, put on his cheap suit jacket and straightened his tie, ran a hand over his ten dollar haircut. When he looked out and saw Altro staring at him, he blushed.

The commotion in the office started again. Everyone closed their laptops. Doolee got up and went into the break room. Sammy took his feet down from his desk. The Princess got up and ran to the bathroom to tinkle and primp for the royal visit.

Altro didn't know how she did it, but Jessica timed it just right again. She came out of the bathroom and smiled as she swiped her card to open the door. It was like she'd heard an inner buzzer announcing the arrival. Jessica was chattering away when she led Governor Listrom into the Team Room, with the Governor's male aide tight on their heels. Altro stood up and straightened her shoulders.

As Listrom made the rounds, introducing herself and shaking hands, Altro could see why Mallory seemed to be so taken with her. Her light gray knit suit fit her just right, just tight enough to reveal the curves without being showy. The blouse she wore had ruffles up the front, and the tall heels of her shoes made her long legs look even longer.

The Princess almost exploded with excitement. Sammy looked shy, and eyed the Governor's legs whenever she wasn't looking at him. Doolee grinned his widest grin and shook her hand with both of his. Mallory stood off to the side and fidgeted, straightening his tie and running a hand over his hair.

When the Governor got to Altro, she didn't hold out her hand.

"How are you doing, Altro?"

"I'm good," she said.

Governor Listrom nodded, then turned to Mallory. "Is there someplace we can talk, Bill?"

Mallory straightened his tie again and pointed to the break room. "Of course, ma'am."

She put one hand on his shoulder. "In private."

Mallory blushed crimson, then led Listrom into his office. She closed the door and Mallory pulled the blinds, but was so clumsy he didn't get them all the way closed. Altro stepped over and watched them through the slits left between the slats of the blinds. They both took a seat, Mallory behind his desk, the Governor in front of it.

Altro watched the back and forth between them. Governor Listrom asking questions, and Mallory answering. Altro couldn't hear what they were saying, but she could pick up the tone of voice. The Governor was intense, leaning forward and using choppy hand movements. Mallory sat erect and rigid, his face unreadable, as he answered her questions.

When the Governor was finished, Mallory talked to her for ten minutes, still rigid, his voice too low to be heard. He opened a drawer on his desk, pulled out the phone and Bluetooth headset he'd stashed in there earlier, and put them on the desk. Mallory talked another ten minutes, gesturing at the phone as he did.

Governor Listrom seemed to relax. She sat back in her chair, crossed her legs and smiled as she talked. Mallory fussed with his tie. Then the two of them leaned in and talked for another five minutes. Mallory did most of the talking, though, and the Governor did a lot of nodding.

At the end of this conversation, Mallory and Governor Listrom stood, nodding at one another. Listrom stepped up to Bill Mallory, took his hand and held it in both of hers. She was smiling awfully big at him. His ears glowed as he smiled back.

"What are they talking about, Ms. Altro?" Jessica whispered.

Altro jumped and waved a hand at Jessica as she backed away. Mallory and Governor Listrom were on their way to the door. When they came out, Altro and Jessica were standing in the middle of the Team Room, trying to look innocent. Mallory pointed to the break room.

"The Governor wants to talk to us all now."

They took their seats, and Doolee insisted on pouring the Governor a cup of his mind-jolting coffee. To her credit, Karen Listrom didn't bat an eye when she took a sip. She looked up at the cameras that were still installed in the corners.

"Are those on?"

"No, ma'am," Mallory said.

"Well they should be. There should be a record of this."

Sammy got up.

"Turn them on and come back in, Sam," Listrom said. "I want everybody to hear this."

Sammy smiled and left. The governor took another sip of the coffee. When Sammy returned, she looked up at the cameras and got down to business.

"I'm here about Martin Woodley. The Attorney General called me and told me you were trying to access Woodley's records. He was quite panicked."

Everyone just sat there. The Governor smiled.

"You all know who Martin is, of course, but there are details you may not know." She nodded Mallory's way. "Bill's already been informed, but I could tell from the Attorney General's demeanor that not all of you have been."

Mallory nodded, and Listrom continued.

"This task force was not Martin Woodley's creation, but he's been an immense help in getting it off the ground. The State is keeping a close rein on funds right now, and the federal budget is in sad shape. To get this going in the short time frame we had in mind was impossible."

Everyone sat like statues.

"Woodley's organization, Free America, came to the rescue," Listrom said. "This building is the property of Free America, and the money to renovate it came from them. The office itself. The phones. The computers. The desks. All of it."

She took another sip of coffee.

"Woodley's been a strong supporter of mine in Washington, and through his contacts with various defense corporations, he's helped me bring hundreds of jobs to Michigan. Not waitresses and busboys, mind you, but high-paying jobs with benefits."

Listrom paused, and looked everyone in the eye, one at a time. When she got to Mallory, he nodded to her, and she kept her eyes locked on him as she spoke.

"As I said, Martin Woodley has been invaluable, to me and to this task force. For this reason, he's been kept in the loop on your organization and progress from the beginning."

Mallory nodded at her again, and the Governor turned her gaze to Altro.

"Now, you may think I'm here to tell you to leave Woodley alone."

Her gray eyes probed Altro from behind the designer glasses.

"I'm not. But Martin Woodley is a citizen of the United States, and has to be treated as such. You don't have to give him preferential treatment, but understand that everything you do must be solidly within the framework of the law. An old newspaper article just isn't enough to go on."

The governor finished her coffee. "Damn, that's good." She turned to her aide. "Matthew, find out how to make this."

And with that, Governor Listrom left, her aide following with his BlackBerry held to his ear.

Chapter 53

When the Governor left, Mallory retreated to his office and closed the door. Everyone else went to their desks and pretended to work. It wasn't long before they gave up the act.

Sammy put his feet up on the desk, put his laptop on his legs and stared at the screen. Doolee muttered to himself in a language Altro couldn't understand. Princess Jessica stared at the door to Mallory's office.

Altro sat and pondered what the Governor said and how she said it, going over every word and nuance. She thought about the private meeting between her and Mallory, him pulling that phone from a desk drawer and sitting rigid as he talked. The way Listrom smiled at him after that. As Listrom was talking to them, she looked to Mallory a couple of times and waited for his nod to continue.

What was up with that?

She was yanked out of her thoughts when SAC Bowman walked into the Team Room.

This moron has access to the Team Center?

Another man came in behind him, a nerdy looking guy who looked like he was fresh out of college.

"I brought our facial composite expert," Bowman said. "Bartley here works in our technical department. We need to work on the composite of this Colonel Nguy."

She shook her head. Colonel Nguy was a nice man, except for his needles, and she didn't want the FBI hounding him.

"I'm busy, Feeeeeelix."

Mallory slumped out of his office, and Altro noticed that the Bluetooth headpiece wasn't in his ear. Mallory nodded to Bowman, pushed his glasses back up on his nose, then faced her. He had that completely unreadable expression on his face again.

"Take care of it, Altro."

She gave him her best glare, the one that almost always made people back down. It didn't work. Mallory just stood there and waited her out. They ended up in the break room.

Altro sat next to Bartley, so she could watch what he was doing on his laptop. Bowman sat at the head of the table, gloating over her downfall. He took a sip of Doolee's coffee, made a sour face and pushed the cup away. Altro tuned the asshole out and watched Bartley work.

The kid was good. He started with a shot from the hospital security camera and worked from there. The surgical mask was taken away, then he put in the lower part of the face, with an Asian mouth and nose. Bartley looked at Altro and raised his eyebrows.

"The mouth is wider," she said.

"We still haven't found the round you fired at Michaels at the drugstore," Bowman said. "The Evidence Response Team is still looking for it."

She ignored him, and pointed at the laptop screen. "The lips are a little thinner, and the nose... just a tad wider."

Bartley worked for a while, then turned to Altro again. It was getting close, and she really didn't know if she wanted it to be any closer. Bowman spoke up.

"I watched the security video from the drugstore, Ms. Altro. Your weapon control was lousy, what we professionals call limp wrist syndrome. It's one of the many reasons I've never approved of amateurs carrying sidearms."

She was getting steamed, but went back to the laptop screen. The chin was a little too narrow on the composite. Colonel Nguy was a block of granite.

"Widen up the chin, and no jowls. Suck in the cheeks. This guy was in good shape."

Altro resisted the urge to stand up and pace the room, drummed her fingers on the table instead. Bartley worked quietly for another ten minutes, then turned the screen her way. Shit. It was the Colonel.

"That's him, Bartley."

Bartley smiled at her and folded up his laptop, then shoved it in the case.

"Now that wasn't so hard, was it?" Bowman asked. "It's quite evident that you were favorably impressed with the kidnappers, Ms. Altro. I still think you should see one of our Psychological Evaluation people. You're obviously not stable."

That was it. She stood up, put her hands on her hips, and went after him.

"You're an asshole, Feeeeeelix," she said. "I know it," She pointed to Bartley. "He knows it." She waved her hands in the air. "Hell, everybody knows it but you. Why do you suppose you don't know it?"

Bowman was on his feet, red in the face, smoke pouring out of his ears. Altro grinned at him. Her death's head grin, all teeth and flat eyes.

"You know what, Feeeeeelix? I think you're too goddamn stupid to know you're an asshole."

Bowman stormed out of the room. Bartley watched him go, turned to Altro and smiled again. He gave her a thumbs up.

"Nice," he said, then followed Bowman out the door.

The Team Room was empty when Altro walked out of the break room. Mallory's office was closed up and the lights were out. Everybody had gone home. She sat down at her desk and started locking up for the night, then heard the bathroom door open.

The Princess walked out of the bathroom, looking like she'd been in there primping and preening for an hour. Her blonde hair was immaculate and she'd freshened her already perfect makeup. The young woman pushed her chair over to Altro's desk, sat down in it and smoothed her skirt.

She was wearing a pale lavender silk blouse and a light gray skirt that was a bit too short and tight by Altro's standards, but certainly looked good on Jessica. Lavender stones hung on delicate gold chains from studs that pierced her perfect ear lobes.

The gold bracelet on her right wrist had stones mounted on it that matched the earrings.

"Ms. Altro?"

The young woman pressed her knees together as she leaned forward in the chair. Altro could smell her perfume. She looked down the young woman's legs to the gray pumps that matched the skirt.

"This must have been so rough on you, Ms. Altro. I mean the shooting... being kidnapped... all of it."

Almost knowing what this was about, and not really ready for it, she just nodded her head and kept her expression as neutral as possible. Jessica's perfect breasts rose and fell while she took a deep breath. Then she continued.

"I thought you might not want to be alone. You know? After all that? If you want, I could come over to your place. Just to give you some company, somebody to talk to?"

Jessica reached out a hand and touched Altro lightly on her shoulder, just the fingertips. Altro flinched at the physical contact and the young woman quickly pulled her hand back. Altro shook her head emphatically.

"No. I'm good, Princess."

Jessica drooped her head.

"Sorry, Ms. Altro. I didn't mean to... I just meant... "

Her words trailed off and it was a few moments before she raised her head again. Altro was a bit shocked to see tears in Jessica's eyes.

"I don't know what I meant, Ms. Altro. You're always so strong, and I'm such a ditz."

"Don't worry about it, Princess."

The young woman pushed her chair back and drew her feet up, preparing to flee. It definitely wasn't in Altro's character to tread lightly but, for reasons she didn't quite understand, she didn't want to hurt her.

"Wait, Jessica."

She scooted her chair over closer to Jessica's and leaned in toward her. "Listen to me. You're not a ditz."

She forced herself to reach out and take Jessica's hand. "You're an intelligent woman, Princess, and we need you here." She took a deep breath and said it. "I need you here."

Jessica had a sad smile on her face as she shook her head, so Altro tried harder. "Look, Jessica, I'm sorry I haven't been nicer to you. Okay? I'm sorry I keep calling you Princess. It's just that…"

It's just that you're so damn pretty! You're like a fairy tale princess to me.

Those were words that couldn't be said, however, so Altro just shook her head. Jessica squeezed her hand and Altro slipped hers away from the tender grip. The young woman looked at her, captured her eyes.

"You really like Michaels, don't you, Ms. Altro?"

"The man saved my life, Jessica."

Jessica shook her head. "I think it's more than that. I feel like you and he really connected."

"No, Princess. It was nothing like that. Nothing physical."

She realized then what she'd just said, that she'd denied the bond between her and John Michaels using terms she'd come to judge all human relationships by. Physical affairs were the only kind she had ventured into for more than ten years.

She struggled for a few moments to straighten it out in her mind so she could put it into words. But it was impossible for her to vocalize the way her spirit had come together with his. There was just no way to convey the way his warmth had flooded into her. Yes, she had thought of him in physical terms. She couldn't help herself. He was unlike any man she had met.

But it was so much more than that, so much deeper. The way their hearts had joined together was beyond physical. She could only describe it as spiritual. No man… no person had ever touched her the way he had.

Teri Altro opened her mouth, but she didn't say anything, just shook her head. Jessica was still staring into her eyes. Altro stood quickly to avoid the gaze.

"I need my space right now," Altro said. "Can you understand that?"

After a few moments, Jessica stood and faced her. They were close, too close for Altro's comfort. Jessica's perfume was making it difficult to think. She stepped back and looked up at the young woman, who was at least six inches taller than her.

"Look, Jessica, I appreciate your offer. Really, I do."

The two of them walked out together in silence, waved back at the deputies in the parking lot. When they got to their cars, Jessica spoke softly.

"I like it when you call me Princess. It makes me feel special."

It was the corniest thing she'd ever heard anyone say, but it touched Teri Altro in the same way being with Walker's family had. She hurriedly got in the ugly rental and slammed the door. As she drove away, Jessica was still standing by her own car, watching. The Princess.

Chapter 54

Teri Altro opened herself to John Michaels, and he poured himself into her. She absorbed him like thirsty soil, then sent her own heart eagerly to his.

A kaleidoscope of sensations filled her. Visions of childhood… aromas of cooking… the sound of voices… the warm closeness of friends and loved ones. The memories of their two very different lives, in snapshots and sound bites, mixed together and blended to form a beautifully cluttered collage. But at the fringe of this peaceful disorder was an icy darkness that belonged to him, and him alone. She reached for it, wanting to see it clearly, needing to know the secret it held.

The alarm jarred her and she groaned at its intrusion. Usually she was eager to get to work, but this morning she hit the snooze several times in an unsuccessful effort to return to the dream. She finally had to admit defeat, and dragged herself from beneath the covers.

After her shower, she stared at the ivory tile that Michaels had given her. She'd left it on the bed stand while she showered, and missed its warmth already. It was hanging from her neck and lying between her breasts without her even thinking about it.

When she began dressing, she smiled at herself in the mirror. She didn't feel at all like her normal self today, and had put on her sexiest black bra and panties. Turning sideways to the mirror, she arched her back, went up on her toes and threw her arms up in gymnast's dismount pose. Her butt still looked pretty damn good.

Wouldn't Sammy just shit?

The ivory tile didn't feel right, though. Altro knew she would want to touch its shape during the day, and she didn't want to be poking a hand between her breasts at work. She tied an extra knot in the back of the leather thong to make it shorter.

There. It sat higher, so she could touch its shape under her blouse without drawing too much attention. She smiled at herself in the mirror again.

A few minutes later, the smile turned into a frown. She buttoned the top button of her starched white cotton blouse, covering the proof of the changes occurring inside her... the lacy black bra and the ivory tile she wasn't going to put back in the drawer today. As she pulled on the business jacket that completed her disguise, she scowled at the two women she saw there.

It was a precarious position she was in, teetering on a knife's edge between the woman she had become and the woman who now struggled to break free. She wondered if the two could exist together, or if this new woman could carry on in place of the old one. The new Teri Altro forced herself to the forefront, even now, and her thoughts drifted.

The ivory tile was warm. The aroma of wood smoke came to her. She could see the laugh lines in John Michaels' face, could hear the even, mature timbre of his voice. He held her hand and the glow of his warmth spread through her. She hugged herself and swayed back and forth like she was dancing.

Her eyes had closed, and she snapped them back open.

Special Investigator Terry Altro took a deep breath and picked up the heavy black shoulder bag that held what had become the sum total of her life. Her credentials, her BlackBerry and her gun.

Chapter 55

Andrea Shellers was sipping her morning coffee and munching a piece of toast with butter and honey. She was wearing her favorite slacks and blouse, her favorite earrings, and drinking her favorite coffee.

Voices were approaching the kitchen, speaking what she now recognized as Hmong. It was Ka and Bao. The bubbling music of the women's voices made her smile.

She had talked to Ka about Bao, was trying to accept her, but she still dreaded contact with the girl. Ka had told her that Bao was "of the Old Ones", descended from what some people thought were the original Hmong.

Andrea had been startled to learn that some scholars thought the Hmong were actually one of the Lost Tribes of Israel, that all Hmong had at one time possessed the light hair and blue eyes that added to Bao's breathtaking beauty. Being a Christian and a bit of a Bible scholar, Andrea had been captivated as Ka related Hmong folklore of the people migrating eastward to Mongolia, then down into China. Ka told her of how the Chinese tried to wipe out the Hmong, due to their refusal to be ruled, how the light hair and eyes made the Hmong easy to pick out among the people they mingled with. The old woman, John's adoptive mother, had a "story quilt" that showed the entire saga, according to Ka.

In her usual joyful manner, Ka bustled in, smiling and chattering to Bao. She was carrying Choua who, by circumstance, was now her younger brother. Bao followed Ka, her blue eyes radiant against her dusky skin. Ka smiled at Andrea and it warmed her. But young Bao ducked her head and went quiet when she saw Andrea. Filling the silence, Ka greeted Andrea.

"Andrea, you look so nice this morning. I love that blouse."

She turned and chattered to Bao, who smiled tentatively at Andrea, then ducked her head again. Ka spoke to the girl again and, at this, Bao walked to Andrea and touched her arm. The girl spoke in Hmong to Andrea, then turned to Ka expectantly.

Ka interpreted. "Bao says she loves your earrings," she said. "You really do have such nice things, Andrea."

Andrea knew her presence made the young girl uncomfortable and she felt a twinge of guilt. It was obvious that Ka was trying to help Andrea grow in her relationship with John's family, but it was hard for her. She touched one of the earrings and smiled at Bao, doing her best, which gave Ka encouragement. Ka moved toward Andrea, and held Choua out for Andrea to see him. The child was beautiful, with his mother's light hair and blue eyes.

"You haven't really met Choua Andrea. Choua is a Hmong name, of course. It means Wind. Father says Choua is the wind of the family's future."

Andrea smiled dutifully. Then Ka held the boy out further.

"Would you like to hold him?"

Trying to hold her emotions in check, Andrea took the child and cradled him. He was wide awake, staring into her eyes unblinking. The whites of his eyes were like robins' eggs. He reached out toward her face with his baby's hand, and Andrea lowered her head to the child so he could touch her. He was so soft and so warm.

"He's beautiful."

Chapter 56

Altro was late for the second day in a row, but she really didn't care.

The dealership left a message the previous afternoon that her XLR was ready, so she drove the ugly rental over to pick it up. It took forever for the idiots at the dealership to get everything done. They fumbled around with the simplest paperwork and insisted on washing her car before she took delivery.

Any other day, Altro would have been pacing with her hands on her hips and chewing ass. Today, she sat quietly in the waiting room, fingering the shape of the ivory tile beneath her blouse and tuning out the special broadcast on television. Martin Woodley again.

When the car was ready, a woman had to call her name twice before she could get her attention. She didn't even walk around the vehicle to make sure everything was back to normal, just got in, started it up and headed for work in a daze.

She should have been elated to have her baby back in one piece. It was a beautiful day, sunny and warm, a rarity for April in Michigan. She should have put the top down and enjoyed the commute to work. But she was distracted by the warmth of the ivory tile lying atop her breasts, lost in her thoughts of the man who had given it to her.

As she drove up US 127, a semi blew past her, and she looked down at the speedometer. 50 miles per hour on the interstate. She tried to concentrate on her driving, but still missed the turnoff on I-96. That meant continuing on to I-496, taking it through Lansing, then back down I-69. It was a miracle she made it to the Team Center without hitting anything.

It was almost ten when she walked in the door. Mallory was hiding in his office again, but the rest of the team was seated at their desks, staring at the flat-screen display on the wall. Dead in the water. The picture of Martin Woodley and Khun Pao reviewing the drug lord's troops was up on the screen. Woodley was smiling. The Drug Intervention Task Force wasn't. They looked defeated.

Altro got a coffee, sat down and put a hand to her blouse so she could feel the shape of the tile. Everybody else continued glaring at Woodley's smiling face until Doolee waved an arm at the screen.

"Sammy, who are the two white men in back?" he asked. " Zoom in, please."

At the top of the picture, almost completely out of the scene, stood two white men. They were wearing uniforms and aviator sunglasses. A red square appeared around them, then their image enlarged to take over the entire screen, pixilated and unrecognizable. Sammy worked at the keyboard and the image cleared up, but was still pixilated. The Princess gave a little squeal and started working at her laptop.

Mallory came out of his office with his coffee cup, talking into the Bluetooth headset he was wearing. He went into the break room for a few minutes, then came out with a cup of Doolee's energy potion. He looked at the screen and stopped in his tracks, then stepped up closer to the screen and peered at it.

"It's Brain and Sledge," Mallory said. "The two spooks who were there when Walker disappeared in Vietnam."

"You sure about that, sir?" Sammy asked. "This picture sucks."

Mallory nodded, then pushed his glasses back up on his nose. "No name tags, no unit insignia, no rank. Aviator sunglasses. It's them, all right. Fucking spooks."

Just then a phone in Mallory's pocket trilled. He started back to his office and touched a hand to the headset to answer. Altro stared at him as he closed the door.

She was certain that Mallory was using the same phone he'd hidden in his drawer when Governor Listrom came by. Altro's suspicion that Mallory was leaking information kept nagging at her, but when he'd shown the phone to the Governor, she'd seemed pleased.

"Ms. Altro! Ms. Altro!"

The Princess was sitting up in her chair like a schoolgirl, waving her hand in the air and waiting to be acknowledged. Altro sighed and nodded at her. Jessica worked at her laptop, and Altro fingered the ivory tile beneath her blouse while she waited. Finally, the Princess pointed a perfectly manicured finger at the flat-screen on the wall.

The screen was now split. On one side was the picture of the two men who accompanied Martin Woodley while he reviewed Khun Pao's troops. On the other side was the picture of the two men who'd caused a disturbance in the hospital lobby.

"The older picture's still pretty bad, so I can't be sure, but don't you think these men look alike?" Jessica said.

Altro stood up and stepped closer to the flat-screen. There *was* a resemblance. In both pictures, one was tall and lean, the other shorter and pudgy. In the older picture, the shorter man looked like he was just beginning to show some premature baldness. Sammy raised his eyes from Altro's butt just as she turned to him.

"We gave their pictures to TSA to try to identify them, right?" Altro asked. "Have we heard anything yet?"

Sam shook his head. Altro stomped a foot and clapped her hands together. "Well, let's get on it!"

Everybody went to work. Altro put her hands on her hips and stared at the flat-screen for a few minutes. Then she turned to Jessica, who had the landline phone cradled against her head and was working on her laptop at the same time. When Jessica looked her way, Altro gave her a thumbs up and mouthed the words. "Good work, Princess."

When the young woman beamed at her, Teri Altro actually smiled back and her ears burned. She scowled at herself as she sat down.

Chapter 57

The members of Kerr-Newman decided to drive, so they rented an SUV big enough to hold them and their gear. They jumped on the Chicago Skyway and took it to I-94 just outside Gary, Indiana. That was slow going, but as soon as they got past the acrid pall of Gary, the traffic thinned out and they made good time.

They checked into their rooms at the Lexington, just outside the Lansing city limits on I-496. Not long after they were settled, Keenan called them into his room. Information was coming in fast. Kerr-Newman usually gathered their own mission information but, in this case, material was being fed to him from two unlikely sources, sources from Keenan's days in Special Forces.

Possum and Buzzard.

Keenan had a map of Lansing spread out on the table, with an arrow pointing to the location of Tommy Mo's Winged Lion.

"So who's this Tommy Mo character, chief?" Geena grumbled.

Geena had her hair in a ponytail this morning, and was flipping it with one hand. When she did that, it always reminded Keenan of a cat ready to pounce. She was leaning over the table with her weight on one elbow, and Keenan could see down the front of her scoop-necked black sweater just fine. He forced his eyes back to the map and answered.

"I'm not sure yet, but I know he's got some muscle in on this."

Prentiss' drawl broke in.

"We're gonna talk to this guy before we deliver him, ain't we, Chief? I still don't like turnin' him over."

"We already talked about that, Prentiss. Nothing's changed."

Keenan moved quickly to cut off any further discussion.

"Asa, you and Prentiss will back up Geena."

He turned to Geena, glad she had stood up straight. He didn't want to be distracted right now.

"You get to have some fun, Geena. I want you to waltz into the Winged Lion. Scope it out. Check out this Tommy Mo's balls, see if he has any."

Geena smiled and placed her hand on his shoulder, pressed her right breast into his arm and batted her eyes. "Ooh baby, you are too fuckin' good to me."

Okay. So much for not being distracted.

"Get everything you can from him," Keenan said. "But what we really want is any information he has on our quarry, Walker."

Chapter 58

Altro was pacing the floor of the Team Room again.

"Sammy? How's it going?"

The only response Sammy gave her was a wave of his left hand. She looked over at Jessica, who was busy at her laptop, then turned to Doolee. He wasn't grinning, for once, but shook his head and placed an index finger to his lips.

Sammy's feet weren't on his desk. He'd been hunched over his laptop for hours, banging keys and rubbing his mouse pad. Jessica had been multi-tasking, talking on the phone, while working her laptop, and occasionally exchanging some kind of esoteric computer jargon with Sammy.

Altro had sent Doolee out to get some lunch for everybody more than an hour ago. She and Doolee ate while Sam and Jessica toiled away. The Mickey D's bag and chocolate shake still sat untouched on the corner of Sam's desk. Jessica's salad was unopened on hers.

Altro continued pacing with her hands on her hips, but Sam didn't even raise his eyes to eyeball her butt. He still didn't react when she stopped in front of his desk and tapped her foot. She caught herself thinking about arching her back and throwing back her shoulders.

Give him a good shot of that tight gymnast butt you've worked so hard on, Altro. That'll get his attention.

But, no. Shaking her head, she sat back down and drummed her fingers on the desk. It was the loudest noise in the room when Sammy erupted.

"Gotcha!"

Jessica squealed like a little girl and pumped a delicate fist in the air. She grinned over at Sammy. "We got him, Sammy! Woo hoo!"

Woo hoo?

The two grinned at each other for a few seconds, then Sammy jumped to his feet and rushed into the bathroom. Jessica opened her salad and started eating it. The Princess was smiling so big that Altro wondered how she could chew.

When Sam returned, he tore open the bag on the corner of his desk and dug into the quarter-pounder, swallowed half of the fries without chewing and drank off half of the shake. He patted his belly and burped loudly, then looked over at Altro. She gaped at him, amazed that a man so small could consume so much food in such a short time.

The Princess giggled at Sammy's burp, then got up to go tinkle. Altro watched the sway of those perfect hips, then drummed her fingers on the desk while they waited for Jessica to return. When she came back, Sammy burped again, then turned to Altro.

"We got him, Altro. You wanna see?"

He didn't wait for an answer, but wiped his hands on his shirt and punched at his keyboard with outright glee. A picture of Martin Woodley came up on the flat-screen, the one of Woodley with Khun Pao and the two spooks from Mallory's tale. The picture shrank and retreated to a corner. A newspaper article, obviously from microfiche converted to digital, now took up the rest of the screen. *The Washington Post.* Sammy took a laser pointer from a pocket and pointed to the article.

"Okay, let's start at the beginning. This article explains what Woodley was doing in Southeast Asia. He was heading a Congressional Oversight Commission on CIA funding of the Hmong insurgency against the North Vietnamese. There were rumors the CIA was using the money from heroin sales to fund everything, but nothing was ever proven."

He pointed the laser at the picture, caressed his mouse pad and hit some keys. The picture zoomed in on the two men in aviator sunglasses. It was much clearer than it had been before, and Altro wondered what he'd done to clean it up so much.

"Now back to these two guys. Jessica ran a program on it to compress it and clear it up. It's a mathematical function, kind of the reverse of when you make a JPG file. Not foolproof, but it worked on this one."

Altro had the just slimmest idea what he was talking about and shot a look over at Jessica. *The Princess did that?* Then she waved a hand at Sam to get on with it. He worked at his laptop again and the rest of the screen changed to two airport security photos. It was definitely the two men from the hospital.

"They flew into Detroit the night of the drugstore shootout, then rented a car and drove over to Lansing. They were booked at the Radisson, but they checked out yesterday."

Sam directed the laser at their names, Wallace Ryan and Theodore Sallison.

"It's Wally and the Beaver," Sam said. "From *Leave it to Beaver*?"

Nobody got it, but Sammy didn't care. He was rolling now. Altro could hear keys clacking as he worked furiously at his laptop. The screen changed to a credit card record. "They paid for their tickets, the rental car and rooms with this card."

Altro stood up and interrupted him. "What about their phones, Sammy? Can you track their location by their phones?"

The Princess piped up, without raising her hand and waiting for permission. "Wallace Ryan received several calls from a number that's registered to Martin Woodley, Ms. Altro."

Altro stomped a foot. "Can you track their location by the phones?"

Jessica pouted for a few seconds before she answered. "I should be able to, Ms. Altro, but there's no signal. They must have turned them off or dumped them."

Altro put her hands on her hips and tapped her foot. Now that his marathon work session was over, Sammy was checking out her butt again, but she let it go. She pointed a finger at Jessica.

"Okay, Princess. Get all the information and their pictures to the Sheriff's Department and the Lansing Police. Have them picked up."

Jessica sighed. "I already did that, Ms. Altro. I sent everything to the State Police too. They said they'd distribute it to Ann Arbor and Washtenaw County."

"Okay. Let's get everything to the DEA and FBI. I want these guys brought in."

She looked at Doolee, who was already making the call. Then she turned to Sam, expecting to catch him in the act of checking out her butt, but he was on the phone, too.

"Good work, you two. Damn good work. Make sure everything gets posted to the case file."

Altro plopped back into her chair and started fingering the tile beneath her blouse again. There was no doubt in her mind. The two men Mallory called Brain and Sledge had come to Lansing to kill Walker, the man who saved her life. These men were definitely tied to Martin Woodley, and were also tied to Khun Pao. It was all knotted together.

Now the Army was trying to hunt Walker down, too. Captain Lafferty called Walker a deserter, damaged goods, but the man she'd met couldn't be a deserter. He was a man of honor, had told her honor is the only thing left in the end.

And the Army's hunt for Walker started with Steadley, Mallory's Commanding Officer in Vietnam, who associated with Brain and Sledge. Steadley was part of this too, somehow. The Army didn't want to take Walker in as a deserter. They wanted to kill him.

She couldn't let this happen. She had to do something. There had to be some way to warn him. A glance at her watch showed that it was past two o'clock.

"I've got to get out of here." She locked up her desk and put her laptop in its case. Jessica stood when she did. "I'll go with you, Ms. Altro."

Altro shook her head at her. "No, Princess."

Sammy and Doolee stood up then, and it made her sigh.

"You will look for him, Altro?" Doolee asked. "We will come. We can help."

She shook her head. "I need you here. I want this all put together — flow charts, timelines, and any conclusions in a wrap up. Make it tight. Maybe we can nail Woodley."

She hefted up the laptop case and her shoulder bag, pushed the straps back and put her hands on her hips. It drew her blouse tight over her chest, but she didn't have time to worry about workplace impressions. *Go ahead, Sammy. Take a good look.*

She looked over at Mallory's office. "Don't tell Mallory anything," she said.

The first thing she did when she got in her XLR was disassemble her BlackBerry, the way Colonel Nguy had left it on her nightstand. If she did find Walker, she didn't want the location pinpointed by the GPS of the device.

Chapter 59

Mallory walked out of his office just as Altro was leaving. Everyone else was standing at their desks, watching her go. She didn't turn around to acknowledge him, just walked out the door.

"What's going on?" he asked.

They all stared at him, trying to figure out whether or not to tell him. He looked at the flat-screen and saw the record for a credit card on the display.

"What are you people working on?"

Nobody said anything, so he stepped up to the display, saw the charges for airline tickets, a car rental at the Detroit airport and two rooms at the Radisson in Lansing. When he turned to them, they were still trying to figure out whether to tell him.

Well, it was out now.

"It's Brain and Sledge. Wallace Ryan and Theodore Sallison," he said, then turned to Sam. "Wally and the Beaver."

Sammy's eyes opened wider, and he ran a hand over his hair. Doolee's face went all hang-dog, and he looked down at his feet. Jessica just nodded at him and sat down. Mallory motioned for Sam and Doolee to sit down, then pushed his glasses up on his nose.

"I was an Army Intelligence officer for thirty years, people," he said. "I know a lot of people think that Military Intelligence is an oxymoron, but if you call yourself that long enough, something's bound to rub off."

He smiled at them, but nobody smiled back. They squirmed in their seats and fiddled around to avoid eye contact. Pointing at the screen, he continued. "This was all obtained legally, right?"

"Yes, sir," Jessica said. "TSA gave us the identifications after we sent over the pictures of these two guys at the hospital. We pushed them pretty hard, but it's all legal."

"The credit card records?"

"We got a warrant from the Bureau, sir. It was no problem."

"And it's all in the case file? Everything is documented?"

"Yes, sir."

"Okay."

Mallory hustled back into his office and closed the door. He was already working on the computer when he called SAC Bowman. There was a chance Altro could lead the FBI to a place that would reveal what was going on.

"Drop your tail on Altro," Mallory said. Bowman sputtered his objections, but Mallory interrupted him. "Drop your tail, Feeeeeelix. Now."

Bowman was still talking when Mallory hung up on him. He used his cold phone to call Buzzard.

"Yeah."

"Possum here. Your people still on Altro?"

"You said to keep an eye on her."

"She's on the loose."

"I know. She just left your office building. Hell, Possum, we got her."

Mallory took a deep breath. It was good to be working with professionals.

"Sorry, Buzzard," Mallory said. "Listen up. I told the Feds to drop their tail, but keep your eyes open for them. And you'd better let Keenan know to watch out for Altro too. She could stumble into something that would gum up the whole works."

Chapter 60

The pilot wore night vision goggles and the copilot concentrated on his helmet-mounted heads-up display. Behind them, their avionics specialist concentrated on the mission status displays. They were flying at "nap of the earth" altitude with no flight plan, on a mission to deliver goods to clandestine drop zones in the mountains southeast of the Golden Triangle.

Darby Parker, an American expatriate, was making a series of deliveries into Laos for the Frenchman, Jean Barouquette. Darby had enlisted a French expat as his copilot, the most capable and trusted man he knew, Jean Levoisse Mantelle. Together they decided to bring in a qualified avionics man, another American they knew from other missions like this one. At his request, they'd never learned his full name, but referred to him only as Pete. With a reliable four-man crew for loading and unloading, they took off.

These men were professionals, part of a close-knit group of men who earned their pay living on the edge of disaster, taking on missions that others in the shadow world of smuggling wouldn't touch. They'd been together on more than a few smuggling missions, but none as lucrative as this one. They were earning the bonus of a lifetime for this job.

Their primary cargo was arms, ammunition and other accoutrements of warfare, destined for clients unknown to them. It was made up largely of the ubiquitous AK47 assault rifle, the cheap and reliable weapon of choice for all manner of terrorists, insurrectionists and despots around the world.

They were delivering 300 of the weapons in total, with five fully-loaded magazines for each weapon. They were also delivering mortars and RPGs, again weapons that were readily available and inexpensive. A consignment of binoculars and radios was included, along with a supply of food and fresh water. They were approaching the last of the seven drop sites for the mission. In the back, Pete was calling out their position relative to the drop site as they approached.

"Twelve seconds, Darby. Bank left 30 degrees and climb 200 feet right after the drop. Right after."

Darby didn't reply, just chewed furiously on the stub of cigar in his teeth. Pete moved his microphone away from his mouth and counted down for the loading crew.

"Five, four, three, two, one. Drop! Drop! Drop!"

The loading crew rolled the cargo out the back in seconds.

"Clear! Clear! Clear!"

The plane banked and rose in altitude. There was a stomach-churning lurch and a sickening metallic scraping sound came from the bottom of the plane. Pete was terrified and, therefore, furious.

"God damn you, Darby! I said 200 feet! Jesus fucking Christ, you scraped the fucking trees!"

Darby couldn't answer. He was choking on the cigar stub he'd almost swallowed. He waved to Levoisse to take the stick, leaned over and puked the cigar into a bucket strapped to his seat for the occasion. It wasn't the first time tonight he'd used it.

Chapter 61

Altro drove aimlessly around Lansing, not really knowing what she was looking for, only knowing she had to warn Walker somehow.

Three blocks east of Sparrow Hospital, she saw a group of Asian men standing in front of an apartment building, talking and smoking. She slowed to a crawl, then stopped at the curb and buzzed down the passenger side window. They all turned and leaned down to look her over and, when she pulled the ivory tile from its hiding place and held it up, they gathered around the car. Several of them bowed deeply, and she lowered the driver's side window to talk to them.

"I need to find him," she said. She held the tile up again. "He's in danger."

They talked among themselves in their own language. One of them pulled a cell phone and walked out into the street as he talked into it. After a brief conversation on the phone, he said something to the others. The men started moving away. Altro opened her door and got out, waving her arms and pleading. At that, they split up and scattered like a flock of startled birds. When she shouted for them to stop, it only made them move faster. She stomped a foot in frustration, got back in her car and pulled away.

She continued cruising the neighborhood, more on impulse than logical thought. There were a number of Asian businesses in the area, nail salons and restaurants, feng shui shops and dry cleaners. A few blocks from the apartment building, she ran across a bar with a sign that read "Tommy Mo's Winged Lion." She pulled into a parking space across the street.

As she sat watching the place, she heard the sound of spiked heels clacking on the sidewalk. A dark-haired woman came up the sidewalk from behind the car, then crossed the street in front of her. Altro caught a whiff of musky perfume. The woman was wearing a very short black skirt and a skin tight black sweater with a deeply scooped neckline. The muscles in her legs rippled and her breasts had just the right bounce as she paraded across the street. In front of the bar, she stopped to adjust her clothing, then wiggled her way through the door.

Altro sighed. *These aren't his kind of people. He's a family man.* Then she swore and banged the steering wheel. The tires of the XLR squawked when she gunned it away from the curb.

*****

The bar fell dead silent when Geena strutted in, but quickly resumed its regular level of noise, with a twist. A whistle here and a "Hey baby" there were added to the usual patter of vulgar conversation. Geena leaned forward on the barstool and twisted just a bit, causing her skirt to rise even higher, almost enough to reveal a cheek. She grinned at the tiny barmaid, and ordered a beer. This was her kind of place, her kind of people, her kind of attention.

Asa and Prentiss came in and took a booth, completely unnoticed.

When she was handed her beer, she turned on the stool to face the crowd. She stuck her tongue into the top of the beer and withdrew it, but let it dangle out of her mouth with the tip covered in foam for a few seconds. She searched the crowd for Tommy Mo, found him immediately, a well-dressed Asian sitting in a booth near the back, talking in the ear of a huge Asian man. She looked Tommy Mo in the eye and raised one leg up, placing her spiked heeled on the upper ring of the barstool, giving him a good look.

The big Asian slithered up to Geena, lion tattoos proudly displayed on his forearms, and gestured toward Tommy Mo with a turn of his head. He was a scary looking guy, with snake-like

269

eyes, but Geena didn't mind scary. She didn't obey, but dipped her tongue back into the beer, drawing out the tease.

Tommy Mo smiled, rose from the booth and sauntered up to where Geena waited, smiling his "man in charge" smile.

"Welcome to the Winged Lion, Miss. I am Tommy Mo, the owner. Please call me Tommy. All my friends do."

"Hi, Tommy. I'm Geena. My friends call me..." She gave a throaty chuckle. "...well, I guess they call me Geena."

"I would be elated if you would join me, Geena."

She stood down from the barstool, took his arm and let him lead her while she pressed a breast against his arm.

"Is there anything I can do for you, Geena? I haven't seen you here before."

Geena took the seat he offered, let him slide in close and put his arm on the back of the booth to stake his claim before she answered.

"I'm looking for a man."

She saw him raise his eyebrows, and raised hers in return, letting his mind wander, letting him listen to his other head.

"I'm a man, Geena. Your search is over."

He laughed, but not too loudly, still in control. She needed to change that, so she dropped a hand down to his thigh. "Yes, you are *definitely* a man."

She squeezed his thigh and looked him in the eye. "But I'm looking for a *particular* man, Tommy. A man called Walker."

Tommy Mo's eyes went flat. She repeated her request. "A man called Walker."

An hour later, she left a disappointed Tommy Mo with a raging hard-on. She'd stoked him and stroked him until his eyes glazed over. She let him look down the front of her sweater at her unfettered breasts, and watched his tongue run across his lower lip in anticipation. With one leg draped over his thigh, she leaned into him and pushed a hardened nipple against his bicep. She had taken poor Tommy Mo to the edge, then brought him back down with a crash.

Through it all, she'd let him know that her primary goal was to locate the man called Walker. If Tommy was a man, a man with balls of steel — she moaned in his ear that she needed a man with balls of steel — he would help her.

She sashayed out, pleased with herself. Game on.

Chapter 62

In northwestern Laos, a group of men were eating a balanced meal for the first time in too long. Walker had been wise to drop food and fresh water with the weapons, for a hungry army always has difficulty performing up to par.

After eating, they prepared to examine the crates that contained the weaponry. All of the crates were marked with a dragon, the Great Za that was the sign of the Valley Walker. The men began discussing these gifts of freedom and honor, and the fact that the Valley Walker hadn't come himself. There were grumbles of fear from some, grumbles that grew louder until one of the younger men stood and beat his chest as he talked.

"The Valley Walker has sent these gifts for us to help ourselves. We will strike the oppressors who place their boot on our neck."

Murmurs arose around the camp and heads nodded in agreement. Throughout their history, the Hmong had risen up against their oppressors, in response to a messiah sent to lead them. This time it was different. Walker would not lead them, but would give them the means to fight for themselves. The young man was right. They were brave and honorable fighters. They had only lacked the means and inspiration.

Truly inspired now, the men opened the weapons crates with gusto and distributed rifles and ammunition. The mortars and RPGs were given to the older men, for they had the experience from the old days. The radios and satellite telephones were handed to younger men, who would be able to learn how to use them more quickly. The binoculars were dealt to those who would hold the key position of spotting their targets.

And, in one particular crate, destined for one particular group that would raid one particular compound, was something other than weapons. The studio quality video camera, complete with satellite uplink equipment was handled with special care. This equipment would record and transmit the end of the oppression they had lived under for decades.

With the weapons distributed and strength from the food and water building in their bodies, the men now held both the means and the inspiration to fight. This would be the end of Khun Pao.

Chapter 63

Tommy Mo felt like a 16 year old boy, just back from a long, hot date without fulfillment. *God damn!* There were things he had to do, but he was so hard he didn't think he could stand. His favorite girl was standing at the bar, talking on her cell phone. When she finished her conversation she turned and smiled at him, and he motioned for her to join him. She slid in next to him, leaned over and placed her hand on his stomach.

"Mmmm… Tommy, you needing me? That girl, she make you hot? You come me, Tommy. I take care you."

She led him by the hand, back through his office to his apartment.

After… She rolled from on top of him and giggled when she bumped her head on the headboard. Then she sat up in the bed and leaned her head tenderly on his shoulder. He remained leaning against the headboard, absently rubbing the girl's thigh as he reached for a smoke. While he smoked, she pulled tissues from a box on the bed stand and dried him, then herself. It had been a flood.

"Ooh, mon cheri. You beaucoup, Amois."

When he'd finished his smoke, Tommy Mo tipped his favorite girl a hundred dollars, kissed her, and sent her back to work. After a quick shower, he went to his desk and called Brain. Tommy came straight to the point.

"There's someone else here in town looking for Walker. I'm afraid you don't have anything to compete with what they're offering. This is the end of our agreement."

Tommy was prepared for Brain's outburst. He was calm now, serene and in charge again. The threats and cajoling of the man barely registered. His mind was occupied with his conversation with Geena, the woman dressed in black. As Brain rattled on, Tommy only half listened, his mind on Geena's hand rubbing the inside of his thigh as she moaned in his ear. He found himself getting hard again.

Less than an hour later, Nab slithered in with Brain and Sledge. The dung eater's lackeys stood there smiling while Nab sized Tommy up through his cold eyes. The snake held a satellite phone out to Tommy.

"Khun Pao," Nab hissed.

It was the General himself, calling from Laos. *Great Buddha, it was 6:00 a.m. there!* Khun whispered threats against Tommy that made him break into a sweat — threats against his mother, his father and his entire family.

When the call was ended Tommy's hands shook so badly he couldn't light a cigarette. Nab just stared hungrily at Tommy, like he was eyeing a tasty rodent.

Chapter 64

Altro drove by Andrea Shellers' clothing store on the way to her condo, still looking for some thread she could follow. She stopped her XLR in a parking space across the street from the store and stared at it. The clock on the County Courthouse gonged the hour, seven o'clock. As the last of the reverberations died away, she looked around the neighborhood. A Thai restaurant was open on her right, and she was hungry. Take-out sounded easy.

She went inside and ordered Yum Talay, a seafood salad, from a young man at the counter. As she sat at an empty table and waited, she fingered her blouse over the ivory tile. Finally, she pulled it out and looked at the dragon etched on it. She noticed the young man who had taken her order staring at her and raised her head to him. He gave a slight bow. She stood, approached him and held out the tile.

"Do you know this?"

He looked away, and she repeated her question, louder this time, almost too loud. "Do you know this?"

He bowed his head, and she reached across the counter to grab his arm. "I have to contact Walker. Do you know him?"

He pulled away, then scurried around a corner to the back. In a quandary, she stood there, sure the young man had recognized the tile. It was almost ten minutes before he returned, accompanied by an old man who carried a sack. They walked around the counter to the table where she had waited, sat down and motioned for her to join them.

She didn't want to pull her credentials, didn't want to frighten them, so she just sat beside the old man and tried to smile. Her throat was constricted and it was hard for her to talk when she held the tile out again.

"I have to warn him. He's in danger. Please don't be afraid. I would never hurt him." Her voice cracked, but she held on. "He saved my life."

The two talked in their Asian language. The old man reached out and put his hand on her forearm, and the young man spoke.

"You cannot help him, ma'am. He is the Valley Walker. Don't you know this?"

He looked at her and waited for her answer, but she had none.

"You have the tile," he said. "He is the Valley Walker. Don't you know this?"

Customers were entering the restaurant and leaving. A couple was standing at the register, waiting to order or pay, Altro didn't know or care which. The three of them sat in a bubble, apart from the world. The two men, the young and the old, talked to each other again. The old man squeezed her arm, and the young one spoke.

"My father says you should go home. He is right, ma'am."

She looked at the old man and he nodded at her. There was a soft buzzing in her ears when she stood. The old man held out the sack, and the young one spoke.

"Your order, ma'am."

She started to reach in her shoulder bag for her wallet, but the young man shook his head.

"You have the tile. You do not pay."

Chapter 65

Brice Keenan and the rest of Kerr-Newman were gathered in his room again. They had their laptops in front of them, with Altro's picture on their screens. Geena looked so intent on her screen that Keenan leaned over to see what she was doing. She didn't have Altro's picture on her screen, but was watching the video of the drug store shooting.

Prentiss nodded toward his laptop display. "I saw this woman at Tommy Mo's, Chief. She was sittin' in a Caddy across the street, watching the place. You see her, Geena? You walked right by her."

Geena didn't say anything, just nodded slightly. It wasn't like Geena to not have some sarcastic remark ready, so Prentiss waited a few beats. When she still didn't say anything, he continued.

"Where you gettin' this info, Chief?"

Keenan didn't answer the question. "Just keep an eye out for her. She's armed, but I don't think that'll be a problem. She's a civilian."

He put up a picture of Steadley. "This is our employer, General Steadley. He works in the Pentagon."

Asa spoke up, his rasping voice so deep it almost rattled the windows. "What's he want our boy for? And don't tell us it's because he deserted. Straight up, now."

Keenan started spoon feeding them. His people had to be all in on this one. It would mean the end of Kerr-Newman.

"Steadley was Walker's Battalion Commander in Vietnam, but it seems that Walker didn't work for him directly. These guys," He put up the airport security pictures of Brain and Sledge. "These guys were CIA, assigned to tracking the NVA buildup in Cambodia. They were in touch with Steadley at the time, since Steadley's command was on the Cambodian border."

"Are they still CIA?" Asa asked.

"No. They were nudged out at the end of the Vietnam conflict. They still hang on the fringe of the military, though, doing some private stuff in Afghanistan."

"Afghanistan?" Asa said. "There's a lot of heroin coming out of there. Just like Southeast Asia during the Vietnam war."

Keenan nodded. "They're employed by Free America, Martin Woodley's organization," Keenan said. He put Martin Woodley's picture up. "All indications are that they were sent after Walker by Woodley before we were called in. They checked out of their rooms at the Radisson and went dark."

Prentiss' ice blue eyes were brighter than usual when he responded.

"Well, shit fire and save the matches! Martin Woodley, huh?"

Prentiss poured everyone a mug of coffee. Geena was still uncharacteristically quiet, almost subdued. Prentiss spoke again, his walrus moustache twitching and his ice blue eyes looking off into the distance.

"You know, I joined the Army when I was 18. I knew it was part of the job, but I didn't join to kill people. I thought I could do something to make a difference in this fucked up world. That's why I'm working with you guys now."

Everyone leaned back in their chairs and raised their eyebrows. Prentiss took a sip of coffee and continued. "I don't want to do this. I mean, snaggin' somebody who wants to blow up the world is one thing, but this guy's like one of us."

"Not quite, Cornpone. That motherfucker's faster than anything I've ever seen."

Geena had broken her silence. She turned to Keenan, the most intense and sincere look he'd ever seen on her face.

"I gotta meet him, Chief. I gotta."

She looked so much like a little girl that Keenan couldn't resist.

"Don't get your panties all wet now, Geena. This guy's way too old for you. Hell, he's even older than I am."

Geena started to come off her chair and go after Keenan, but Asa saw it coming and pinned her arms from behind. His rattling voice was playful as he held her.

"Hey now, Geena. You know we all love you."

She struggled only a little, then relaxed. Asa let her go. Keenan reached over and squeezed her shoulder, and she patted his hand before she pointedly removed it. After an appropriate time, Keenan asked the question.

"I take it we're all thinking the same thing. We don't want to take this guy in?"

"Fuck no," Geena said. "The whole thing sucks, Chief."

Asa agreed. "This is all about the heroin. Money and power."

Okay. Everyone was on the same page. It was time to bring things out in the open.

"I was kind of wondering, you know, if there's anything we might do to help him out. He's up to something, and it's gotta be good."

There was a soft knock on the door.

Keenan looked through the peephole and saw an Asian man standing outside, holding rolled up sheets of paper. Keenan held a fist in the air, then made a circling motion with his index finger. His three companions drew their weapons and melted away. Keenan opened the door.

"Good evening, sir. I am Colonel Nguy Bo, retired from the People's Army of Vietnam. I am Walker's friend. May I come in?"

Keenan let the man in, then took a step back to give Geena a clear shot.

"Walker sent me to talk to you." Colonel Nguy said. "We were wondering if we could enlist your assistance."

Keenan eyed the rolled up sheets of paper. Nguy nodded, and placed the rolls on the floor.

"You should have one of your associates come out and examine these, so we can talk," Nguy said. "They are maps of the area."

Asa moved from his position in the bathroom, picked up the rolls of paper and looked them over. "Maps, Chief."

Nguy bowed to Asa. "Yes. I would like to show you what Walker has in mind. If I may?"

He reached out slowly and took the rolls from Asa, kept his eyes on Keenan for a second, then moved to the coffee table. He knelt, unrolled one of the maps and spread it on the surface of the table. Prentiss came from the bedroom, tucking his pistol into the back of his pants. He walked up to Nguy and held out his hand.

"I'm Prentiss, Colonel."

Nguy stood, shook his hand and bowed. He then offered his hand to Asa and Keenan in turn. After kneeling again, on one knee now, Colonel Nguy turned back to the map and pointed out a building that was circled in yellow highlighter.

"This is the Winged Lion."

Geena emerged from the bedroom. She held her pistol loose at her side.

"How'd you find us?" she asked.

Nguy stood again, turned to face her and bowed. "My men followed you back from the Winged Lion."

Geena's hand tightened a fraction on her pistol.

Nguy turned to Keenan. "Buzzard said to tell you hello, Mr. Keenan."

Keenan cocked his head. "Did he now?"

"Actually he said things I don't want to repeat in front of a lady."

Keenan chuckled. "Yeah. That sounds more like the old reprobate."

At that, Geena put her weapon away and held out her hand. "I'm Geena, sir."

The Colonel didn't take Geena's hand, but bowed to her. He cleared his throat and pointed to the maps. "Back to the Winged Lion, then. We have a low-light capable, wireless surveillance camera set up on a building across the street. There and at a warehouse of interest."

Keenan nodded.

"We have people who are very talented with computers and electronics." Nguy said. He shrugged. "I'm afraid that my own training has always been in more primitive skills."

Geena nodded and pumped a fist in the air. "Fucking A right," she said. Then she dipped her head and grimaced. "Excuse me, sir. My training has been similar."

"Ah, yes. Your talents are well-known, Geena," Nguy said. "That was good work in the Winged Lion, by the way. Poor Tommy, he is so confused now."

Keenan couldn't believe it, but Geena was blushing. "You saw?" she asked.

"We have someone in place there," Nguy answered. "A waitress who is Tommy Mo's favorite. She recorded everything on her phone."

Geena hung her head. "I was just... Well, my actions had a specific purpose, sir."

"Please, Miss, I don't mean to detract from your tactics. They were very effective."

Instead of railing at Colonel Nguy for calling her "Miss," Geena smiled. "Thank you, sir," she said. "I'm glad you understand."

"In fact," Nguy said. "Walker said he would like to meet you."

Geena looked immensely pleased, like a high school girl who had just made the cheerleading squad. Keenan was perplexed. He looked at Prentiss and Asa, who both raised their eyebrows. They needed to cut to the chase, though, so he pointed to the table.

"Why don't we clear the computers off the table?" he said. "We can spread the maps out there, and you can tell us what you have in mind."

Chapter 66

Altro was sitting at the kitchen counter in the tee-shirt she wore for pajamas, glaring at the smiling image of Woodley on her laptop. She felt a slight tremor in the building. The world shifted, and Walker was there, standing in her kitchen, just across the counter.

He was wearing faded blue jeans and a long-sleeve cotton pullover. He smelled of freshly laundered cotton and wood smoke. She inhaled deeply, reveling in the aroma. He smiled at her and she felt heat in her cheeks.

Teri Altro wished that she hadn't pulled her hair into the lame ponytail. She wished that she'd taken a shower and put on fresh underwear, that she'd worn something else besides this ratty old tee-shirt. Her arms crossed over the swell of her breasts, so obvious beneath the thin white cotton, but he didn't seem to notice what she was wearing. He continued smiling at her, and her face got hotter. Then he spoke.

"Hello, Teri. I hear you've been looking for me."

Her mind shifted gears quickly, and she blurted it out. "There are two men out there looking for you. I can't prove it yet, but I'm sure Woodley sent them."

He nodded his head and held a hand in the air. "I know they're here."

"The Army sent someone too. From General Steadley. He called you damaged goods," she said. "He said you're a deserter and the Army wants to take you in, but I don't believe him."

He just nodded again.

"They'll kill you," she said.

He shook his head. "No, Teri."

Altro stared at him, and he stared back. He was so calm that it warmed her. Her hand went to the shape of the ivory tile beneath the tee-shirt.

"I'm glad you're wearing it," he said.

"You shouldn't have given me this. It must be priceless."

That came out all wrong. She tried again.

"I know the cost doesn't matter to you. You don't have to tell me that. It's just that… Well, it's yours, John."

She'd called him John, and he smiled at that. It made him look younger. "I wanted you to have it."

She smiled back at him. "I'm proud, you know, that you gave it to me."

He smiled wider, and looked even younger. Then his smile vanished and he turned serious. Walker. She tensed up.

"I want to talk to you, Teri."

She gave a sigh of relief. *Good.* She wanted to talk to him too.

"The things I set in motion at the drugstore are coming together," he said.

What? She didn't want to talk about that, about the war he came here to begin. What she wanted to talk about was how warm the ivory tile felt against her skin. She wanted to talk about how she'd felt when he looked inside her, how she felt when she'd been able to see back inside him. She wanted to talk about the oneness she felt with him. Her lip quivered as she started to speak, but he broke in.

"Your team will have a lot of work to do tomorrow night. You should sleep in."

Sleep? She didn't want to sleep. She wanted to talk to him, to touch him and hold his hand and feel his warmth. But he continued talking about those other things, pushing aside her wants.

"Tomorrow, it will all come to a head. In Laos and here."

It took her a few moments to surrender. She took a deep breath.

"What's going to happen?"

"Khun Pao will be destroyed. You'll see it on the news, I'm sure."

"What about here?"

"They'll come after me. Woodley's men. Khun Pao's men. I'll wrap them up and hand them over to you."

The danger seemed very real to her, but he talked like it was nothing to him. Then she thought of how easy it was for him in the drugstore. She had to say it.

"Please don't kill anyone. Not here."

It wasn't the potential victims she was worried about, but the implications their deaths would have for his future.

He was quiet for a while, one of his pauses. "That's important to you."

She lowered her head and nodded stupidly, like a cow. He sighed before he replied.

"You're right. I've done things the old way too long." Another pause. "Do you remember when I told you that honor is all that's left in the end?"

She raised her eyes to him again. His eyes glistened.

"Well, I was wrong," he said. "I've been so driven. So angry."

Altro knew all about being driven. She knew all about being angry. Those two feelings had been her primary motivation for the last ten years. He smiled again, sadly now, as he continued.

"There is friendship. There is love. There is family."

Teri Altro had seen how much his family loved and respected this man. She reached a hand across the counter, wanting to touch him, but he was too far away.

"You have a wonderful family, John."

"You're family now, Teri."

She touched the form of the tile again beneath the tee-shirt and tears came to her eyes. He was reaching out, touching her secret places, and she let him. Gladly. She started to reach out to him, but he interrupted her when he spoke.

"Teri? You don't have to hide in your shell anymore. It's always better to feel something... anything... even pain... than nothing at all."

His words affected her so deeply that she lowered her head again, unable to look at him. The ivory tile's heat filled her. She pulled it from its hiding place and looked at it, almost expecting to see a glow. The dragon etched in the ivory seemed alive. She touched it, but it didn't move. She looked up, and the question slipped from her heart to her lips.

"John, what will happen after... to you, I mean... after all this?"

Suddenly he looked tired. The grief on his face was the grief of the ages, fallen on the shoulders of a mere man, after all. His shoulders slumped and a sigh came from somewhere deep inside him. He spoke quietly.

"Two salt tablets, a canteen of water and push on."

It was the second time she'd heard him say that. She wondered what he meant, and he felt the question in her mind.

"An old saying of mine," he said. "There were days, humping that rucksack through the jungle. I'd get so tired that all I could do was shift the load higher on my shoulders, lean into it and push on." The question remained, and he continued. "It's been a long hump for me, Teri — a long walk in the valley. I can't tell you what it's been like, having such strong ties to this world — trying to live in it, but having no real place in it. I'm tired now. So tired that you'll have to finish it with Woodley and Steadley. I'm going home."

Home. Her eyes opened wide. She wanted to ask if she would ever see him again, but he was gone. Poof. She looked around frantically.

"John?"

Nothing. She tried again.

"John?"

She shouted at the ceiling.

"Damnit, John!"

She stewed in the emptiness he left behind, overcome with fear and longing. Then Special Investigator Teri Altro took a deep breath, straightened her shoulders, and picked up her BlackBerry. She didn't trust Mallory, so she didn't call him. If he thought she was going around him, too bad. She called the other team members and let them know it would be a long night tomorrow. They should sleep in and report to the Team Center at noon.

She didn't doubt the wisdom of the move at all.

Slaying the Dragon

Chapter 67

Altro spent another sleepless night, worrying about John Michaels. His confidence calmed her while he was at her condo, but as soon as he left she began to fret and worry. Her entire night was spent theorizing about the events that would unfold, worrying about the effect those events would have on John's life. Toward dawn her mood darkened. She started worrying less about his future, and more about his survival.

She carded herself into the Team Center at 7:30. The remote for the flat-screen was sitting on Sammy's desk. Altro picked it up, studied it until she figured out how to turn the TV on, then started surfing the national news channels, looking for any news coming out of Laos. When nothing came up, she went to the break room to make coffee.

Doolee was sacked out in there. He'd pulled a chair into the corner and had his feet up on another. A pillow was wedged into the corner behind his head. Altro tried not to make any noise, but he opened his eyes and smiled at her.

"Altro. I knew you would come. I will make coffee."

She protested, but it didn't do any good. He stepped in front of her to take over, and when the pot was underway, headed for the bathroom. Altro was sitting down at her desk with a steaming cup of Doolee's go-juice when Sam and Jessica came in. It was eight o'clock on the nose. Doolee and Sammy did their high-five.

"Sammy Lu... how are you?"

Jessica made her way to her desk. The Princess looked perfect, as always. She had a cup of Starbucks she'd picked up on the way in, probably a flavored latte with extra sugar. Jessica had never even tried to adjust to Doolee's coffee.

"I told you people to sleep in," Altro said.

Sammy rolled his eyes, then ambled over to the break room for coffee. The Princess took a sip of her latte, flounced her hair and beamed at Altro.

"We talked it over after you called last night, Ms. Altro, and decided we'd come in anyway. There was something we were working on anyway. I hope that's okay."

Altro noticed Sammy and Doolee's chairs were both pulled up to Jessica's desk. She wondered what was up, but movement on the television screen caught her eye and she looked away. The rest of her morning was spent that way, surfing the news channels and searching the internet on her laptop. She paced and glared at the television, willing it to come up with something.

She just about ignored her co-workers, and they reciprocated. They ended up taking their laptops into the break room, in fact. Every time Altro went in for more coffee, Jessica smiled at her, then put her pretty nose back to her laptop. Their conversation was quiet and intense, but the three of them weren't talking to her.

About ten, it registered on Altro that Mallory hadn't come in, but she was too engrossed in the TV to think about it. At noon, the three of them came out of the break room. Altro was still pacing, but she was running out of steam.

"You want to go get something to eat with us, Ms. Altro?" Jessica asked.

Altro shook her head and continued her lap around the office. Not long after they were gone, she realized how tired she was getting, and Doolee's makeshift bed in the break room came to mind. She switched off the TV, walked into the break room and took their laptops back out to Jessica's desk. By the time she'd carried the laptops out, one at a time, she was exhausted.

In the break room, she closed the door behind her. After fluffing up Doolee's pillow, she sat down, leaned back into it and put her feet up on the other chair. The ivory tile was warm, so warm that she pulled it out and held it tight. Its warmth spread through her, strong and confident. She was asleep in seconds, the smell of wood smoke filling her mind.

Chapter 68

Andrea hadn't seen Ka and Bao since early morning. Nor had she seen Neng Cheng, John's adoptive mother. She hadn't seen John since he came to her room.

She left her room, looking for some human contact. As she walked down the hall, she heard the voices of the women, coming from the room where she'd seen John covered in demons. Resolutely, she turned to the voices, went to the place that had brought such terror to her. Thankfully, the heavy drapes that covered the windows were pulled back, and the room was lit with sunlight.

After a few steps into the room, she stopped, and they all turned to her. Ka didn't have her usual radiant smile, but was more subdued. Bao gave Andrea a tentative smile, then lowered her head. Choua, the baby, was lying on a blanket on the floor, content to watch his grandmother. The old woman was standing on a stool, straightening a large painting of a dragon on ecru cloth.

As Andrea looked at the painting, she recognized the dragon, a painted image of the dragon that had possessed John. She gasped, uneasy at the likeness, but smiled weakly at the old woman, trying to dampen the fear.

The old woman climbed down from the stool and tottered over to Andrea, chattering in Hmong. She took Andrea's hand and gently led her toward the painting, all the while speaking in Hmong. Andrea was disturbed at the life in the painting. It seemed to move, to breathe. The eyes followed her.

Neng Cheng stopped her in front of the beast, and began a soft chant, a rhythmic sound that made Andrea begin to feel calmer. She heard Ka's voice then, not the ebullient joyful Ka, but quiet, almost serene.

"We're going to pray, Andrea."

Andrea, still calm, didn't understand.

"Pray?"

"Yes. It has begun."

"What's begun? Is John in danger? Where is he?"

Ka moved closer, turned and spoke to Bao, who moved closer to Andrea too. Bao raised her head and looked directly into Andrea's eyes then, the first time the girl had done this. Ka spoke again, so quietly, so serenely that Andrea wasn't sure she heard her correctly.

"You can join us if you wish. You can bring your Bible."

She was beginning to be afraid again, but not for herself. It wasn't fear of the dragon. It wasn't fear of these people and their alien ways.

"He *is* in danger, isn't he? You're going to pray for his safety."

"We don't pray for his safety, Andrea. You know it's too late for that."

Andrea flinched and took a step back, breaking the gentle grip of the old woman. Blind terror overtook her immediately. Her breath came in gasps. She broke into sobs, unable to speak, unable to move. The old woman took her hand again, and she was calmed again by her touch.

She felt herself being led from the room, down the hall to the room where she slept, where her things were. The old woman crooned to her, chanted in the soft rhythms that seemed to soothe her. She led Andrea into her room and sat her on the bed.

There on the nightstand was her Bible. The old woman picked it up, opened it and placed it on Andrea's lap. She bent and kissed Andrea on the forehead, released her arm and smiled to reassure her. Andrea's eyes were pulled to the Bible, open on her lap. The 23rd Psalm. "Yeah, though I walk through the valley of the shadow of death..."

Mother was talking to her, in Hmong again, but Andrea understood every word.

"There, Daughter. You pray your prayers, to your own God in your own way. The Hmong side of the family will do the same."

Chapter 69

A look at her watch told Altro she'd slept for more than three hours. She stood up, worked the kinks from her back and neck, and walked from the break room. After using the bathroom, she walked back into the Team Room. They were waiting.

Doolee's eyebrows shot up. Sammy rubbed a hand over his outlandish hair and looked at her. The Princess sat up straight in her chair and hit her with the question.

"Ms. Altro? What's going to happen?"

Special Investigator Teri Altro straightened her shoulders and put her hands on her hips. First things first.

"If anybody needs a nap, they can sack out in the break room. Doolee, you'd better get some coffee going. We're going to need it."

Doolee grinned and stood, but Altro held a hand up.

"Right now, I'm going to run out and get something to eat. Then you people are going to show me what you've been working on."

Thirty minutes later, Altro was finishing a sandwich while Sammy was putting data up on the flat-screen. He had the record of the credit card Brain and Sledge used up again, his laser pointer aimed at the screen.

"Okay," Sam said. "Back to Wallace Ryan and Theodore Sallison. Brain and Sledge. We were talking about the credit card they used when you left yesterday, Altro, so we didn't get a chance to go over everything with you."

There wasn't the slightest hint of reproach in Sammy's manner over the way she'd walked out on them yesterday. Altro looked at the others and saw no bad feelings there, either. These were good people.

"The card was issued to Free America, Woodley's organization," Sam said. "It turns out they're employees of Free America. Tactical Consultants."

Altro stood and put her hands on her hips and glared at the screen. She saw Sammy start eyeing her butt out of the corner of her eye, and turned a bit to give him a better look. Hell, he deserved it.

Doolee spoke up. "Tell Altro about the money, Jessica. The money is important."

The Princess waited for Altro to nod at her before she began.

"Well, we were looking into Free America, where all the money goes, you know. They took in a ton of money during this whole mess with the heroin. The TV ads?"

Altro remembered Martin Woodley's public plea to the Governor, how he'd offered his help and the resources of Free America to combat the "epidemic." All the TV ads, even before the Task Force was formed, gave a toll-free number and a website asking for donations. The contributions must have rolled in. Altro thought it over and shook her head.

"It's all about money for Woodley and Free America."

The Princess nodded. "And power. Martin Woodley gets to look like a hero," she said.

Yes. Woodley was on television all the time now. He was being pumped up by the media as the savior of America's college youth.

Sammy piped up. "But you'll never guess where a big chunk of the money goes."

She turned to him as he drummed his hands on the desk, giving himself a drum roll.

"Marbley Logistics," he said.

"The lobbying firm?" Altro asked.

"Correctomundo. And the real beauty of it is... Are you ready for this, Altro?" Another drum roll. "Marbley Logistics is wholly owned by Free America."

The Princess was practically jumping out of her chair.

"And, Ms. Altro, Marbley Logistics works exclusively for defense corporations, including the companies that make up the New Defense Corridor north of Detroit."

Altro chewed on it. The heroin sold on college campuses was dirt cheap and uncut. They had to know there would be overdoses. The deaths of those college kids were deliberate, and had indirectly profited an industry that provided security for the nation. And good jobs to Michigan residents. The New Defense Corridor. The Governor.

"I know the Governor said that Woodley's been a supporter, but I just can't believe she's involved in this," Altro said. "She told us Woodley's been kept in the loop from the beginning. She made sure everything would be recorded before she did."

Sammy and Doolee were nodding their heads, but the Princess answered.

"We don't think that was meant to cover her butt, Ms. Altro. She was making sure the information would go in the case file."

"But the weird thing about that recording is," Sammy said. "Mallory moved it to a different directory in the filing system, a directory with limited access. He did the same thing with just about anything referring to Woodley, Brain and Sledge."

"We've been looking at the files," Altro said. "How come we can read them?"

"He must have set it up so we're the only ones who have access," Sam said.

"He could do that?" Altro asked.

"It would take some doing," Sam said. "But yeah, he could." He smiled then. "I looked at the method he used to create the directory and limit access. Pretty slick."

Altro shook her head. "Mallory?"

"He was Army Intelligence, Altro," Sammy said.

Altro nodded slowly. "You're sure nobody else can see them?" she asked.

"Nobody but Task Force team members has access to them," Sam said.

"The Governor," Jessica said.

"Oh yeah," Sam answered. "I forgot about her."

Altro crossed her arms, tapped a foot and stared at her shoes while she tried to figure it out.

"Oh, it gets better," Sam said. "When we found all this out, we started looking at what else Mallory's been up to." Sam smiled when Altro turned to him. "He called Steadley at the Pentagon from his landline here," he said. "Just before he told us Steadley's aide was coming over. We're thinking he's the one who got Steadley and the Army into this."

It didn't make sense. Altro suspected Mallory was the leak in the Task Force. His contacting Steadley fit her theory, but him hiding files from everyone but Task Force members didn't. She put her hands on her hips and opened her mouth, but the Princess spoke up before she could say anything.

"Tell her about the guns, Doolee."

Instead of exploding when Jessica interrupted her train of thought, Altro took a deep breath. She'd cut them off and rushed out the door before they were finished telling her everything yesterday, and she didn't want to do it again. She nodded at Doolee.

"I finally traced the serial numbers of the pistols he used in the drugstore," he said. "They were reported stolen from the armory of the 519th Military Intelligence Battalion in Vietnam in 1970. They were assigned to a Green Beret on temporary duty with the unit. His name is Arlo Goodrich, but the code name he went by back then was Buzzard."

Altro shook her head. "Buzzard?" she asked. "Jesus. Did everybody go by code names back then?"

Doolee shrugged. "It seems that way, doesn't it?" He continued. "Anyway, the Bureau is trying to track him down, but he has dropped out of sight."

Jessica broke in. "The 519th, coincidentally, is the same Army Intelligence unit that Mr. Mallory was assigned to in Vietnam."

"Coincidentally, my ass," Altro said. "What the hell is Mallory up to? The man's not stupid. He had to know that call to

298

Steadley would be logged. He had to know we'd find out he tampered with those files." She turned to look at the office. "Where the hell is he, anyway?"

"Let me check," Sammy said. He bent over his laptop for a few minutes. "Uh, I hate to tell you this, Altro, but his ID says he's here. He carded in yesterday, but never carded out."

Altro strode over to the office, opened the door and turned on the lights. His BlackBerry, and ID were sitting there on the desk. *Damn.* How the hell did he get out of the building without his ID? You had to swipe it to get out, just like you had to swipe it to get in. She picked them up, walked out and handed the BlackBerry to Jessica.

"See if you can find any more surprises in there, Princess."

"Can Sammy and Doolee help?" Jessica asked.

"Hell yes, Princess. This is the Team Room. We're a team."

Princess Jessica smiled at Altro. Altro blushed and turned away, then went to get some more coffee. As she was walking out of the break room she heard Jessica's voice.

"The battery's dead, guys."

"I'll get the charger," Altro said. She went back in the office, rummaged around the desk and found the charger in a side drawer. The cord was wrapped around it and held in place with a rubber band. The rubber band was also wrapped around a yellow sticky-note.

Looking for this, Altro?

I sent an encrypted video file to my BlackBerry. The key is Possum, but don't post it until this is finished. If you do, Woodley will see it.

I'm not the leak, Altro. Woodley is, and he has access to our files.

Mallory

"Jesus H. Christ, Mallory," she muttered. "You and your damn sticky-notes." She carried the charger out and tossed it to Doolee as she started a lap around the office. He caught it in one hand, looked at the note and gave her his widest grin. The BlackBerry buzzed as soon as the charger was plugged into it.

"His BlackBerry's locked," Jessica said. "Oh. Wait a sec."

Jessica thumbed in a password. "Got it," she said. "The same password as the key to the file. Possum." She smiled, not her usual beaming smile, but a private acknowledgement of something she did right. "I just knew Mr. Mallory wasn't the leak," she said.

Altro stopped her pacing. Jessica's face was screwed up as she thumbed the BlackBerry. Sam and Doolee were looking over her shoulder, and both of them frowned at the remark.

"You knew there was a leak, Princess?" she asked.

"Well, duh," Sammy said. When Jessica punched him in the shoulder, he smiled and rubbed his shoulder.

"How else would they know where to find you?" Jessica asked "How else would they know where Ms. Shellers lived?"

"You didn't say anything to me," Altro said.

"Well, you have to admit, Altro," Sammy said. "You're not the easiest person to approach."

Jessica scowled at Sammy, then turned to Altro. "And you've been through a lot, Ms. Altro. Anyway, it wasn't until yesterday that we were certain the leak wasn't someone on the Task Force," she said. "And that was after you left."

"Sammy and I thought it was Mallory," Doolee said. "The way he's been locked in his office, using an unofficial phone."

"But I just knew it wasn't him," Jessica said.

Sam rolled his eyes. "Yeah, yeah. Princess Perfect."

Jessica stuck her tongue out at Sammy. Doolee arched his eyebrows, frowned and waggled a finger at him. Sammy smiled and raised his hands in surrender. The three of them went back to studying Mallory's BlackBerry.

Altro walked over to her desk, sat down and thought about everything she'd just learned. It could explain why the Governor had looked so agitated when she was talking to Mallory during that private meeting in his office. Listrom had suspected they had a leak and confronted Mallory about it. When Mallory pulled out that phone and showed it to her, he'd been explaining what he was doing. That's what had made her smile so big, take his hand in both of hers and hold it so tight.

From the inception of the Task Force, Altro had resented Mallory. Then she'd been almost certain he was the leak. But a grudging respect was pushing aside her aversion for the man, confidence replacing her suspicion. She'd underestimated the Princess all along, after all, had underestimated everyone on the Task Force, in fact. Teri Altro realized now that she'd really underestimated Bill Mallory.

But she still had only the vaguest idea what Mallory was up to.

"Whoa," Sam said. "You have to see this, Altro. But it's just too good to watch on the BlackBerry. We need to put this up on the flat-screen." He grabbed the BlackBerry and unplugged the charger. "I'll plug it into my laptop. It'll keep charging through the USB port."

He went to his desk, pulled a USB cord from a drawer and in less than a minute the video was up on the flat-screen. It was a view of a bar in Lansing, Tommy Mo's Winged Lion. It showed Altro's XLR parked across the street, while a woman in a tight black skirt wiggled past.

"See, Altro? That's your Caddy, " Sammy said. "But who's that other hottie?"

Sammy zoomed in and paused it as the woman stopped to straighten her dress before she went in the Winged Lion. He whistled. "Wow."

After an appropriate moment of silence, in deference to the woman's figure, Sammy started the video again. Altro's car drove away. The video was cut, then came back in to show two men entering the bar. Sammy stopped the feed and zoomed in again.

"That's Brain and Sledge," Jessica said.

Altro started to call the Attorney General, but stopped herself. A warrant would be posted in the case files, and Woodley would have access to it.

Chapter 70

Tommy Mo tossed his phone on the desk. He'd been trying to contact Geena all day, but there was nothing he could do if he reached her. He was committed to the dung eater's lackeys. The threats of General Khun and Nab, the fucking snake, made his cooperation mandatory. He yelled at the walls.

"They own me!"

He was quickly working his way through a bottle of scotch, and poured himself another drink. As he poured, the ground trembled a bit, and Walker was standing in his office.

Tommy felt himself being assessed, judged. He reached behind his back for his Glock, but the ground shook again, and Walker had the weapon in his hand.

"Tommy. What will you do now?"

Tommy knew the man wasn't talking about the weapon. It was his commitment to the dung eater's men, the threats of Khun Pao, his desire to help the beautiful woman. The man knew somehow.

"I can't do a fucking thing. I'm trapped. You know that."

Oh, he knew all right. Walker's face showed it all.

"It's time for you to think, Tommy. Who is your enemy?"

"They own me, Walker. My family… You've seen haven't you?"

Walker spoke quietly to him, like a man soothing a frightened animal. "Khun is finished, Tommy. He won't be able to follow up on his threats." Then he moved to Tommy's desk and put a piece of paper on it.

"Call this number, Tommy. Talk to Teri Altro, the woman you tried to kill. Tell her about the dung eater's lackeys. Tell her about Woodley. But you have to hurry. There's not much time."

Tommy picked up the paper. There was a phone number and another number, a series of numbers separated by dots. He looked up at Walker with a question in his eyes.

"That's an IP address. It will be streaming a video feed of your warehouse and the apartment building you have your men watching."

Tommy looked up at Walker again. The man who had killed three of his best men and raised the hackles of Khun Pao gazed back at him kindly.

"I'm not your enemy, Tommy. The woman you tried to kill isn't your enemy. That old man in the Shan, Khun Pao... He's your enemy."

The ground shifted again, and Tommy Mo found himself alone. He took a drink, then decided on another. The bottle was almost empty when he picked up his phone and called the number.

*****

Altro was trying to figure out what to do about the Winged Lion when Tommy Mo called and said he wanted to come in. It took Altro about two seconds to decide. The Team Center location still wasn't public, but this was going to be over quickly. Tommy sounded a little drunk, so she sent Doolee to pick him up.

Even as Doolee walked him in, Tommy was already blabbering about Walker coming to his office. Altro held out a hand like a traffic cop to stop him.

"He came to see you?" she asked. "When?"

Tommy screwed up his face. "I don't know... maybe a half hour ago?"

Altro touched the shape of the ivory tile beneath her blouse. She wanted to ask him more, but shook it off and turned to Sammy.

"We'll do this in the break room. Set it up, Sammy."

Sam started the recording and they settled in. Tommy opted out of calling his lawyer, and Altro started the interrogation.

"You came here voluntarily, Mr. Mo, but we'll report everything you say. You'll probably be arrested. Do you understand that?"

He nodded quickly. "I know. Can you protect me?"

Thinking Tommy Mo was planning long term, Altro shook her head slowly. "We may be able to get you into the witness protection program, but I can't promise you that."

"No, I mean right now. Tonight. These people are dangerous, Ms. Altro. No offense, but I think Walker's the only one who can protect me. Maybe the only one who can protect you. He scares the hell out of me, but I trust him. Is there some way you can contact him?"

Altro thought of the men in the drugstore, the men that went after Andrea Shellers. She was armed and the deputies were outside, but she didn't think it would come to that. She shook her head at Tommy.

He sighed, then pulled out a slip of paper with numbers written on it. Walker had told him the numbers were a website the task force should look at right away. They all rushed back out to the Team Room. Tommy's interview would have to wait.

Sammy opened his laptop and navigated to the IP address. When he put it up on the flat-screen, half of the screen was a video feed of what looked like a small warehouse. The other half was a video feed of an apartment building.

"Good picture for at night," Sammy said. "The cameras must have some killer sensors."

The picture *was* good, so good that Altro recognized the apartment building immediately. It was the place where she'd talked to the Asian men yesterday afternoon.

Chapter 71

The Valley Walker sensed two guards standing in the shadows by the warehouse. He looked deeper, into the corners, into the darkness, to the roof of the building and inside. He saw everything, saw the lack of thought in their defenses, the futility of their attempts at preparation.

He was across the street from the building where Colonel Nguy's men had tracked the survivor from Andrea's house. That man was inside now, with the man he let live at the drugstore. He could see these men had not regained the entirety of their soul, that they never would. They would live in fear for the rest of their days, jumping at imagined noises and movements and feelings.

He reached out, felt the rhythm of the building and the surroundings, found the space that lay between places. He slipped through it, touched the guards at the front of the warehouse with a hand on each temple and they collapsed soundlessly.

The Great Za was fully awake and reached the peak of its power quickly, with no conscious thought from him. It roared, and Walker went through the front door as it disintegrated. He moved into the building and met the others. They were helpless as he drifted in and out among them, and fell as he reached out to them, one by one.

The power was raging in him now, its fire eager to be set free. He let it reach out to the walls as he moved through the main floor where the men slept. On to the office. Again the Great Za roared, and the walls and door of the office disintegrated as he walked through them. Here were the most trusted men, and he let the dragon take them to the edge of hell, inhaled the aroma of burning flesh. He broke their will and held them with their spirits shattered and bleeding.

When he left, he looked up into the eye of the surveillance camera and smiled. He'd killed no one. Teri Altro would be pleased.

*****

Tommy gave them the location of the warehouse, and Altro was already on the phone with the Lansing Police when she saw the action begin. Walker popped into view in front of the building, and the two guards at the door collapsed with just a touch. There was no visual evidence of the dragon on the feed, but Altro knew it was there, could almost feel its power. The door exploded as Walker went through it.

Doolee jumped to his feet. Jessica turned to Altro, her eyes wide. She had a delicate fist to her mouth, and bit at the knuckle of her thumb. Sammy sat spellbound, completely missing Doolee's effort to give him a high-five.

It was over so fast there was no way to mark the time. The entire building shuddered. Shards of glass and pieces of wood and sheet metal were hurled from the building. The roof buckled and caved in. Walker left the building in almost the same moment he entered. And as he walked away he looked up at the camera, directly into her eyes, Altro thought, and he smiled.

Jessica gasped. Doolee laughed and tried again to give a rapt Sammy a high-five.

Altro was still talking to the Lansing Police about the warehouse as she watched Walker enter the apartment building with his longtime friend and comrade, Colonel Nguy Bo. She said nothing to the police about this.

"Altro?" Sammy said, but she shook her head. Doolee sat down, leaned back in his chair and stroked his mustache. The Princess stared at her for a few seconds, then turned her attention back to the screen.

Minutes later, a van pulled in front of the building. Men dressed in tactical gear piled out and trotted toward the building, three to the front and three to the back. Except for lights in the entryway and hallway, the building looked deserted. Three men went in the front door, and Altro saw the flash of gunfire in the hallway, then more from a window at the back of the building.

Beneath her blouse, the ivory tile grew very warm for a few seconds, then went heavy and cold. Her stomach lurched. She stood up. The phone slipped from her hand as she reached for the tile. It was as cold as death.

Chapter 72

At his compound in the mountains of Laos, Khun Pao was sitting outside by a smoky fire. Gathered around him were a number of his officers, discussing a disturbing development among the subjects of his heroin empire. His adjutants were complaining that many of the men and women in the work force were disappearing from the fields. Khun took a drink of lao-lao and half-listened to their senseless chatter. Didn't he have enough trouble without his laborers shirking their duties?

First, Woodley wanted him to back off from his pursuit of the Valley Walker. The cursed white man had brought in a team of specialists, and wished to give Khun's long-time enemy over to them. He had to feign loyalty to the dung eater to keep his supply lines open, a humiliating experience. Then his man in the States had thoughts of handing Walker over to someone else. This took a call on his satellite phone, and a visit from Nab, to remind the underling of his place.

It was madness. Everyone wanted the Valley Walker, it seemed, but Khun Pao desired the pleasure of meeting his nemesis at the gates of Hell for himself.

As Khun Pao stewed, a soldier from his army's ranks brought a field worker who'd been caught sneaking away from his village forward. Though the laborer's hands were tied, the soldier seemed more afraid of Khun than the worker. The laborer held his head high and looked Khun in the eye, while the soldier kept his eyes lowered as he spoke.

"This man will not answer our questions, General Khun. We beat him, but he still refuses to talk."

A lieutenant stepped forward and struck the laborer in the face with his fist.

"Why do you refuse to kneel before your leaders? What do you think you will accomplish?"

With a jutting chin, the worker spat his answer back at the officer. "My leaders? You will not lead much longer."

The laborer glared openly at Khun. Out of the corner of his eye, Khun saw Neng Jou, the Dark Shaman, making her way toward them. He rose and took a step forward as he pulled his pistol. He calmly shot the laborer in the head, then turned the gun on the lieutenant and aimed it between his eyes.

"You are my officers," Khun said. "I expect you to take care of these things." The lieutenant stood wide-eyed, his mouth open. "See to it," Khun said, "or you will meet the same fate."

Khun shooed the officers away, then turned back to the approaching hag. Neng Jou was still making her way, so he waited. When, at last, she arrived, Khun offered her a stool. She lowered herself onto it with a groan.

"It is time," she said. "Nab, the snake, faces the Valley Walker and his dragon now."

Khun smiled. At last he had good news. He would be rid of the Valley Walker. He sat beside the ancient woman, handed her a pipe of opium and held the flame of his lighter to it for her. She drew the smoke into her lungs, held it, and exhaled.

"Now, snake," she chanted. "Slay the dragon."

Khun held his lighter to the opium again. The Dark Shaman took another lungful of smoke and exhaled. She made a grating, humming sound while the smoke hung in the air. The smoke grew thicker and swirled into the shape of a snake. The old hag's humming grew louder and the snake solidified into an image so real that Khun leaned away from it.

Neng Jou began nodding her head to an inner drum beat. Her voice quavered as her chanting grew louder. She nodded faster. Then, though her legs were still bent, the dark old witch rose in the air from the stool. She nodded faster and hummed louder.

The snake was completely solid now. It coiled around the Dark Shaman and held her as she floated in the air above the stool. Its tongue flicked out. It opened its mouth, drew back its head and struck.

The hag stopped her nodding and chanting. A smile twisted her face as she floated above the stool.

"The Valley Walker is dead," she said.

Chapter 73

Tommy Mo's man parked the van in front of the apartment building. Just minutes ago, Walker was spotted entering the building with Colonel Nguy, and neither were seen leaving.

Brain and Sledge were sitting in the rear of the van with Nab and three more of Tommy's men. They were geared up like a SWAT team, suited up with ballistic vests and gas masks. Each man in the assault group carried an H&K MP5 K. No chances would be taken. It was time to take Walker and Nguy down for good.

Brain and Sledge headed toward the front of the building with Nab, the snake man. The three other men went around back, to cut off any escape.

Nab slid into the entrance vestibule ahead of Brain and Sledge, then opened the hallway door. There was movement at the end of the hallway and Nab opened fire as someone ducked into the apartment there. Sledge covered Brain and Nab as they scurried down the hallway, then followed them to the apartment door. Brain and Sledge lined up on either side of the door, and Nab kicked it in.

They pulled down their gas masks, tossed in CS canisters, then concussion grenades. Brain and Sledge ducked into the apartment behind Nab. All three of them slid along the outer wall with their backs tight against it, firing indiscriminately. The 19-round magazines of the MP5s were empty in just over a second.

They were fumbling to ram in another magazine when a deep rumbling, droning sound began around them. The sound grew in intensity until it shook the walls and drove all three men to their knees before they could reload. The floor began to ripple and a tearing noise filled the air, a fighter jet ripping overhead at tree top level. Through the fog of the gas, Walker seemed to rise directly from the floor, a corpse rising from the grave.

A beast from their darkest nightmares grew from the fire of him, a great dragon that coiled around him, its wings spread above him. Walker's voice was like hot iron, a voice that echoed from the depths of Hell.

"I am the Valley Walker."

Brain and Sledge were locked in terror, but Nab struggled to his feet and removed his gas mask. Something glowed bright in his flat eyes as he slammed the magazine of his weapon home. He smiled, thumbed the bolt release and the safety, then emptied the weapon at Walker. Nab grinned, and the world dimmed and blurred.

Then the room came back into focus. Walker reappeared. His body showed no ill effects from the rounds fired.

The dragon's head shot forward and struck the big Hmong under the chin. Nab's head snapped backward and twisted with a crackling crunch. The snake man fell to the floor and went into death spasms, was still twitching as Walker turned back to Brain and Sledge.

The dragon's wings beat at the air. Flames engulfed the terrified men. The smell of burning flesh and the sound of fat popping in a fire filled the air. The dragon reached out and ripped the melted gas masks from their heads. Clumps of burnt hair and flesh stuck to the masks and were ripped from their heads. The two men stayed on their knees, in supplication now.

They could smell rotting flesh, could feel the movement of maggots inside them, dining on their wasted flesh. They looked down and saw that their clothing was rotted away and yellowed shards of ribs protruded from their chests. Flies buzzed everywhere. Worms crawled out of them. They could hear the sound of screams echoing from deep within the blackness of Walker's eyes and realized the screams were their own, that their voices were hoarse and raspy from screaming.

The two men couldn't breathe. Their chests heaved as their mouths opened and closed like fish stranded on the shore. They lost control of their bodily functions, shit themselves and urinated down their legs onto the floor. Vomit spewed from their mouths, ran down the front of their rotting chests.

Chapter 74

In Laos, the Dark Shaman floated above her stool, caressing the snake coiled around her.

The witch's smile vanished when the earth shook in an explosion, a great clap of thunder. The snake disappeared and the old woman fell back to the stool with a thud. A hush fell over the encampment, an eerie, unnatural quiet that chilled the air. The hag spun around to face Khun Pao, her eyes wide. Khun had never seen the old witch show fear. He bent over her.

"No!" she hissed. "The Valley Walker is dead, but still lives. The Great Dragon comes!"

There was a flash of light, brighter than the sun. Then, though it was the middle of the day, a gloomy darkness fell on the compound and surrounding mountains. Another clap of thunder shook the earth.

The old hag screamed. Smoke rose from her clothing and scarf, smoke that smelled of sulfur. The crone screamed again as flames engulfed her. Her skin blackened, bubbled and peeled away. Her flesh burned away to ashes. Hoarse screams came from the mouth of her skull and flames shot from her empty eye sockets. The fire was so hot it consumed the bones, and the Dark Shaman was gone, leaving behind a thick cloud of yellow smoke. The stink of sulfur permeated the air, so heavy it was hard to breathe.

A low reverberation began in the hills around the encampment, an indistinct vibration that grew in intensity until it shook the earth. The rumbling rose in pitch until it took on the sound of the great horn at the Buddhist temple, carrying through the air, echoing off the sides of the surrounding mountains.

Men lost their footing and fell. Shouts for help were heard as the power of the vibration and sound grew. Khun Pao looked up and saw flashes of light in the gloom of the mountains, but heard only the deep thrumming that overpowered all other sound. Then the vibration and overwhelming sound stopped.

The silence was short. From the sides of the mountains came the hollow chunks of mortar fire. Khun understood that he had seen the flashes of the mortars firing, and the sound was just reaching his ears. He scrambled to his feet and made a dash for a depression in the ground he spotted, determined to make it to some minimum cover before the shells fell on them.

The first salvo came schussing down in the darkness and fell on the clearing where many of Khun Pao's adjutants were standing, paralyzed in fear. It was a "fire for effect" salvo that spread itself around the clearing and wreaked havoc on the men there.

Shrapnel tore into bodies and carried pieces of bone and flesh with it as it ripped out the other side. Whether the pieces were large or small depended on how close the body was to the detonation. Some men were only slightly wounded, while others lost limbs or were killed instantly. Khun Pao saw the flashes of the mortars again, as they began their second salvo.

These rounds landed in and around the buildings in the compound. There were direct hits on the barracks that housed some of Khun's private army. Men stumbled out, followed by the screams of the less lucky still inside. Then the mortars began to fire continuously and the rounds walked their way to buildings, or fell with uncanny accuracy in the clearing. Khun Pao knew there were spotters who were bracketing the targets and communicating with the mortar teams to correct the fire.

General Khun Pao crouched in the depression and watched helplessly as the mortars destroyed the buildings of the compound, one after another. The laboratory where the final refining of the opium took place disintegrated in a ball of flames, as the chemicals used in the production of Number 4 heroin exploded. The last building to fall was Khun's own residence, and he stood in the depression to shake his fist at the sky.

"Valley Walker! Show yourself!"

RPGs whooshed into the compound, exploding randomly and adding to the bedlam. The kak-kak-kak of AK47s began around him, and what men were left standing fell to withering fire that rained in on them. Armed men ran out of the darkness, yelling and screaming as they charged into the encampment to kill anyone left alive. Khun Pao watched as the people he used as forced labor stormed into the compound to have their revenge.

There was no real battle. The slaughter was violent and short. The initial heavy fusillade died down to sporadic firing in minutes, and the avengers began moving from place to place, making certain their tormentors were dead.

When the gunfire stopped, it dawned on Khun that he was still alive, that he'd been spared — through luck or the gods, he couldn't tell. Men and women of the Hmong villages he so mercilessly exploited gathered in a circle around him, began to close the circle until Khun stood face to face with them. Khun's pistol was taken and he was hauled from the depression to stand in the center of the clearing.

The darkness that had fallen lifted and the sun reappeared. Off to the side, Khun saw a video camera set up on a tripod, a parabolic dish set up on another tripod. A man stepped in front of him and pulled a sheet of paper from his pocket.

"These are the words of the Valley Walker that will be read to you. He has written these words and we the People, the Hmong, will execute them."

Khun could not believe these ragamuffins would rise against him. "Where is the Valley Walker?" he shouted. "Let me see his face!"

The man with the paper raised his chin in pride.

"He is not here. We have done this ourselves, Khun."

Khun Pao sucked air in through his teeth. The man with the paper began reading.

"These are the charges brought against you, Khun Pao."

You have lived a life full of evil.
You have used the Dark Ways.

You have taken the freedom and joy of the Hmong people for profit and power.
You have treated the people as if they were not human beings, only objects to serve you.

This last is the most evil of all your evils.

The reader and the entire front line of the group stepped to the side. An old Hmong man holding a crossbow stood there. The speaker continued.

"You have been found guilty by this court, Khun Pao, and are sentenced to death. You will die here."

The speaker raised his hand in the air and held it while the old man with the crossbow took aim.

"And know this, Khun Pao. This is taking place in all of your encampments across the Shan country. Your army is being wiped out and your laboratories are being destroyed. The Hmong will be free of you from this night forward."

He dropped his arm. The crossbow clacked and hummed. A great shout went up from the people, a shout that echoed from the mountainsides.

Khun Pao was shot through the heart. He dropped to the ground and lay there, his arms and legs flailing, like a rag doll being shaken by a dog. When the spasms ended, Khun's body was dragged to the depression where he hid during the attack. His lifeless form was tossed in, and every man and woman in the group took turns urinating on him. Then the cut-off drums from the privy were dragged over and the dung dumped on the corpse. Diesel fuel for the compound's generators was poured on the stinking mound and lit with a torch. The smoke rising from the fire was thick and black, carrying the stink of burning human flesh and excrement.

The old ones who'd served in the CIA's secret army smiled their old men's smiles at one another and nodded their heads. The shit was being disposed of, burned up like it was in the old days. It was as it should be.

Chapter 75

Jessica took the call. John Michaels' body was found in the apartment building.

Altro felt the ivory tile, cold and heavy on her chest. "I have to see him," was all she said.

Jessica quietly told the caller to hold the body until Special Investigator Altro arrived, then turned back to Altro, the phone still in her hand. Altro just sat and stared off into space. Things needed to be done before she could leave, but Altro made no move to do them. The rest of the team took over.

The Princess told the Lansing Police to hold anyone arrested and any witnesses. Doolee called the FBI to inform them of Tommy Mo's presence at the Team Center. Sammy went out and asked one of the deputies in the parking lot to come in and guard Mr. Mo. This took a radio call to the Sheriff's Department for it to be cleared by the man's superior, who wanted another deputy sent to the parking lot. It all took time, but Altro didn't pace the room with her hands on her hips. She didn't tap her foot and glare at people. She sat quietly and let the others take care of it all.

Doolee told her she could leave when everything was done. With no response from her, he said he would drive her. She just nodded.

It looked like the whole neighborhood was out to watch the show at the apartment building. The entire block was cordoned off and Lansing Police cruisers were everywhere. An ambulance and a Medical Examiner wagon were parked on the small lawn. Emergency lights flashed off the brown brick of the apartment building.

Doolee and Altro ducked under the crime scene tape and held up their credentials as they made their way through the officers toward the building. The uniforms were all chatting and drinking coffee, their eyes wide and alert.

Doolee led the way through the doorway into the building, then to the end of the hall. The sharp odor of tear gas hung in the air. He talked quietly about the lack of any sign of flash from an explosion as they picked their way through the wreckage. It was just like the drugstore, he said. No pattern that would indicate an explosion, but clear evidence of a shockwave. Altro said nothing.

A man in a white lab coat was standing in the apartment doorway, scribbling on a pale green form on a clipboard. He moved out of the way so they could get by him, and Altro saw the words "Medical Examiner" stitched over the left breast pocket of the lab coat as she squeezed by. Altro had met the Ingham County ME while working cases, and wondered if this was his assistant. The man appeared to be in his forties, lean and hard looking compared to the doughy ME she knew.

She made her way through the rubble to the body of John Michaels. He was on a gurney, a lifeless lump in a black bag. Altro knelt down, took a deep breath and unzipped the bag.

His hands were crossed on his chest, one of them clutching the red cloth bag. He was wearing the same cotton pullover and faded blue jeans he wore to her place last night. His face was calm and serene. There were no wounds she could see, though she opened the bag all the way and looked closely. Her hand went to his face, and she felt the cold deadness of the ruined flesh.

The lights dimmed and hummed. Time stood still, while it rushed forward and backward. Teri Altro came and went while the universe blurred and ran, watercolors thrown on the face of her existence.

John Michaels looked young again. *God, he was just a boy!* She looked into his wide open eyes and felt herself falling. Knowing what was happening, she didn't try to fight it, but allowed her heart to merge with his.

She stood on the skid of the Huey as it nosed up over the LZ.

Green tracers raced toward her. Rounds snapped overhead, then knocked into the side of the chopper. The door-gunner started banging away. Hot brass fell on her and made its way down the back of her fatigue shirt. She leaned out, judging the drop. Fifteen feet maybe? She was ready to jump. No way they would risk the bird by landing.

Her breath exploded from her in an animal grunt as rounds penetrated the useless fucking flak jacket. She was falling back inside the chopper, but it tilted crazily and she was back outside as it slid away. Another round knocked the steel pot from her head, just as she slipped from her perch on the skid.

She bounced off the skid, spun in the air and slammed into the ground. A broken toy. The web gear dug into her shoulders and the downdraft from the chopper blew dust and grit into her open mouth and eyes. One arm was useless, but she tried to drag herself away with the one that responded. Her hand couldn't get a good grip on the ground. Her feet scrabbled at the earth in a ridiculous pantomime of running while she lay on her side. Dying.

Altro jumped when a gentle hand touched her shoulder. A deep, gravelly voice spoke.

"Ma'am? I'm sorry, but we have to move him now."

She turned and looked into the kind face of a giant black man who knelt beside her. A Medical Examiner technician, in a lab coat so tight it looked ready to split at the seams. His hand was still on her shoulder, and she shrugged it off.

"I had to see him," she mumbled. "He saved my life."

"Yes, ma'am. We'll take good care of him. You have my word on that."

The big black man looked into her eyes and she saw the truth in them.

Another ME tech, a white man with icy blue eyes and a walrus mustache, stood on the other side of the stretcher. He nodded at her in reassurance. The big hand cupped under her elbow to help her stand. The two men raised the gurney and the huge black man zipped up the bag.

He was gone.

In the Dragon's Wake

Chapter 76

The emptiness Teri Altro felt as they took him away was worse than any physical pain she could imagine. She pulled the ivory tile from its hiding place and squeezed it, but it remained cold, like the cold face of John Michaels. She felt so disoriented that she lost her balance and almost fell, but Doolee was there. He caught her by her shoulders, held her up until she regained her footing, then turned his back to her.

Special Investigator Teri Altro crawled back into her shell. She straightened her shoulders, hiked up her shoulder bag, and went about her duties with grim purpose.

Three Asian men were under arrest at the scene. None of them provided any information or answered any questions. They were docile, empty hulls that stared off into space and said nothing. The Lead Detective at the scene explained the men were found in back of the building, incapacitated by tranquilizer darts. They were sent to Ingham County for holding.

There were two white men Altro recognized as Brain and Sledge, the two men who had come to kill Walker. They were kept off to the side, and when Altro approached them she understood why. They reeked of urine, vomit and what could only be their own feces.

They blubbered and ranted incoherently, their eyes wide and wild. They twitched spasmodically and jerked their heads around to peer over their shoulders. They were already handcuffed and, as Altro watched, a uniform put plastic restraints on their feet. They went to County, too.

There was another body that had been left behind by the ME techs when they took John away, a huge Asian man who looked like his neck was broken. Altro wondered if John had killed him, but it didn't matter. John was dead. They couldn't hurt him now.

She drifted off for a few moments, then shook her head and signaled Doolee that it was time to go. The other body could rot where it was, as far as she was concerned.

SAC Bowman was at the Team Center when Altro and Doolee arrived. He was standing in front of Jessica's desk, trying to chat her up. Altro gave Bowman a stiff nod, then strode to the break room for coffee.

Tommy Mo was sitting in the break room, with Sammy and two more Feds. The deputy brought in to guard him sat in the corner, reading a gun magazine and looking bored. Altro nodded at them, got her coffee and walked back out to the doorway. She pointed at Tommy Mo.

"We'll do the interview of Mr. Mo now. Jessica and Sammy? Set it up."

The Princess looked relieved and mouthed a "Thank you" as she sashayed over to the server room.

"Doolee, you'll join me and Feeeeeelix for the interview."

Tommy was Mirandized and offered a lawyer. When he declined, one of the Feds produced a form from his briefcase and had him sign. The interview began.

Bowman started by asking Tommy who he was, and quickly learned that Tommy Mo was Khun Pao's right-hand man in Lansing. The Detroit SAC immediately phoned the U.S. Attorney in Detroit and, after a brief conversation, offered Mo a deal if he would cooperate in the investigation. Tommy agreed eagerly, signing the agreement that one of the Feds pulled from a briefcase. Altro drummed her fingers on the table.

When things finally got going, Mo opened by saying they weren't making any money on the sale of the heroin, were taking a huge loss, in fact. They were practically giving it away. Khun Pao didn't conduct business this way, but squeezed every cent he could from his product.

"Who else would order this?" Doolee asked.

Tommy didn't know the answer to that. He told them about the warehouse, that he ran things from his office at the Winged

Lion. Then he went off on a tangent about a man named Nab, the snake. He was at the apartment building, he said. Altro zoned out, thinking about John Michaels' cold flesh. Doolee stepped in, and when Tommy described the man, Doolee told him Nab was dead.

Tommy took a deep breath and smiled, then proceeded to tell them about Brain and Sledge. He said Brain and Sledge were sent to oversee Walker's murder. They had relayed the information about Walker's woman, Andrea Shellers. This led to who had sent them, who had given them the information. Altro and the others on the task force knew already, but it was a shock to Bowman and the other Feds.

The Hmong all called him the dung eater, but Tommy was high enough in Khun's hierarchy that he knew his real name. Martin Woodley.

Bowman turned a putrid shade of green and waved his arms in the air. "Hold everything! I need to call the Director about this."

Altro slapped a hand on the table. "This is my interview, Feeeeeelix. Mr. Mo came to me. The Bureau can conduct their own interview when I'm finished."

Tommy spoke up. "I will tell you anything you want, Agent Bowman. But Walker wanted me to talk to Ms. Altro, and this is what I will do. Otherwise, our agreement is off. I will take my chances in court."

Bowman sulked, but to keep Tommy as a non-hostile witness, he had to agree.

The one question Altro didn't think she already knew the answer to was the assassination attempt. She asked about that. Tommy said the order came from Khun, but the drug lord told him the idea to kill a member of the task force originated with Woodley. Bowman held up a hand, but Altro pushed ahead.

"How did you know I would be there?" Altro asked. "You were tailing me?"

Tommy nodded. It had to be a public execution, so they had her tailed and were waiting for their chance. Then they received information that she would be stopping at the drugstore, that it would be a lengthy stop. This turned out to be true. It was more than enough time for the shooters to be called in.

"But why me?" she asked. "Why not Mallory? He was leading the damn Task Force."

Tommy shrugged. He was told Mallory was Woodley's man, that Altro would be the true danger to their operations. She was a driven person, and would push the investigation relentlessly.

Altro stared at the table. She was definitely a driven person, and the Governor had insisted Altro be a member of the Task Force for that very reason. True to form, she had pushed the Task Force team along certain lines, but felt like the end results had slipped beyond her grasp, that she'd been a mere observer in a chain of events completely beyond her control. Doolee coughed.

Altro looked up at Tommy. "Thank you for your assistance, Mr. Mo. That's all the questions I have." She waved a hand in the air. "He's all yours, Feeeeeelix."

Bowman took over the rest of Tommy's interview. When it was completed, Bowman, sullen and scowling, had him sign more forms, and the deputies took him to County for holding. After Bowman and his entourage filed out, Altro got herself another cup of coffee and sat down at her desk. Her BlackBerry buzzed. It was the Lead Detective from the apartment building scene.

"Somebody stole the Ingham County Medical Examiner's wagon," he said.

The ME wagon dispatched to the apartment building had come across a gray sedan with the hood up, blocking the road. When they stopped, a dark-haired woman in tight black clothing got out of the car and trotted up to the side of the vehicle.

"The techs' description of the woman is one for the records," the detective said. "They just kept saying 'She was hot.' The idiots rolled down their windows, of course, and the woman shot them with a tranquilizer gun. Same make of darts the men at the apartment building were shot with."

At the same time, according to the ME, an Asian man climbed into the back of the vehicle, overcame the ME and stuck a needle in him. No one was seriously hurt when they all woke up on the side of the road, but their lab coats and the ME wagon were gone.

An alternate vehicle, an ambulance, was eventually sent to the apartment scene. Two fresh ME techs checked their orders and said a body was missing. The officers on the scene insisted the missing body was taken away by the Medical Examiner's wagon earlier. When it was all straightened out, the detective realized the body of John Michaels had been stolen while he watched.

Chapter 77

Altro sat numbly in her chair. She and the rest of the task force were watching the news on the flat-screen. It was the beginning of the morning news hour, and a story about some violence in Laos was hitting the airwaves.

"This is George Kuzman, reporting from Vientiane. It appears that violence has broken out in the mountainous region of northwestern Laos. Details are sketchy, but the Laotian Government has contacted Interpol with a plea for help. They are urgently seeking their cooperation in trying to locate this man... "

An old picture of John Michaels filled the screen, then shrank to an inset, allowing the world to continue watching the reporter live.

"... John Michaels. A government official said Michaels is a rogue CIA agent who returned to Laos to overthrow the communist government there. According to this official, Michaels served in Laos during the Vietnam War and, I'm quoting the official now, 'has held a longstanding grudge against the righteous communist government the people chose after their glorious victory over the imperialistic American Armed Forces in Vietnam'."

Altro went to get more coffee. It had been a long night. She'd been on the phone with the Lansing Police through most of it, receiving reports of their findings at the warehouse and apartment building. A substantial cache of heroin and cash was seized at the warehouse. A number of weapons were confiscated at both sites and more than twenty arrests made.

The body of John Michaels was still missing.

She was just sitting down with her coffee when Mallory's BlackBerry buzzed. It was back on Jessica's desk.

"The caller ID says it's General Steadley, Ms. Altro," Jessica said.

Altro grabbed the remote and muted the television. "Put it on speaker, Princess."

Jessica punched a button and put the BlackBerry on her desk. "General Steadley. What can I do for you?"

"Who is this? I need to speak to Mallory."

"This is Jessica Harmon, General, Michigan State Police. Mr. Mallory's not available. What can I do for you?"

There was a pause. "Where's Walker?"

Altro stood and stepped over to Jessica's desk. "Special Investigator Altro here, General. I'm with the Michigan Attorney General's Office. John Michaels is dead."

"I heard that, and I don't believe it. You people get off your asses over there and find him."

Altro shook her head.

"He's dead, General. We don't work for you. If you need someone to chase his ghost, I suggest you find someone else."

Sammy piped up. "Ghostbusters maybe."

Altro leaned over and hung up on a cursing General. Jessica burst out giggling. Sammy and Doolee were giving each other high-fives and grinning ear to ear. Teri Altro didn't smile. She couldn't.

"You people want to go home?" she asked. "I know it's been a long night. I'm going to stay a while, answer the phone, maybe watch some more TV."

Doolee shook his head. "No, no. I will stay with you, Altro. You may need me, huh?"

Sammy picked up his laptop, put his feet up on the desk and leaned back in his chair. The Princess beamed at Altro, flounced her hair and shook her head.

Altro turned up the television volume again. A picture of an Army officer was on the screen, and an anchorman's practiced voice was talking in the background. "We haven't been able to reach General Steadley for comment."

So that's Steadley. He looks like a toad in full-dress uniform.

"Meanwhile this same site is streaming information that details a long standing relationship between these two men and Martin Woodley, the chairman of Free America."

The General's image faded to a picture of Brain and Sledge, which shrank down to a corner. Woodley's image took over the screen.

"For those of our viewers who are unaware, Free America is a non-profit organization with the stated objective of stamping out illegal drug use in America."

Woodley's image shrank down to line up beside the pictures of Brain and Sledge at the bottom. The anchorman's serious face took center stage.

"We haven't been able to reach Woodley either, but his attorneys released a statement, saying the website's allegations are libelous and a lawsuit is being filed. Statements by the website include accusations of facilitating the flow of heroin to American soldiers during the Vietnam conflict. Another assertion says that Woodley was instrumental in smuggling heroin into the United States in the last few months."

The anchorman, eager to continue, barely took a breath before launching into details.

"We've tracked down the owner of the website who, coincidentally, is the same man the Laotian government is seeking in reference to the violence that reportedly broke out there."

The picture of Walker came on the screen, then shrank back to the bottom.

"John Michaels is being sought..."

Altro flipped through the news channels. They all were running the same story except the local news, which had paused in their national coverage to air reports of the warehouse bust and apartment building violence. The camera showed the outside of the warehouse.

"Miraculously, no one was killed in the explosion, but 18 dazed men were arrested at the scene. According to a Lansing Police spokesperson, a large amount of heroin was confiscated, along with a substantial amount of cash and a number of firearms.

In a bizarre side note, 300 pairs of athletic shoes were found inside the building. The shoes were new, piled up with the boxes at one side of the warehouse. All of the arrested men were wearing the same type of shoes, incidentally."

The camera switched to the reporter holding up an iridescent athletic shoe. "Nikes. Police are looking into whether these are the same shoes stolen from a Howell warehouse a week ago. The same warehouse reported another theft of Nikes six months ago."

Damn! Sammy's been going on about those Nikes for days!

Altro hit the mute.

"You were on to something, Sammy. 300 pairs of new Nikes. Hell, they must have been bringing in the heroin in the shoes, or with them."

Sammy pumped his fist in the air. "I knew it!" he said. "They're made in Ho Chi Minh City, what used to be Saigon. That gave Khun Pao almost the same smuggling route to the States as the old days."

Jessica and Doolee both applauded. Doolee and Sammy did their high-five. The celebration was short, however. The screen switched to a view outside the apartment building. Altro waved a hand for them to quiet down and brought the sound up again.

"In another incident of violence, a shootout occurred in this apartment building a few hours ago. Police arrested five men, and confiscated automatic weapons and sawed-off shotguns. And listen to *this*, folks. Three of the men arrested were found incapacitated with tranquilizer darts behind the building. Two bodies were recovered at the scene. One body was identified by members of the Drug Interdiction Task Force as John Michaels. Michaels was being sought in connection with the drugstore shootout that occurred in Mason last week."

Damnit! Damnit! Damnit!

She wiped at her eyes with her sleeve, turned off the TV. The Princess stood and started toward her desk, but Altro sent her back with a wave of her hand. She took a deep breath and straightened her shoulders.

"They're hiding the fact that they lost the body," Jessica said.

"Of course they are," Altro said. "You think they're going to admit to that?" She turned to Sam. "Sammy, can you find anything on the videos they're talking about in the news?"

Sammy had his mouth open, like he wanted to say something nice, but Altro shook her head. He took a deep breath and she shook her head again. He nodded and turned back to his laptop.

"Sure, Altro. The whole thing'll go viral, I bet."

John Walker Michaels appeared on the flat-screen. This wasn't an old photo, but a recent video recording.

"My name is John Michaels, and this is a message to the president of the Lao People's Democratic Republic."

He paused, just slightly, not one of his long pauses while he gathered his thoughts. This was rehearsed.

"Sir, I have no intention of interfering with the workings of your government. I acknowledge the proud past and hopeful future of your country and its peoples. What I have done is give the Hmong the means to rid themselves of the tyranny of Khun Pao, a vicious drug lord who preyed on these people for his own profit and amusement. By the time this is aired, Khun Pao and his army will be defeated. His heroin producing facilities will be destroyed. Enough armaments and ammunition were given to the Hmong to accomplish this, but no more."

What followed was a video of the trial and execution of Khun Pao. He was shot in the chest with a crossbow. His body was rolled into a shallow hole, urinated on and covered in what looked like excrement. Then fuel was poured on the mess and it was burned. The yellow glow of the flames reflected off heavy black smoke. People clapped their hands and cheered.

The Princess sat wide-eyed. Doolee was stoic, with one eyebrow raised and one hand stroking his moustache. Sammy shifted uncomfortably in his seat as John Michaels came back on the screen.

"I have been adopted by the proud Hmong people. I have a stake in their future, and so with the future of Laos itself. The People's Republic also has a stake in the future of my adopted people, and I know they will work tirelessly to ensure that the future of the Hmong is bright."

By noon, the Drug Interdiction Task Force had ground to a halt. Altro declared an end to the day and told them to pack it in. Sammy and Doolee stumbled out the door, but Jessica lingered, puttering away at her desk. Even after a twenty-eight hour day, the Princess still looked fresh and beautiful.

Teri Altro walked over, timid and unsure of herself.

"Princess?"

The young woman turned and Altro was relieved to see the ready acceptance in her eyes. She took a deep breath. This was so hard for her. "I was wondering if you could come over to my place. I mean, if you still want to."

Jessica stood, started to reach out to her, but stopped herself. "I've been keeping some clothes and stuff in the car, Ms. Altro. Just in case, you know. Are you sure?"

Terry Altro stuck her head tentatively out of her shell. "Please? I don't want to be alone."

When Jessica smiled at her, it was sunshine, pure and simple. Teri Altro reached out, took Jessica's arm and leaned into that sunshine. With her head on the young woman's shoulder, she whispered. "I can't believe he's gone, Princess."

Jessica pushed her away and held her shoulders, looked into her eyes. Teri Altro saw the strength and wisdom in those beautiful young eyes.

"I can't pretend to understand everything that happened between you and him, Ms. Altro, but I've looked pretty hard at all the events. He started this by announcing himself, knowing people would come after him. He had to know how it would turn out."

Teri Altro wanted to disagree, to argue the point, but she couldn't. Walker told her he would wrap them up and hand them over to her, but she would have to finish it. He was going home. She remembered how tired he said he was, and the look of exhaustion on his face. That same exhaustion fell on her then, like a truckload of sand, weighing her down, pinning her limbs and filling her mouth. There was nothing she could say, nothing she could do. She was done.

She let the Princess lead her out of the Team Center like an invalid, then sat numb and speechless while Jessica drove her home. Altro's baby, her shiny Cadillac XLR convertible, was left without ceremony in the parking lot.

Chapter 78

Khun Pao was a Dark Hmong, but even the Dark Hmong heart is made up of more than one soul. When Khun was killed, his souls left his body and made the journey across the twelve rivers, across the twelve valleys, to the cold and misted valley of the dead. His passage was swift and painless, but he was met there by the person he feared the most.

The Valley Walker waited there, clothed in the Great Dragon, facing the very man who boasted that he would meet him at the gates of Hell. The Great Za flapped its wings, fanning fire over Khun's cowering souls. Quivering moans circled their way up to the earth, causing leaves on the trees to tremble.

The wings of the dragon gathered in the singed and smoking souls of Khun Pao, and the Valley Walker shoved them into his black bag that admitted no light. He took the wailing souls deeper into the valley, the valley he had walked so long and knew so well. He carried them to the den of Ndsee Nyong, the Soul Devourer, and called out to the monster to wake it.

"Hoy to you Ndsee Nyong! I am the Valley Walker. I have brought the souls of one who fed his heart with the fear of others. His feeble mind dreamt he was made strong by bathing in the darkness, but he was only a pig wallowing in its own dung. Now I hold his sniveling heart in my bag. I offer it to you."

The Soul Devourer opened its maw in anticipation, and the reek of decaying flesh drifted from its mouth. Lodged in the teeth of the monster, the litter of bones, hair and shredded parts of others it had devoured were rotting and putrid. The drool that hung from the jowls of the nightmare was the blood of its victims, as old as the ages, freshened to liquid by its hunger for more.

The Valley Walker reached into the bag and brought out the souls of Khun Pao, one at a time. He tossed each soul to the monster like he was tossing a treat to a dog. Ndsee Nyong caught them in the air, snapped its jaws shut and chewed, cracking bones and slurping as it savored the evil stink and foul flavor. Between treats, the monster burped, and screams echoed up from its bowels. When only the Winjan, the primary soul, of Khun was left, the Valley Walker held it out and waved it.

Ndsee Nyong rose on its hind legs, and the Valley Walker tossed the last that remained of the once powerful drug lord at the monster's feet.

The claws of Ndsee Nyong slashed at the Winjan. Bowels sagged out through the cuts, then spilled over and lay on the ground. Ndsee Nyong slurped greedily at the loops of intestines, sucking them down its throat like egg noodles. When it was done with the entrails, it popped the remainder of the Winjan into its mouth and ground it between its teeth like a piece of candy. The screams of pain were so great they were heard echoing through the mountains of Laos. Hmong there smiled and celebrated the agony of the man who had enslaved them.

The appetite of Ndsee Nyong is never truly satisfied, however. When it finished its feast, the monster turned its greedy attention to the Valley Walker. The strength of the Valley Walker's heart brought its hunger back, even stronger, but the desire of the beast would not be realized.

The claws of the Great Dragon swiped at the monster's face and one eye was ripped from its socket and dangled on Ndsee Nyong's scaled cheek. With a groan of acceptance the monster coiled back into its lair and lay down to digest its meal.

Chapter 79

The press conference celebrating the heroin seizure was held on the steps of the Michigan State Capitol. It was a beautiful day, but Altro took no enjoyment in the weather or the moment of fame being forced on her.

The ivory tile still felt cold and heavy. She still felt empty and directionless, and numbly let Jessica hold her elbow and guide her through the throng to the podium. Sammy and Doolee walked ahead of the two women. A squad of State Police formed a ring around the group to keep reporters out of their faces.

News media people were everywhere, hustling about with their camera crews and tablets while they tried to glean information. Every major television network was on hand, along with the local stations. Anchor persons stood in front of cameras looking important and saying important words. It was a media extravaganza. The image machines of the various law enforcement agencies involved had made sure of it.

There were four police chiefs present — Lansing, East Lansing, Ann Arbor and Mason — along with the Ingham and Washtenaw County Sheriffs. The Michigan Attorney General was there with his entourage of toadies. People from the Detroit offices of the FBI and DEA were in attendance, eager to bask in the fleeting glory.

SAC Felix Bowman was there, of course, oozing personality as he slid through the group, networking with everyone he thought worth the trouble. Altro watched him press himself on Governor Listrom, then saw the Governor wipe her hand on her skirt after shaking his hand. As they approached the podium, the Governor waved their group over, then led them aside. Her aide and the State Police kept everyone at bay, while the Governor gave them a private conference.

"I wanted to tell you people myself what a fine job you've done. You've done an enormous service to the people of Michigan, and I won't let them forget it. You'll hear it in my speech, of course, but I wanted to shake your hands personally."

She shook every hand of the Task Force until she got to Altro. The Governor just nodded at her. "It was a damn good job, Altro. You should be proud."

But Special Investigator Teri Altro wasn't proud. She let herself be led to the designated seats for the task force members — five chairs, all marked with their names. Bill Mallory's chair was empty.

The Governor introduced all the law enforcement heads and gave her sincere thanks. Everyone had a chance to say a few words, but no one mentioned General Steadley or Martin Woodley. No one mentioned Bill Mallory. No one mentioned John Walker Michaels. When everyone had said their piece, Governor Listrom took center stage. She put on her designer glasses and faced the cameras and microphones.

"You've heard all the details from the major players, so I won't bore you. I do want to express my deepest gratitude to the people who made it all happen. A lot of the credit for success should be given to the Drug Interdiction Task Force and the man who led it, Bill Mallory."

This was their cue, and Altro readied herself. As the Governor read off each of their names, she pointed to them and they rose from their seats.

"Special Investigator Teri Altro of the Attorney General Office — Abdul Korszctani of the FBI — Sam Lu of the DEA — Jessica Harmon of the Michigan State Police — and the Task Force Leader, Bill Mallory, U.S. Army retired. They did a lot of the real work, and without their dedication, the end goal would not have been reached."

The Governor started clapping then, and the crowd joined in. When the applause died down, she nodded at them and they sat back down.

"Due to pressing family matters, Bill Mallory couldn't be with us today, but he gave me the words he'd like to say to all of you, and I'll read them in his place."

Karen Listrom held up a piece of paper, then read Mallory's statement.

"I sincerely hope that the efforts of myself and the fine people I worked with have not been in vain, that parents out there can sleep a little easier at night. The war is not over, but a major campaign has been won, and my part in the fight is done. Now it's time for me to go back to the quiet retirement I left when I accepted Governor Listrom's challenge. Thank you everyone for the opportunity to be of some use to you and the great state of Michigan."

Listrom lowered the paper to the podium.

"As Bill said, this war is not over. We must face the continuing problem of illicit drug use head on, and use our resources wisely. We cannot — CANNOT — allow this to happen again."

Applause broke out. The governor waited for it to die down.

"One more name needs to be made public," Listrom said. "A name no one else has mentioned, but a name I think you should know." She looked over at Altro. "This man saved Special Investigator Altro's life." Altro lowered her head. The governor turned back to the cameras and glared at them. "And without his help, I don't know if we would have been able to accomplish what we did."

The crowd grew quiet.

"John Walker Michaels," she said. "Thank you, John. We, the people of Michigan, owe you."

The Governor strode off the stage with her aide tight on her heels.

Chapter 80

The Task Force members went straight from the news conference to the Team Center. They were supposed to be wrapping up the investigation and turning everything over to the Attorney General's Office, but no one felt like working.

Altro didn't either. Now that it was over, she just felt empty. Walker was gone. John Michaels was dead. She sat at her desk and stared at its surface. After a few moments, she noticed the silence in the room and looked up.

The others were all watching her, but when her head rose, they looked away from her to each other. Then they all nodded in unison. Sammy took his feet down from his desk and picked up two brown folders.

"Michaels' service records came in."

There was intense pressure between her eyes and a hollow feeling in her chest when Sammy stood and brought the folders to her desk.

"You've already looked at them?"

Heads nodded but no one spoke. Altro opened the larger of the two. It was full of acronyms she didn't understand, but she got the gist.

John Walker Michaels had enlisted in the United States Army at the age of eighteen, in September of 1967. His Basic Training was completed at Fort Campbell, Kentucky, in November of 1967. His test scores were high, and he was actively recruited for Special Forces and OCS, Officer's Candidate School. He'd chosen the Infantry instead. He graduated from his Infantry Training at Fort Bragg in February of 1968, then volunteered for Vietnam. He took a thirty-day leave to get married in June of 1968, just before the Army shipped him out to Vietnam. A Bronze Star with V device and Purple Heart had been awarded. Altro flipped pages, needing to see on paper what she already knew in her heart.

He was reported MIA, missing in action, in April of 1969 after a failed helicopter insertion along the Cambodian border in March of 1969.

March of 1969. When Andrea Shellers said he came back home. Before his tour was over. Still in his fatigues. Filthy and unshaven, looking like he just stepped out of the jungle.

His status was changed to KIA, killed in action, after his body was recovered in January of 1970.

When Mallory said his unit recovered the body along the Cambodian border.

She tossed the folder aside and picked up the other one, his medical records. She flipped through the pages in a frenzy to the final page. The corpse was almost completely decomposed, bits of matter clinging to bone, but was identified through dog tags. Ribs had been nicked and broken, which indicated bullet entries and exits. A crude diagram showed their locations. Her head swam.

The wounds were in the same places as the scars she'd seen on Walker as he sat on the mat in the candlelit room. The wounds the nurse at the hospital said no one could live through. The places she'd felt the bullets hit her own chest before she tumbled out of the chopper.

How much of the filth on his fatigues when he went home was blood? His own blood.

She read the final entry in his records four times. Corporal John Walker Michaels died of apparent trauma to the thoracic cavity, the result of gunshot wounds. She stood up and looked at the others. None of them would meet her eyes.

"You knew this, didn't you Sammy? I saw it in your face, when you said they were mailing his records."

Sammy looked up and nodded.

"Sorry, Altro. I thought it was some kind of mistake. I mean, everything was kept on paper back then and… Well, it had to be some kind of clerical error. Hell, I still think it has to be some kind of foul-up."

Doolee tried to smile but couldn't quite manage it. "It's an interesting problem." Then his face took on its Bassett Hound look. "They will want the body. They will dig him up to make sure."

Sammy nodded at Doolee and turned to Altro. "His ex-wife buried somebody in Mason, in May of 1970. The cemetery gave me the name, John Michaels. It all fits. It's him, but it just can't be him." He shook his head. "Damn. I sound just like his ex-wife sounded when we interviewed her."

"Not his ex-wife, Sammy," Jessica said. "The FBI never found the divorce filing at the Ingham County Courthouse. They finally learned that Ms. Shellers never divorced him. She just changed her name five years after she'd buried him."

Sammy and Doolee nodded, and Jessica continued.

"She never said he was her ex-husband to us. In fact, she shook her head forcefully when we used the term. She never even said the word divorce. We just assumed."

Altro remembered her confusion over just who Andrea Shellers was, and Ka's words. *Second wife.* She walked over to the table, sat on the corner and crossed her legs. She sat there staring at her feet, trying to think, but her thoughts kept going back to John Michaels, the Valley Walker.

"Ms. Altro?" Jessica asked. "You met him. You talked to him. What do you think?"

Memories of the man came to her. His rising so effortlessly from the floor. The way his touch sent warmth through her. His family. Her final talk with him. The two men taking him away in a body bag.

"Ms. Altro?"

She dragged herself back to reality. "I don't know, Princess. I just don't know."

They were waiting for more, so she tried. "The man I met was a man of honor. It was very important to him."

Her hand went to the ivory tile under her blouse, but it was still cold.

"He was polite... kind... gentle."

She pulled the tile out for them to see. The deep breath she took came in a shudder. "He gave me this. It was his."

She thought of the veins that pulsed on his temple... that took on shape and moved... the dragon that came alive.

"He was driven, and so angry that it was frightening."

The emotions that overcame him, that changed so suddenly. His tears.

"But he was tender too, soft-hearted, I guess. He actually cried, just because I was afraid of him."

Altro looked up to the others, then at Jessica. "He was a lot of things, Princess. I'm afraid you only saw one side of him. I wish you could have seen the others."

Jessica's eyes were still searching hers. "But... but..."

Teri Altro could see Walker's feet scrabbling on the floor of the drugstore, then on the waxed and polished hardwood floor. She saw his arm reaching and trying to drag himself away. Then she could feel her own feet scrabbling and her own arm reaching, could feel the downdraft of the chopper blowing the grit and dust into her open mouth and eyes as she lay dying.

"Ms. Altro?"

She looked away from Jessica's piercing gaze, shook her head and held the ivory tile tightly in her hand. It remained cold.

"I touched him," was all she could say. "He was real."

Her BlackBerry buzzed. She pulled it out and looked at the display. It was the Attorney General. She waved a hand at the others as she plodded toward Mallory's office to take the call in private.

"Altro here."

The AG babbled on while Altro's mind wandered. She caught words here and there, but it was all a blur. At the end of the conversation, she came back to earth in time to absorb what the AG was saying. Bill Mallory had limited access to case files on the Team Center server without authorization. He'd called the AG on an untraceable phone and made threats about making Task Force case files public.

The FBI would be at the Team Center tomorrow. They would bring an Evidence Response Team and a team from their Regional Computer Forensics Laboratory. They would be going through the entire building, and would confiscate all of Mallory's computer equipment. Special Investigator Teri Altro would make herself available. She would be helpful and courteous to SAC Felix Bowman. There would be no excuses.

Altro didn't tell the Attorney General, but she wouldn't be available tomorrow. She had other plans. Tomorrow was the day of John's funeral.

Chapter 81

The announcement for the funeral of John Walker Michaels didn't come in the mail. It was hand-delivered by an older man with a bald head and a beak of a nose.

Jessica, who was all but moved into Altro's condo now, took it from him when he rang the doorbell. The only thing the man said was, "For Teri Altro." The Princess called Altro, handed her the envelope, told her how it came and walked away to give her privacy. Inside was the announcement, along with specific instructions on how Altro could get there.

The day of the funeral, Altro drove her XLR to a parking structure on Grand River in East Lansing. The black shoulder bag that held her credentials, her gun and BlackBerry was left at home, at Colonel Nguy's request. She walked in the front door of a Vietnamese restaurant across the street from the parking structure, and a man at the counter motioned toward the back with his head. Altro walked behind the counter, then wound her way through the kitchen and out the back door.

Colonel Nguy was waiting for her in the alley in a nondescript sedan. When she got in, he handed her a blonde wig and an over-sized pair of sunglasses.

"No shot today, Colonel? No hood?"

Colonel Nguy smiled his kind smile and shook his head. "He said you are family now, Teri."

She reached out experimentally to touch his arm, then turned her face away quickly.

He waited until she donned her disguise before he put on his own, an oversized baseball cap and sunglasses. The drive took them south, out of town, into the countryside. On a long straight stretch, he passed a car and sped up considerably, looking in his rearview mirror as he talked on a cell phone. She realized he was watching for tails.

"They have a composite picture of you, Colonel. I'm sorry, but I had to help them with that."

He smiled. "Don't worry, Teri. I spent years living in tunnels while the United States spent millions of dollars trying to find me and kill me. I will be fine."

They were silent for the rest of the trip, which seemed meandering and directionless. They were deep into farm country when they finally turned into a long blacktop driveway that ran through a wooded area of mature maples. The car was stopped by two Asian men in suits, and Altro could see three more in positions back in the trees. The men recognized Colonel Nguy and saw the ivory tile that Altro was wearing openly for this day. After a brief discussion between themselves, they apologized profusely and bowed deeply to Altro before they waved them on.

They both removed their disguises when Nguy parked the car on a section of freshly mown lawn in front of a rambling ranch house, an area outlined by yellow rope strung between young trees. There were a lot of cars.

Colonel Nguy walked with her across the lawn to a large concrete slab between the house and a white pole barn. There he introduced her to "Captain Kangaroo," the owner of the house, then excused himself and walked back toward the men stationed in the trees.

The "Captain" was so rotund that his suit jacket wouldn't button. His gray hair was combed down in bangs that covered the top of his forehead, his mustache neatly trimmed. He pointed to a neatly mown area out beyond the house. Situated around the area, tents made of heavy white canvas had been erected, the type rented for graduations and weddings.

It was yet another beautiful day and the tent sides were rolled up, turning the tents into awnings . Beneath these white awnings, folding chairs and tables were set up, with food and drink set out. A number of women sat in groupings around the tables, a large number of Asian women and a few older white women.

The Captain said she could find the family on the far side of the lawn, close to the fire pit where the bonfire had already been laid in. The fire would be lit later, he explained. A bull would be sacrificed and there would be feasting. It was a variation of the Hmong way, since the Hmong were his adopted people.

She started walking, skirting the tents, making her way around the outside of the gathering. There were a number of white men who looked to be in their sixties in attendance, clustered around large orange coolers, smoking and drinking and talking quietly.

As she was passing one gray-haired group, she caught a whiff of cigarette smoke. The need hit her and she turned subconsciously toward the knot of men. One lean man, with hawk-like features and cold eyes, held out a pack of Marlboros to her. She took one and he lit it for her, using a battered Zippo with engraving on the side. He saw her interest in the lighter, moved his thumb and tilted it so she could see the letters clearly.

Snake Eater

She nodded her thanks, took a hit and was instantly dizzy from the rush of nicotine. Another drag and she was nearly swooning. She saw Mallory standing about 30 yards away, talking with a man who looked vaguely familiar. The cigarette man's cold eyes followed her gaze, and she turned to look at his face. One corner of his mouth turned up and his cold eyes twinkled a bit.

"You know Mallory?" she asked.

"Possum?" he said. "He speaks highly of you. Says you're a pain in the ass, though."

Altro rolled her eyes, then grimaced and nodded. "Possum," she said. "That figures."

"Yeah. He got that handle because he rolled over and played dead back in the old days."

Altro cocked her head.

"Possum was Army Intelligence, so he knew a lot of the Snake Eaters," he said. "That's what they called us Special Forces types back then. We're a pretty tight group, and we've stayed in touch over the years. All the time he was playing dead, Possum was working behind the scenes, running quiet operations. Nothing as big as this one, though."

A woman and two men joined Mallory and his companion. A beautiful dark haired woman, a giant of a black man, and a white man with ice blue eyes and a walrus mustache. The black man turned to Altro and nodded, and recognition came to her. The men were the ME and techs from the apartment building. The woman was the one she'd seen outside Tommy Mo's Winged Lion.

Altro looked around at all the gray-haired men, wondering what part they'd played in this. She turned to the man who gave her the cigarette and looked him over, taking in his hawk-like features. The bald head and hooked nose. The Adam's apple that protruded from his thin neck. He was Buzzard, she realized. Arlo Goodrich. The two pistols Walker had.

"Did you know Walker?" she asked.

Altro searched his face for acknowledgement, but his eyes had lost that twinkle and returned to their cold stare. She let him keep his secret and turned back to the cigarette.

The next hit she took was shallow, but she was still reeling. She didn't want to pass out, and looked around for a place to get rid of it. Buzzard just took it from her hand and put it in his mouth. She stood there for a minute, getting her bearings back, letting the effect of the nicotine abate. He waved a hand at her mumbled thanks as she walked away in search of the family.

Hmong and Vietnamese and Thais were everywhere, in far greater number than the gray-haired men. They too drank and smoked and talked, either in their native language, or a pidgin that contained words she recognized as French. Some nodded at her as she passed. Some even turned and gave a slight bow.

She completed her walk around the gathering and approached a huge stack of wood, arranged in a conical shape in a shallow hole dug in the ground. Near there, beneath the largest of the tents, the immediate family was gathered. Andrea Shellers and

Ka. Bao with the baby and John's adoptive mother. They all looked serene and at peace, and she couldn't understand their apparent acceptance of the loss.

She stood there stupidly, looking around for a casket or a funeral urn, any sign of where John's body may be, but there was none. Ka rose from the group to meet her with a soft smile and a hug, pulled her to a seat apart from the others and held her arm.

"He's not here. They brought him to Mother and she took him home."

Home. Alto's mouth moved, but no sound came out. Ka took her hand.

"How are you, Teri?"

Altro couldn't speak, just shook her head. The ivory tile hung cold and heavy, reminding her of his absence.

Colonel Nguy approached them, stopped in front of Altro, then sat on the other side of her. The granite was gone from his face. "Teri, he was my friend, my brother. I'm happy that I was able to know him. Now I am so sorry for our loss."

Altro remained silent, words failing her. Tears formed in her eyes, but would not fall. She sat in a heavy haze of grief, longing for the warmth of him, incapable of questioning the depth of her feelings for a man she had known for such a short time.

Teri Altro suddenly wanted to talk with his family. She wanted to talk to Bao and Andrea. She rose to do so, and Ka went with her, Colonel Nguy, too.

Altro dragged her chair in front of Andrea, Mother and Bao. She sat and faced them. Ka and Colonel Nguy stood on either side of her, each with a hand on her shoulder. But words failed her, so she leaned in and put her arms around Andrea. In turn, she put her arms around Bao, Walker's beautiful butterfly, and then around Mother. Still, the words she sought stuck in her throat, and still her tears would not fall.

She stood to leave them, but Mother stood with her, and Bao, and Andrea. Mother held up the red cloth bag that had hung around Walker's neck, the bag he had held so lightly in the drugstore and the hospital, in his hideaway, and in death. The old woman pulled Altro's hand to the bag, then closed her hand around it. Ka placed her hand over Altro's, Colonel Nguy placed his hand over Ka's. Bao put hers on Colonel Nguy's and, after a nod from Mother, Andrea put her hand on Bao's. They all stood with their hands wrapped around the course cloth bag, joined by the memory of the man who wore it.

Altro stood mute, in the center of John's family. The ivory tile grew warm again, then warmer, so much warmer. She thought she felt the dragon that was etched on it move, felt its power.

Mother began chanting, a low lilting sound in a language that was not Hmong. It was more guttural, without the Asian tonal vowels, but with drawn out "K" sounds that came from the back of the old woman's throat. The chant infused Altro, filled her with quiet, stilled her heart.

Then, from the farmlands around the tents, came a deep resonating vibration, the sound or feeling she had encountered in the drugstore. The sound she had heard or felt or dreamt when Walker had been in the throes of the Great Dragon. Hope rose in her. She stood on her tiptoes, looked frantically around her, trying to find the source of the sound.

"Is it him?"

Ka shook her head, smiling even though tears flowed freely down her cheeks. Then Ka started reciting a poem, her voice barely audible above the resonance of the sound.

Where he has gone, you may not follow.
He has left no footprints.
Where he has gone, no one may find him.
You cannot catch him, even if you ride on horseback.
Where he has gone, you may not follow.

Mother's chanting ended at the conclusion of Ka's poem. The great vibration stopped.

Teri Altro wept then, in great, gulping, uncontrollable sobs that shook her. The tears that would not fall now ran through the fingers of her hands as she pressed them to her eyes, rolled down her cheeks and fell to the ground. She felt the warm weight of the arms of Andrea and Bao and Ka on her heaving shoulders and felt them sobbing with her.

Finally she was empty. She wiped her face with a sleeve and looked into the kind knowing eyes of Mother. The old woman took Teri Altro in a fierce hug — she was surprised at the woman's strength — and deep within her something warm and alive moved.

It was him.

He rushed into her, filling her with his warmth until she could see him, hear him, feel him touch her again. He was a spark that ignited something deep in the core of her. It was knowing — knowing that he was in her — knowing that he knew her and she knew him.

The feeling grew inside her, until there was nothing else.

Chapter 82

The funeral lasted through the day and night. When the service was over, a long line of Asians and gray-haired white men filed past the family, quietly giving their condolences. At the end of the line was Bill Mallory. He was with a tall Frenchman he introduced to Altro as Jean Barouquette.

The sun was nearing its peak when the family left. Altro went with them. She was part of the family now. At John's hiding place, Mother ushered Altro into the candlelit room with the polished hardwood floor, the room with the cast-iron brazier in the center, and the dragon painting on the wall. Her gauzy eyes were filled with tears as she held up the red hemp bag, but a smile of pride was on her face.

"This is my son," she said. The old woman spoke in Hmong, but Altro understood her perfectly. Mother reached into the bag and pulled something out of it, then held it out to Altro.

"He wanted you to see this. He took it from you, and it became part of him."

It was a bullet, a spent round. Altro saw that it was a 9 mm Hydra-Shok, the very bullet she'd fired at Walker in the drug store. She'd seen many spent rounds presented as evidence over the years, and could plainly see that this round was pristine, had never hit anything. She smiled at Mother through her tears. The beautiful old crone clucked her tongue and hummed as she put it back in the hemp bag.

Then Mother's tears returned, and the smile of pride, and she looped the leather thong around Altro's neck. The bag came to rest on her chest, next to the ivory tile with the dragon carved on it.

"He is with you, Daughter. You are with him."

Then she sat Altro down in front of the brazier that was the centerpiece of the bare room, on the same mat where she'd first met John. The old woman started beating her little drum and chanting. Altro could feel the warmth of the fire at her back and smell the aroma of wood smoke. Time was slashed and bled down the walls of eternity. Years passed and ran backward.

The cries of the families of the students who had died came to her. Their moaning and weeping rang in her ears until she could hear nothing else. Their tears fell on her in a river that permeated her until their grief was her own. Teri Altro knew the reason for the deaths of those young ones, and it made her angry. Very angry.

Her anger grew in her until it was a pressure in her brain that forced her eyes to mere slits, and she felt herself falling into a cold darkness. As she tumbled through the darkness, a tiny point of light appeared in front of her. She reached out, took the light in her hand, and her fall was arrested. The light was warm, and she held it tight until its warmth spread through her.

She opened her hand and the light lay there in her palm like some shining jewel. Inside this gem she saw the essence of her character, her need to do the right thing. Her honor. But she also saw herself as she used to be, with a young heart filled with hope and wonder and love of life. The layers of scar tissue didn't cover her heart. The walls weren't built to keep others at bay.

She placed the glowing nugget in the red hemp bag, closed her hand on the bag and clutched it desperately, promising herself she would never let it go. The great foghorn sounded, the world vibrated and something stirred deep inside her. Birth.

The rhythms of the eternal struggle to remain pure of heart built up in her until she could feel life breathing inside her. She opened her eyes to look at the painting of the Great Dragon that hung on the wall, saw that it breathed in unison with her. It wasn't just a painting on the wall anymore, but a living thing that entered her. The power of the Great Za grew inside her, filled her, running rampant through her heart until her fingertips glowed.

She wasn't afraid of the dragon's power anymore. Instead of fear, she felt a fullness of heart she hadn't felt in years, and smiled at the dragon in thanks. The tiny red points in the dragon's eyes glowed with life. And it smiled back.

Chapter 83

Teri Altro found the space that lay between places, slipped through it, and she was there. Mallory's office at the Task Force Team Center was empty now.

Through the office door window, she saw that the entire Team Center was being stripped. The flat-screen, desks and phones were gone. The only remaining furnishings were the chairs and the folding table. With the flow of heroin stopped, the Drug Interdiction Task Force was being disbanded.

Jessica, Sam and Doolee had pulled their chairs together in the middle of the floor. They all looked angry, and Altro knew why.

She'd gone to her condo to pick some things up and saw two unmarked sedans parked on the street. When she checked her BlackBerry for messages, she found texts from the Task Force members, asking her to meet them at the Team Center. She disassembled the device immediately, then came to see them.

Like her condo, the FBI had the Team Center building under surveillance. The Bureau had questions, and they were using the team members as bait to draw her back to the Team Center.

It made Altro angry, too. She reached for the red hemp bag that hung from the leather thong around her neck and gripped it. A buzzing began in her ears. Her head thrummed and her temples pulsed. She could feel the veins in her arms rising to the surface, moving and taking shape. Focusing on her center, she slowed her breathing, regained her rhythm and quieted the beast.

She walked from the office, went to the table at the side of the Team Room, then leaned back against the corner of the table and crossed her legs. Mallory style.

The Princess came out of her chair. "I'm sorry, Ms. Altro. They used our BlackBerrys to message you, then told us to wait here."

She waved at Jessica to sit down. Sammy sat there with his mouth open, rubbing a hand over the yellow brush of his hair. Doolee just looked at her and smiled, shaking his head. He was still smiling when he spoke.

"The FBI is looking for you everywhere, Altro. They are looking for many people, in fact." He held up a hand and ticked the points off on his fingers with the other. "Mallory, Walker's body, Ms. Shellers, Colonel Nguy, the pharmacist."

Doolee ran out of fingers, so he put his hand down. "They couldn't find anyone, so they used us to find you."

Doolee paused for breath, arched his eyebrows and stroked his moustache. "How did you get in here, Altro? They're waiting for you outside."

The light came on in Doolee's eyes. He shook his head again and smiled even wider, waved a hand up and down at her. Then he looked pointedly at Altro's attire, back up to her face and raised an eyebrow.

Teri Altro had her shoulder bag, but she wasn't wearing her business suit today. She wore black slacks she would have considered too tight a few days ago. Her platform shoes were replaced by mid-height boots, the starched white cotton blouse with black silk. Four-inch silver hoop earrings dangled from her ears, and an array of silver bracelets adorned her wrists. The red hemp bag and ivory tile hung in the open from her neck. She shrugged her shoulders and smiled back at Doolee.

"I went to his funeral," she said.

"Ms. Altro?" Jessica said. "The whole report we put together, all the information and conclusions implicating Woodley? Well, Mr. Mallory got access to it, even though they'd locked him out of the system. He put his name on everything, then added some information about when this building was renovated for us. The renovation was completed before the Task Force was formed, Ms. Altro. Even before the first student overdose."

When Teri Altro just nodded, Jessica sighed before she continued. "Well, he copied the file from our server, then called the Attorney General and threatened to leak everything to the press if Woodley isn't investigated."

Altro smiled a tight-lipped smile. "Bill's a good man."

Mallory did it that way to put full responsibility for the report on his shoulders, to protect the other members of the Task Force. Both he and Governor Listrom were working very hard to protect them, in fact. That was the reason for the Governor's private meeting with Mallory, the reason she'd been so animated. It wasn't about the leak, as Altro had thought. Karen Listrom had been chastising Bill Mallory for his failure to keep them out of trouble.

Woodley was a powerful man, and their attempt to dig into Woodley's records could have ruined the four of them. Even if they didn't end up incarcerated, their careers in law enforcement would be over. Bill had shown Listrom the phone and explained what he was doing to calm her. Then they'd cooked up the scheme to tell the rest of the Task Force to back off.

"They're looking really hard for him, Ms. Altro," Jessica said. "If he sends anything to the media, they'll press charges. He signed a non-disclosure agreement."

Altro nodded and frowned. They would put Bill Mallory away if he stepped out of bounds, but would never go after Martin Woodley. Every organization involved in the War on Drugs depended too much on Woodley's power and connections for that to happen. He was untouchable.

But twenty-seven Michigan college students had died of heroin overdoses. Lives were forever changed. Families were still grieving. The thought of people who would use the misery of others in their endless quest for profit and power brought a weariness that bore down on her until she didn't think she could carry it. Her shoulders sagged. Her head drooped.

She caught herself before she faltered, took a deep breath and straightened her shoulders. The power of the red hemp bag drew her. She touched a hand to it and murmured the words Walker had passed on to her.

"Two salt tablets, a canteen of water and push on."

Their confusion was evident. Altro would explain it to Jessica later, but first she had to get something settled between them. She walked over and absently started stroking Jessica's flawless hair.

"My name's Teri, Princess. And I won't let them harm Bill."

Sammy and Doolee were staring at them. Then they looked at each other and arched their eyebrows. She stopped stroking Jessica's hair and turned to them.

"You guys, too. Call me Teri. Please?"

The two of them looked shocked, then confused, but the Princess beamed over at them so brightly, they couldn't help themselves. They smiled back.

"What are you going to do, Teri?" Jessica asked.

"I have to stay off the grid right now."

Jessica frowned, so Teri explained.

"Just for a couple of days, Princess. I've got some things that need to be taken care of. You'll still be at my place when I get back won't you?"

Jessica beamed and took Teri's hand. Sammy and Doolee were looking at each other and raising their eyebrows again. She slipped her hand from Jessica's and turned to them.

"Did they dig up John's body yet, Sammy?" she asked.

Her use of Walker's first name confused Sam momentarily. She waited while he sorted it out.

"They scheduled it for later in the week, Altro... Teri." Sammy cocked his head to one side. "Teri, huh? I don't think I can ever get used to that. I mean, you've always been such a hard-ass." He blushed and shook his head vigorously. "No, I didn't mean that in a bad way, Altro. And I didn't mean your ass. Well, it *is* real nice, but... "

He struggled for few seconds... until Teri smiled at him. Then he gave up.

"Come on, Altro! Give me a break!"

Still smiling, she turned to give him a good look and arched her back just the right way, went up on her toes and tossed her arms up in a gymnast's dismount stance. It wasn't a ten, but it was pretty damn good. Her chin was raised and pointed correctly. The unfolding of her arms was timed right. Her pinkies were separated from her other fingers, with just the right gap.

Sammy didn't notice the nuances of her stance, though. He took a long look at her tight gymnast butt, turned a bright crimson and broke into a grin that was almost as wicked as Doolee's.

Jessica giggled. Doolee gave Sammy his most wicked grin and held up his hand for a high-five. The two of them slapped hands and Jessica giggled again. It was nice to see them smiling so wide, but she had things to do. She turned serious on them.

"I don't have much time, but I wanted to thank you guys for all your hard work," Teri said.

She stepped over to Doolee.

"Did you find the bullet?" he asked.

She touched the hemp bag.

"He had it all along?" he asked.

All she could do was nod. He nodded back, stood up and held out his hand. She shook his hand, then leaned in and went up on her toes to kiss him on both cheeks. Sammy sat there, looking at her with a question on his face. She took the few steps to his chair and ran her hand over that ridiculous yellow brush of hair. He was wearing a pair of bright neon basketball shoes. Nikes.

"You and those shoes, Sammy. You sure called that one right. I should have listened to you. I guess I haven't been the easiest person to approach, like you said."

He smiled and did a little tap dance with his feet.

"You know what, Sammy? I think I'm actually going to miss you staring at my butt all the time."

To her delight, Sam stood up and hugged her. She hugged him back, but when his hand started sliding down her back she pushed him away and waggled a finger at him.

"Don't even think about it, Sammy."

He blushed again, then shrugged his shoulders. "Too late, Altro. I already thought about it."

Jessica giggled again. Dooley laughed.

It was time. Teri Altro stepped back and gave them her very best smile. And then she was gone.

Chapter 84

Jarvis Willcote, a Founding Partner at Marbley Logistics, was waiting patiently in Martin Woodley's study. Willcote had formed the lobbying firm with some of his cronies when he retired from the U.S. Senate. His work on the Defense Appropriations Committee transferred nicely into the business of working with present members of Congress to make sure the corporations Marbley represented continued to thrive.

The War on Drugs provided a viable enemy for the masses, a focus for their anger. It made people willing to part with a higher percentage of their income, and the money provided law enforcement agencies with state-of-the-art drug detection equipment. It gave corporations the means to put satellites into space, to build and program powerful computers to sift the data those satellites intercepted. The War on Drugs was big business.

Willcote was at Woodley's Virginia estate to discuss the upcoming campaign, a campaign to assure that the flow of money from the pockets of American taxpayers into the coffers of the corporations his firm represented continued. They were all defense contract companies, of course, and included most of the corporations located in the New Defense Corridor north of Detroit.

General Steadley had finally arrived, and Woodley was in the drawing room with him. Willcote supposed the two of them were comparing notes to make sure they had their story straight. Well, that was a big part of the image business and Willcote could easily understand their concern. The public's perception of the two men was in danger.

The allegations against Woodley and Steadley made by that website in Thailand had truly gone viral. YouTube and Facebook were swamped with copies of the recordings. The sharks of the Fourth Estate smelled blood on the water. *The Washington Post* and the rest of the liberal rags were in a feeding frenzy, and the latest spate of special reports aired on the national news presented a huge problem.

The same talking heads who had lauded Woodley a short time ago were now digging into his past and slinging the mud they found across the airways. Steadley, that pompous ass, was being summoned to an Inspector General Hearing for an accounting. With men like these involved, it wouldn't be an easy campaign, but it was doable.

He'd already convinced the agencies involved in the Task Force investigation not to probe into Woodley's affairs. With enough money and pressure, the news media could be brought under control, and the public would believe what they were told. All they had to do was tell them often enough. It would be an expensive campaign, but there was certainly no shortage of money to fund it.

Willcote sat in a deep leather armchair with his feet up on a padded leather hassock. A snifter of brandy that had been discreetly served to him sat on the end table, and he rolled a fine cigar between his thumb and two fingers. The fireplace popped and crackled with a pleasantly aromatic cherry-wood fire. Precious art adorned the walls and a rich Persian rug covered the fine oak flooring. Handsomely crafted oak finished the fireplace, the walls and the thickly padded door. Martin Woodley knew how to live.

As Willcote sipped his brandy, considering the massive amount of money his firm would take in, a tremor ran through the ground. The ashtray and bottle on the serving table vibrated, scooted across the surface and stopped. He sat up straighter in his chair as the tremor began again, this time stronger. Was it an earthquake?

No, it was some great foghorn, but much deeper than a foghorn. The sound was everywhere, vibrating so strongly that it penetrated Willcote himself. Books started falling from the shelves. His chair bucked and moved. The brandy bottle slid across the table and fell over. The deep resonance of the foghorn broke his consciousness. His vision blurred and he lost sight of the room, then lost sight of the world altogether. Finally, there was only the continuing vibration inside him.

He awoke — he had no idea how much time had passed — when he became aware of Woodley's valet vigorously shaking his shoulder. The old fellow was breathless, and appeared to be on the verge of a stroke.

"Excuse me, sir, but I've been trying to wake you. Mr. Woodley and the General seem to have fallen ill. I've called for an ambulance."

"Both of them?"

"Yes, sir. There was a noise, sir, perhaps an earthquake. I'm not sure what happened but, in any case, they're in the drawing room."

Willcote stood and rushed to the drawing room. There he found Martin Woodley lying on the floor, looking like some human scrap cast carelessly aside. General Steadley, in his full dress uniform, looked like a broken action figure a boy had tossed into the corner.

Vomit stains were on the carpet next to Woodley and down the front of the General's uniform. On closer examination, he could see that both men were quite literally covered in their own spew. It also smelled like the men had soiled themselves, and he could plainly see urine stains on the General's trousers.

The odor in the room was overpowering. Willcote pulled his embroidered handkerchief and clamped it over his nose in a vain attempt to block the stench. He backed out of the room to stand in the hallway and, as he stood there absorbing the repulsive scene, he could almost see the campaign to save these poor creatures' reputations fading away. A potential gold mine lost.

Both men's eyes suddenly snapped open. Woodley sat up and looked at General Steadley. The General looked back at Woodley. In unison, they screamed at each other.

"Walker!"

Then the great foghorn started sounding in the distance again, and the two men seemed to have some kind of seizure.

They twitched and convulsed, thrashing their arms and legs about through their own vomit.

The foghorn grew louder until the walls vibrated with it, until the whole building shook. Willcote put a hand to the wall to steady himself, but it didn't do any good. The sound grew in intensity until he felt himself falling under its power, slipping away from his own world into some netherworld below.

Just before the sound overcame him, he heard an old woman chanting. And as the curtain of darkness closed down on him, as he started tumbling through a never ending blackness that swallowed him completely, he smelled wood smoke.

Chapter 85

Terri Altro was tapping a foot and drumming her fingers on the table when SAC Bowman barged into the conference room. She was seated facing away from the door, and turned to watch as his eyes darted around, taking everything in.

They were in Conference Room A at the FBI's East Lansing Office. A large flat-screen on one wall was lit up. One half of the display was taken up with the face of Governor Karen Listrom, the other half with the face of the Director of the FBI. Senior Resident Agent Furlow was seated at one end of the table, with Altro and Mallory on either side of him. Andrea Shellers and four attorneys from a D.C. law firm sat at the other end. The Frenchman, Jean Barouquette, was standing behind Andrea with his hands on the back of her chair. Barouquette walked toward Bowman with his hand extended.

"Special Agent Bowman? I am Jean Barouquette, an old friend of John Michaels. He left instructions, to be executed at his demise, that I should intervene on behalf of his family. When I received news of his death, I hurried over."

Bowman looked the Frenchman's impeccable suit over before he extended his hand.

"I heard they may be in legal difficulty, so I retained the Bachman Law Office to represent them," Barouquette said. "Perhaps you've heard of them."

"Of course I've heard of them," Bowman snapped. "They're well known trouble makers." He turned to Furman. "We're supposed to exhume Michaels today. His body is scheduled to be shipped to Quantico for analysis."

Furman motioned toward Andrea with his head. "Ms. Shellers is contesting our right to the body, sir."

Bowman scowled. "We need to know who's buried there," he said. "The lab at Quantico will get to the bottom of it."

All eyes turned to the flat-screen when the Director of the FBI cleared his throat.

"In light of recent developments," the Director said. "I think we should acquiesce."

Teri Altro struggled to keep the smile from her face. Recent developments? It was a media shit-storm. And it seemed that Martin Woodley, General Steadley and Jarvis Willcote had recently acquired the IQ of turnips. All three had been found in a catatonic stupor at Woodley's estate and were being treated in the Psychiatric Ward at Bethesda Naval Hospital. The prognosis was bleak. Too bad.

Bowman opened his mouth to protest, but the Director held up a hand and interrupted him.

"Ms. Shellers will allow us disinter the body, but only to ascertain identification and death. No autopsy will be performed. The attorneys of the Bachman firm will observe all procedures to ensure we keep our word. After that, John Michaels belongs to his family again."

Bowman's shoulders sagged. He waved a hand around the room. "These people were being sought for questioning, sir."

"We've already debriefed Altro and Ms. Shellers. They will no longer be considered persons of interest, and are free to go," the Director said. "Colonel Mallory was questioned by Agent Furman, with Governor Listrom and myself present. He is free to go, also."

"When did this all happen?" Bowman asked.

"Yesterday, sir," Furman replied.

"But Mallory signed a non-disclosure agreement," Bowman said. Governor Listrom broke into the conversation.

"Bill made threats to leak the Task Force findings," she said. "But didn't follow through. The Michigan Attorney General hasn't filed charges, since he broke no laws. The Director agreed with me that Bill's outstanding service in the Army and his invaluable contributions as leader of the Task Force far outweigh any conduct perceived as out of bounds by the Bureau."

The Director nodded solemnly while Bowman shook his head emphatically. Listrom kept her gaze on Mallory until he blushed. Altro couldn't hide her smile any longer.

Listrom had bullied the AG into submission, then threatened the Director of the FBI with a press conference, a conference which would reveal that the FBI's tactic to use Altro as bait had backfired and resulted in her being abducted. Listrom had exerted all of her power as the Governor of Michigan to intervene on Bill Mallory's behalf.

Altro's smile got bigger. Karen Listrom, an attractive and powerful woman, seemed to have a thing for Mallory. Good old Bill, with his clunky glasses slipping down on his nose, his cheap suits and cheaper haircut.

Bowman didn't find it amusing at all. He stood stiffly erect and nodded his head toward Altro. "Why wasn't I notified of this, sir? I wanted to be in on Altro's interrogation."

"It wasn't an interrogation, Agent Bowman," the Director barked. "It was an interview. You weren't included in her interview because you're no longer working on the case." The Director paused, took a deep breath to calm himself, then said, "Your actions are under investigation, as a matter of fact. The Office of Professional Responsibility will be interviewing you this afternoon in Detroit. You'll have to hustle to get back there in time."

The Office of Professional Responsibility was the FBI's equivalent to a police department's Internal Affairs. Being investigated by the OPR was the worst thing that could happen to a Special Agent, but Altro didn't feel sorry for Bowman. A lot had changed since Teri Altro met John Michaels, especially her, but some things were constant. Bowman was still an asshole.

He was staring at her, his eyes so wide that she could see the veins in their whites. She gave the moron her death's head grin, the same one she'd given him after working with the facial composite expert. All teeth and cold eyes. He just continued staring, so she winked at him.

That did it. Bowman's ears turned a bright red. His eyes went to slits and his mouth turned down in an ugly grimace. He raised an arm and pointed a shaky finger at her.

"Bitch," he said.

"Feeeeeelix," she answered.

A few hours later, they were in Sparrow Hospital's morgue. Altro stood next to Andrea Shellers, who stood next to Barouquette. The Bachman lawyers spread themselves around the room. The Ingham County Medical Examiner and Agent Furman hovered close to John's casket, while a technician worked to open it.

The coffin, a bronze-unit, was discolored but remarkably clean, due to the care the cemetery crew had taken. The director of the cemetery oversaw everything personally, even had them hose the casket off and dry it before it was loaded in the ME wagon.

The casket sat on a gurney and the technician was using a battery powered drill to loosen the fasteners that held the lid closed. The technician undid the last fastener, put down the drill and looked at the Medical Examiner. The ME nodded, and the technician opened the lid. The pleasant aroma of wood smoke wafted from the casket, overpowering all the other odors in the room.

Furman moved in closer. So did the ME. They leaned in and took a good long look.

"What the hell?" Furman said. Frowning, he reached out and touched the body.

Altro took a few steps in closer so she could see what she already knew.

This wasn't the body of a young soldier who'd died decades ago. It was the body of an older man, with laugh lines at the corners of his mouth and eyes. It wasn't a corpse that had rotted for months in the jungle, tatters of putrefied flesh clinging to a skeleton. It was a man who'd died very recently, the skin not even discolored and sunken yet. The body of John Walker Michaels looked perfectly preserved, like he was still alive.

Muttering to himself, Furman lifted a thumb and pressed it against a mobile scanner. He put that in his pocket and took a few pictures with his BlackBerry while he waited for the results. When the scanner beeped in his pocket, he pulled it out and frowned.

"John Walker Michaels," Furman said. "The thumbprint matches the one taken at the drugstore. And his Army records." Then he shook his head. "It's him, but it can't be him. It just can't be."

Altro could understand Furman's confusion. She'd watched them dig up the coffin. The men had stopped the digging to cut through tree roots as big as her arm with a chain saw. There was no way John's grave had ever been disturbed.

But there he was, wearing freshly laundered blue jeans and a plain cotton pullover, looking serene and at peace in this cold and antiseptic place of death. His hands were clasped together on his stomach and his head was tilted up a little, so he looked like he was napping on the couch, blissfully unconcerned about the activity around him. There was even a hint of a smile on his face.

Furman stood there muttering to himself. The ME tech stepped up with an infrared thermometer and held it out to the ME. The ME took a body temp, then checked for pulse and respiration. Furman kept muttering, "It can't be him."

"This man is dead," the ME said. "Whoever he is."

Furman and the ME began a lively discussion of the accuracy of the mobile scanner versus the ME's infrared thermometer. Andrea Shellers cleared her throat. One of the Bachman attorneys moved in and spoke quietly to the two men. They shuffled away, still arguing. All four Bachman lawyers closed in on Furman and the ME then. The room went quiet.

Andrea stepped up to the coffin, leaned in and spoke to the body. "I didn't tell you before, John, and I wanted to be here so I could." She reached in and put a hand on his shoulder.

"Welcome home."

They took John back home that afternoon.

It was a quiet spot in Maple Grove Cemetery, in a clearing surrounded by towering trees. Maples, of course. The clock on the County Courthouse rang five times. The echoes died away slowly.

Teri Altro stood on one side of the grave, Andrea Shellers and Jean Barouquette on the other. Bill Mallory stood stiffly behind the headstone. At a discreet distance, Furman sat in a Bureau sedan, taking pictures with a long-lensed camera.

It was chilly and wet, so a canopy had been set up to cover the grave site. Thunder sounded in the distance. Rain drummed on the canvas and ran in rivulets from the edges of the awning. The beautiful weather had moved south. Springtime in Michigan was back to normal.

The casket was lowered slowly into the grave with a hand-driven winch device, the cemetery director watching and giving hand signals to the operators. The coffin settled, the straps were removed and the director nodded to Andrea as he and his men moved away.

Bill Mallory pulled a small American flag from a pocket of his cheap suit coat, bent over and placed it in a bronze holder next to the headstone. When he stood, he pushed his clunky glasses up on his nose, came to attention and snapped a crisp salute. He held the salute briefly, dropped it and turned to Andrea.

"I had to be here, ma'am," he said.

"I know," she said. "I'm glad you came, Bill."

The rain pelted down on Mallory as he marched away. His cheap suit, already water-spotted, was getting soaked, but it didn't seem to bother him in the least. He was smiling, in fact.

A small ceremonial pile of dirt was on a stand next to Andrea. She scooped up a handful and tossed it into the hole. At the hollow sound of the dirt landing on top of the casket, she broke into sobs. Jean Barouquette put an arm around her shoulders, opened an umbrella and led her away through the rain.

Teri Altro stood there alone. The rain beating down on the canopy fell into a primal rhythm, a tribal drumbeat on the canvas, echoing the ebb and flow of elements in the universe. Something fluttered inside her, a slight stirring that grew until it turned into a familiar warmth. She reached a hand up, clutched the red hemp bag and held it tight.

Time became a blur. The dragon etched on the ivory tile spread its wings and soared within her. The pleasant aroma of wood smoke and the sound of Mother's chanting filled the air. Teri spoke to him like he was right there, because he was.

"Hello, John."

He smiled, looking so damn young again.

"You can rest easy now," she said. "Your long hump is over. You're home."

She paused while she sorted her thoughts, and he waited patiently.

"And, John? You don't have to be angry anymore. You don't have to carry the weight of the world on your shoulders any longer. I'll take it from here."

He cocked his head for a moment, then spoke slowly, like he had in the candlelit room, a professor explaining an important point. She broke into a smile and clutched the red hemp bag even tighter.

"You're right, of course. You'll always be with me." Her smile got wider. "We'll do it together."

But he wasn't done yet. She listened again, then nodded. Serious now.

"I know. There are others, just waiting to take Woodley's place, people completely without honor." She took a deep breath. "Knowing that does get heavy, but I'll remember. I'll always remember."

Teri Altro shifted the weight higher on her shoulders and leaned into it.

"Two salt tablets, a canteen of water and push on."

Acknowledgements

Thanks for taking the time to read this. You're invited to take a look at my second novel, *Five-Toed Tigress*, available at Amazon.

I have to say thank you to Becky Tsaros Dickson for her editing skills. She helped me make this a better work, and I learned more from her than I could ever say.

I also have to give thanks to my wonderful wife for living with me through the work that went into getting this done. She was an immense help in the proofreading and editing. Her ideas were solid, and she caught me in mistakes I probably never would have seen. Finally, she helped with the cover design.

About the Author

T. W. Dittmer's full name is Timothy Watson Dittmer.

He was raised in Gary, Indiana, the son of a steel worker who turned to preaching the Gospel. After high school he joined the army, volunteered for service in Vietnam, then reenlisted for service in Vietnam. When his time with the army was over he studied music, digital electronics and information technology.

He started writing music and poetry in high school, and has carried the love of those arts through his life.

He now lives quietly with his wife in Michigan.

Made in the USA
Las Vegas, NV
15 November 2021

34497396R00213